MW01064716

HOT DAYS AND LIGHTNING BUG NIGHTS

A Novel By
Jake Keeling

ISBN: 978-1-936497-38-6

Photo credits:
Mary Curry and Sarah Dowden Mault

First Edition: September 15, 2018

Searchlight Press
Who are you looking for?
Publishers of thoughtful Christian books since 1994.
PO Box 554
Henderson, TX 75652-0554
214.662.5494
www.Searchlight-Press.com
www.JohnCunyus.com

Dedication

With love and appreciation to Sandy Simmons Gatlin
and Jennifer Davis Green

Jenny, you put as much effort into this project as I did. I am grateful for your quiet, unruffled assurance that I would eventually get it right and for the wonderful memories we made along the way. I treasure your friendship.

Ms. Sandy- my pastor's wife, my cousin, my dear friend- I'm never quite sure how to introduce you, but I know without your initial read-through and favorable opinion this manuscript would never have seen the light of day. Thank you for your tireless encouragement, your listening ear, and your faithful example.

Table of Contents

Chapter One

L ook, Jenna, the boy's seen a psychiatrist, a toe doctor, and everything in between."

I sat alone in the next room, an insecure thirteen-year-old boy, rearranging my large herd of model horses for the umpteenth time and listening to muffled footfalls as Dad paced nervously up and down. My parents' rare fights always started over me and my lack of improvement.

"Exactly what are you suggesting, Terry?"

"Why not give Sis a chance? C.J. is the colonel's grandson, blood kin. That's enough for her."

Dad built his career and our lives on a sea of concrete and asphalt just three hours by car but worlds away from Colonel Chester Durham's rural home. Aunt Sis, though, stayed hand in glove with the old man until he passed away. Nobody ever used her given name, Serena. I knew her only as a soft, throaty southern drawl on the other end of the phone line, but as I would soon learn, Sis Durham was much, much more.

"Is she still smoking?"

"I expect so; Sis don't much cotton to change. Speaking to me just might be the only thing she ever quit in her life."

Despite tension within the family and the lack of her physical presence in our lives, Aunt Sis held a special place in my heart. She started my collection with a bluish black plastic horse from an obscure World War II era toy company. I still have that pony along with the tear-stained card.

> To C.J. Ches Durham on his first birthday in memory of Colonel Chester Durham. He loved you more than you will ever know. Ride 'em cowboy
> -Sis Durham, McKendrick, Texas.

Aunt Sis became my chief supplier of antique model horses, and Papa Joel took care of the necessary restorations. Mom's father and a retired machinist, he found his true calling with model horses. When we decided to build a few original models,

Aunt Sis condensed her lifetime of experience down to a couple of rough sketches on a paper napkin, and some telephone time. Her insight and Papa Joel's craftsmanship produced amazingly lifelike horses.

"Your sister still speaks to us, and you know it," Mom corrected. "It may not be anything we care to hear, but she speaks."

"That's true enough," Dad answered, "but mostly she says, 'Please put my nephew on the line.'"

"Considering her lifestyle, I'm reluctant to allow C.J. even a short visit. What can she do for him that we can't?"

"Which side of this argument are you on?" Dad wondered. "She might not do anything for his leg muscles or his balance, but those aren't the only things crippling him. I guarantee you Sis will expect more of him. He just might live up to those expectations and be proud of himself for it. The average mule could take stubborn lessons from Sis, but that doesn't necessarily make her a bad influence. With everything he's got to face, our boy could use an extra dose of determination."

"Injuries happen so easily around livestock. The last thing C.J. needs is a broken bone, and you know what they say about second-hand smoke."

"I know it ain't healthy for him to stay cooped up in that room with those dust-gathering fake horses."

"Please don't say ain't, dear."

At the accounting firm where he worked Dad's speech sounded almost as proper as Mom's, but around the house he sometimes slipped back into the easy, drawling slang of his East Texas youth. Now, his words caused me to take an honest look at myself. I'd been a fairly happy little kid with a sharp mind and lots of personality. As I grew older, though, the realities of life with cerebral palsy sent me scurrying into the protective shell of indifference.

"Working with animals is always chancy," Dad admitted, "but Sis is a sure-enough horse hand. She won't let him get hurt if she can help it. Besides, everybody needs a little risk."

A mixture of fear and excitement boiled in my stomach. Life in a wheelchair is tough, even within the comfortable parameters of a familiar environment. I tried to explain this to my doctors.

"I'm not crazy. I'm not even depressed, though I probably should be. I just want my life as steady and dependable as possible."

"Okay," they answered all too often, "Why don't we try this new pill?"

I usually had to take a few of the darn things before Dad got fed up with all the side effects and flung the rest into the garbage disposal.

A visit to Aunt Sis was sure to disrupt my settled existence, but such a trip promised the chance to get out in the world and live a little. Not just any old world, either, but the world I had always dreamed about. I'd smell real, honest-to-goodness horse sweat.

Gathering my courage, I put a little forward pressure on the joystick, guided my motorized wheelchair into the center of the living room, and surprised my parents speechless.

"I'll do it. I'll go see Aunt Sis if she'll have me."

Natural beauty lay over sleepy little McKendrick, Texas like a blanket in mid May of 1999. The green, gently rolling landscape looked as different from the rugged western-movie scenes of Monument Valley, Utah as it did from Dallas skyscrapers. My aunt lived among tall pine trees and fertile pastureland.

"No point going to the house on a Friday evening," Dad said, gesturing toward the white-painted frame home that stood on a little knoll. "We'll find Sis holding court down at the barn."

"What if Y2K hits early and I'm stuck out here in the boondocks?" I asked, gazing around uncertainly at all the empty countryside.

Dad threw back his head and laughed.

"That's all a bunch of hype. Besides, I can't think of a better place to ride out a tech crisis than here in Mac Town. Sis keeps her records with a fountain pen on a Big Chief tablet. If every computer in the world crashed, she'd sigh and allow herself a little smile. 'If they don't figure some way to get the gasoline flowing pretty quick, the horse markets apt to take a jump.'"

The sale barn wasn't exactly swarming with activity, but I saw a few people on horseback and others unloading their animals. A tall, lean man in a starched western shirt and blue jeans met us just inside the front entrance.

"Terry Durham… It's been a long time, little brother."

Little brother? I knew Dad didn't always see eye to eye with his family, but surely this wasn't an uncle that nobody ever bothered to mention.

"Hello, Jim Rex. You haven't aged a day since I left."

"If hard work ages a body, I'll be young as long as I live."

"Yeah; you'll probably make it 'til a shade tree falls on you. Meet my son."

The man's green eyes twinkled as he grabbed my hand to shake. "Good to know you, Ches. I've heard an awful lot about you. When you were born, the colonel went around passing out cigars for a month. Why, I wound up with a double handful myself." Then his attention shifted back to Dad. "It looks like I may outlive that sister of yours. She's a-runnin' herself ragged."

"Sis loves the horse business," Dad answered with a shrug.

"I'll say, but there ain't no real money left in it. She won't turn her help loose, either, not even a little bit. She's doing everything the colonel ever did plus what she's done all along. My daughter and the other girls up front just sit around and gossip. Sis won't leave a blessed thing for them to do."

Jim Rex led us down a narrow hallway and opened the office door to reveal a pretty, petite lady. At first glance, though, Aunt Sis looked more like an overworked secretary than the high-riding cowgirl of my imagination. She sat behind an antique roll-top desk in a leather armchair that all but swallowed her dainty frame.

Stiff posture and faint circles beneath her eyes told a story of stress and strain. Dark, coffee-colored hair, the same shade as my own, showed the first faint streaks of gray. The old-fashioned bobbed-off hairdo barely reached past the nape of her neck, but plenty of big, springy curls softened the chiseled beauty of her face.

During many of our telephone conversations, I'd heard Aunt Sis complain that too much time behind a desk had made her fat, and yet her jaw line stood out sharply, showing more than a hint of stubbornness but not the least trace of a double chin. She held a regular, corded phone against one ear, balanced a cellular phone on the other side, and rifled through paperwork as if searching for something important.

"Durham Auction Company, how may I help you?" Then into the other phone, "…pick up two mares and a stud out of the Parmalee bottom. Giles is bringing the gelding himself. You know how the old goat is; he wants everything done yesterday. No, sir… No, sir," and she let out a musical little laugh. "I would never call you an old goat. Still, you guaranteed the horse sound. An examination by a reputable vet showed otherwise. The horse is lame, sir. If you don't refund the buyers money you'll never sell another one at my barn; it's as simple as that."

Then she glanced up and saw us. Her deep brown eyes flashed with joy and excitement.

"Hi, Aunt Sis," I mouthed.

"Thank you, sir, I'm sorry things worked out this way, but you made the right decision. It's the only way to do business." She hung up one phone, jotted something on a piece of paper, and then, "You'd best blow the cobwebs out of that old Dodge. Those Parmalee horses need to bring top money, and they won't do it late in the sale."

The mobile phone rattled to the desktop as Aunt Sis sprang from her seat. She was only 5' 3" and delicate in appearance, but boy could she hug. Squeezed tightly against her, I caught the distinctive mixture of sweet perfume, wintergreen mints, and cigarette smoke that was her smell.

"Oh, I love you, Ches. I'm so very glad to have you home."

"It's…good to…see you…too" I managed in a muffled voice.

"Still dressing up for sale night, I see." Dad said with an odd little smirk.

"The colonel believed a lady ought to look like one. I generally wear a skirt on sale nights and a dress to church."

"Church I understand, but a skirt never seemed too practical for the horse sale."

"Walk soft, little brother," Jim Rex warned under his breath, but Aunt Sis ignored the criticism.

"We're shorthanded as usual, Terry. I'm busier than a one-eyed cat watchin' two mouse holes. Will you work in the ring tonight? I'll pay."

"It's not the money. It never was. I've put all that behind me, now, and I wouldn't be much good to you. Besides, Jenna's expecting me back."

Hurt and anger showed in my aunt's large, expressive eyes, but she reined in her temper and spoke quietly with a gesture in my direction.

"Did you take his things up to the house?"

Ignoring her reasonable question, Dad spoke in a mocking tone.

"Don't worry; you'll have C.J. trained in no time. Everybody pulls his weight at Durham Auction Company."

"Well," she huffed, "I'll have the boy's throw your weight right out of here if you get too smart with me."

"No you won't." He laughed and squeezed my shoulder but never took his eyes from hers. "You couldn't stand the humiliation. However mad you get, I'm still your little brother and Colonel Chester Durham's son. You'd not let a one of them touch me."

Aunt Sis froze for several long seconds but finally turned away to gaze out the window.

"I need a cigarette," she groaned, and her rigid shoulders drooped ever so slightly.

Though I'd never spent time around a smoker, several adjectives popped automatically into my head: nasty and unhealthy and socially irresponsible and...

But this was my wonderful, sweet aunt. Her unfailing love spanned a mysterious family rift as well as the miles between us. Now, she searched the pockets of her long denim skirt, checked her pearl-snap blouse, and whirled frantically back to us.

"Don't look at me," Jim Rex said. "You stuck 'em somewhere in your desk, told me you planned to cut way down while Ches was here and probably wouldn't even miss 'em. Sound familiar?"

"Go ahead and laugh, Jim Rex McKendrick," she retorted, yanking out the top right-hand drawer. You don't know how it feels."

I knew all the negatives associated with cigarette smoking, but I also wanted Aunt Sis to feel better as soon as possible. Jim Rex seemed to share my sudden pang of sympathy.

"I've poked fun at everything and everybody I ever knew," he murmured softly, "but not you, Sis, never you."

Three unrelated facts clicked in my mind. First, this cowboy wasn't really my long-lost uncle, second he carried the same name as the town, and finally, he thought an awful lot of his boss. Aunt Sis ignited a silver-plated lighter made in the shape of a western saddle and let out an eager little moan as she brought it up to the cigarette between her lips.

In my world ninety percent of businesses enforced a tobacco-free policy. Here, Miss Sis Durham owned the barn. Any unpleasant limitations on her habit were self imposed.

"Smoking less is probably a really good idea," I ventured, "but, Aunt Sis, you don't need to change for me. I love you just the way you are."

She spoke in a constricted voice, still holding the smoke in her lungs, but fixed me with a misty-eyed, adoring look.

"Thank you, Ches. That's a very grown-up attitude and one of the sweetest things anybody ever said to me."

"Sometimes C.J. acts older than I do," Dad joked.

"That wouldn't push him much," Aunt Sis said coolly.

"I know," he admitted in a serious, almost sad tone of voice. "The bossy big sister in you never fails to bring out the worrisome kid brother in me. I am sorry. Thank you for making C.J. welcome; it means an awful lot."

"Hush, Terry. You'll have the boy thinking he's a burden. This is as much his home as it is yours or mine."

"Thanks, Aunt Sis." I said, considerably reassured.

Dad and I said our goodbyes and then...

"You're getting old, Sis, old before your time. Why work your fingers to the bone for so little return? The colonel's got a nice headstone, and that's monument enough for anybody."

As an accountant, Dad always advocated sensible business practices and healthy profits. The part about the grave marker, though, I filed away for further consideration. Aunt Sis turned her head, but I caught the sound of tears in her voice.

"Stop by the café on your way out, Terry, no sense leaving hungry."

"All of C.J.'s stuff is in the van. I'll leave it so you can move his wheelchair around. Could you let me have one of the pickups or something else to drive?"

"Show him the little car, would you, Jim Rex?" Aunt Sis cleared her throat, squared her shoulders, and tapped her cigarette on the edge of a heavy, cut-glass ashtray as the two men trooped out of the room. "I still can't believe you're actually home, Ches."

"Yes ma'am, I'm here alright."

"The colonel wanted you in McKendrick so badly... He wanted you to grow up here, but if one summer's all we've got, we'll just have to make the best of it. Come on and let me show you around before things get too crazy."

"How many horses do you usually handle?" I asked, looking over the covered pens at the rear of the facility where horses were kept before and after each sale.

"Anything less than a hundred is a mighty poor run, but if we break two-hundred, it's something special."

"Wow, that's a big bunch of animals to deal with every week."

Farther down the alley, a red-headed boy about my age struggled to groom an uncooperative Shetland pony.

"This is Scooter McKendrick, Jim Rex's youngest boy. He rides for the barn," Aunt Sis said as we approached the tussle. "Scooter, meet my nephew, Ches Durham."

"Hello, Scooter."

"Name's Scott," he grunted, barely glancing up from the tiny black bronco. "This thing bites hard, Miss Sis. Your new vet chickened out and wrote adult for his age."

"Well, of course he bites. He's a Shetland." Aunt Sis stepped forward, caught the pony's upper lip expertly, and pulled it upward. "'Bout fourteen," she stated matter-of-factly. "Tell 'em I said mark it down."

"He drives that thing pretty good," Scooter observed, watching me navigate the narrow alley in my wheelchair, "but don't let him come out back by himself. He might get trampled with horses going every which-a-way."

"He ain't deaf," Aunt Sis said sharply.

"No'm, I didn't mean… I didn't think…" He raked some shavings around with the toe of his boot and then stepped up to me. "Sorry, bud," he said, offering me his hand. "Like Miss Sis told you, my friends call me Scooter. Reckon we can just start again?"

"Sure," I answered a little uncertainly, trying not to wince from his strong grip.

To my surprise, Scooter stuck the pony back into a pen and followed us. Being an only child and somewhat isolated, I felt more at home with people my parents' age and older. Still, this kid had an honest, likeable way about him.

Aunt Sis showed me the sale ring, a small indoor pen with wooden bleachers around it and an auctioneer's box high up over one end. Everything seemed functional but a little plainer and more rundown than I expected.

My aunt moved through the place without noticing its shortcomings, though, and her enthusiasm soon rubbed off on me. We only saw a few people, but they all clamored for her attention, running up with questions, complaints, or just a quick hello. Each time, she proudly introduced me as her nephew.

"There sure are a lot of kids around here," I observed, looking to Scooter for an explanation.

"You betcha; we carry saddles and stuff in and out for the tack sale and a few of us- the ones who are good enough- ride horses through the ring."

"Is there any way I can help, Aunt Sis?"

"You don't know how much you help me just by being here. We'll find plenty of work for you in the sale, but not on your first night. Your welcome to sit up in the box with me and Jim Rex, but you might learn more beside one of the regulars out in the crowd."

"Wherever you want me, that's where I want to be."

Holding a freshly lit cigarette at arm's length, Aunt Sis leaned in and placed a peck on my cheek.

"You hungry?"

Scooter glanced away, assuming I'd be embarrassed by the kiss, but he snapped back to attention in time to answer her question.

"I am!"

"I watched you put away two heaping plates and scarcely thirty minutes ago, too. Since when did I start paying you to tag after me? Now, scat, and find something to do."

"You probably think she's some kind of grand lady, Ches, walking around in a cloud of that old White Soldiers perfume with her hair all fixed up. Shucks, she ain't nothing but a slave driver."

"White Shoulders, not soldiers, goofball!

"Catch you later, Ches," Scooter called as he dodged her playful swat and took off for parts unknown.

The café turned out to be a separate little business within the sale barn. If Dad ate there, he didn't linger because there was no sign of him when Aunt Sis breezed in with me following close behind.

"This's my nephew, Terry's boy," she said to an elderly woman behind the counter. "Ches, Mrs. Crawford is my pastor's wife and one of the sweetest ladies you'll ever know."

I spoke up and shook hands with Mrs. Crawford as she fussed over me. Apparently healthy and strong in her early to mid eighties, she performed her job with quick efficiency.

"This is good," I said, swallowing my first bite of smothered pork chop.

"That's the way I remember it," Aunt Sis answered, glancing wistfully at my plate. "We've got some mighty good cooks at McKendrick Missionary Baptist. Whatever they earn from this café benefits the church, building fund one week, extra missionary support the next, and so on."

"Is everything around here named after Mr. McKendrick?"

"Who, Jim Rex?" she questioned with a laugh. "No, bless his heart, there's nothing named after him unless it's somebody's lazy old hound dog. But his family founded the town and owned our only bank for years."

"If he's rich, how did he end up working for you?"

"Money runs through his fingers like water through a sieve, but Jim Rex is as good as gold." One of her frequent throat clearings acted as punctuation, and she changed the subject. "If you want more food or a bite of dessert they'll bring it to you. I make a donation after every sale to cover what the barn help eats."

"But I'm not barn help, not until you put me to work. Dad gave me some money."

"I'll say you're not barn help! You'll own this place one day if you want it. As far as I'm concerned, you own it now. I'm just holding things together like the colonel would want done."

"Wow, Aunt Sis, I don't know—"

"Whatever you want or need, don't be scared to ask. A lot of the folks running around here work for us, and most of the customers are longtime friends. Come find me before the sale starts. I'll point out somebody for you to sit with."

The smattering of people I'd seen when we first arrived somehow swelled to an overflow crowd before I finished my berry cobbler. As I made my slow, careful way from the café to the sale ring, I thanked my lucky stars for an electric wheelchair. My forearm crutches are great for covering short distances, but it's easy to get knocked down in a crowd.

I usually tried to avoid strangers, especially in large groups. However, the thought of watching a live horse sale pushed this anxiety to the furthest corner of my mind. Aunt Sis glanced at her small silver wristwatch and smiled down from the auctioneer's box. I felt loved and protected under that smile, but wondered offhandedly how she managed to keep her teeth so nearly white despite years of smoking.

"Did you change your mind about me sitting up here?" I wondered when she beckoned me up a brand-new ramp to the auctioneer's box.

"No, son, I'm just fixing to introduce you." Then into the microphone: "Good evening, folks. Most of you know me. I'm Sis Durham. On behalf of Durham Auction Company, I'd like to welcome you to McKendrick, Texas and our horse sale. I also want you to meet a very special young man this evening."

"Aunt Sis," I whispered, "this is a little embarrassing."

"Just grin big," she told me without any effort to lower her voice. "Ain't nobody out there but homefolks and horse traders. This is Colonel Durham's grandson and my nephew, Ches Durham. Ches marks our third generation in the horse and mule business right here at this barn, and he's as much an owner as I am. Y'all don't wear him out on the first night, though. If you enjoy the sale, tell him about it. If you've got a bur under your saddle, come see me." Aunt Sis smiled and patted my shoulder as she waited for the scattered applause to die down. "Brother Crawford, would you start us off with a prayer, please sir?"

After the prayer, Aunt Sis instructed me to park on the front row next to Giles Parmalee.

"The old goat?" I questioned with a sly grin.

"Yes, but he's raised and bought and sold enough fine horseflesh over the years to remount the whole U.S. Calvary." Then, she spoke into the microphone. "Take care of him, Giles, and explain the sale as we go."

"I'm no babysitter, Aunt Sis, but if it'll make you hush and start the sale, send him along."

I winced as my aunt's warm laughter gave way to a nasty-sounding cough, but one close look at my "babysitter" pushed my concern for Aunt Sis to the back burner.

Mr. Parmalee's nose looked to have been broken several times over his seven decades of life, and his sheer size intimidated me. A younger man in a light grey designer suit sat on the other side of him. This tall, slender fellow smiled a greeting as I backed my chair into place, but the broad old giant only grunted.

"Y'all heard the man," Sis gasped, reaching for her Diet Coke. "Let's have a horse sale. Here's Jim Rex."

"Thank you, Aunt Sis."

Jim Rex emphasized the aunt just as Mr. Giles had done, but she rolled her eyes at him and took another sip of the fizzy liquid. He gave her hand a half-apologetic squeeze, called out his Texas Auctioneer's license number, and started the tack sale. Aunt Sis watched the tack auction, everything from expensive saddles to used lariat ropes, with proprietary interest, but her excitement seemed to redouble when they started on the horses.

Gates clanged open and shut. A strange combination of odors: horse sweat, ammonia, and manure filled the air. If an occasional whiff of cigarette smoke cut through the other smells, it soon got drowned out. I took everything in rapidly, adjusting to the quick pace of the sale, and the gleam in my aunt's eye assured me this thrill would never grow old.

"Jim Rex is easy to understand," Mr. Parmalee said into my ear, "but he can't auctioneer his way out of a paper sack. Sis is feeding him numbers, guiding every move he makes, and keeping the books besides."

"Well," I questioned, "if he's got the chanting thing down, doesn't that make him a good auctioneer?"

The old man snorted, but refused to comment.

"There's a little bit more to it," his well-dressed buddy suggested gently.

This guy stood out like a sore thumb. I doubted if horse sales were part of his regular routine, but evidently he'd seen more than I had.

"Auctioneer's got to know what a horse is worth and how to work a crowd to get the money," Mr. Parmalee finally added, "unless he's got Sis Durham whispering in his ear. Your granddaddy was a topnotch auctioneer. Jim Rex learned to mimic his sound but never picked up the knowhow to go with it."

"Did you know the colonel?"

"Yep."

"When was he in the military?"

"Chester served in the Second World War, same as me. But the army didn't make him no colonel; little Miss Sis done that. Colonel is kind of an old-timey courtesy title for an auctioneer. Sis Durham didn't need anybody to tell her there was something special about her daddy. She latched onto that colonel business and made it stick."

"I never knew—"

"Hush a minute and look at that son-of-a-buck turn around. You talk about a horse…" The next thing I knew, his hand was in the air. Jim Rex sounded as smooth as honey and as insistent as a jackhammer.

"Eight and a quarter… Now, eight and a half… You're out, Giles. Yah, eight and a half… Now, nine... We're gonna sell him, boys; he'll get a new zip code tonight." The bidding climbed to $1,250 where it stalled out with someone else on top. Jim Rex worked for $1,300, but Mr. Parmalee shook his head. "Don't miss this one, Giles; I'm fixin' to sell him. All in, all done?"

"Talks like a man in the driver's seat, don't he?" Mr. Parmalee asked from the corner of his mouth. "You watch."

Sure enough, Jim Rex rattled around until Aunt Sis tapped lightly on the tabletop.

"Sold," he shouted. "Put him on buyer number 322, and thanks to both you gentlemen."

"I saw it," I assured my reluctant tutor. "Sorry you didn't get the horse."

"I'm not," the old man harrumphed. "That's one of my nags, and I sure didn't want to haul him back home."

"If Aunt Sis would just learn to chant like Jim Rex," I said, after taking in his admission, "she could do the auctioneering herself."

"Son, she'd have to back up to chant like Jim Rex. She can run circles around him now."

"Why won't she do it?"

"Sis started writing tickets and keeping books for the colonel at about sixteen. Before that, she rode horses through the ring. She's a wonder, but to auctioneer and keep books at the same time would be almost impossible."

"Why not hire someone to do the paperwork?"

"Partly because she don't want nobody else poking their nose into her business, but mainly because Chester never considered auctioneering very ladylike work. Kind of a narrow-minded view, I'll grant you. Still, Sis always counted his word like gospel. Now, shut your trap. Yonder comes my other horse."

Aunt Sis caught my eye with a wink or a smile several times throughout the night. She looked happy and carefree, except in those moments when the auction stalled. She'd reach over and pluck the microphone from Jim Rex's hand.

"Bring one… Don't go to sleep on me back there. I need to see a tail goin' out and a head comin' in!"

Somehow this sounded more like encouragement than scolding, and her lilting voice never failed to galvanize the tired workers. I sat there spellbound, amazed at the assortment of horses, mules, and donkeys parading through the ring. Some were ridden in under saddle, others were led in by the halter, and the youngest or wildest were shooed in and out on their own.

I watched with particular interest every time Scooter rode into the ring and also noticed an older rider who favored him.

"Seth McKendrick's the top barn rider," Mr. Parmalee explained. "His little brother Scooter's starting to make a hand, too. Both them boys come through Sis Durham's school of riding, the 'You jerk on that horse's mouth one more time, and I'll wear a quirt out across the seat of your britches,' school."

"But Aunt Sis is so sweet."

"I reckon there's a little more to the story," he admitted. "It's also the 'What in the cat hair's wrong with… Oh, honey I didn't mean… I'll swan; youngsters today are awfully tenderhearted,' school."

"That sounds more like it."

"Good morning, sonny," he quipped later as we listened to Aunt Sis thank the crowd and invite them all back next week.

"I'm not asleep. Is that all the horses?"

"That's all. I never said you was asleep, but it's morning just the same."

A glance at my digital watch backed him up, 12:51 a.m.

"Kind of a light run, but they had some pretty fair nags tonight. You've probably seen enough horses to last you from now 'til Christmas."

"No sir!"

"Well then, you'd best hit the hay. If you liked tonight, you'll love tomorrow. They'll load horses in the morning, serve dinner in the café at noon, and start the playday after that."

"Playday?"

"Say, you are green. A playday is like a little rodeo without the rough-stock events. They put one on every Saturday afternoon following the horse sale on Friday. The barn help and folks from the community enjoy it, but nobody loves to fool with a horse anymore than Sis. I guess it's what you'd call informal, no entry fees, no real prizes, and not too many rules."

Sometime around 2 a.m. Scooter brought word that Aunt Sis wanted me in her office.

"I know you're ready for bed, Ches. We're just about—"

A heavy-handed knock on the doorframe cut her greeting short.

"You in there, Miss Sis?"

"All the checks are cut, and we're through loading for the night. Your horses are gone, Giles. It's way too late to pull them out of the sale."

"Why is it you always expect trouble from me? I just came to introduce you to your new neighbor."

"Andrew Hollister, ma'am," the suit said. "It's a pleasure to meet you."

Aunt Sis rose to her feet and offered her hand in one graceful motion.

"Welcome to McKendrick, Mr. Hollister. I'm Sis Durham, and this is my nephew, Ches."

I caught a roguish flicker in Giles Parmalee's eyes as I shook hands with the suit.

"When I say neighbor, I mean neighbor. Andrew's gone and bought Uncle Doc's house, the ground around it, and half of the bottomland."

"I see."

Most of the color drained from my aunt's face. Her eyes flitted longingly to a half-forgotten cigarette resting in the ashtray, but she refused to show the least sign of weakness.

"Don't give me that deer-in-the-headlights stare, Miss Sis."

"Why, Giles, I never…"

"Want to hear her thoughts, Hollister?" the old man asked with a sly smile. "I'll translate as best I can. 'You unreliable old reprobate! The Parmalee family has owned that bottom forever and a day, and the house sits on Durham land.'"

"Durham land?" Andrew demanded, seeing a potential cloud on his title.

"Well, it was," Giles clarified. "My Uncle Doc married a Durham, her great aunt."

"I reckon poor Doc probably blew a gasket?" Aunt Sis questioned.

"Not yet; I ain't told him."

"Oh, Giles," she moaned, sinking suddenly into her chair as if the strength had gone from her legs. "How could you? That land's been out of Durham hands for a long time. I'm not worried about the place or whatever else I might get, but my heart breaks for Uncle Doc."

"You know the funny thing, Sis?" Giles asked, his expression clouding over for a moment, "I believe you." All signs of regret vanished as he continued. "Hollister here's got an option to buy the rest of the old place as soon as I kick the bucket."

"What about your girls," Aunt Sis asked in a tired and somehow deflated tone.

"Shoot fire, as far as they're concerned, my land's just holding the world together. The Parmalee name's played out, and you're in just about the same shape. Ches sure seems like a good kid, but just what do you think he's gonna do with your little kingdom? Hollister's a money man, and a likable young fellow besides. If you knew what he paid me…"

"I assure you, Miss Durham," the suit put in, speaking up for himself, "I'm not here to concrete over half that bottom and plant ornamental kudzu vine on the rest of it. I'm a country boy, born and raised in North Georgia."

"That's all very nice but—"

"I took a corporate job right out of college and moved to Houston. The job has been good to me but city life… Your East Texas piney woods remind me of my home, and I need a weekend place to pursue my passion for fine birddogs."

"I'm afraid you're about twenty-five years too late to shoot quail around here, Mr. Hollister," Aunt Sis said a little too happily.

"Oh, we'll raise our own birds and release them."

"Get yourself set for another shock, Sis. His next big plan takes in your holdings: sale barn, homeplace, and all."

Chapter Two

Mr. Parmalee obviously expected my aunt to go off like a rocket. She held herself in check, though, as if determined to prove him wrong. Her pretty face turned bone white, but she spoke in a controlled tone.

"No. Thank you for your interest, sir, but I absolutely will not sell."

"Don't you even want to hear my offer?"

"I do not, but my good friend Giles Parmalee's doing his dead-level best to give me the heart failure. Maybe you can deal with Ches."

I'd only been there for a matter of hours. I still don't know exactly what came over me, but I rolled forward and put a hand on her shoulder.

"The answer wouldn't change, Aunt Sis. Durham Auction Company's not for sale."

Hollister's hair was jet black, and his eyes matched the expensive-looking cloth of his suit jacket. When he glanced in my direction, I caught a warm smile in those grey eyes.

"Good man." Then to Aunt Sis, "I was a fool to let Mr. Parmalee persuade me to talk business at such an hour. May I call on you tomorrow afternoon?"

"The time of day has no bearing on my response."

"I hear you loud and clear, ma'am, but I'm also in the market for some gaited horses. Tennessee walking horses, to be exact."

"Well... I suppose that's a different matter," she answered with a measuring look. "Drop by any time it suits you. If you don't find us around the barn, come up to the house."

Old and tired-looking, Giles Parmalee hesitated regretfully at the door.

"Hope I haven't burnt any bridges tonight, Sis."

"No, I reckon not, but our so-called friendship will likely be cut short when Uncle Doc shoots you for an egg sucking dog."

"Don't worry your pretty little head about that, and don't bother slipping him a gun, either. He shakes too bad to hit anything."

Aunt Sis choked back a snort of laughter and turned apologetically to me.

"I'll smoke just one more before we go out to your van. This one's burned plumb away."

"Yes ma'am," I said automatically and then out of simple curiosity, "how many do you normally…"

"Around a pack and a half a day, honey, and sometimes it's not nearly enough."

"Today?" I pressed dubiously.

"Hey," she protested with a mischievous wink, "that's hardly a fair question. We've already started tomorrow."

She was Dad's sister and naturally tight with a dollar, not to mention the seemingly painful consequence of running out of cigarettes. Admit it or not, Aunt Sis knew exactly how much she smoked.

"Just wondered," I mumbled suddenly embarrassed by my own prying questions.

"Well, I don't have to smoke in the house if it bothers you."

"It seems kind of selfish to keep you running in and out of your own home."

"I'll make it a point to keep the smell out of your automobile and bedroom."

"The van belongs to my parents, but I don't actually have a room in your house."

"Oh, fiddlesticks, your dad's old room or any other that suits your fancy is yours for as long as you want to stay. If you take a liking to mine, I'll move out of it tonight."

"You're awfully openhanded with a virtual stranger, Aunt Sis. When and where you smoke is your own business."

Wry, knowing humor twisted my aunt's mouth.

"Your mother would pitch a regular hissy fit if I lit a cigarette in that van or in a room where you slept. Why, she wouldn't even approve of you sitting here with… But tell me, what did you think of our little country sale?"

"I loved the excitement, and I learned a lot from Mr. Giles, too."

"Like what?" she wanted to know.

"Like, you're a better auctioneer than Mr. McKendrick."

"Shush, honey, a lot of people don't know that, and Jim Rex is one of them. I meant for Giles to teach you something about the horse market, not sit there and run poor Jim Rex down."

"He talked a little about the different classes of horse stock and their value, too, but you shouldn't be ashamed of his compliments if they're true."

Aunt Sis continued the conversation in a low voice as we crossed the gravel parking lot.

"Frankly, Ches, I'm good enough at what I do without Giles Parmalee singing my praises. The only thing Jim Rex has ever been any good at is being Jim Rex, that slow smile and those laughing green eyes." She gave an unconscious sort of sigh and then continued. "He's a dear friend. I wouldn't hurt his feelings for the world, and I won't stand for anybody speaking unkindly of him."

"Yes, ma'am," I answered rolling my wheelchair onto the lift, "but what do you mean he's only good at being Jim Rex?"

"He's a fine conversationalist and quite the ladies' man, too, but… Have you ever seen ribbon roping?"

"I don't think so."

"It's calf roping for youngsters who aren't big enough to throw one down and tie him. When a boy rides out and catches his calf, his girlfriend, or sister, or somebody runs down and snatches a ribbon off of it. Once she crosses the finish line with his ribbon, they call time. Nobody loved ribbon roping anymore than Jim Rex, but he just about couldn't hit the ground with a lariat rope. I'd be sitting on go, ready to run after that ribbon—"

"You were his girlfriend," I guessed, teasing her a little.

"Oh, he had a dozen or more, but I stuck it out as his ribbon runner after the others got too embarrassed or bored waiting for him to catch something. He'd throw a loop big enough to catch a car, and sure as you're born, the calf would run right through. It got so bad that Mr. McKendrick, his own daddy, asked me why I bothered to take off my spurs."

"Why did you?"

"Well, I figured he was bound to catch sooner or later. I wanted to be ready to run. Anyhow, Jim Rex's life has turned out kind of like his ribbon roping. It's not exactly his fault… Like I said, he is awfully good at being Jim Rex."

"Who did he finally marry?" I asked.

"He married three times, and none of them had the sense God gave a goose. I guess they aimed to marry money but… Anybody who can't hold her head up without money has got no business with it."

"Kids?"

Her expression softened into a fond smile.

"You saw Seth and Scooter riding for me tonight. Their half-sister, Serena Kate, fell between the two boys, and she works the pay window in the front office. None of them have the same mother. Still, they're as close as brothers and sisters get, and a mighty fine bunch if I do say so."

"Old Jim Rex named his daughter after Aunt Sis," I thought, "bet that went over like a rock."

A pack of barking dogs greeted us in my aunt's front yard.

"Do they bite?" I asked, concerned.

"Not you," she answered with a laugh. Then to the dogs, "Y'all hush that racket."

"They sure love you," I observed as they wriggled around her feet.

"This is old Rhett," she said, pausing to stroke a particularly rough looking animal with tattered ears and scars around his graying muzzle. "He's been with me a mighty long time, especially for a working dog."

"Red?" I asked, observing his dingy russet color.

"No, Rhett, like Rhett Butler."

"I hear you, now, but who's Rhett Butler?"

"That leads to a long string of questions. Who's Clark Gable? Who's Margaret Mitchell?" Laughing, she ran a hand over my head much as she had done with the old dog. "We can't undo a lifetime of ignorance on your first night."

"Well, thanks for putting in so many ramps," I said uncertainly and gestured to the one at the front door.

"This old house will creak and moan," she warned, standing beside my wheelchair in the old-fashioned parlor, "but you're safe here. Pretty soon those sounds will act like a lullaby."

"I may not hear anything tonight," I answered with a yawn.

"Bless your heart," she said and smiled kindly. "Your bedroom's just across the dog run, and the water closet is next door. Holler whenever you need my help, or at least let me look in and say goodnight."

"Yes ma'am."

I didn't even attempt to figure out what running dogs had to do with it but followed the direction of her vague gesture across the open-air hallway, assuming the so-called water closet must be something like a bathroom. Closets in general are pretty tight quarters, so even though the doorway was wide enough to accommodate my wheelchair I dropped lightly out of it onto the worn planks of the hall.

"Heavens to Betsy!" The sudden cry turned me around, and the pounding of boot heels across the floor made me scoot out of the way. "What's the matter, child? Did you fall?"

"No, Aunt Sis, it's called knee walking. I get around this way a lot," I explained.

"Well, I declare; give me a little warning next time and spare me the heart palpitations. Don't these hard old floors hurt your knees?"

"No ma'am, my knees are tough and callused, but the soles of my feet look like a baby's bottom."

"Maybe I can put down some nice, thick rugs. For now, though, you go on in and take care of your business while I try to settle these runaway nerves of mine."

If I've ever seen an antique commode, my aunt owned it, along with a claw-foot tub and a pedestal sink. Once in the bedroom, I parked my wheelchair, climbed into the center of a mattress at least twice my age, and called to her.

"I'm ready, Aunt Sis."

I heard her footsteps coming across the hall but sensed sleep crowding in on me. Barely aware of her scent and a loving presence in the room, I felt a light kiss on my forehead.

"Goodnight, honey, and welcome home," she murmured.

I slept like a rock and woke to find a note on my bedside table.

Gone down to the barn to get things started, but I want to cook breakfast for you. Call when you're ready. Surely they can manage without me for a few minutes. 898-2355 XOXO

Left alone in our pleasant suburban neighborhood, I bolted the doors and watched the clock until one or both of my parents returned. Here, in my aunt's home, I felt completely safe without actually thinking about it. I lingered over my morning routine but finally motored into the kitchen to call.

"Good morning, Aunt Sis. You really don't have to cook for me, but I could use a little help with my socks and shoes."

"I'll be right there, Ches. Breakfast is just about the only time I cook, so you'd better take me up on it."

Socks are the most difficult part of dressing. A lot of people have put mine on over the years, but nobody ever did it quite as meticulously as Aunt Sis. Not a single wrinkle eluded her gentle fingers.

"Sorry to pull you away from your work," I apologized.

"Don't worry your head about that." Then, gazing doubtfully at my tennis shoes, she said, "We've got to get you to the western wear store. In the meantime, I think there's some old stuff of your dad's around here."

She disappeared into my room and came back loaded down. She carried a pair of expensive-looking cowboy boots and a hand-tooled leather belt along with a western shirt straight out of the '70s. No pants, though, so I assumed my jeans measured up okay.

"I feel almost like a real cowboy now." I said, topping off the western getup with my Texas Rangers ball cap.

"Clothes don't make a cowboy, honey, but if blood has anything to do with it, you ought to be a jim-dandy. Do you like to watch baseball?"

"Dad kind of likes the Rangers. He's not nuts about it or anything, but we go see them at Arlington every once in a while."

"I scarcely ever turn the television set on except to look at the weather or Horace McQueen's Farm and Ranch News. We get three channels, and two of them stay fuzzy. If you ever want to watch a ballgame, though, just let me know. We'll turn the antenna and get you a clear picture."

My ears caught an unfamiliar chime as Aunt Sis left the room. A quick glance at her boots showed me a pair of well-worn spurs that jingled with every step. Cable TV helped pass the long summertime hours back home, but I smiled to myself, wondering how anybody with an aunt who cooked breakfast in her spurs could possibly want for entertainment.

I followed her into the kitchen and watched as she paused before a 1970s era stereo with turntable and eight-track player. She selected a record, an actual vinyl record, from the stack, placed the needle carefully, and then turned a knob.

Suddenly, Old-time gospel harmony filled the room. At least four voices sounded from the record player, and my aunt's deep but feminine tones blended right into the mix as they sang about the Jericho road.

"You sound really good," I told her as the song ended. "How do you stay with one part, though? I'd be all over the place."

"Well, honey," she answered, slicing bacon into an iron skillet, "I grew up on this kind of music. I know the songs, too, and that helps. I've sung alto for so long that it just comes naturally."

"What's alto?" I wondered.

"That's the line you heard me singing," she explained, "the lower of the two ladies' parts. In a mixed quartet the tenor singer and the bass are men while the soprano and alto are women. What do you think of the Chuck Wagon Gang?" she asked, gesturing toward the stereo as they moved into "When the Roll is Called up Yonder."

"It's pretty," I decided," but they don't sound much like cowboy singers to me."

"The Gang sang their way out of the West Texas cotton fields a-way back in 1936. They recorded a few western ballads in the beginning but went all-gospel a long time ago."

Aunt Sis cooked enough food to feed an army, singing all the while. Finally, she shut off the stereo, laid a hand on my shoulder, and offered a short prayer of thanks. Pan sausage, bacon, fried eggs, homemade biscuits, and gravy lay ready on the table before us, but she settled down with a cigarette and a cup of coffee to watch me eat.

"Aren't you hungry," I asked.

"Always, but I'm not likely to starve."

"There's no way I can eat all this. Won't you have some?"

"Your dad and I don't agree on much these days, but he's right about me getting old. I'm old… and fat, Ches. We ate this stuff every morning for years, and I never gained an ounce. Now, just the sight of it makes my hips spread. I've got a closet full of things that ought to still fit. They don't."

"Probably her clothes from high school," I guessed, smiling at the thought.

"It's not one bit funny," she chided, though I hadn't spoken aloud.

She wore a red and white bandana-print shirt, and even in a pair of snug-fitting blue jeans, the extra weight she fretted over hardly showed at all.

"You look just fine to me, Aunt Sis. Besides, you've got to eat something."

"Now you sound like the colonel."

"Is that a bad thing?"

"No, honey, it sure ain't," she said, clearing her throat as she reached for a biscuit. "It's been a long time since anybody worried about me."

The telephone rang then, and she started from her seat.

"Finish that biscuit, young lady," I teased. "I'll see who's on the phone."

"Yes sir," she quipped with a perky little salute.

"Durham residence, this is—"

"Hey, sport. It's good to hear your voice."

"Papa Joel!"

"It's me alright. How are you and Miss Serena making it down there?"

"Good; I over slept a little after a late night at the horse sale. We're just sitting down to breakfast."

"Well, I won't keep you from it. Take good care of yourself and Miss Serena, too. You know I'm just a phone call away, right sport?"

"Yes sir," I answered with a lump in my throat. "Try not to worry. So far, I'm having lots of fun."

When I rolled back to the table Aunt Sis looked up sheepishly from spooning gravy onto a second biscuit.

"How's Mr. Joel this morning?"

"He's fine; just checking in."

"I figured as much. Your grandpa loves you a whole lot. Now, he's getting a taste of the lonesome feeling I've known all these years. I wouldn't wish it on a kicking mule," she added with a humorless little smile.

"I never realized…"

"Do we need to take the van and your chair down to the barn, or do you want to bring your crutches and ride the Mule?"

My heartbeat quickened.

"Can we get me up in the saddle? How well-trained is your mule?"

"I'm sorry, honey," she said, chewing her lower lip as she tried not to laugh. "This one runs on gasoline."

I walked out to the side-by-side in my customary crouch, and Aunt Sis eyed my permanently bent legs uncertainly.

"Do they pain you much, honey?"

I finally processed that tender but countrified question into, "Do your legs hurt?"

"No ma'am, there's no pain at all. I get a little sore if I walk a lot farther than normal, but your muscles would probably ache if you tried to run a marathon."

"Pshaw, I'd end up in bed. This girl does her running a'horseback."

Down at the barn, I soon found myself absorbed in watching all the activity. Horse trailers pulled in and out all morning. Aunt Sis and an elderly black man she introduced as Nash Holloway worked right through the noon meal, but I took dinner with the rest of the crew.

When the stream of trailers finally slowed, my aunt's voice came over the loud speaker.

"A-l-l-right, y'all, catch your fastest pony and gather up for the playday." I soon heard her again, this time at normal volume from the back of the barn. "Nobody's gonna ride the little bay mare?"

Craning my neck, I caught sight of her standing in an alleyway.

"They're not crazy," Jim Rex answered. "That little booger's plumb hostile."

"Five years old with saddle marks… She may be a tad spoiled, but there's nothing wrong with her that a few wet saddle blankets won't cure. I'll bet she's quick as a cat, too."

Aunt Sis reached up and reset her narrow-brimmed straw Stetson. She placed the hat just so, a little forward and tilted rakishly over her right eye, then pulled it down tight and flashed a grin in my direction.

"Get that look off your face," Jim Rex ordered half heartedly. "You've got plenty of gentle horses to ride, and there's no need to show out just because Ches is here. You're getting too ol— Well, anyway, where'd the rest of us be if you broke that pretty little neck of yours?"

"Your concern for me is heartwarming, Jim Rex, but I happen to own the horse and the ground she's standing on. I guess I can ride her if I take a notion."

"I'll ride her for you, Miss Sis," Seth McKendrick offered. "She don't scare me none."

"Thanks, Seth, but you're maybe half a minute late. Jim Rex thinks I'm about ready for a rocking chair. What do you think?"

"Well'm, I'd hate to see you get hurt, but I'm not about to bet against you."

"I guess you expect us to stand around and cheer while you act a fool," Jim Rex grumbled, throwing his hands up in disgust.

"All I'm asking you to do is stand back out of the way," she quipped, then rose on tiptoe to give him a rare peck on the cheek. "Nash, you feel like earing this little kitten down long enough for me to throw a saddle on her and step aboard?"

"You bet, Miss Sis. We'll show 'em how it's done!"

All of a sudden, Scooter shoved his way up from the back of the bunch.

"What you're fixing to do, Aunt Sis, it goes against all them natural training methods."

"I'm not your aunt, Scooter McKendrick, and you know better than to spout that stuff at me. It's natural for a horse to graze and romp and kick up his heels and gat about wherever he wants to go. A natural horse is no earthly good to anybody but himself. I've heard the colonel say it many a time; if you want to teach a horse something, get in the middle of his back and stay there a while."

"Scooter got some of those training tapes for Christmas," Seth explained with a grin. "He's been agitating Miss Sis ever since, and having a big time with it, too."

Old and arthritic, Nash didn't look much more physically able than me, but he stepped into the pen and caught the little mare without a hitch. He twisted her right ear, bit down on it, and wrapped a muscular arm around her neck. Aunt Sis never once hurried or fumbled but saddled the horse in no time flat. She vaulted up like an athletic teenager and settled easily into place.

"Careful," I called at the last minute, but she only nodded and spoke to the old man.

"Turn 'er loose, Nash."

My heart rose into my throat as the animal bellowed and leapt high off the ground. Strong, agile, and scared out of her wits, the little horse resembled a stick of dynamite, but before long, even I could see she was outmatched.

"Stay with it, Sis," Jim Rex yelled, now caught up in the excitement. "Look at her, Ches, spurring every jump!"

The show lasted three or four minutes, and by the end of it Aunt Sis panted harder than the tired horse.

"Good thing this little girl's change of heart came when it did," she wheezed, walking the mare slowly around the pen. "I give out faster than I used to."

This admission, probably meant for Nash's ears alone, did nothing to dim my glowing pride. The barn help hooted and cheered, Scooter loudest of all. The next thing I knew, Jim Rex stepped into the driver's seat beside me and slung an arm around my shoulders.

"How about our girl, Ches, ain't she something?"

"She sure is, Mr. McKendrick."

"Call me Jim Rex. Everybody else does."

"Thanks, I'll try to remember that."

"There's no sound system for the outdoor arena, so they usually get my loud-mouthed self to do the announcing at these playdays. I'll help you walk up to the platform if you'll keep me company."

The little mare's bay coat matched Aunt Sis's dark brown hair. Both horse and rider possessed a great deal of athletic ability in a small, pretty package. The two of them made a good team in fast paced events. Jim Rex operated the stopwatch, shouted out times, and explained the different forms of competition to me. I'd seen barrel racing on TV, but pole bending, ribbon roping, and the keyhole were all new to me.

"Man, Aunt Sis can ride," I observed after her barrel run.

"Yeah, but that little bay rocket don't know nothing about chasing trashcans. She shied away from the barrels and wasted several seconds. That's alright, though, Sis is likely to win the keyhole and maybe the poles, too."

"You two are pretty close, huh?"

"Me and Sis? I don't have much family left, but she… She's always here. We grew up together. You know something else, Ches? It's good to see her happy. You're just what the doctor ordered."

"Me? I'm only making more work for her, and she's way too busy as it is."

"Sis is as busy as she wants to be, son. She'll always have time for you. With two years of college and the Durham head for business, she could get a good nine-to-five job."

"What for?"

"Well, she'd have plenty of money, an air-conditioned office, an hour for lunch, and the evenings free to go riding or just put her feet up and rest. But no, she'd rather squeeze every nickel to keep the colonel's business alive, breathe in the smell of horses with every breath, and supposedly, do as she pleases."

"I never thought about it like that."

"You wouldn't, not listening to her. Sis has got a one track mind, and this darned old horse sale stays on it most of the time."

"You sound like my dad."

"Maybe so, but I stayed around." I felt myself stiffen a little, but he went right on talking. "I'm not saying anything against your daddy, you understand. Terry was the kid brother I never had. I let him drive my hotrod car when he could barely see over the dash. Heck, he even went along on most of my dates."

"Dad never talks much about growing up in Mac Town, but when he does, he usually mentions you."

"Watch that Mac Town business around your Aunt Sis," Jim Rex warned. "Speaking as a McKendrick, it doesn't bother me one little bit. For some reason, though, it just crawls all over her. The name of our little town is McKendrick, and nobody had better forget it in her presence."

"But Dad always calls it Mac Town."

"Yeah, I never quite understood why Terry loved to get her goat. He had it pretty tough, I reckon, living in Miss Sis's shadow. A perfect little southern lady and fearless on a horse, she was the colonel's pride and joy."

"Daddy's little girl," I said with a laugh.

"Not that she was afraid of him, you understand. Rebellion never even crossed her mind. Oh, she enjoys her cigarettes, but the old man smoked like a chimney. Mighty few in his generation found any fault with it. Besides, she shared his notions of family loyalty and community pride. Nearly every move Terry made looked rebellious alongside that, right down to the way he parted his hair."

"Gosh," I said, not sure whether to laugh or cry.

"Sis is sweet, not put on, but the deep-down good-hearted kind of sweet. Even so, when it came to pleasing the colonel or doing a job right she set high standards. I've seen her snap at little brother like a biting dog. 'If you can't handle a horse any better than that, Terry, get off and work a gate.'"

"Jim Rex, are you running that stopwatch or yakking," Aunt Sis called lightheartedly as she hooked a leg over her saddle horn.

"You best watch that little mare," Jim Rex answered. "She's still apt to jump out from under you."

"Some people are born worriers," she teased, laughing at him with her eyes.

"Yeah, and other folks never worry until they're looking around wondering what just happened. Ever seen anybody run the keyhole, Ches?"

"No, what is it?"

"Simple, really, whoever can run into the arena, turn a tight circle, and make it out again in the fastest time wins. Doesn't sound like much, but it's fast and fun to watch."

The pounding hooves and flying dirt reminded me of a western movie, and the little bay mare with all her heart and fire made my model horses look like the empty shells they were.

Finally, I watched my aunt pay her barn help. They formed a rough line from her desk out into the hallway, laughing and joking with each other while they waited. Aunt Sis signed checks, or in some cases, counted bills out of an old cash box and spoke warmly to each one as she handed over their wages.

"Twenty'll do me good, Miss Sis," Nash told her. "Put the rest of it down in your book."

"He uses her like a savings account," Jim Rex said with a grin. "Now me, I'd draw all of mine and his too if she'd give it to me."

I wasn't the one who'd worked all day, but by the time evening rolled around, I felt thoroughly worn out. Aunt Sis unpacked the last of my things and perched for a moment on the edge of the bed.

"What's in the book," she asked, gesturing toward my thick binder.

"Records," I admitted shyly, "records for my model horses."

Each 8"x11" sheet included a picture, breed info, model horse show rankings and notes on origin for a single model. Aunt Sis flipped curiously through the laminated pages.

"Heavens to Betsy, I don't keep this much paperwork on my live horses."

"Dad says I get a little carried away."

"Nothing wrong with it as long as you enjoy yourself."

"I do, Aunt Sis, but model horses are a girl's game. I was too little to realize it when I started. There are a few old men who've been collecting forever and a day, but when I go to shows, I compete against girls and most of the judges are women."

"Look at it this way, Ches. You'll have a plenty to choose from when you get ready to find yourself a lady."

"I guess," I answered, laughing a little, "but I don't know if model horses will ever look the same after being around the real, live animals."

"I reckon we'll cross that bridge when we come to it, honey."

Aunt Sis seemed genuinely interested in my model horse hobby, but her thoughts kept straying. Finally, realization dawned. She wanted a cigarette but wouldn't allow herself one as long as we stayed in my bedroom.

"How about showing me around your property," I asked.

I felt awfully close to exhaustion in the face of my aunt's boundless energy, but I knew she'd feel better outside with a cigarette in her hand. Driving the Mule to the edge of her yard, she stopped to open a gate.

"Pull it through," she called cheerfully as if this were nothing.

"Me?"

"Sure, Ches. Don't they ever let you drive?"

"No ma'am, Dad mentioned it a time or two, but Mom says I don't have enough strength in my legs."

"Well, I never! It's not exactly like playing an old-time pump organ. All the new cars have power brakes, and there's nothing to mashing the accelerator."

"I really don't have a safe place to learn in the city."

"We've got plenty of room out here. Don't get excited, honey. Just knock it out of gear and let it roll through."

I scooted reluctantly across the seat, and my heart raced as the side-by-side coasted down the small incline and through the gate.

"How… How do I stop it?"

"Mash the brake," Aunt Sis sang out, and then with laughter in her voice, "Whoa, mule. See there; easy as pie." To my amazement, she stepped casually into the passenger seat. "Now, start the thing and put it back in gear."

"Hold on tight," I warned.

"You can't scare me, honey child. Just keep it right side up and steer clear of the pine trees."

As we bounced along through the afternoon sunshine, Aunt Sis proved a calm and remarkably patient teacher. She whooped and squealed with girlish high spirits when I sent the machine plunging forward in wild fits and starts but never once laughed at me. Her dogs kept us in sight most of the time but stayed well out of my erratic path.

"Your property must go on forever," I said, looking around in wonder once I finally got the hang of driving.

"It's ours, Ches, the Durham place. There's 467 acres here, but that counts everything. The house, outbuildings, and corrals take up some little bit, and the sale barn sits on a pretty good chunk of ground. Considering the scattered patches of timber, there may be 315 acres of pastureland. It's a fair-sized chunk for our part of the country."

"Do you call it a farm or ranch or what?"

"Well, I'm ranching, that and running the horse sale, but they farmed this land up until about the time I was born. The colonel- and my granddaddy before him- raised cotton for a cash crop, feed for the livestock, and vegetables for the table. I mostly just call it the place or sometimes the homeplace."

"You say it belongs to us. I thought you bought Dad's part?"

"I didn't give him much choice about it, either," she admitted. "Couldn't have him selling out to somebody else, now, could I? Still, this is our home. Your daddy can come back anytime he wants and you... Well, you have come, haven't you?"

The famous line from a baseball movie flashed through my mind, but my aunt probably heard the colonel's voice.

"Hold what you've got, darling; they'll come home one day."

"Raising cotton, the way we done it around here, took a right smart of work. They broke ground, planted, and plowed with mules and horses, but the hoeing and picking called for hand labor. Several families, black and white, lived here on the place and worked for a share of the crop. In the spring of the year you can still see scattered patches of yellow jonquils and a few white ones, too. Those mark the old house sights."

"How many homes..."

"Eight, for sure, not counting the big house."

"The big house? Like prison?"

"No, honey, I mean the house where the family lived; my house."

"All three bedrooms of it?"

"It's changed some since Great-Granddaddy Durham built it. The kitchen used to be in a separate building out back. The old home was never very large by today's standards, but compared to the little shotgun houses scattered over the place, I reckon it looked fair sized."

"How did the colonel go from row-crop farming to the horse business?"

"My granddaddy farmed, but he was something of a horse trader, too. The colonel said they never had anything really broke to work the crop with. By the time they got a bunch of mules and horses trained right, Granddaddy would swap them off for some fresh stock."

"Seems like that would slow the work down," I observed.

"Maybe, but Granddaddy figured if his plow hands had to trot to keep up with their mules, they'd cover more ground." She laughed at the little joke I didn't quite get and then continued her explanation. "The boot, or cash difference, he drew on his trades provided an extra income. Besides, the colonel and several of the hands enjoyed the challenge."

We passed several small bunches of horses running loose. Aunt Sis told me to slow down and skirt around them. Her left hand bobbed up and down rapidly as she counted, and her eyes swept over them, taking in every detail. She followed the same routine with a herd of cattle in the next pasture. Every field, every little rise or low place, held a story: a tale of her granddaddy, the colonel, or a stocking-legged sorrel mule. As the memories flowed from my aunt, I began to understand why the thought of Doc Parmalee, Giles's blood uncle but a fairly distant relative of hers, losing his land hit her so hard.

"What happened to the people," I asked when we finally headed back, "the people who used to live here?"

"I kept up with some of them for a while but… The old folks are dead and gone. And their children have pretty well scattered, except for Nash. Nash's quite a horseman, so him and the colonel always got along real good."

"You mean he's lived here all his life?"

"Yes; they say he had a wife once but no children. 'Yonder's the road,' he told her, 'if you got the itch to go. I ain't living nowhere folks don't know a good horse hand when they see him.'"

"Wow," I said, "that's pretty extreme."

"Mmm," Aunt Sis murmured thoughtfully, "this old East Texas red land gets in your blood."

"I'd get lost riding around out here without you," I admitted.

"Oh, you'll learn your way around."

"You make everything sound so simple, Aunt Sis. Who's truck is that?" I asked, catching sight of a late-model silver pickup as we neared the house once again.

"Company's come," Aunt Sis answered and removed her hat long enough to smooth the wind-blown curls beneath it. "Oh, it's just that Hollister fella."

He walked down to the gate and swung it open for us to pass through. When Aunt Sis motioned me over to a patch of shade, he shut the gate and followed. She reached across me to kill the motor, and our visitor stood on the driver's side, casually resting a foot on the floorboard.

"I hope I'm not troubling you, Miss Durham, but I've got some man-to-man business with your nephew."

"Well," she said, arching an eyebrow, "never mind little-old me. Y'all go right ahead."

"See there," he said lightly to me, "a real lady never forgets her place."

A smile twitched at the corners of my aunt's mouth, but she banished it with an almost imperceptible shake of her head. Mr. Hollister's voice turned level and direct. "Seriously, Ches, I admire the way you stood by your aunt last night. Y'all must be close."

"Yesterday is the first time I actually remember seeing her. We've been apart for most of my life, but Aunt Sis is… She's pretty special."

"I can see that."

"I'll play the meek little woman any old time," Aunt Sis quipped, "if I can get a couple of gentlemen to take turns bragging on me."

"Nah, that's enough man-to-man talk. Your name's on the deed, and I think we'd better bring you back into the conversation."

"My name's on the deed, alright, and I aim for it to stay there. I thought I made that clear, Mr. Hollister."

"Please call me Andrew, both of you."

"Ches can do as he pleases, but Mr. Hollister suits me fine."

"Answer me this, ma'am. How's the Durham Auction Company faring financially?"

"Didn't your mama ever tell you not to poke your nose into other folks' affairs? I'm not in business to lose money."

I usually hated conflict of any kind but found myself enjoying the back-and-forth exchange between these two sharp-witted individuals. Mr. Hollister's arguments sounded smooth, persuasive, and not at all threatening. Then too, I felt secure with Aunt Sis, safely on the winning side.

"Perhaps you're not losing money," he admitted, "but managing to support yourself and break even is hardly the definition of success."

"I don't know, Mr. Hollister. The definition of success depends a great deal on one's goals. How much money will your birddog operation bring in?"

"Birddogs are my hobby, a regular money pit, but I don't call them a business. Your sale barn would make an ideal gathering place during field trials and a great venue for indoor bench shows. I need the added acreage, too. Of course, whatever my needs, your property belongs to you."

"Come up to the house?" she invited, probably from an ingrained sense of hospitality rather than any real warmth. "I believe you mentioned some walking horses to ride behind your dogs."

"Thank you, but I won't impose. We can do our horse trading under this old shade tree."

"I'm satisfied right here if you and Ches are comfortable."

I told her I was fine, and Mr. Hollister got down to business.

"A cousin back home wanted to sell me some horses, but I've already bought eleven dogs. Moving them from Georgia will be expensive enough."

"Mercy," Aunt Sis said with a spark of genuine enthusiasm in her voice, "I thought I was dog poor."

"I count four," he said gazing around at her little pack, "fine looking animals in lean working condition."

"Thank goodness you approve. They're blackmouth curs, working dogs. All my girlfriends and even some of the men folk are used to looking at fat little lap ornaments. They accuse me of starving my so-called pets. Of course, I could do more to ease their minds. When they ask what I'm feeding I say, 'cow tracks and creek water.'"

"That's a good one!" Mr. Hollister laughed and slapped his knee. "Why, anybody ought to know from the shine on their coats that those dogs are healthy."

This praise won him a tiny smile.

"That cow track and creek water business is just one of my daddy's old lines. They eat a plenty and run most of it off working stock or following me around."

"Exactly; they burn calories and build lean muscle doing what they were bred to do."

"I can probably find some horses to suit you. We've always been quarter horse people, but I've got some contacts in the gaited horse business."

Mr. Hollister talked for well over an hour about the kind of horses he wanted and about the similarities between East Texas and the North Georgia countryside he'd romped over as a boy. Eventually Aunt Sis began to fidget. Several times, I saw her hand stray to the pocket that held a pack of cigarettes. Finally, Mr. Hollister noticed.

"My grandmother smoked, Granddad, too. You certainly won't bother me if—"

She folded her hands demurely in her lap.

"I do enjoy an occasional cigarette, but I'm fine right now."

A glint of grim determination showed in her eyes. We received his order for three good Walking horses, but Aunt Sis strained the limits of her willpower. As we watched Mr. Hollister drive away, she let out a frustrated groan, swooned and threw her head back against the seat.

"What is it, Aunt Sis?" I yelped, heart pounding. "What's the matter?"

Chapter Three

H is grandmother… I declare, Ches, if people are going to treat me like some kind of anachronism, I may just have to quit smoking."

"I hate to say it, Aunt Sis, but you aren't off to a very good start."

She glanced down at the cigarette between her fingers as if surprised to see it there.

"Well, maybe not today but… No girl wants to remind a nice-looking fellow of his grandmother! People take such a childish attitude toward smoking these days. It's not something they choose to do, so a cigarette between my fingers must make me evil or at least backward."

Some people might consider her habit rude and off putting, but Aunt Sis drew her manners from a bygone era, a time when gentlemen still offered a lady a light and the rare nonsmoking host provided ashtrays out of common courtesy to his guests.

"I think Mr. Hollister just wanted to put you at ease," I suggested gently.

"That man doesn't care how I feel. He's got a greedy arm stretched out to sweep this place into his pile, and I'm standing in the way. Of course, since I'm so grandmotherly, he may decide to just wait until I expire from old age." She exhaled a long stream of smoke and seemed to blow all thoughts of Mr. Hollister away with it. "Do you want something for supper, honey?"

"Not much," I answered.

"I brought leftover cornbread home from the café. I'll fix you some in a glass of buttermilk if you want it."

"Cornbread in a glass?"

"Poor deprived child, we'd best start you off with sweet milk."

Back up at the house, Aunt Sis pulled my boots off and disappeared long enough to bathe. I enjoyed the odd but surprisingly tasty snack and then called my parents. Dad laughed when I described my supper, but Mom fretted about a balanced diet.

"Serena agonizes over every added ounce, yet she flatly refuses to give up the foods her parents and grandparents ate. You need to be careful, son. Any amount of excess weight will make it harder for you to get around."

"Yes ma'am."

"It's been a while since I heard that, quite the refreshing change from 'Oh, Mom.'"

Dad chuckled. I could almost see him in his recliner with one leg thrown carelessly over the other knee while Mom held another phone and tapped away on the computer.

"Miss Sis Durham draws good manners to the surface like the sale barn draws flies. I'm telling you, Jenna, we grew up together, but she's more a product of Daddy's time, or even Granddaddy's, than mine."

Laughing, Mom admitted that there might be a few positives associated with living in the past. I bit back a surprisingly automatic defense of my aunt, and we finished our conversation without a fuss.

"Now, Ches, I don't mind helping you any way I can," Aunt Sis said when she reentered the living room.

"Thank you, but I can manage most things myself."

She made a delicate little noise, not the usual necessary throat clearing, but her acknowledgement of a somewhat awkward subject.

"If you ever want help from a man, don't hesitate to tell me. I'll get Nash or Jim Rex up here right away if it makes you more comfortable."

"I reckon we'll cross that bridge when we come to it," I said, smiling as I parroted her phrase.

"Sounds like a plan," she answered with a laugh. "Now, we'd best get some sleep, church tomorrow."

"I thought we might rest after the sale and every—"

"We'll rest, between morning and evening services. I'd shut the sale down in a heartbeat if I thought it kept folks out of church," she declared.

"Strong words," I thought, "considering her love for the Durham Auction Company."

Mom and Dad belonged to a large church with a catchy name, professional musicians, and several well-known members sprinkled through the massive congregation. I attended along with them. We went once every couple of weeks, but Aunt Sis operated on an entirely different game plan.

I jolted awake out of a deep sleep and stiffened in fear of rolling off the unfamiliar bed. When my eyes finally adjusted to the semidarkness, I recognized my surroundings and relaxed. Unfortunately, the sound of loud, prolonged coughing from my aunt's room scared me all over again.

I'm slow, painfully slow, at dressing myself. Putting on my own socks meant an all out struggle, rolling around on the floor. A pointless struggle, really, when Aunt Sis would gladly help me with them, but in my sleep-clouded mind I wanted to be fully clothed and ready to face whatever emergency I found down the hall.

Call it respect or embarrassment or whatever you like, but the half-open bedroom door stopped me for a moment. Aunt Sis lay propped against her pillows, her naturally fair complexion flushed red from coughing. She finally caught sight of me and tried to smile.

"Come... come in, honey."

She pulled the bed sheet up over her already modest nightgown and motioned me inside.

I rolled through the door and glanced uncertainly around her room. A large, antique vanity with a leather padded bench sat against one wall, and a matching wardrobe stood across from it. Only a few scattered patches of the rose-covered wallpaper showed between black-and-white snapshots, blue ribbons, and yellowed newspaper clippings featuring Durham Auction Company. I even spotted a young Jim Rex, sitting his horse next to Aunt Sis near the center of a large group of mounted kids.

Though my aunt was hardly an indoor person, this space fit her like a well-worn coat. Most of the pictures showed the colonel, usually on horseback and flanked by either or both of his two children. A few caught him on the ground with one arm around my grandmother, and these startled me. The Aunt Sis I knew looked just like Grandmother. Only that half-dangerous little grin and the way she wore her Stetson marked her as the colonel's daughter.

"Are you okay," I eventually asked.

"I... I'm fine," she managed, dabbing at her lips with a lacy handkerchief as the current spasm eased. "How'd you sleep?"

"Not quite as well as I did last night, but I feel rested enough. You don't sound fine."

"Believe it or not, I'm a morning person. I've always loved this time of day, but five or six hours without a cigarette..." She trailed off with a little shutter, reaching for the pack and saddle-shaped lighter on her nightstand.

For the first time since my arrival Aunt Sis actually looked middle-aged or maybe even a little older. She leaned back on the pillows, closed her eyes, and drew deeply on her cigarette. Relief flooded her expression. However, I saw weariness there, too, a deep-seated weariness that didn't belong in the face of a relatively young, energetic woman waking from a nights rest.

"All better now?" I asked, but she totally missed my sarcasm.

"Oh, honey, you just don't know how much better I feel. Now, if I had a cup of black coffee..."

I left the room in a huff, wondering how she could take so much pleasure from something that was obviously bad for her. Out in the hallway, though, I remembered Jim Rex's passing reference to her father's attitude about smoking.

For most people my age, cigarettes represented rebellion, a bad-girl or bad-boy image. For Aunt Sis, though, they were her tie to a simpler, happier time. Her body demanded a certain amount of nicotine, but perhaps more importantly the familiar habit reminded her of the colonel and of her young, vibrant self.

As crippled and near-helpless as I was, I never saw anything but loving pride in my aunt's eyes when she looked at me. Who was I to criticize her only apparent weakness? Her morning seemed off to a rough start, and if a cup of coffee would help... Well, how hard could it be?

"Here you go, Aunt Sis," I said a few minutes later, carefully handing over a cup of the steaming liquid. "I never made any before so..."

I wrinkled my nose as the bold aromas of coffee and cigarette smoke mingled in the air, but the combination wasn't exactly unpleasant.

"Thank you, Ches. The way you took off, I figured you must be put out with me."

"I can't decide whether I am or not," I answered, smiling at my own confusion, "and it doesn't much matter."

"Ahh, coffee's just right."

I suddenly realized she'd say that, even if it tasted like dishwater or road tar, simply because I made it for her.

"You could quit smoking, Aunt Sis. I know you could. You're the kind of person who can do almost anything once you make up your mind."

She smiled gently and shook her head.

"Thanks for your confidence, Ches, but I once heard the colonel describe me in horse terms. 'She's a fine, spirited filly,' he said proudly, 'but just a mite too high-strung for her own good.'"

"What does that have to do with—"

"I think about quitting every now and then, but the thought rattles me so badly... I reach for a cigarette every time. I'd be a nervous wreck without them. Probably let myself get as big as a barn, too. I don't want to see you take up the habit, honey, but you don't want to see me try to stop, either. It wouldn't be a pretty sight."

What do you say to something like that?

"Yes ma'am," was all I came up with.

"The colonel had a cure for this cough," she said with a tight little smile after enduring another harsh bout of it, "but I'll not start my mama spinning in her grave. It will ease up on its own. I'm feeling better already."

"Whatever you say," I agreed reluctantly.

She lit another cigarette almost immediately, but you couldn't stay worried around Aunt Sis. Besides, she was right. The cough gradually disappeared, except for her regular throat clearing. Soon enough, she shooed me from the room.

"Time we got our day started. I'll be out directly."

"Okay, if you're really feeling better, but that cough of yours is pretty scary."

"You'll get used to it, honey; I did."

"Wonderful," I groaned. "That just solves everything."

Aunt Sis laughed off my remark, but her kind eyes seemed to acknowledge the concern that lay behind it.

"How about riding out to the pens with me," she asked after breakfast. "You can stay in the Mule and won't have to dirty your good clothes."

"Sure," I agreed.

"There's no such thing as a day off, not with livestock on the place."

Aunt Sis drove to a set of corrals not far from the house, and her dogs trooped along. Rhett led the way while the others followed behind us. She retrieved a square bale from the little shed, broke it open and tossed hay to several horses.

"Are these your horses?"

"Some of them are. I try to clear the sale barn out by Saturday afternoon, but there are nearly always a few head left, not counting whatever I bought in the sale. We move everything up here to empty the barn. That-a-way it's ready to clean out and wash down come Monday morning. Plus, it makes it easier for me to feed. I don't work my help on Sundays, except for emergencies."

Back at the house, Aunt Sis fed and watered the dogs and then excused herself for a few minutes. My aunt never seemed to wear much makeup, but she surely knew how to use the stuff. She reappeared ready for church and looking like Colonel Durham's youthful darling, without a line or wrinkle in sight.

Yesterday's shirt and blue jeans were gone, too. She wore an old-fashioned dress of light blue with a narrow white belt at her waist and white crocheted gloves to match.

"Wow," I said. "You look like a living, breathing picture from an old-timey catalog."

"Yes, well," she apologized, glancing down at her outfit, "such things fell out of favor a long time ago, but I still like them."

"Oh, I think you look very pretty. That's all I meant."

"Thank you, Ches. It's a shame I don't even know you well enough to recognize a compliment when I hear it. There's something else, too. I don't exactly know what you can and can't do. Would you like to use your wheelchair at church, or do you want to walk on your crutches?"

"That's alright, Aunt Sis. How could you know? We've never really spent any time together."

"Oh, honey, I was a stubborn fool not to visit you in Dallas. I wanted you here on the homeplace where you belong, but—."

"Well, you're awfully busy here. Besides, you and Dad don't exactly…"

"Gee-haw," she supplied.

"Whatever you say," I answered, laughing. "My balance and stamina aren't the greatest, but it's good for me to use the forearm crutches. I'll take the wheelchair today and look things over. Then we can go from there."

McKendrick Missionary Baptist, or at least the white frame church house, sat on a double lot near what had once been the center of town. Instead of driving straight to it, Aunt Sis showed me around.

"There sits the old bank building, and over yonder was a grocery store."

"Not much left in Mac Town, is th—"

Remembering Jim Rex's warning, I bit the sentence off, but Aunt Sis only sighed.

"I don't have to ask who taught you that piece of foolishness," she said, cutting her eyes at me before returning them to the road, "but I live in McKendrick, Texas. Good Lord willing, I hope to die in McKendrick. I never heard of Mac—any such place."

"Yes ma'am… I mean no ma'am. I…"

"Don't let me upset you, Ches. It's not your fault. Now, to answer your original question, the church is still fairly strong. Then there's that new Exxon out on the highway."

"That gas station didn't exactly look new."

"Well, I guess… They put it in not long before Mama died."

"I wasn't even born then," I said as we pulled up to the church. "Don't you think the new has worn off?"

"Smarty britches," she quipped, but she laughed when she said it.

I noticed an obstacle right off. Concrete steps led up to a wide front porch.

"Uh oh," I thought, "here's one place Aunt Sis couldn't just snap her fingers and order a ramp."

"Go on around to the other door," she said as if reading my mind. "I'll unlock it from the inside."

Aunt Sis glided up the steep stairs like she'd been born in a pair of high-heeled shoes. They made a nice clickety-clack sound on the steps, too. She paused at the top to remove a key from her white handbag, and I wheeled off in the direction she had indicated. Sure enough, a steep wooden ramp afforded me access to the side door.

Aunt Sis sang softly to herself as she adjusted the thermostat and started a pot of coffee in the fellowship hall.

"Rock of Ages, cleft for me, let me hide myself in Thee."

The older couples who drifted in first looked like an altogether different crowd from those who attended the horse sale. Still, these church folk had at least one thing in common with that tough bunch of kids, tack peddlers, and horse traders. They all clustered around Aunt Sis and hung on her every word.

Even when she withdrew to the shade of a large oak tree for one last cigarette, they tagged along, most for the simple pleasure of her company. My aunt introduced me over and over again, beaming with pride, and the church family seemed pleased at her obvious joy.

"Ches, this is Uncle Elmer Blakely, my mama's only brother. That makes him your great uncle. He leads the singing for us."

A tall, gaunt man with snow-white hair, he shook my hand and never batted an eye at the wheelchair.

"I saw you once or twice as a baby, young man, but you've grown a sight since then."

"It's nice to meet you, sir. I've heard Dad mention your name."

Uncle Elmer said something else, but I missed it, distracted by the sight of a familiar figure waddling rapidly in our direction. I'd forgotten about Great-Aunt Hattie. Well, not forgotten about her exactly, forgotten that she lived in McKendrick. Heavyset as she was, the summer heat didn't agree with her. The short walk left her huffing and puffing but failed to check the rapid flow of unnecessary advice.

"Just wait until I get through with your daddy. If he wants you to spend some time around here, I've got a perfectly good spare bedroom. Why send you a-way out yonder in the sticks to stay with Sis when she never even bothered to come up and see you."

Aunt Sis stiffened visibly and took a possessive step toward me, but Hattie blocked out everything else as she swooped in for a hug. The old lady might not squeeze as tight as Aunt Sis, but she kind of folded you in like a great big tent.

"I like staying with Aunt Sis."

"Ridiculous; you'd be better off with Elmer. Not that he ever drove three hours one way to come to your birthday party anymore than she did, but he's got a nice brick home with central heat and air right across the street from me."

"Mornin', Aunt Hattie," Sis finally said, greeting her mother's youngest sister dryly and without much enthusiasm.

"And you," Hattie snapped, whirling around, "you might have let me know C.J. was coming."

"Yes'm," was all Aunt Sis said, but I glimpsed a dangerous spark in her eyes before Uncle Elmer stepped between them.

"I'm mighty glad to see the boy, Hattie, but I don't recall inviting him as a houseguest."

"Elmer Blakely, you mean to tell me you'd turn our own dead sister's grandson out in the street?"

"He ain't in the street, Hattie. He's out there on the Durham place with Miss Sis."

The old lady pinched my cheek, nodded briefly to Aunt Sis, and went on inside. The coolness she showed her niece startled me a little because most of her generation regarded Aunt Sis as their own special pet.

"Good mornin', young man." The hardy greeting and a slap on the shoulder took my mind off Aunt Hattie's strange attitude. "My name is Carlton Crawford. I'm the pastor here, and some way or another, I missed you at the horse sale on Friday night."

"Yes sir, I saw you there and heard your prayer. It's nice to meet you."

"Nice to meet you, too, Ches. I remember your daddy well, and it's good to have you with us."

A little later, I watched a cute redhead wiggle her way through the crowd of old folks and up to my aunt. Though not seriously overweight, this girl had packed on more pounds in her sixteen or seventeen years than Aunt Sis had accumulated in twice that time.

"Miss Sis, I'm leaving for Six Flags tomorrow with a friend. Daddy promised me some spending money, but you know how that goes."

Aunt Sis turned a warm smile on the girl but stiffened a little at the sight of hip-hugger jeans.

"Oh, sweetheart, where are those darling dresses I sent over for your birthday?"

"In the closet, I guess. What am I supposed to do for money?"

"Well, I've got a horse or two that'll make your stomach drop down to your toes for free and give you the whiplash to boot."

"Really?" the girl groaned with a roll of her eyes.

"Jim Rex may make it yet," Aunt Sis observed with a glance at her watch. "I doubt he'd miss church on Ches's first Sunday in McKendrick."

Recognition dawned suddenly. Serena Kate, the daughter Jim Rex named after my aunt.

"If he shows up at all, he'll probably be broke," she answered tartly.

"Now, sweetheart, that's not funny or very nice, either."

Aunt Sis spoke kindly, but I could almost hear the colonel's voice echoing in her head.

"Bullwhip's hung on the wall too long."

Nevertheless, she dug something from her white handbag.

"Here's fifty dollars. Surely that'll do it."

"Oh, thank you!" Serena Kate squealed in delight and accepted a hug along with the money.

"You're welcome, sweetheart."

Just like that, all was forgiven; the attitude, the jeans, and the fifty dollars she'd never see again. Aunt Sis obviously had a soft spot for this girl. I felt a twinge of something like jealousy, but just then she turned around to look for me.

"Ches, come meet Miss Serena Kate McKendrick. You already know her brothers, but she was busy in the office." Suddenly, her attention swung back to the girl. "I thought you were supposed to be with your mo…gone this weekend."

"Yes, but I wanted to come over here and get some extra…see you."

"Hi, Serena Kate," I put in a little stiffly, examining the girl's blue jeans and bright green t-shirt.

I couldn't see anything particularly racy about the outfit, but it contrasted sharply with my aunt's Sunday-go-to-meeting dress. Anybody bold enough to ask Aunt Sis for money could certainly make a little more effort to please her.

"Hey, Ches."

I didn't intend to like her one bit. I really didn't, but she dropped to her knees to look me in the eye as she smiled. She even gave me a quick hug, a lot of attention for a thirteen-year-old kid. Her hair smelled good, too.

"Hi," I stuttered again.

"It's fun to watch the little ones on the swing set out back unless you'd rather hang out with the smokers. I'm afraid I make Miss Sis puff a little harder sometimes, but I really do love her."

My aunt swatted playfully at the back of Serena Kate's head but ended up stroking her hair.

"I guess I'll stay close to Aunt Sis for now, but thanks."

Serena Kate opened her mouth to respond, but Aunt Sis spoke first.

"Here's Jim Rex now."

The girl stood up, glanced toward her father's battered pickup, and shrugged, but a loving smile tugged at the corners of her mouth as she turned away. The three of us waited there together while Jim Rex ambled across the yard.

"Didn't expect to see you this morning, sugar bear," he said, putting an arm around his daughter and then turned a beaming smile on me and Aunt Sis. "We'd best get us a seat 'fore they're all took up."

The large shotgun-style building smelled of furniture polish and ladies perfume with a musty hint of age. I didn't see any great danger of all the seats being taken, but Aunt Sis stepped carefully to avoid sticking one of her high heels in the gaps between worn floorboards.

Sunlight danced prettily off the highly polished wood surfaces as my aunt led us straight down front. She put Serena Kate next to Jim Rex, placed her bible in the aisle seat, and motioned me to park alongside it.

Amazing me yet again, Aunt Sis walked primly up to the piano. She laid her handbag and gloves atop it and settled herself on the bench. At Uncle Elmer's nod, she tore into Amazing Grace. Though she sat still and dignified with her back straight, her fingers flew over the keys with the same controlled energy I'd seen when she mastered the bucking bay.

Remembering my aunt's love for the Chuck Wagon Gang, I pictured the old upright piano standing in one corner of her parlor. Miss Sis Durham's musical abilities shouldn't have come as any surprise, but they didn't necessarily fit the cowgirl image.

"Glad to see each one here this morning," Uncle Elmer said, stepping to the microphone. "Find a songbook, if you would, and turn to hymn number eleven."

"I heard an old old story, how a Savior came from glory…"

Mom and Dad's church switched to praise music when I was five or six, and Papa Joel gradually quit coming. "Same seven words eleven times," he often grumbled. The old hymn sounded fresh and new to my ears, but there was something else, a timeless quality.

The age-cracked voices around me weren't polished to perfection, but it hardly mattered. My aunt's romping piano style covered most of the bobbles while Uncle Elmer kept everyone more or less together. One arthritic hand swung back and forth through the air, beating time, and his voice rang out clear and strong.

"Oh victory in Jesus, my Savior forever, He sought me and bought me with His redeeming blood."

Living side by side for years, generations really, little squabbles like whatever lay between Aunt Sis and Aunt Hattie were bound to come up. As I listened to the sweet harmony of their voices, though, I realized such trifling disagreements could never erode the deep family feeling these people held for each other. They came together every Sunday for a single purpose, worship.

When the song ended, I anticipated more of the same. As it turned out, though, I had a while to wait. Someone got up, read a verse or two out of the King James Bible, and delivered a short devotional.

"Go along with Serena Kate," Aunt Sis instructed after the speaker closed with prayer. "She'll take you to your Sunday school class."

"Thirteen, right?" Serena Kate asked over her shoulder as we made our way down a narrow hall.

"Yeah, I'll be fourteen next month."

"You'll be in class with me. There aren't enough teens here to split into smaller age brackets."

"Okay," I answered casually.

In truth, though, I felt relieved to keep my new acquaintance in sight. As silly as it seemed, this was the first time since my arrival I'd faced any kind of crowd without the comfort of my aunt's presence. I never felt weak, crippled, or out of place with Aunt Sis. By her side I took on the qualities she expected me to show. I became capable and determined, Colonel Durham's grandson.

After Sunday school I made a bee line for the old oak tree where I found Aunt Sis visiting contentedly with Mrs. Crawford and several other ladies. The music of her laughter soon chased away my unreasonable fears. I drifted close enough for her to reach down and place a hand on my shoulder but didn't interrupt the conversation. Eventually, Mrs. Crawford motioned me a little apart from the other ladies.

"We're glad to have you with us, Ches, and not just at church. Carlton and I fretted terribly over our Miss Sis, living up on that hill above the horse sale all by herself."

"Thank you ma'am, but I imagine she could handle whatever trouble came her way."

I bit the inside of my cheek to keep from laughing, not only at the lady's notion that I could somehow protect Aunt Sis but also at her possessive affection for my aunt. Just then, several pickups and a battered car or two pulled into the yard. Familiar faces from the horse sale and playday piled out, taking off hats as they entered the building.

"Do you know what draws the horse people to church?" the preacher's wife asked. "This particular church, I mean?"

"No ma'am, what?"

"Who, I should say," she corrected and then answered her own question. "Your Aunt Sis does."

"Really?"

"Yes, she tells them they're welcome here anytime and then never says another word about it. Still, they know how exhausted she must be after a Friday night sale, Saturday checkout, and the playday. It doesn't take long to figure out church is important to her, so I suppose they come to see what it's all about."

"That's pretty neat."

"It certainly is. Of course, your aunt's most important contribution is to help create a welcoming environment. Most of those folks know Carlton from his opening prayers. He hardly ever misses a sale. A good many are members now, and they invite other people."

I spotted Scooter, excused myself, and started over to speak to him, but Aunt Hattie swooped down on me.

"Is she treating you alright, son?"

"Who?" I wondered.

"Sis, of course."

"Oh, yes ma'am. She is wonderful."

"She's a sweet girl," Aunt Hattie admitted. "She really is, but there's too much of

Chester Durham in her. That dratted horse sale comes first, ahead of everyone and everything else."

"That's not exactly—"

"Don't try to tell me about my niece, young man. You may think she's all honey and light, but Sis can be mighty cold and hard when it suits her."

I dodged around the old lady then and headed inside. Horse-sale folks swelled the congregation considerably. I knew them, or at least their faces, and felt no crowd-induced anxiety. Besides, there sat Aunt Sis with back straight, head held high, and a contented half smile on her face, hammering away at the piano. Eventually, she made her way back to the pew, and Brother Crawford drew his sermon from Luke 12:4-7.

> And I say unto you my friends, be not afraid of them that kill the body, and after that have no more that they can do. But I will forewarn you whom ye shall fear: Fear him, which after he hath killed hath power to cast into hell; yea, I say unto you, Fear him. Are not five sparrows sold for two farthings, and not one of them is forgotten before God? But even the very hairs of your head are all numbered. Fear not therefore: ye are of more value than many sparrows.

Aunt Sis traced the lines in her Bible for my benefit. The lettering, red in color to signify the spoken words of Jesus, stood out sharply against her white-gloved fingertip.

I prayed for salvation somewhere around the tender age of six and felt at the time that God had truly changed me. As I grew older, though, I became more aware of my challenges. Thoughts of how much easier God could make my life if He chose to heal me soon led to doubts about my relationship with Him.

"The Lord cares for each and every man, woman, and child individually. His greatest desire is to save us from our sin and shelter us protectively in his mighty hand. Satan, on the other hand, wants to destroy us and any chance we may have to honor and glorify God."

Brother Crawford had a habit of removing his glasses to fix me with that piercing blue gaze. Sometimes his voice rang from the rafters, but all too often, it went deathly quiet, sending a shiver up and down my backbone. Even that shiver, though, couldn't erase a certain question from my mind. If The Lord God cared so much about me personally why wouldn't he fix my body?

"How many crippled sparrows are out there flying in circles with just one good wing?" I thought sourly.

When we finally got home, Aunt Sis fixed me a grilled cheese sandwich for lunch and made funny faces over her weight-loss shake. These expressions, downright hilarious on someone as dignified as Miss Sis Durham, helped take my mind off the troubling sermon.

"Those things taste awful," she said dabbing the corners of her mouth with a paper napkin as she eyed the empty can, "but I need to cut calories."

"You're beautiful just the way you are. I can't see any reason to make yourself miserable, but it is awfully entertaining to watch you drink that stuff."

"Aw, thanks, Ches." Then in sudden confusion, "What do you mean, entertaining?"

"My grilled cheese tasted good," I assured her. "At least one of us is full."

"Do you want a nap," she asked, making quick work of my dishes, "or do you feel like sitting out on the gallery with me."

After a couple of days keeping up with my whirlwind of an aunt, the idea of a nap sounded pretty good. Suddenly, though, the words "with me" registered. Aunt Sis was an exceptionally busy person, and I realized she was finally ready to unwind a little. A lot of people value their alone time, but she wanted me by her side.

"I'll sit with you, Aunt Sis."

Leaving the wheelchair inside, I followed her on my knees. The old-fashioned dog run always seemed to draw a breeze, and a wide rear porch, which Aunt Sis called a gallery, offered a swing and plenty of shade from the late May sunshine.

Taking a deep breath of fresh air, I marveled at the profound quiet and sorted through several unfamiliar smells. A faint scent of manure drifted up from the sale barn, but the honeysuckle vine on the yard fence overpowered it.

Aunt Sis held the swing while I climbed into it and then sank down beside me.

"You ought to stay off those knees. They'll be worn plumb to the bone by the time you get to be my age."

I grunted noncommittally, and she started a steady pumping motion with one high-heeled shoe, causing the swing to rock gently. The click of her lighter followed by a deep, satisfied sigh told me this might be as good a time as any to ask some difficult questions.

"What's the matter between you and Aunt Hattie?"

"Aw, honey, don't you know some of the butter has slid off her biscuit?"

"Well," I said, laughing, "I never heard it put quite like that."

"Aunt Hattie loves you; bless her heart. You needn't worry over how she feels about me."

Satisfied, at least for the moment, I moved on to a more pressing question.

"Aunt Sis, do you ever get scared?"

"Of Aunt Hattie?" she asked, giving me her that'll-be-the-day look.

"No, I mean do you ever get scared of anything. Like, were you scared yesterday on that bucking horse?"

"No," she said with a dismissive laugh, "I don't have sense enough to be afraid of a horse. There are times, though, when I'm scared half to death. I'm afraid nobody'll want this place when I'm gone," she answered. "What if I've worked and scrimped and saved… thrown away the opportunity to be a wife and mama all for nothing?"

"Don't worry, Aunt Sis. I'll—"

"Your life may go off in a different direction, Ches, and that's fine. Those things are in the Lord's hands, not mine. Nine times out of ten, our fears are things we can't control."

"If it's alright for me to take another path, how come you got so angry with Dad?"

"I'm a long way from perfect, Ches. I'm stubborn and prideful and when people I love disappoint me, I don't handle it well. Terry left here mad. It never bothered me to admit that I might be in the wrong, but for him to go against the colonel…"

"Wouldn't you get angry with me if I let you down?"

"I'm older, Ches, and maybe even the tiniest bit wiser. Most of the resentment I felt toward your Dad is faded and gone. Of course, my blood pressure still jumps a little every time I think of the way he left me alone after we lost the colonel."

"I thought Dad left here a long time before the colonel died."

"He did," she said with a nod.

"Well, then, what do you mean the way he left you afterwards?"

"I figured he'd move home and take on a share of the responsibility for Durham Auction Company."

"And we all know how that worked out."

"He and your Mom showed up at the funeral home just in time for visitation and then spent one night out here with Jenna pouting and working up a fake cough every time I lit a cigarette."

"You and Mom are kind of hard on each other, aren't you?"

"We tend to look at things differently, and by things, I mean almost everything. She loves you and your daddy, though. That's good enough for me. Terry left home of his own accord. Jenna met and married him without the least notion of his deep family roots. Nobody could accuse her of stealing him away. And maybe, just maybe, those coughing fits weren't as put on as they seemed."

"But you had just lost the colonel," I said, and this little bit of understanding earned me a grateful smile.

"If I ever needed my cigarettes, honey, I needed them that night. Terry finally saddled a couple of horses and asked me to ride out with him."

"Well, play like Paul Harvey. Let's hear the rest of the story."

"They left the next day, not two hours after we laid the colonel to rest. I was sitting right here on this old swing with you in my lap when Jenna swept past, grabbed you up, and said, 'take care of yourself, Serena.' That's exactly what I've had to do ever since."

"What did Dad say?"

"Nothing; he got up off those porch steps, kissed me on the top of the head, and followed after his wife and baby. The Durham Auction Company never missed a sale, Ches, not even one. I settled the estate, mailed Terry a check that left me with precious little to operate on, and slowly clawed my way back up to what the colonel built. To sit here and watch y'all go, though, that nearly tore the heart out of me."

"You're still young enough to get married and start a family."

"I turned forty this year, Ches. If Mr. Right don't come high loping in here pretty quick... Besides, I'm too set in my ways. When I go to sell a horse or buy some cattle or light a cigarette, I don't look around for anybody's permission. No man worth his salt would want to put up with me."

"You don't know that, Aunt Sis."

"You're right, I suppose. I'm meddling in the Lord's business again, and it's awfully easy to do."

"I guess…"

Aunt Sis seemed to draw a lot of comfort from her relationship with God, but my own uncertainty on the subject proved as worrisome as a sore tooth.

"Now, enough about me," she said, dropping her spent cigarette into the coffee can she kept for the purpose. "What is it that's troubling you?"

Chapter Four

I'd hate to shame you," I said reluctantly. "You deserve so much better than a coward for your nephew."

"Honey, you're all the nephew I'll ever want, and there's not a cowardly bone in your body. Bravery doesn't mean you're never scared. It means you get as scared as the next fellow but keep on keepin' on. You do that about as well as anybody I know."

"Maybe it seems that way to you," I said, half wishing I'd never started this conversation, "but I get scared for no real reason. Take this morning; I got scared, or maybe nervous is a better word, just leaving your sight to go to Sunday school."

She sighed, shook a fresh cigarette from her pack, and finally answered.

"Ches, I can't tell you which fears are reasonable and which aren't. You saw how stressed I let myself get in the office, but when it comes to a ruckus with a bad horse or facing somebody over the barrel of a gun—"

"What!"

She gave a little shrug of her shoulders and chuckled at my shocked expression.

"I'm a mite touchy when it comes to my territory. Nobody's gonna come on this place and threaten me or mine. Why, I couldn't call myself the colonel's daughter."

"Oh snap," I thought, "My aunt's part cowgirl, part southern belle, and part gangster."

"Safe and sound behind a desk," she continued, "my nerves are a regular train wreck. Let real trouble come, though, and I'm as cool as a cucumber. What kind of sense does that make?"

"Not much," I admitted.

"Look, honey, I'm blessed with the colonel's quick reflexes and a fair amount of agility. I can take a bullwhip and flick flies off a horse's rump without touching him, or I can make my whip draw blood at every lick."

"Yes but what—"

"Some of the things I do that might look bold or even a little crazy to you are nothing more than day-to-day chores. They don't require any bravery because I'm reasonably sure of my abilities within the situation. You on the other hand… Every time I see you try something new or push out of your comfort zone, my heart fills up and my eyes sting. You're the brave one."

"Sure I am," I muttered as she rose to her feet.

"As Mama used to say, I feel a sinking spell coming on. Can I bring you a glass of tea, Ches?"

She didn't ask if I wanted my tea sweetened or unsweetened, but that stuff had enough sugar in it to float a silver spoon. A bright yellow wedge of lemon perched on the side of each glass. I seldom drank tea and never sweet tea with lemon. After the first refreshing sip, though, I wondered why?

"Talking about fear," I ventured, "I love horses, or at least the idea of them, but I'm too scared to ride."

"You've got horses in your blood, Ches. It's only natural they'd peak your interest, but riding in your condition is an uncertain proposition at best. I don't intend to push you, but I'm here to help. You'll overcome the fear if you really want to ride. Just look how quickly you learned to drive the Mule. I never in my life saw the colonel afraid of a horse, no matter how wild or crazy, but he wouldn't go within ten foot of a three wheeler."

"I don't want to let you down, Aunt Sis, or disgrace his memory."

"If you ride, Ches, it's got to be for your own enjoyment. Riding's not a necessary part of life like it was during the colonel's growing-up years. If you don't like it, there's no use fooling with it."

"Yes ma'am, I understand."

"I hope you do. I'll always be proud of you, and the colonel… Oh, Ches… He—"

Voice choked with emotion, she discarded a half-finished cigarette and immediately reached for another one.

"Aunt Sis, I didn't mean to upset you."

"It's not your fault," she said, wiping fiercely at the tears on her cheeks. "I'm just a silly old lady."

"Old lady my eye," I shot back, and she laughed.

"Now, about your handling horses, the thing to do is ease into it. Let me study on that for a while."

"I got kind of a funny feeling at church," I admitted, changing the subject.

"What kind of funny feeling? You seemed to enjoy yourself."

"Oh, I did. I loved the singing, but to think that all those people have known our family for years and years... They're total strangers to me, and it just felt odd. I didn't even know you played the piano."

"I muddle through," she said dismissing her tremendous talent as offhandedly as she flicked the ash from her cigarette. "I wish you could've heard Mama play."

"She couldn't have sounded any better than you; there's no way."

"You're awfully sweet to me, but I promise you there are a bunch of pianists who play better than I do."

"Well," I decided, "I don't ever want to hear one of them."

"Why not?" she asked, puzzled.

"I'd either jump up out of my chair, cured, or die of over excitement right there. It's just too big of a risk."

Aunt Sis threw back her head and laughed so loud and long that her dog Rhett padded around the corner of the house to investigate.

"I'm... alright... old fella," she said, speaking in short bursts and stroking his ragged ears as she caught her breath.

The battle-scarred veteran of many a fight reached his nose over to snuffle me but

I shrank back with an undignified yelp.

"No, get back boy. Get away from me."

"Don't you like dogs, Ches?" Aunt Sis wanted to know.

"I don't know. I've never been around one except for those little yip-yap types people keep in the house."

"Well, we can sure remedy that. Old Rhett's no yip-yaper. He's loyal to his last drop of blood, and He'll come to love you because you're part of us."

"Yeah, well…"

"As far as getting personally acquainted with the church folks, that'll come in time. They know who you are, and it's not your fault you weren't raised here at home."

"Thanks, Aunt Sis. I felt welcome and all, but it made me think of one of those TV characters who comes down with amnesia. You know, they sit there in the middle of their friends and family and don't recognize a soul."

"I reckon you miss your pals from Dallas, huh?"

"What pals?" I asked a little bitterly. "I miss Mom and Dad, but even if I were home, I'd only see them for a few hours in the evening. Now, Papa Joel…"

"Oh, I know you miss your grandpa. Why don't you go in and give him a call?"

"Yes ma'am, I will, but can we sit here just a little longer?"

"I don't see why not," she answered lightly. "It's a pleasant spot."

"Sure it is, but that's not all. I like sitting here with you. You've finally stopped long enough for me to catch up."

"Oh, honey," she said with a pained look, "I never meant to neglect you."

"No, no, it's not that at all. You've done nothing but look out for me and entertain me ever since I got here. It's just… You never move any slower than a good spanking trot. I like talking to you without half a dozen other people waiting their turn, too. You should let yourself relax more often."

Aunt Sis smiled as she ran her fingers through my hair.

"A good spanking trot, huh? You're starting to talk like a horseman already. It feels good to rest a minute and gather my thoughts. I'm enjoying our visit as much or more than you."

"Brother and Mrs. Crawford mean an awful lot to you, don't they?"

"They've been mighty good to me. Mrs. Crawford was my first Sunday school teacher, and I was saved under Brother Crawford's preaching at nine years old. He preached Mama's funeral and then the colonel's. It was Mrs. Crawford who first suggested the church ladies take over the concessions for the sale."

"Really?"

"Uh huh, she said I had too much on my plate and the café was something they could handle. Of course, she intended to do it for nothing as a sort of temporary relief for me. I fleshed out the notion of using the proceeds to benefit the church and making it a permanent situation. Brother Carlton and Miz Edna are two of the finest people I know. You like them, too, don't you?"

"Sure, sure I do. That sermon, though…"

"That one struck me as pretty tame, all about the Good Lord's love and care. When he really gets too preaching on Hell, honey, you can smell the smoke." She nodded her head in definite approval and something very near enthusiasm. "The truths of God's word ought never be watered down."

"I guess not, but sometimes I wonder. If God loves me so much why'd he stick me in this broke down body? It makes me question whether I'm really one of his at all. I mean, what if I'm missing the boat here?"

Aunt Sis nearly dropped her glass of tea. Recovering, she set it down carefully, and I saw tears gathering in her eyes as she took one of my hands into both of hers.

"Why, bless your sweet heart. No wonder you're scared. We all need to be rock-solid sure of our salvation. Terry told me you took care of that years ago, but it's not for him or me to say. Can you remember a time and a place in your life when you repented and asked the Lord to save you?"

"Yes ma'am… I mean, I think so. I'd gone to some kind of church camp. While I was there, I mainly wanted to go home, but afterwards I couldn't stop thinking about the things they taught us."

"Yes, honey?"

"On my second or third night back, I got up and went into Mom and Dad's room. Instead of waking them up, though, I prayed at the foot of their bed. I felt something… But that doesn't help much in the here and now. I still can't walk."

"Ches, there are some things I can't explain because I don't understand them myself. I do know I've prayed and prayed for you since before you were born, and I truly believe the Lord answered my prayers because you are a fine young man."

The tears spilled over onto her cheeks, and each one fell like a tiny hammer on my heart.

"Aw, don't cry, Aunt Sis. I can't stand it. I think I'm saved, I really do, but I'd like to understand God's plan for me a little better."

"The thing is, honey, you've got to do more than think when it comes to your spiritual condition. The Lord wants you to know for certain. He gives His children the Holy Spirit to guide, comfort, and reassure us."

"But how do I know if I've got it?"

"He, the Holy Spirit, speaks to our hearts in a still, small voice. Please don't let a crippled body stand in the way of your eternal salvation, Ches. Somewhere in the book of Romans, Paul asks, 'Shall the thing formed say to him who formed it why hast thou made me thus?'"

"Well, that's about as clear as mud."

"He goes on to compare God to a potter and us feeble human beings to hunks of clay. A potter exercises power over his clay and can do as he pleases with it. The Lord's not out to get you, honey. There's a reason for every burden he's laid on you. We may not always understand his reason, but you can rest assured he's got one."

"If you promise not to cry anymore of those big, pitiful tears over me- not even into your pillow- I'll do some thinking and praying about all this. I might even get saved again."

"No, honey, that's not possible. If you were ever saved, you're still saved today. Jesus Christ did the work to save us, and he's the one who keeps us."

"Alright, I'll figure it out. Just don't worry yourself sick in the meantime. Remember, no more tears for me."

"Well, I'll try to leave it in the Lord's hands. I love you so much, though, and worry has always been a weakness of mine. You may not think we know each other all that well, but you can talk to me anytime about anything. I do favor that spanking trot or even a flat-out run. Still, I've got a good whoa with the right hand on the bridle reins. Just say, 'Aunt Sis I need a minute,' and you'll see a pretty fair slidin' stop."

The next few days passed pleasantly enough, but despite my best intentions I mostly avoided thinking about God or my relationship with him. On Monday I watched Aunt Sis attack her housework with the same ferocious energy she put into every other task. I helped as best I could and lured her out to the gallery a time or two for short rests. Late in the day, we checked her livestock, inspected the freshly cleaned pens at the sale barn, and bought three horses from Nash's nephew, Little Herman.

"How come y'all call a grown man Little Herman?" I asked over the hum of the crickets as we settled back into the porch swing. "He's not even particularly small."

"His daddy was Big Herman, so I reckon he'll always be Little Herman."

We watched the fireflies, Aunt Sis called them lightning bugs, in silence for a while until she cleared her throat to speak.

"Say, Ches, when was the last time you went fishing?"

"Try never," I said with a snort. "We visited a hatchery one time where they let kids fish but you had to climb these steps and get up high enough to let your line down into a humongous glass tank."

"Good gravy," she said half under her breath. "What's wrong with that brother of mine?" Then realizing I'd heard her, she backtracked a little. "I'm a fine one to talk. We've got three ponds here on the place and I haven't wet a hook in the last ten years. I guess I'm as tied up with horses and the Durham Auction Company as he is with other people's money. Still, if I had kids…"

The next morning after breakfast Aunt Sis fixed us a picnic of thick-sliced bacon on her buttermilk biscuits. She threw in several cans of Diet Coke for herself, some Orange Crush for me, and a jug of ice water for us to share.

"No iced tea?" I asked jokingly.

"Goodness knows it tastes better than this stuff," she answered, scowling at the Diet Coke in her hand. "I always seem to have a frog in my throat, though, and the bubbles feel nice."

"Why not drink Orange Crush, real Coca-Cola, or another carbonated drink you might actually enjoy?"

"All that sugar," she explained with a pitiful little sigh, "they might as well label that stuff Figure Flaws in a Can."

"If sugar's to blame," I thought silently, "your tea is nothing but Homemade Figure Flaws in a Pitcher."

"Besides, if a sodee-water tasted good," she reasoned, "I wouldn't know when to quit."

We loaded some dusty old fishing tackle and three lawn chairs into the bed of her '70 model Ford pickup, and she casually told me to drive. Just then, though, Nash strode into the yard.

"Morning, Miss Sis. I dug some worms and brought along that new line just like you asked me."

"Thanks, you might as well come with us."

The old man hemmed and hawed, perhaps realizing he wouldn't get paid for a day of fishing, but he soon relented.

"Y'all may need somebody to kill a snake. Reckon we can swing by the house to pick up my pole and a few little groceries?"

"We'll swing by; grab the pole and something to wet your whistle. I've got a plenty of bacon biscuits here."

The old pickup's transmission was automatic, but I managed to make it buck and jump across the pasture like a standard. My foot slipped off the accelerator every fifty feet or so. I'd stomp around looking for it and then accidently jam it to the floor. Aunt Sis laughed good-naturedly and gave me an occasional gentle pointer, but Nash voiced a mild protest when we finally arrived at the pond.

"You make it almighty rough for a body tryin' to ride the toolbox."

"Toolbox is safer than the tailgate," Aunt Sis quipped. "You might land in the bed of the truck instead of falling plumb out."

"Not if I get throwed over the side."

He restrung the two rod-and-reels, grumbling about newfangled contraptions, while Aunt Sis picked out a shady spot and set up the folding chairs.

I breathed in the exotic, muddy smell of the pond and settled in for a long wait, but five or six minutes after my red-and-white cork hit the water, it disappeared.

"Reel," Aunt Sis squealed gleefully, "reel hard."

The tip of my rod bent toward the water as something flopped around on the other end of the line. My heart hammered with an excitement I'd never known. I barely heard my aunt's instructions, but I felt her hand on my shoulder, felt her there with me.

"Good frying size," the old black man observed, "but nothin' to write home about."

"This is his first catch, Nash," Aunt Sis said, still laughing as she took it off the hook.

"Well, yes'm, we ain't been here ten minutes."

"No, this is the first fish he ever caught, first time he's ever fished."

"Go'on away from here," he retorted incredulously, and a grin spread slowly over his face. "Big as he is and ain't never been fishing?"

"I reckon it's hard to raise a boy right on concrete, Nash."

"You're sure right about that, Miss Sis, right as rain!"

After that, Nash laid his own pole aside on the bank and took an active interest in my fishing.

"That's a whopper." I observed when Aunt Sis pulled in a large catfish.

"I used to bait her hook when she was little," he said, chuckling fondly at her excitement. "We'd ride horseback to whatever pond she wanted to fish, and I'd help her down. 'Tie my pony up good, Nash, and be sure to loosen the girth.' Her a little bitty mite of a girl and a-telling me every move to make but sweet as molasses candy about it."

I smiled at the mental image of a dark-haired little princess toddling around handing out her sugarcoated orders. We fished for a couple of hours before I heard someone holler from across the nearby fence.

"Can I see your fishing license, young man? I believe y'all are having more fun over there than the law allows."

"Ches is a Durham, Mr. Hollister. As long as I hold the deed to this place, he don't need any dratted license."

Despite her cold response to the little joke, I noticed how quickly Aunt Sis parted company with her freshly lit cigarette and buried it in the soft dirt of the bank.

"I really wish you'd call me Andrew," he scolded, ducking between strands of barbwire.

He stood around visiting until Aunt Sis offered him her rod and reel. Nash nodded a farewell then picked up his trusty cane pole.

"Believe I'll try my luck over yonder by the dam."

Andrew Hollister carried on a rather one-sided conversation with my aunt while he fished and she sipped daintily at her Diet Coke. His eyebrows shot up when she started to re-bait my hook.

"Ches is a big boy, Aunt Mama, you don't have to do everything for him."

"Today's his first time fishing," she explained defensively. "I don't want him to hook himself."

"If he was on a horse and I said something like that you'd say, 'Aw, Hell, let him ride. He'll figure it out.'"

Mighty few people actually stood up to Aunt Sis, and I caught a fleeting glance of the pleasure and amusement that crossed her face.

"I don't talk that-a-way," she answered a little haughtily.

"Probably not," he conceded, "but whatever you said would carry about the same meaning." Then without missing a beat, "Tell me something, Ches, our lily-white lady enjoys more than the occasional cigarette, doesn't she?"

"I sure hope you wouldn't call my Aunt Sis a liar," I said sternly.

"Never," he assured me. "Just answer the question."

"Well, let's say those occasions roll around fairly often."

"That's what I figured," he said with a nod. "Look, Miss Durham, I find your company rather enjoyable, but you'll soon dread the sight of me if you force yourself into nicotine withdrawal every time I show up. Just go ahead and puff away. It'll make things easier for everybody."

"You certainly don't show much concern for my health," she said tartly.

"Don't get me wrong. If you actually intend to quit, I think that's just wonderful, but when we both know you'll reach for that next cigarette as soon as I leave…"

"You're a persuasive man…Andrew."

He smiled broadly at the use of his first name, and Aunt Sis finally allowed herself another cigarette. We fished a while longer then divided the bacon biscuits among the four of us.

"I haven't had a biscuit this good since I left Georgia," Andrew admitted. "It sure didn't come out of any can."

"Mama'd roll over in her grave if I whopped a can of biscuits on her counter," Aunt Sis answered with a laugh. After dinner, she watched fretfully as Andrew tried to teach me how to bait a hook. "His fingers don't work quite right; he'll stick himself sure as the world. Besides, he doesn't need to bait his hook. I'll do it for him."

"Maybe she's right," he finally told me. "Save that determination for the struggles that really matter. You cast fairly well; let's keep working on that."

Suddenly, Aunt Sis glanced at her watch.

"Mercy, I've got to run. You boys want to keep on fishing?"

"I started out to walk my line fence," Andrew said, "but it'll be there when I get to it."

"I kind of like fishing," I admitted.

"Might just as well keep on," the senior member of the group agreed, making it unanimous.

"Come go with me right quick, Nash, so you can bring the Mule down here."

"Why the rush?" Andrew asked.

Nash smiled knowingly and spoke up before Aunt Sis could answer.

"Tuesday afternoons is beauty shop time, come hail or high water."

Andrew's jaw dropped, and he stared at her.

"Don't say it," I thought. "Please don't say it."

"He's kidding, right? You have your hair done every week?"

"Shampooed and set, at least," she answered matter-of-factly.

The word I'd been dreading popped right out of his mouth.

"Grandmother and all her friends kept standing weekly appointments with their beauty operator, but I don't know of a woman anywhere near our age who—"

"Maybe you think I ought to visit a gym once a week instead, or should I go every day?"

"Well, I—"

"Don't you dare answer that! I won't pay good money to sweat like a field hand and gasp for my breath in front of a bunch of strangers. Not only can I sweat for free, working cattle or schooling colts, I can generate a little income. I may never have a perfectly flat tummy, but I will have my hair fixed nice and pretty."

"Yes ma'am," Andrew answered with a broad grin. "I reckon you will. Your aunt is quite a woman," he observed as the pickup pulled away.

"One of a kind," I agreed with a smile, and then decided to throw him a tip. "You know, she hates being compared to your grandmother. It just flies all over her."

"I loved my grandmother," he protested.

"Sure, and Aunt Sis would have too. I don't know… She's middle-aged, still single, and, in her eyes anyway, not as pretty or as thin as she once was. She is proud of her old-fashioned ways and ideals but more than a little sensitive about the old-lady tag."

"Miss Sis never married? I just assumed she was divorced or maybe a widow."

"Do you really think she'd be the kind to divorce?" I asked, raising an eyebrow.

"Not if she could help it," he admitted. "She must've had plenty of chances to marry. And as for her aging, if she was ever any more attractive than she is now…"

"There's some history between Aunt Sis and her auctioneer, Jim Rex McKendrick. I'm sure she had other suitors, but from what I can figure out she just never took the time to marry."

"Now, that right there is what you call too busy."

"There's something else, too. Maybe she never found a man to equal the colonel.

Her father, I mean."

"Yeah, I bet he was a sight. You don't have to know Miss Sis very long to figure out a couple of things. She was Daddy's pride and joy, and Daddy was the big bull of the woods."

"You're not saying she's spoiled?" I asked a little sharply.

"No," he said with a quick shake of his head. "She's worked too hard for that. Besides, some people are too sweet to spoil. She's bossy and independent, though. No use denying it. Miss Sis took her orders from one man and one man only. Evidently, he's been gone a long time."

"You're pretty observant," I admitted. "Have you ever been married?"

"I had a few girlfriends in high school and college but none I wanted to make a life with. From grad school on, I focused on building my career."

"You couldn't get over the fact that Aunt Sis never married," I said with a chuckle as he slid my fish onto the stringer, "and now, I find out you traveled a different fork in the same road."

Andrew grinned sheepishly and re-baited my hook.

"Too much talk will scare the fish away," he huffed, making a joke of his sudden wish to end the conversation.

About that time, we looked up to see Nash coming on the gasoline Mule. He pulled down as close as he could, probably for my sake, and then walked over to join us.

"Step careful around Miss Sis, young mister," he said flatly to Andrew. "There's a lot of us around here won't take it none too kindly if you trifle with her feelings."

"I didn't mean any harm, old timer. Remember, I never said one word about the gym."

"I ain't worried about no little spat, but I made the colonel a promise before he died. Let's just say if you ever hurt Miss Sis or break that tender heart of hers, you won't like what happens. Now, get on with your fishing. I won't hinder you no more."

"Well," I thought wryly, "old Nash's got a little gangster in him, too."

Maybe gangster's not the right word. It's certainly not a word the folks around McKendrick would have chosen, but I was starting to learn a thing or two. These people didn't back up, and they didn't holler for outside help, either.

Nash kept back a mess of fish for his supper, and we cleaned the rest for my aunt's deepfreeze. Andrew hinted that he'd rather wrangle an invitation to her table than take any of the fish home with him.

Aunt Sis returned from the beauty shop wearing the same 1950s hairdo, freshly teased into place, and brimming over with harmless, gossipy news. A few words and a catchy tune ran through my mind as we settled into the porch swing.

"You'll never hear one of us repeating gossip, so you'd better be sure and listen close the first time."

Before I knew it, the Friday night horse sale rolled around again. Mr. Parmalee greeted me with a mischievous grin. I waved and spoke, but somehow I didn't really want to sit with the old rascal. Disappointing Aunt Sis, not to mention purposely goading her, carried a sort of social stigma. I guess Andrew felt it, too. He exchanged a few words with the elderly horse trader and then strode over to sit by me.

"When's the fish fry?" he asked with a wink.

"Anytime's fine with me, but we better run it by the boss lady. Drop a couple of hints if you can catch her tonight."

Suddenly, Aunt Sis materialized at my shoulder.

"Hello, Andrew. Catch who? Look here, Ches, I need you to take some phone bids for me tonight." She held out her cell phone and a paper napkin from the café, but she finally noticed my blank look. "I've got a gentleman calling in to bid. Here are the tag numbers on the horses he's interested in," she added, shaking the napkin for emphasis.

"I don't know enough about—"

"Don't be silly; you'll do fine. Just give him the tag number and a brief description.

Tell him where Jim Rex is, and if he wants in, you bid for him."

"But what if I buy the wrong horse or something?"

"We all make mistakes, more so when we're just starting out. Sometimes they're costly, but don't worry about being hung out to dry. If he turns a horse down I'll back your bid until the barn goes broke."

I think it was supposed to comfort me, but her confidence only added more pressure. Even so, I took the telephone and the piece of café stationery. Favoring us with a quick smile, she glided away up to the auctioneer's box. Hard knots of fear formed in my stomach, but I told myself Aunt Sis wouldn't give me the job if she didn't think I could do it.

Ready to perform my assigned task and put it behind me, I chaffed at an unexpected delay between the tack auction and the horse sale.

"Miss Sis tells me we've got a few items to sell outside," Jim Rex drawled into his microphone. "There's a stock trailer, a couple of golf carts, and even a surrey with the fringe on top. We'll meet y'all at the east end of the barn."

"Surrey with the fringe— What did he say?" I asked Andrew.

"It's a kind of buggy. You know, a horse-drawn buggy, and a pretty nice one. I looked."

"Are you interested in a buggy?"

"I might be, if the price is right. Miss Sis hasn't bought my horses yet, so I could ask her to get one that's trained for driving."

"I believe I'll come along and watch," I said, momentarily forgetting my anxiety over the telephone bidder.

"Lookey here; lookey here." Jim Rex called after making quick work of the other junk. "This is a slick little rig, boys. The spokes are tight, and that strip of rubber over the wheels really cuts down on the racket. We'll have a fine trotting horse and a fancy set of harness for sale inside. Now, what do y'all want to give?"

"Nine hundred," my aunt's words came softly but distinctly through the night air.

Andrew bid a thousand, and on up to twelve hundred before he turned to me.

"I can't see who's bidding against me, can you?"

"No sir, I don't think it's anybody standing under the nightlight."

"Twelve fifty," he called.

Suddenly, it dawned on me. One of my aunt's hands rested lightly on Jim Rex's arm as if the uneven ground might be too much of a challenge in her high heels, but I knew better. Right after Andrew bid, she squeezed that arm almost imperceptibly. Jim Rex took her bid and kept climbing.

"Fourteen hundred once, fourteen hundred twice, put the shiny little buggy on buyer number two!"

"I still don't know who bought the thing," Andrew said on the way back to our seats, "but they can have it."

"Yes sir, I reckon they can!"

It didn't take me long to figure out what Aunt Sis might want with a buggy, and I liked the direction of her thoughts. In fact, the tension over my coming task evaporated in the rush of excitement.

My telephone customer bought two of the five head we bid on and thanked me for the help. I got quite a thrill spending his money for him but kept an eye peeled for the trotting horse. Finally, they led him into the ring.

"Alright now folks, here's a sure-enough fancy trotter, come right along with the buggy we sold earlier. He's a registered standardbred gelding by the name of Dandy's Delight. They say he'll get down the road at something close to thirty miles an hour. Just look at the shine on that coat, black as the night, and his high-dollar harness sells with him."

Jim Rex wasted his sales pitch on me. I was ready to buy the moment Dandy stepped into the ring, walking on egg shells and tossing his head proudly. The young woman leading him had to run flat out as he trotted around the ring. My breath came rapidly, and my heart hammered in my ears.

"Six and a half," Aunt Sis opened.

Jim Rex got $700 and rolled away. I saw three or four bidders in the crowd, but Andrew stayed out. So, apparently, did Aunt Sis. I watched her like a hawk without detecting the slightest sign of a bid. For a minute there I considered bidding myself.

"No," I thought, "that would be pretty stupid. If she's bidding, I'd raise the price on her, and if she's not, she's got a good reason."

Still, my heart sank like a rock when Jim Rex charged the horse off to a strange buyer for $950.

"You look like your dog just ran over the mailman or something," Andrew quipped.

Distracted, I barely heard him. A wink from Aunt Sis captivated my attention. Except for that single lightning-quick gesture, her expression remained deadpan. No trace of her usual loving smile, no nothing.

I spent the rest of the night trying to decipher her message. A smiling wink, I could have read like a newspaper. "Don't worry about the buyer's number. I got him," but that pokerfaced signal... Finally I settled on, "Everything's alright; trust me."

"You did a fine job with that phone bidder, Ches," she praised, lighting a much-needed cigarette after the sale.

By that time, I'd started to doubt my own eyes. Buyer number two could be anybody, so I concocted a roundabout question.

"Is it considered honest and aboveboard to buy something out of your own auction?"

"There's nothing wrong with it," she assured me. "If I'm the top bidder, I've paid the fair market value."

"Do we... Do you keep a buggy horse?"

"I've owned some in the past," she answered rather evasively.

"You did buy that surrey, didn't you?" I finally blurted.

"I did," she said with a smile. "You've got a good eye. Not that it's any big secret, but if the crowd doesn't know I'm bidding, they can't hold back out of fondness for me or jack the price up from spite."

"Why'd you buy the buggy?" I asked, trying to sound casual.

"Oh, I thought I might know somebody who'd like a ride. Any ideas?"

"Plenty," I answered, taking up her teasing tone, "if we only had a horse."

"Honey, we've got plenty of horses. I could put the craziest fool here tonight in harness and make her work, but that's not what I'm after. You'll need something dependable. Speedy Delight, or whatever his name was, ain't it."

"He sure was pretty, though."

"Pretty is as pretty does," she said tightly, holding onto the smoke.

"Yes'm," I said, slipping naturally into her vernacular.

"Why don't you go look at your buggy while I finish up here? Find Scooter and take him with you. Climb in and try out the seats or whatever; the rig belongs to you."

"Oh, Aunt Sis, that's too much money."

"Horse feathers," she said dismissively and leaned down to accept my hug. "We'll try to go and see Brother Crawford tomorrow."

"The preacher?" I asked, suddenly confused.

Before she could elaborate, Scooter trotted up to her side.

"There you are, Miss Sis. They've got trouble in the office."

"Oh, for pity's sake," she muttered, "can't a girl get a minute's peace around here?"

She hurried off, high heels clicking on the rough concrete, and left us to follow in her wake.

"What's up," I asked Scooter.

"Hitch a ride?" he asked in return. "I'm about worked down."

"Sure," I answered, and he stepped quickly onto the coaster wheels designed to keep my chair from tipping over backwards.

"Some tough guy's hollering at Serena Kate because she won't take his check," he explained as we zipped along behind Aunt Sis.

"Doesn't the barn accept checks," I wondered.

"Yep, we take them from people on the ledger."

"What's the ledger?"

"It's an old book about three foot thick. If their name ain't in there, we take cash on the barrelhead until they bring a letter of credit or somebody puts in a good word for them."

"I've bought horses all over five states," a man's voice thundered as we neared the office, "and I've never had my check refused."

"What seems to be the trouble here, Serena Kate?"

As she spoke, Aunt Sis boosted herself up into the pay window and perched on its ledge. This move placed her protectively between the bellowing customer and the teary-eyed girl seated on the other side. At the same time, it made the man look up slightly to meet her gaze.

"I bought seven head here tonight, and this brat of a girl won't take my check."

"I'm talking to my office manager right now," she said in a controlled tone. "You may certainly state your difficulty after we've finished."

I doubt whether Serena Kate knew she was the office manager until that moment, but it sounded more dignified than the girl who works the pay window and was easier to explain than the daughter of my old flame. Though the stranger's mouth popped open again, Miss Sis Durham's cold stare snapped it shut.

"He… he's not in the ledger, and there's nobody to vouch for him."

"Giles Parmalee knows me," the man protested. "I came here with him tonight."

"You know how Mr. Parmalee is," Serena Kate retorted, gaining confidence under my aunt's protection. "He says he knows this gentleman, alright, but he won't stand good for anybody."

"And this gentleman bought seven horses tonight?" Aunt Sis asked over her shoulder, bearing down ironically on the word gentleman.

"Yes ma'am."

"I sure did," the stranger verified, "and I'll leave 'em here if you ain't careful. I don't have any cash on me and wouldn't give it to you, now, if I did."

"Come along, sir," Aunt Sis said, issuing an order, not an invitation. "Surely we can resolve this without holding up the line."

She flicked her glance at me, letting me know I was included in this little conference. Just then, I noticed that Scooter had stepped off my wheelchair and disappeared. Aunt Sis led the irate man into her private office, and I followed.

"Look, lady, don't you hear good? You can take this check and like it, or I'll leave you holding those nags. It's as simple as that."

"Mister," Aunt Sis answered, taking a seat behind her desk, "this sale runs off a straight eight percent commission. I make my money, what little there is of it, from volume. Unless you're an awfully poor excuse for a horse trader, I can make more on the animals you bought than I could on those seven commissions."

"Why, you little—"

The office door flew open and slammed back against the wall, cutting off his insult.

Chapter Five

I turned my head, expecting a rescuer, but saw only Scooter. His tone was level and business like as he spoke to my aunt, making no attempt to be funny or disguise his message.

"I couldn't find Pop, but Nash is watchin' the front. Seth's got two of them Clark boys out back with him."

"That'll do nicely," Aunt Sis quipped with a hard-edged smile I'd never seen before.

"I don't know," Scooter said doubtfully. "Nash is getting pretty old. Do you want me to—"

"I said that'll do."

"Say, what kind of deal is this?" the would-be horse buyer demanded, his bluster wearing a little thin.

"Didn't anybody ever tell you," Aunt Sis asked sweetly, "not to chase a dog to his doorstep? You could cheat me at somebody else's sale, and I'd chalk it up to experience. But, mister, I call the shots around here."

"I'm a good mind to show you who's calling the shots."

"Scooter is a crafty little booger," she said conversationally. "He laid a mean-spirited trap for you when he dropped that hint about the man out front getting old and feeble. In the event you decide to snatch me out of this chair and slap me around a little, Scooter's hoping you'll make your brake in that direction. Those young men out back are perfectly capable of stopping you, but Nash worked alongside my old daddy. He's apt to be a little rougher about it."

Slapping the joystick, I propelled my wheelchair forward and made the bully leap away from my aunt's desk. I didn't care how rough Nash might get with him afterwards; nobody was going to hurt Aunt Sis unless they dealt with me first. Seconds later, though, I watched in open-mouthed disbelief as a real, honest-to-goodness smile spread across his face.

"Little lady, you and these two snot-nosed kids show more brass than the average marching band. Let's go have a look at the nags I bought, and then you tell me how this deal's gonna work."

Aunt Sis brushed a hand lightly over my shoulder as she passed. Scooter and I waited for her latest admirer to follow and then brought up the rear.

"You can sure pick 'em, mister," she said in a conciliatory tone as she ran a hand down the shoulder of a big, brown gelding. "They're on the cheaper end of the sale tonight, and you bought them right. Three or four might fit an order I've got for some summer-camp horses. Like I said, I'll make more money if you dump them on me than I will if you pay for what you bought."

"Why do you think I'm still here?" he asked with a grin.

"I like a sharp trader," she told him, laughing a little. "I'll hold the horses at no cost to you until your check clears."

"Checks no good," he said in a careless tone, "but if you'll hold 'em 'til Monday, I'll get the cash for you."

"Talk about brass," Aunt Sis yelped. She cleared her throat then and regained her ladylike composure. "I'll hold the horses for you, but you're gonna apologize to my office manager and tell her that check's hotter than a firecracker."

"Can I whisper in her ear?"

"Not the apology, but the hot check business… I suppose so."

"Tell me something, missy. Are you as rough as this old cutthroat you're supposed to have working for you?"

"I'm every bit as rough as I need to be," she said in the same light tone she might have used for, "Why, sir, a lady never tells her age."

"That was close," I observed with a shudder after he'd gone.

"Nah," Scooter answered, "I've seen them closer."

"Ches," Aunt Sis pointed out gently, "I have parents and grandparents come here looking for a child's first pony. Most of the traders are decent folks, too, but there are always a few who want to push. You'll find that kind in any business, and a body'd best know how to push back." Then to Scooter, "Run tell Nash and the boys to stand down."

"They're really out there?" I asked.

"You better believe it, and that little pull out drawer right under my hand holds a .38 caliber colt revolver. I can't tell you how much it means that you'd place yourself between me and harm, but next time get off to one side a little and give me a clear shot. He wasn't fixing to snatch me out of that chair."

"Why didn't you let him know?"

"A gun can make a bad situation worse, and threatening somebody with one of the cotton pickin' things is for the movies. He wouldn't have seen my pistol until he heard it go off."

"Wow…"

"As it stands now, he's leaving happy. He'll probably come back, too, but he sure better come with cash money in his pockets."

By the next afternoon I'd forgotten all about my aunt's intention to call on the preacher. She rode in the playday as usual and then asked Jim Rex to hook the bumper-pull stock trailer to her pickup while she ran to the house to freshen up and change.

"Where're you off to?" I asked.

"To see a man about a horse," she answered briefly, "and you're coming along."

Jim Rex let out a knowing chuckle as we watched her pull away on the Mule.

"The colonel always popped off that-a-way when somebody asked where he was headed. You never knew for sure whether he really intended to make a trade or was just telling you to mind your own business."

"That's pretty funny until you want to know the plan," I said dryly.

"When you go off with somebody like the colonel or Miss Sis you've got to think on your feet and follow their lead, but you'll never be bored. Say, I think I'll meddle a little."

"Go ahead," I answered with a shrug.

"I heard that weekend farmer from Houston went fishing with you and Miss Sis?"

"Andrew's originally from Georgia, but yeah, he happened along and joined our little crew."

"Mighty convenient," he grunted, "happening along that way. What's he like?"

"He's sharp. I've never seen him get the best of Aunt Sis, but he can just about match her. I think she kind of likes the challenge. Anyway, I'll probably invite him to supper one night."

"You really think Sis'll cook for that pilgrim?" he asked, a cloud of concern darkening his usual happy-go-lucky expression.

"She can, you know."

"She don't, though, not without a good reason. Ches, old buddy… How about asking me to supper, too?"

"On the same night?" I questioned, raising an eyebrow.

"Anytime," he clarified, "but especially when he comes."

My aunt came back a few minutes later wearing a floral-print skirt. It differed significantly from the long, western-style garments that made her look like a movie cowgirl from yesteryear. Though this one could hardly be considered short, she wore it with a pair of nylon hose. A ruffled white blouse and a single strand of pearls completed the outfit.

Her land, our land, ran along both sides of the road for a good little ways, and I studied it silently while she depressed the trucks cigarette lighter and drummed her fingers impatiently on the steering wheel. With that little chore out of the way she cleared her throat and recaptured my attention.

"You know, Ches, the day you were born me and the colonel and Uncle Doc Parmalee all piled into this very pickup and headed to Dallas before daylight."

"Mr. Giles's uncle?" I asked.

"Don't forget, he was the colonel's Uncle by marriage and our family doctor, too. I ought to take you by to meet him, but it breaks my heart to see him in that nursing home."

"You brought a doctor with you?" I asked, snorting with laughter as I thought about the extensive medical community in and around Dallas.

"Brother and Mrs. Crawford offered to come," she added, "but you were born on a Wednesday. The colonel figured they could pray for your safe arrival just as well without canceling midweek service."

"Why all the fuss?"

"Your mama was a spindly little thing. Raised on Post Toasties and rice, the colonel always said."

"Do what?" I blurted.

"You know, Post Toasties, like Cornflakes. His theory was that city people, especially the girl's, didn't eat right and couldn't stand up to hard work. Good, fresh produce and fried meat with plenty of biscuits and cornbread thrown in was his concept of the ideal diet."

"Sounds tasty, anyway," I observed.

"Oh, it's delightful," she said with a sigh, "and perfectly alright for growing children and hard-working men. When a girl reaches a certain age, though, Post Toasties and rice are a lot easier on her figure."

"If hot buttered biscuits, homegrown vegetables, and bacon grease contributed anything to your figure, they ought to put it in all the beauty magazines."

My face burned from the moment of unguarded honesty. In our short time together I'd developed a deep-seated admiration and respect for Aunt Sis. Her kind of beauty started on the inside. Somebody needed to clue her in about the nice-looking outer package, but a nephew probably wasn't supposed to notice such things.

"You're a silver-tongued little scamp, Ches Durham," she said with a gentle sort of chuckle." Some nice girl will count herself awfully lucky to have you one day."

"Who'd want to be tied to me for the rest of her life? Talk about baggage."

"Oh, honey, I'm sure the Good Lord has somebody out there just for you."

"He doesn't always," I wanted to point out. "What about you?"

Aunt Sis must have read the look on my face because I never spoke the thought aloud.

"I have yet to marry because the right man's never come along at the right time. If that's not a part of God's plan… Well, riding a good horse out across the homeplace is joy enough for me. But, Ches, I know He's got somebody special for you. You'll carry on the Durham name."

"Anyway," I asked, steering her back to the original subject, "what about Mom?"

"Well, sickly as she was, she like to have worried us to death the whole time she carried you. Uncle Doc operated a car the same way he drove a buggy horse, just sort of point her down the road and let her go, and the colonel's health had started to fail. Naturally, I did all the driving. "Lord," she added with a shutter, "that Dallas traffic."

"Did Dr. Parmalee deliver me?"

"No, honey, but he acted as a go between for us and those big-city doctors. One of them would come out from time to time and spout off a bunch of medical terms. Uncle Doc never batted an eye, just fired back a string of questions."

"Bet they liked that," I chuckled, having had more than a little experience with modern medical professionals.

"The delivery lasted for hours, and sitting in a hospital waiting room is awfully rough on the nerves. The colonel and I took turns stepping out to smoke so that one of us would be there all the time. Uncle Doc finally got enough of that and scolded us pretty good."

"Well, naturally, a doctor—"

"The old rascal wasn't worried about our health, just aggravated. He'd be talking along to one of us and look up to see the other one sitting there instead. Late that night, after I finally got to hold you, Uncle Doc caught my eye and jerked his head toward the nearest exit."

"Giving you permission to have a cigarette?" I asked.

"Not exactly, but I took full advantage of the opportunity. He wanted a word with me. 'Now, Sis,' he said, and I can still see the sympathy behind his stern expression. 'These white-coated wonders won't never admit it, but that birthing took too long, way too long. If baby Ches comes out alright, it'll be the Lord's doing and none of theirs.'"

"He knew," I breathed, but Aunt Sis didn't seem to hear me.

"What do you mean if? I demanded. You saw him yourself; that precious baby's nothing less than perfect. Then he told me there could be any number of problems that might take months to show up. He even hinted that you might turn out a little slow," she added apologetically.

"Doesn't bother me," I answered gazing out the lowered window at the highline poles as they slid passed. "Cerebral palsy affects people in all kinds of different ways. As it happens, my mind came out okay, but my balance, muscles, and motor skills..."

"You didn't particularly want to be a mechanic anyhow, did you honey?"

I bent double in the seat and slapped my knees as laughter came in waves.

"No, no," I hooted, determined to explain in spite of my amusement. "Motor skills have nothing at all to do with a car engine. Climbing up to the auctioneer's box or riding a pitching horse takes gross motor skills. You use what they call fine motor skills to fasten those fancy little buttons on your blouse, bait a fishhook, and play the piano. Mine, gross or fine, don't work too good."

"Sorry, Ches," she said with a chuckle. "Remember, I'm just a dumb little country girl."

"Oh, yes'm," I agreed sarcastically. "The last fellow who believed that tale came out on the short end of a horse trade."

"What causes it, cerebral palsy, I mean?"

"You know," I answered thoughtfully, "that may be the first time you've ever asked a question about my disability when it didn't relate directly to what we were doing."

"It's not from lack of interest, honey."

"If you're afraid of hurting my feelings—"

"No, not exactly... I just... As far as I'm concerned, your wheelchair will never define you. Cerebral palsy is something you have to deal with, not the thing that makes you who you are. I don't even think about it unless it effects the situation at hand."

Tears stung my eyes, but I fought them off with a laugh.

"You may be the only one who feels that way, Aunt Sis."

"Bloodlines can make all the difference in a horse, and you'll never convince me they don't mean something when it comes to people. You're a Durham, out of mighty good stock if I do say so myself. Besides, Ches, the Lord made you special."

"'Specially useless, or sometimes I feel that way."

"Don't even think such things," she said almost harshly. "Do you believe me when I tell you something, Ches?"

Wanting to lighten up the moment, I drew out one of Dad's sayings that never failed to make Mom roll her eyes.

"If you tell me a chicken dips snuff, I'll get outta the way before she spits."

"Then listen to this," she answered firmly, only the ghost of a smile disturbing her intent expression. "You're gonna be more of a man with two crooked legs, no balance, and not enough motor skills to change a sparkplug, than many a jaybird out there with all the advantages of a healthy body."

Completely floored by this impassioned little speech, I drew in a deep breath and answered her original question.

"Lack of oxygen to the brain, either during delivery or some time before the birth, that's what causes cerebral palsy." a grin spread across my face then as my thoughts returned to the night of my birth. "I wouldn't relish the idea of standing in front of twenty-seven-year-old Sis Durham with the pronouncement that her brand-new baby nephew might turn out to be a brick or two short of a full load. How'd you take it?"

"I'd have probably slapped anybody else from pure reflex, but Uncle Doc got by okay. 'Not a word of this to Chester,' he warned. 'His heart's weak as it is. We mustn't add to the strain.'"

I felt tears sting my eyes, not for myself but for Aunt Sis.

"You knew all the time and couldn't say anything?"

"I knew there might be problems; that was all. I passed the word to Terry and told him to watch close. Then I came on back to McKendrick, cried a lot, prayed more, and took many a long ride by myself."

"The colonel never suspected anything?"

"No, at least I don't think so. When I started smoking a little more, he noticed that, but I just made some kind of cute little remark about not letting him outdo me."

"You two were so close; keeping such a secret from him must have been horrible."

"It wasn't easy, but in the end Uncle Doc was right. The colonel died before you ever showed any symptoms. " Then, suddenly, she laughed at herself. "Well, that's certainly a cheerful way to wrap up our little talk, but here we are."

"Don't worry about cheerful, Aunt Sis. You've told me part of my life story I never heard before. Guess I should be thankful I've got all my marbles, huh?"

"You've got a head full of good sense," she assured me, guiding the pickup down a rutted dirt driveway, "and that's worth more than two or three pair of strong legs."

A yard full of guineas, ducks and free-ranging chickens offered their clamorous welcome as we parked in front of a modest frame house.

"Who lives here?" I asked, suddenly realizing we had passed right through McKendrick and back into the countryside.

"Why, Brother Carlton and Miz Edna," my aunt answered. "I told you we'd pay them a visit."

Aunt Sis glided around the pickup to steady me as I slid down and worked my crutches into place.

"Come in this house," Mrs. Crawford called from the doorway. "Won't y'all eat a bite of dinner?"

"Thank you Miz Edna," Aunt Sis said, returning the older woman's hug, "but they put out a fine spread at the café."

"Land sakes, this being my Saturday off, I reckon the café slipped my mind. I've got a chocolate sheet cake here, fresh from the oven, and some Blue Bell ice cream."

"It sounds awfully tempting. I don't need another bite, but I'm sure Ches would love some."

"I'm the one who ate in the café; you never even—"

My aunt cut me off with a look, but I guess Miz Edna got the message. She fixed four bowls of cake and ice cream, stepped to the back door, and called the preacher.

"Hey there, Ches," he said as he washed his hands at the sink. "Whatcha up to?"

"Nothing much, sir, I'm just following Aunt Sis around."

"That sounds like a fulltime job," he observed with a grin. "Pick you out a chair, and I'll bless our cake and ice cream before it goes soggy."

He offered a simple, sincere prayer of thanks, and then we divided our attention between eating and visiting.

The old couple wanted to know all about me, my parents, and Dad in particular because they'd watched him grow up. For someone who supposedly didn't need another bite, Aunt Sis made short work of her cake. When her spoon scraped against the empty bowl, she laid it primly on her napkin, sighed deeply, and looked up with a smile.

"I declare, Miz Edna, you've done it to me again, but I always enjoy your sweet treats."

"I'm sure thankful for Ches. You try to subsist on cigarettes, black coffee, and pure Durham hardheadedness, but as long as you're cooking for him you might accidently eat something once in a while."

"Coffee and cigarettes didn't change my dress size," Aunt Sis quipped regretfully, even as such motherly concern brought another smile.

"No, darling, time took care of that, time and nothing else."

Brother Crawford hadn't lived into his eighties without gaining some wisdom, and he quickly changed the subject.

"Say," he asked, "y'all visited your new neighbor yet?"

"We haven't paid a call on him at Uncle Doc's place if that's what you mean, but he's been around some."

"Now, Miss Sis, that place doesn't belong to Doc Parmalee anymore. Change is never the easiest thing to accept, but that's no reason not to welcome this young fellow into our community."

"Andrew wants to come to supper," I volunteered, "but he's too polite to invite himself."

"A polite, hungry bachelor," Miz Edna cried in delight. "What more could you ask? Remember, Sis, the way to a man's heart is through his stomach."

"I'm pretty sure the way to this one's heart is through a large bank balance. I certainly don't have one of those, and if I did I wouldn't use it to catch the likes of him. I'm sorry, Miz Edna, but there's no need to get your hopes up."

"Jim Rex wants to come, too," I supplied helpfully, and my aunt's head snapped around.

"Both of them togeth…" She trailed off, reaching up automatically to check her meticulous hairdo. Then after a moment's thought she gave a reluctant nod. "Nash sets out trotlines on the river whenever he takes a few days off, and he generally brings me a good mess of catfish. I suppose we might have us a little fish fry one of these days."

"Let's do it soon," I suggested.

"Miz Edna," Aunt Sis admitted after a moment's hesitation, "I'm not sure I can handle something like that alone. Besides, the colonel wouldn't much favor the notion of me playing hostess to a houseful of men all by myself."

"We'll be glad to help, darling. I'll bring over a pot of beans and something sweet."

"Bless your heart," Aunt Sis gushed. What would I ever do without you? I'll let you know if we decide to go through with it."

Mrs. Crawford patted my aunt's hand but spoke to me.

"You may not realize it, Ches, but you're really bringing our sweet Sis out of her shell."

"For pity's sake, Miz Edna, you make it sound like I've been hiding under the house."

"I'm not exactly convinced you haven't; how else does a beautiful, kind hearted, smart girl stay single for so long."

My aunt's cheeks flamed red.

"I manage, somehow I manage."

"The neighbor's name is Andrew, I gather?"

"Yes sir," I said in answer to Brother Crawford's question, "Andrew Hollister."

"Did you invite the young man to church, Miss Sis?"

"No sir," she admitted, raising a hand pitifully to her forehead, "and I'm plumb ashamed of myself. The first time we met I was mad as a hornet over Giles selling out Uncle Doc. Next time I saw him, we conducted a bit of business, and the last time… Well, I just don't have an excuse. I'll certainly invite him the first chance I get."

"She gets kind of flustered around Andrew," I announced, trying to provide some small justification for my aunt.

"Don't make me sound like a giddy schoolgirl, Ches," she said in a tone of gentle correction. "He may get on my last nerve, just like any city slicker who comes in here throwing money around and thinking he owns the world, but flustered is hardly the word I would choose."

"I see you brought the trailer along," Brother Crawford observed diplomatically, gesturing out his bay window.

"We did," Aunt Sis said with a nod. "Have you made up your mind yet to sell me old Mable?"

"I'm sorry, Miss Sis. The mare's not for sale, but we might as well have a look at her."

"Take Ches in my pickup. I'll help clean up the kitchen and then walk on down there."

"No need for that, darling," Miz Edna protested.

"I may go against all my better judgment for chocolate cake and ice cream," Aunt Sis said with a teasing smile, "but I'll not go back on my raising."

"I suppose not. Still, I don't want you walking clear down to the barn in those heels."

"Maybe a little walk will undo some of the damage," Aunt Sis answered, laughing as she indicated her empty bowl.

"Oh, hush that silliness, and tell me some more about young Mr. Andrew Hollister."

Plenty of women and girls showed interest in and skill with horses, but most of the wheelers and dealers in my aunt's circle were men. Up to that point I'd never really watched her interact with another lady. Caught up in their lighthearted chitchat, I almost hated to leave the table.

Even so, my curiosity stirred as I followed Brother Crawford to the truck. A small white donkey greeted us outside the weathered barn, and Brother Crawford dismissed him with a friendly slap on the rump.

"Get outta the way, Snowflake."

The old preacher had a likable way about him, seemingly at odds with the stern presence that made me so uncomfortable from the pulpit. When he led me into the ramshackle barn, I caught sight of a sorrel mare standing tied. Her golden mane and tail showed a fresh trimming and her dark red coat glistened from recent brushing.

"She's beautiful," I breathed.

"She don't look bad for her age, not bad a-tall. I raised fifteen fair-sized gardens behind her before Edna and a newfangled doctor decided hard work might be fatal. And son, you talk about travel down the road with a buggy, she'll flat get it. Don't misunderstand me, though, she'll walk as slow and easy as you might care to go."

My heart leaped into my throat, but then I remembered something.

"You say she's not for sale?"

"A pastor tries not to have favorites among his congregation, but Miss Sis… Well, Edna and I love her like a daughter. Not that I'd ever use that phrase with her, she wouldn't take kindly to anybody crowding into the colonel's place."

"Probably not," I agreed, "but she sure thinks a lot of y'all."

"Anyhow, I hope you'll understand. I mean no disrespect when I say she's very much accustomed to get her own way."

As he talked I eased up to the old mare, balanced on one crutch, and reached to stroke her graying muzzle.

"Hello, Mable," I whispered, feeling her warm breath on my hand and inhaling the musty but somehow fresh and exciting odor of horse.

"Miss Sis says, 'Brother Carlton you ought to sell me your Mable for Ches,' and in her mind that's the end of it. If for some reason that don't get it done, it's, 'Miz Edna I sure need that old mare. She's just standing around in the pasture going to waste.'"

"I guess I can sort of see your point."

"Your aunt's right, as usual. Mable is going to waste. Still, it's up to those of us who love Miss Sis to keep her feet on the ground."

I nodded my reluctant understanding just as Aunt Sis strode into the barn.

"Hello, old lady," she crooned, placing a hand on the mare's shoulder, and Mable turned a big, kind eye toward the familiar voice. "Brother Carlton went to an awful lot of trouble cleaning you up, not to sell you to me; yes he did."

A smile flitted around the corners of my aunt's mouth as she cut her eyes toward the preacher.

"Ches and Mable get along fine together," he admitted.

"What'll you take for her?" Aunt Sis asked confidently.

"I'm sorry, darling. I can't sell her to you at any price."

His gentle words carried overtones of kindness and regret, but Aunt Sis flinched like he'd slapped her.

"I… I don't understand. Why would you even show her to the boy if—"

"I can't sell Mable because I don't own her anymore. She belongs to Ches here."

It's a good thing my aunt's weight problem existed almost entirely in her imagination because she ran about five steps and jumped up into the old man's arms.

"Way to keep her feet on the ground," I said with a smile as he caught her around the waist and dangled her at arm's length like the little girl he remembered so well.

"Oh, Brother Carlton," Aunt Sis said through laughter and tears, "a man oughtn't to be a preacher and a scoundrel at the same time. For shame, fooling me that-a-way when you knew perfectly well what you planned to do." Then, turning serious as he set her gently down, "I don't mind paying for the horse."

"You've got no part in this deal, Miss Sis, and it's already done."

"Brother Crawford," I said, hobbling over to stick out my hand, "I don't know how to thank you. I'd love to have Mable and learn to drive her, but I'm sure she's worth some money. You hardly know me."

"Don't you fret about that, son," he said returning the handshake. "I know Miss Sis, and I know Terry. I knew Chester, his daddy, and some of his aunts and uncles. I'd say I know you pretty well even if we're just now getting to enjoy each other's company. Have you got a set of harness to fit her?" he asked Aunt Sis.

"I've got some I could make fit," she answered, "but I'll give a couple of hundred for her buggy harness if you've still got it."

"Kept it oiled, too," he said with a nod and then turned to me. "My old buggy kind of rotted down, so I sold it for yard art. Mable will make a pretty picture in front of that fancy surrey of yours."

"My mare… My surrey… Y'all give wonderful gifts around here, but I may have a hard time fitting my new treasures onto Mom and Dad's half-acre lot."

Aunt Sis reached reflexively for a cigarette, and repeated her view on the subject.

"We'll cross that bridge when we come to it, honey."

"Watch Mable, Miss Sis," Brother Crawford advised as he shut the trailer gate. "I don't think she'd act ugly, but it's been over a year since I did anything with her. I'd hate to see that pretty surrey all smashed up."

"This old lady?" Aunt Sis asked skeptically. "Why, she's got perfect manners. I'm sure we'll get along fine, but I'll make a circle or two before I let Ches in the buggy."

Aunt Sis and I arrived home to find Scooter waiting on the porch steps.

"They run off and leave you?" my aunt inquired teasingly.

"Shucks, Miss Sis, Seth left here bound for his girlfriend's house to play volleyball. He's a fine horseman, a real credit to the family, but he looks plumb goofy running around in them shorty britches after a cotton pickin' ball."

Aunt Sis laid a hand on his shoulder and spoke in the kindest tone I'd ever heard her use with him.

"Child, you may be spending too much time with me. Not everybody eats, sleeps, and breathes horses. That doesn't necessarily make them tetched in the head."

"Don't it?" he asked, grinning up at her.

"Keep Ches company while I slip on some blue jeans, and we'll head down to the barn."

"The cab stinks like your precious cigarettes," Scooter explained a few minutes later, vaulting into the bed of the pickup.

"Don't hold back," my aunt quipped, laughing at him. "Tell me what you really think." Then after a short pause, "At least you're not copying all my ways."

Pointing the truck and trailer downhill, she reached for her pack almost immediately but stopped short.

"Go ahead, Aunt Sis, if you want."

"I can't smell anything in here, Ches, but if it bothers him, it must bother you, too."

"To be honest, I've learned to like the smell of a burning cigarette. Just the smell and nothing else," I added quickly as she opened her mouth to scold me. There's a stale-smoke odor, though, that kind of hangs around."

"Oh, honey, I'm so sorry. Why didn't you tell me before?"

"What could you do about it besides worry yourself into a nicotine fit? If you won't quit for your own health, you might as well enjoy your cigarettes without feeling guilty. My nose ain't all that delicate."

Scooter brought me a chair out of the sale barn, and I watched excitedly as they fitted Mable with her harness. Straps and buckles seemed to go every which way, and I wondered if we'd ever get to ride. Really, though, Aunt Sis straightened the mess out fairly quickly.

"You've put on a few pounds, old lady, just like me, but the collar still fits. Now,

Scooter, hand me the hames and traces."

"Miss Sis, I don't know what none of this stuff is called. It ain't on my saddle."

"Well, you'd better learn. Who do you think's gonna hook this rig up every time Ches wants to ride."

"Maybe short britches ain't so bad after all," he muttered under his breath.

"Those two metal rods are the hames, and the traces are already buckled onto them. This is what does your pulling," she explained buckling the hames into place on either side of the collar.

"I'm starting to see how all this junk comes together," Scooter said, more interested than he cared to admit.

"I'll drive her around a minute before we hitch her to the buggy," Aunt Sis said, and then clucked to the old mare. "Step up, Mable." The horse walked around calmly, turning as directed and even backed up on command. "She ain't forgot nothing. Besides, walking is hardly my favorite pastime. Let's hook up and ride in style." She backed the mare into place between the shafts, tossed the driving lines into the buggy, and hooked the traces.

"Need help, Ches?" Scooter asked.

"No," Aunt Sis answered for me. "He's sitting this first round out. Hold her head and talk to her while I get aboard."

"Want me to twist an ear?" he joked.

"You twist that old lady's ear, and I'll twist yours. Does she look like a bronc?"

Scooter made a show of speaking to me, but he meant for Aunt Sis to hear.

"I'd better stop complaining about those cancer sticks. She's bad enough now, but without some nicotine in her system…"

I shrank from the term cancer sticks and all of its cruel possibilities, but Aunt Sis just snapped back.

"Either get in the buggy or step out of the way. This mare's not wearing shoes, and I'd hate for her to bruise a hoof against your hard head."

"She talks tough," Scooter told me, planting a big sugar smack on my aunt's cheek as he hopped up beside her, "but she loves me. In fact, I'm her all-time favorite sale-barn brat."

Mable took them for a big, uneventful circle and plodded back again. A familiar prickle of fear suddenly tainted my joy and excitement, but Aunt Sis smiled reassuringly.

"There's no such thing as a bombproof horse, Ches, but Mable is as close as they come. I'll be right here beside you if you'd care to go for a little drive."

"Yes ma'am," I answered, swallowing hard.

"What's to be scared of?" Scooter asked incredulously.

"Hush your mouth," Aunt Sis scolded. "Ches can't jump out of here like a cat squirrel if something goes wrong."

"Aw, I wouldn't jump."

"Pshaw, I can hear you now. 'The last time I seen Miss Sis, the preacher's old mare was really taking her yonder. Maybe we can find some tracks.' Sit here and hold the lines while I help Ches."

"Yes, oh queen; your wish is my command."

She stepped down in one smooth motion, and, though not as graceful as her, I managed to climb in without too much trouble. Scooter had moved over to make room for me, but now, she circled over to his side of the buggy and fixed him with a look.

"You're in my spot."

"I don't want to ride on the back seat."

"You can run alongside if that suits you better."
"Reer," he squalled, imitating an angry cat and even making a clawing motion with

his hand.

"Well then," she retorted, "go play volleyball."

"And there we have the reason I put up with your moody self."

"Why's that?" I asked, hoping to break up there constant back and forth.

"See," he explained, "go play volleyball was the nastiest thing she could come up with off the top of her head. We think alike."

This won him a smile from Aunt Sis.

"The buckskin colt could do with a ride. I'll wait just five minutes for you to catch and saddle him. Then, this wagon train's pulling out."

Sure enough, we drove off and left poor Scooter.

"You cut my time by thirty seconds," he complained when he caught up to us.

"Yes," Aunt Sis admitted breezily, "and if you hadn't meddled around looking at your watch, you might've been ready."

"Let's show Ches the swimming hole," he suggested, and my ears perked up.

"I love the water. It gives me some freedom of movement, but we've been so busy, I haven't even thought about swimming."

"There's a pretty good road running down to it," Aunt Sis said, considering. "We might as well swing by."

"Yeah," Scooter cheered, pumping his fist in the air.

Road, in this case, didn't mean blacktop but a fairly smooth path through the pasture. As we jostled along it, Aunt Sis gave me tips on driving a horse and buggy.

"When and if you start riding, I'll put you on a horse with a good solid neck rein. That'll feel more like the joystick on your wheel chair. Just move your hand in the direction you want him to go, laying the off rein against his neck. In the buggy, though, you'll need to plow line."

"Ma'am?"

"If you want to go right," she explained, "loosen up on the left line and tighten the right one. It may not take a lot, but pull her head around in the direction you want to go. You can talk to her, too. Gee means turn to the right, and haw means step to the left."

"Now, how in the world am I supposed to remember that?"

"Somebody once told me to think of a man talking to his wife. 'Gee, honey, you're right.'"

"If the man and wife thing don't work for you," Scooter offered, "you can picture just about anybody talking to your aunt. 'Gee, Miss Sis, you're right.'"

Aunt Sis muttered something under her breath and to my complete surprise handed me the driving lines.

"Put your hands just in front of mine," she instructed, "and feel how much pressure I've got on her mouth. You don't want to fight with her or get in her way, but you may need to collect her at a moment's notice. Steady, Mable. Stay with it, old lady."

The next thing I knew her hands lay folded neatly in her lap, leaving my sweaty, uncertain ones to set our course.

"Aunt Sis, I don't know how—"

"You're doing just fine, honey, and I'm right here."

"If you weren't my good buddy," Scooter called, "I'd be awful jealous of such tender encouragement. She'd tell me to, 'quit whining, and get it done.'"

Aunt Sis smiled innocently, but all three of us knew he spoke the truth.

Just when I thought I had the hang of driving, we started down a small incline. The swimming hole, a small and remarkably clear spring-fed pool, lay at the bottom. About to run out of road, I hauled on the right line and spoke to the mare.

"Gee, Mable, gee."

She geed, alright, whipping the buggy around as she lunged back up the hill. The right front wheel made a horrendous scraping sound against the side of the buggy, and I knew in that moment that I'd turned us a flip.

Chapter Six

I'm not sure why my aunt's laughter surprised me, but it did.

"Loosen up on that line, Ches. Let her go back up the hill before we upset this applecart."

Her warm, loving voice penetrated the icy fear that gripped me. I followed instructions, and the faithful old mare dragged us safely back to level ground.

"I'm sorry, Aunt Sis. I don't know what happened; I'm just so sorry," I blubbered and tried to hand her the driving lines.

She threw an arm around my shoulders and squeezed me to her.

"No, honey, I'm sorry. There's no harm done, but the whole thing was my fault. I should have prepared you for that little dip and the dead end into the swimming hole."

Scooter hooked one leg over his saddle horn in unconscious imitation of my aunt.

"That sounds so much nicer than, 'You came mighty near getting my hair wet. Try it again, and I'll ring your neck for you.'"

His joking around cheered me up when her soft comfort couldn't quite do the job, and Aunt Sis laughed with us.

"The way the surrey's built," she explained, "it won't turn but so far. They put rollers on the sides to keep the front wheel from skinning up the wagon box."

"It sounded like the whole thing was coming apart," I admitted.

"Not hardly; now, let's ease back down there."

"Don't you think you'd better drive?"

"Not hardly," she repeated with a smile. "This time make a slow quarter turn instead of wheeling us plumb around. The buggy will sit there on that little sidling place, and you can look at the water just like we originally planned."

I felt my own hands tremble, but I also felt her steady one on my shoulder. Gaining strength from that grip and from her musical drawl as she talked me through the maneuver, I pulled it off without a hitch.

Another Sunday church service brought on a fresh crop of confused feelings, but Aunt Sis took me for a buggy ride afterwards and showed far more kindness and patience than I had any right to expect. She taught me a great deal about how to enjoy my new pastime safely. At the same time, she provided a priceless example of unconditional love.

"I really like driving Mable," I told her. "It's awesome to think that I can guide such a large animal wherever I want her to go."

"I know you like it, honey. The look on your face makes it all worthwhile. I wish we could stay out longer, but this is the hottest part of the day. It won't do to over work the old lady."

"No ma'am, we don't want that."

"I'll get Nash to shoe her early Tuesday morning. There's a younger shoer does most of my work, but Nash will still nail a set on when I need them in a hurry."

I'd picked up enough information about horses to know that people who trimmed hooves and fit horseshoes were called farriers, but Aunt Sis said horseshoer or in this case shoer with the familiarity of one who'd dealt with such folks all her life.

"There's no real hurry on Mable's shoes, is there? Seems like it would be easier on Nash to wait for the other fellow."

"Well, I moved my afternoon shampoo and set up to the cool of the morning."

"What in the world do my mares shoes have to do with your beauty appointment?" I asked jokingly.

"Nothing, smarty britches. Once Mable's got her shoes on, we can work her down the blacktop. Miz Lillian's beauty shop is fairly close by. If it's not too awfully hot we might take a buggy ride over that way."

"Sounds fun," I said, "but what about the traffic?"

"There's not too many cars, and they don't bother Mable. Still, you've got to really watch yourself anytime you ride on a public road. Some folks are totally ignorant when it comes to horses, and others just don't care."

The next day I took the Mule down to the sale barn to watch the shoveling out and hosing down process while she threw herself into house cleaning. My idea for a fish fry seemed to hang over her like some kind of threat, and she doubled her usual efforts in expectation of company. When we finally settled together in the porch swing, she seemed glad to get off her feet.

"You look tired, Aunt Sis."

I spoke in a gentle, concerned tone but regretted the words almost immediately.

"Oh, Ches, your aunt is old and getting older every day. I used to ride horseback

alongside the colonel from daylight to dark and then do the housework after he went to bed. Now, the house takes a solid day. Why, I'm still out of breath and my energy is flat gone."

"You could work most of the people I know right into the ground," I assured her. "I don't suppose you stopped to eat anything at noontime?"

Her mouth formed an O, and her eyes widened as she turned to look at me.

"Dinner; I'm so sorry. What did you do for a meal?"

"Nash made peanut-butter-and-syrup sandwiches for everybody who wanted one. They tasted great, but the syrup seemed… I don't know, pretty strong."

Aunt Sis threw back her head, giving her curls a little toss as she laughed.

"That's ribbon cane syrup, homegrown, ground in a mule-powered mill, and cooked off last fall. Thank goodness for Nash and his cane patch. I just can't believe I forgot to feed you." Pulling a familiar red-and-white package from her shirt pocket, she shook it and appeared to examine the contents. "I'd like to sit here all evening, honey, but that's not going to happen. This is my last pack of cigarettes."

"We can take your truck if it's easier on you," I offered.

"Don't be silly. If you have your wheelchair, you can come in the store with me. I'm not about to leave you sitting in a hot pickup just so I can smoke on the drive. We'll manage."

"You know," I ventured on the way to town, "that swimming hole looked nice and cool."

"I bet it feels good for you to get in the water and kick around."

"Yes'm. I can even walk without my crutches, but the water level has to be just right, shallow enough for me to touch bottom and deep enough to hold me upright."

"Plenty of daylight left," she observed. "If you feel like a swim this evening, we'll swing by Jim Rex's and see if we can't scrounge up a lifejacket from his ski-boat phase."

"A lifejacket, for me?"

"Yes, because the water's deep in spots, and I'm not going in with you."

"Don't you swim?"

She cleared her throat, coughed, and turned her face away but not before I spotted the tell-tale color in her cheeks.

"Of course, I do. Right now I just… Oh, Ches, I can't fit into the last bathing suit Mama made for me, and I wouldn't be caught dead in one of those scandalous things they wear nowadays."

I turned my own head then, hiding my amusement as I asked a question.

"How old were you when Grandmother took the measurements for it?"

"Oh, eighteen or nineteen, I guess, old enough to want a cigarette pretty badly by the time she finished checking and re-checking them. Say, not to change the subject, but I've been promising you a trip to the western store."

"That's nice of you, Aunt Sis, but it might cut into my swim time. If you're not too awfully embarrassed by my clothes, we'll wait until another day."

"Honey, I doubt you'd ever wear anything to shame me, but if you did, you'd know about it. In case you haven't noticed I don't suffer in silence very well."

We drove sixteen miles to the county seat, and as soon as Aunt Sis stepped out of my van in front of the tobacco outlet sunlight flashed off her silver-plated lighter.

"Do you want me to wait here or come with you?" I asked.

"It's awfully hot out here, honey, but I'll leave the van running if you'd rather stay."

"I've kind of gotten used to tagging after you," I said, and she let down the wheelchair lift with a smile.

"Hey there, Miss Sis," a lady clerk called warmly over the sound of a little bell that announced our entrance. "Who's this handsome fellow?"

"Hey, Margaret, I'd like you to meet my nephew."

An encouraging glance from Aunt Sis sent me rolling forward to shake and howdy.

"I'm Ches Durham, ma'am."

"Oh, Miss Sis, he's just about the cutest thing I've seen lately. There surely is a family resemblance. What can I get you, the usual?"

"You know me," my aunt answered with a short laugh, "steady and dependable, but don't ring them up just yet. Ches wants me to open the old home to a bunch of company. I'm not fully committed yet, but I'd like something to freshen up the house, you know, hide the smell."

"Well, Miss Sis, maybe you should invite people who bathe regularly," Margaret joked.

"Ain't that the truth," my aunt said with a sigh before selecting an air purifier and several different kinds of room spray.

"You don't have to—"

"Hush, Ches. Let me do what I can."

After dashing through Winn Dixie for a few groceries, we made our way back to

McKendrick and stopped in front of a rundown old house, mansion really, just off the deserted square. She walked briskly up onto the columned porch and knocked on the once-white door. Nobody answered, and to my surprise, she let herself into a shed at the side of the house and came out with lifejacket in hand.

"So that's the old McKendrick house?" I asked as we pulled away.

"Uh huh," she said pointedly, "all that's left of a medium-sized fortune."

"Are you trying to tell me something?"

"There are at least two lessons here," she answered. "First, divorce is quite painful and expensive. Second, working for me doesn't pay any too well."

"At least you're honest about it."

I carried groceries in, balancing plastic sacks on my lap and hanging others from the handlebars on my chair.

"That's the last of it, honey," my aunt called as I bent double to pick up a fallen slip of paper. "You're quite the gentleman to help out, but I hate to make a pack mule of you."

"Good grief, Aunt Sis," I yelped, staring in disbelief at the receipt for her cigarettes.

Rushing to my side, she glanced down at the crinkled paper in my hand.

"Well… They don't give those fancy air cleaners away," she retorted saucily.

"Or anything else in that store, either," I observed, indicating the total on five cartons.

"I know, honey, but they'll last me a while. Maybe one of these days… Right now, though, they're worth every penny."

The look in her eyes when she finally glanced up at me held a hint of embarrassment and a silent plea for understanding. I shook my head with a wry smile but reached for her hand and squeezed it.

"I'm ready for that swim if you really feel up to taking me."

"Nothing to it," she assured me. "I'll rest while you exercise."

True to her word, Aunt Sis found the shadiest spot on the bank and settled down happily with a tattered paperback.

"You don't know what you're missing," I called. "This is better than our neighborhood pool."

"You're enjoying it enough for both of us, honey," she answered, laughing at my antics as I splashed around in the water.

"I bet somebody's got a line of old-school bathing suits." I saw her stiffen and felt like biting my tongue. Instead, I forced myself under the water. When the lifejacket popped me up again I sucked in a deep breath and changed my adjective. "Ladylike, I mean ladylike bathing suits. We can order one out of a catalog, or I'll ask mom to look on the internet. It'd be a lot more fun if you swam with me."

She allowed the old-school comment to pass, but I knew I hadn't helped my case.

"Sorry, honey. I'm awfully comfortable right here. Besides, I'd sooner try to swim in a ball gown than admit to your mother that I need a larger bathing suit."

"How many people do you think really stay the same size for their whole adult life?"

"I'm not swimming, Ches, not until I lose the tummy. I've always been a tad bottom-heavy, but this layer of flab around my middle... Well, you don't want to hear all that."

"Andrew and Jim Rex seem to approve of your shape," I shot back.

"Why, Ches, what a thing to say! In any case, they both seem fond of you. I'm glad you've got a few men friends around here and won't be stuck with your old maiden lady aunt all the time."

"If you think they hang around because they're fond of me, you're crazier than I thought. I don't have an old maiden lady aunt, and I may not have a maiden lady aunt at all very much longer the way those two are buzzing around."

She blushed slightly but then winked at me.

"We'll see."

"Whatcha reading?" I asked later, watching as she smiled and sometimes chuckled over the pages.

"Oh, this is Ben K. Green's first book. I must've read it a hundred times. Terry's got copies of all his stuff because I gave them to him."

"I've never seen one," I admitted.

"That boy," she sighed in frustration, and I felt reasonably sure she wasn't talking about me or this Ben K. Green. "Mr. Green was a cattleman, horse trader, and sometime veterinarian from up at Cumby, Texas. He traded horses and mules in and around Fort Worth during the 1920s and '30s. He published Horse Tradin' in 1967, and several other books followed."

"Sounds like an interesting man."

"Oh, honey, you talk about a character. Reading one of his books always makes me think of the old timers who used to hang around our sale; good memories. I always thought somebody ought to write about Daddy. Lord knows there's material enough."

"Hey," I observed, still kicking my legs in the water, "that's the first time I've heard you call him anything but colonel."

"Slip of the tongue," she joked. "I've got all of Mr. Green's books and several more pertaining to this way of life. Maybe they're not high-toned literature, but I think you'd enjoy them."

"Well," I said uncertainly, "I don't read very much. The muscles behind my eyes tire easily. They call it strabismus, but I suspect it's another gift from the cerebral palsy."

"There's nothing wrong with my eyesight as yet. If you want, I'll read them to you."

"Oh, Aunt Sis, I'm already so much trouble to you."

She closed the book, rose from her lawn chair, and cleared her throat as she searched for the right words.

"Honey, you must not know what it is to be lonely. I love the horse sale and enjoy running it, but working all by myself… It's been an uphill battle. I'm afraid I didn't take time for much of anything or anybody else. Miz Edna hit the nail on the head. Slowly but surely, you're bringing me out of my shell."

"What about Jim Rex, Nash, your customers, and your church family? A lot of people love and depend on you."

"Maybe, but somehow I managed to fill my role and shut them out at the same time. I've told more of my true feelings to old Rhett, and whatever horse I happen to be riding, in the last ten or fifteen years than to any human being."

I choked on the lump in my throat and felt my eyes sting. Another quick plunge beneath the surface gave me a few seconds to gather my thoughts, and when I reemerged, the water running off my head masked the tears on my face.

"I reckon I know a thing or two about loneliness," I said, and we both smiled because my I reckon sounded so much like her. "Mom and Dad are great parents. They work hard, love me, and provide anything I might need, but their jobs keep them away all day. Papa Joel's always there for me, but I never really felt like a necessary part of anything until I got here."

"I told myself I enjoyed peace and quiet. If some people didn't appreciate the joys and tribulations of a weekly horse sale or thought me too old fashioned or didn't like the smell of cigarette smoke or… Well, they just didn't have to come around."

"Sounds reasonable to me," I admitted.

"Reasonable, maybe, but it's not the most welcoming attitude. Now, with you to think of, I'm ready to invite a house full of folks over for supper. You're no trouble to me, Ches. You're a blessing."

"I'd like to help out with more of the chores and such but…"

Aunt Sis dabbed at her eyes with a handkerchief, ground out a spent cigarette with the toe of her shoe, and seemed to study the horizon.

"Cloud coming up," she observed. "We sure need a good shower, but let's get you out of there before the lightning starts."

"Want to go out on the porch?" I asked when Aunt Sis offered to read a little before bedtime.

"That's alright, honey. Climb on into bed where you can stretch out and get comfortable. I'll sit in Granny Mert's rocking chair."

Her grandmother's old rocker sat in a corner of my room, or the room where I slept, but Aunt Sis moved it closer to the bed. Settling herself comfortably, she opened Horse Tradin' and started to read.

Though Ben Green's tales had taken place seventy or seventy-five years earlier, they seemed part and parcel of my aunt's world. She explained a few obscure details, but a good story is a good story. We laughed so hard together that I finally rolled over and pounded my fists against the mattress.

"Listen," I gasped after one of these laughing spells. "Is that your telephone ringing?"
Laying the book carefully aside, she bounced up out of the rocker and took off in the direction of the kitchen. The sound of her running steps as she re-crossed the dog run a minute or so later set my heart to pounding. Aunt Sis always traveled briskly, but run? Knowing her scorn for pointless exercise, I felt my heart hammer with fear and adrenaline.

Mac McKendrick's cows are out on the highway, and he took his wife and grandkids to Galveston for a week," she gasped, collapsing on the foot of my bed to swap her moccasin-style shoes for riding boots. "I've got to tend to this, honey. It ain't like the old days. Traffic travels faster, and some of these young deputies don't know come-here from sic 'em about livestock."

"I understand," I lied, still trying to process it all.

"Nash is hooking up the trailer now. Do you want to come along, or stay here?"

"Sounds like a big job for just you and Nash."

"I'd take that old man over half a dozen drugstore cowboys, but Jim Rex and Seth are on their way. You coming?"

Even as she spoke the question, Aunt Sis snatched up a pair of my blue jeans, and I took that as a strong hint.

"Yes ma'am. You sure I won't be in the way?"

"No more than Jim Rex," she joked, sliding the jeans on over my pajamas.

I expected another ride in the Colonel's old pickup, but we piled into a slightly newer one-ton truck. The diesel motor roared and the windshield wipers slapped away a heavy drizzle as Aunt Sis drug the long gooseneck trailer with its live cargo of horses and dogs down the road.

"So many horses come and go around here," I observed. "Do you keep one in particular for times like this?"

"I've had a couple of mighty solid using horses in my day," she answered. "Mostly, though, I'm betwixt and between, riding whatever comes through the barn or tuning one up for somebody else. We don't do much stock work in the hot summertime anyhow."

"Kill a horse or a cow right quick a-pushing on them in the heat," Nash explained.

"It can sure happen," Aunt Sis agreed. "Most folks sell one or two horses at a time, but sometimes we get called out to gather a sizable bunch. There's nothing quite like bringing in a big herd of horses on a cool fall morning, nothing in this world, Ches."

"Wouldn't you be a lot safer riding one dependable mount?"

"Now, don't you start on me. It seems like all I hear anymore is, 'Stay off those bad horses. Stay off the bad ones, and quit smoking.'"

Nash, who never spouted such advice, offered a reasonable suggestion.

"Those folks just want the best for you."

"I like the bad ones," she declared with a defiant little toss of her head, "and I enjoy my cigarettes. Mercy sakes, you'd think I was the only one who ever took chances in her work or indulged a less than popular habit."

"I know, Miss Sis. I know," Nash said gently.

"I'm sorry, Aunt—"

"None of that was aimed at you, honey, or at Nash, either. Sometimes the grouchy old lady in me just has to let off a little steam."

"You're not grouchy or old," I protested. "Fiery might be a better word." Then, changing the subject, "Who's cows are we after?"

"Mac McKendrick," she reminded me. "He's a first cousin to Jim Rex's daddy," Aunt Sis explained. "He's got plenty of cattle and very little fence, but he would help any of us out of a bind."

"Would and has," Nash agreed.

"Pull it over right along in here," Jim Rex called as he flagged us down," and turn your flashers on if they're working. I parked on the other end. Seth and Scooter are trying to get around that bunch of wild cattle on foot, but you know how that'll play out."

"You get Scooter out of the highway this instant, Jim Rex McKendrick. He's not old enough to be out here chasing cattle in the pitch-black dark."

"Yes, Mama," he quipped. "And how am I supposed to find him?"

She withered him with a look, and let out a couple of high-pitched, wordless yells.

"If I heard a noise like that on a dark night," I thought, "I'd run all the way home."

Soon, though, we heard the pounding of booted feet on the asphalt shoulder.

"Well, I'll be darned," Jim Rex said, tossing me a wink. "She's got them boys trained near-about as well as her dogs."

By the time they appeared in the headlights, Aunt Sis was swinging onto a rangy cream-colored gelding.

"Darn it all, Sis, I'd walk before I rode that ugly white rascal," Jim Rex observed ruefully.

"I don't much care for him myself," Aunt Sis admitted. "A white horse will have more eye and skin trouble every time. This one's broke solid, though, and he ought to show up good out here in the dark." With that, she turned her attention to

Scooter. "Turn them dogs out and then get in the truck with Ches."

"One of the dogs is apt to get run over, Miss Sis," Nash cautioned.

"That's a chance we'll have to take; these boys already scattered the cattle."

"I don't wanna stay in the truck," Scooter protested.

I stared round-eyed at him, considering the fine line between bravery and stupidity, but Aunt Sis didn't have to think about it long.

"Do you want to feel my bridle rein across your backside?"

"No'm," he yelped, unlatched the trailer's escape gate, and let it swing.

My aunt repeated what I could only describe as her war whoop, and this time tacked a few words onto it.

"They're out there, Rhett. Go to 'em. Get around!"

"Old Rhett don't have no business out here," Scooter confided, sliding in under the wheel. "He'll never hear the car that hits him. The same goes for Nash, but at least his horse might jump clear. Miss Sis just can't deal with the fact that all her standbys are aging out on the job. They say she liked to have come unhinged when the old colonel died."

"Shut up, Scooter, or talk about something else."

"Say," he drawled, sounding almost pleased, "you are kin to her." We sat there in silence for maybe five minutes before he spoke again. "I hope they don't have to rope nothing."

"Why? Looks like it would make a lively show if we could see it."

"Yeah, but that wet highway is slicker than goose grease. I don't want to see a horse crippled or some of our folks busted up."

"Oh," I answered, my enthusiasm flattened, "I never thought of anything like that."

Just then, a car zoomed past us. Scooter slammed the heel of his hand into the steering wheel and swore bitterly. My head snapped around more from surprise than disapproval, but he looked kind of guilty.

"Don't tell Miss Sis I said that word, but how do you miss this big old truck and trailer with all the lights flashing. Some people are just too stupid to be running loose. Well," he added disgustedly, "whoever it is better try to take Miss Sis and Nash out together. If he gets just one of them, he's apt to bring down some rough justice."

I gripped the door handle until my knuckles went white, but it didn't do any good. Finally I hung my head out the open window and heaved my supper into the road ditch. The thought of any of them, but especially Aunt Sis, getting mowed down on the highway made me literally and violently sick. Scooter placed an uncertain hand on my back.

"Gross, man, are you okay? You can't pay no attention to me. Everybody knows I talk too much. They've dodged many a car before this."

"Sorry about the mess, but I suffer from severe anxiety," is not something one thirteen-year-old boy wants to say to another, so I said something else. "Dig around; Aunt Sis is bound to have a few mints stashed in here. I need something to take this taste out of my mouth."

"Here's a cigarette?" he offered jokingly. "Nah, I'll keep looking."

We found part of a roll of Breath Savers and got me about halfway straightened out, but the sight of red and blue lights in the rearview mirror started my stomach churning again.

"Quick," I said hoarsely, "slide over here by me."

"What for? I might need to move the truck."

"If he thinks you're driving this freight train, he'll throw us both under the jail."

"Nah, they're all pretty leery of your aunt. A city-bred highway patrol jumped all over her about some horses in the road while the colonel was getting over one of his heart attacks. She was gathering them as fast as she could, but this fellow talked real ugly to her."

"And…"

"Oh, the old colonel got wind of it and made a few phone calls. The Parmalee bunch, Mac McKendrick, and all the old timers like that forgot to shut their gates. Pop turned out the Durham stuff, too. Nash might not have done it without running the plan by Miss Sis, but Pop never did much give a care. The stunt happened way before my time, but they had open range all over this end of the county for nearly a week."

"You're kidding."

"Nope, if your aunt ever knew they done it all on purpose, she kept her cool. A couple of guys from the cow sale usually catch livestock off the roads, but they were plumb swamped. The county ended up paying Miss Sis and some of the Durham hands to help straighten out the mess."

When the officer cleared his throat at the window I nearly jumped out of my skin.

"What say, Scooter?"

"Hey, Mr. Wallace. How you been?"

"Fair to middling," the big man answered. "Mac's cows out again?"

"Well, sir, I couldn't say. There seem to be some cattle on the roadway, but they are awfully hard to identify at night."

"Sure," Deputy Wallace agreed with a grin. "Mac got everything under control?"

"He's not here, but Miss Sis is up there somewhere. She's got Pop, my brother, and old Nash Holloway, all of them horseback."

"No trouble then?"

"None, except for some idget in a blue Nissan."

"That'd be the young fellow who called it in, said his life flashed before his eyes."

"He must've been right busy watching it 'cause he never even tapped the brakes."

Officer Wallace through back his head and let out a booming laugh.

"You're a pistol, Scooter. I'll stop traffic on this end until they clear the road. One of our part-time guys is coming in from the other direction. I'm surprised Miss Sis didn't park this truck and trailer across the road."

"Ever heard of precious cargo?"

"You?" Wallace asked with a dubious snort.

"Not hardly. Meet her nephew, Ches Durham."

My stomach still churned, not from fear of good-natured Officer Wallace, but from visions of what could happen to Aunt Sis and the others out on the dark, rain-slick pavement. I managed to return his greeting. Finally, though, he went back to his patrol car and Scooter fell quiet.

"Dear God," I prayed for the first time in a long time, "please watch over them, especially my sweet aunt. I need her, Lord, and I couldn't stand it if anything bad happened to her."

"Pop was down at Nacogdoches working a car sale the night my mom finally left us," Scooter said out of the blue. "After an hour or so, we all got hungry, and Serena Kate decided to cook supper. Did you ever try to eat scorched beanie weenies?"

"Can't say I have."

"Well, Seth's the oldest you know. He took one bite and headed for the phone to call Miss Sis. Your aunt made the drive from her place into McKendrick in no time flat. She put together a meal out of whatever we had in the kitchen. I don't remember much about it, but it was hot, filling, and not the least bit scorched."

"Must've been a tough night for you," I ventured, not knowing anything better to say.

"Serena Kate remembered her mama leaving, and Seth had seen it twice before. Of course, I figured my mom was different. I guess she was different in one way. She got worried about us and came back; that's more than the other two ever did. Miss Sis had us tucked away in bed at her house by that time, but Mom left a note."

Suddenly, I realized how much of my prayer had centered on me and decided to try again.

"Oh, Lord, I'm so thankful for my solid, dependable parents and for Papa Joel. Aunt Sis, too; thank you for giving me Aunt Sis and this time to spend with her. I've been so focused on my cerebral palsy and other hang-ups I never stopped to appreciate the blessings you gave me. Open my eyes, God, and let me know if I'm one of yours. If I'm not, I sure want to be, 'cause Aunt Sis is going to Heaven and I want to go with her. I ask these things in Jesus name, Amen."

I'd like to say that a sudden peace filled my life, but there wasn't anything quick about it. Scooter was still talking, so I tuned his voice back in and listened.

"I thought I was way too old for it, but Miss Sis rocked me on her lap. She always mothered the three of us as best she could and kept Pop in work. He'd leave to try something like the car auction, but she'd take him back onto the payroll every time."

"Aunt Sis may have her faults," I admitted, "but she won't quit on a friend."

"I'll never forget what Seth told me that night, 'We may have different mama's, bub, but we've all got the same Miss Sis.'"

"You've known her a lot longer than I have, really."

"I went to work for her when I was nine years old. I'll tell you something, Ches. My mom hardly ever swatted me, but when she did it was because I inconvenienced her. Now, Miss Sis, I've had her to snatch me up and go to work on the seat of my britches with whatever she had in her hand, but I always knew it was because she loved me."

"That keep you from kicking and hollering?" I asked with a smile.

"I hollered loud and kicked hard," he retorted. "You would too if some crazy lady attacked you with a lariat rope, or a curry comb, or... Well, you get the idea."

"I reckon," I admitted but stopped short at the urgent barking of dogs and the cracking of my aunt's whip.

"Look yonder," Scooter said with excitement in his voice, "they've got 'em all wadded up nice and neat."

Straining my eyes, I saw what really did look like a wad of cattle, moving calmly through a gate and back out into the pasture.

"How do they do that?" I wondered.

"It's mostly the dogs. Once a bunch of cattle is dog broke, two or three half-decent mutts can put them in a herd. Miss Sis never fed a half-decent dog in her life, and none of the riders are too shabby, either."

"Now, maybe we can go home."

"Don't get in too big of a hurry. I figure Miss Sis will push them way back into the creek bottom for tonight. Somebody'll have to patch fence tomorrow. I've got a real bad feeling it'll be me and Seth. Your aunt will come out at all hours of the night in any kind of weather if she can be the heartbreakingly beautiful hero up on her horse, but pounding fence posts ain't her style."

I punched him lightly in the shoulder, laughed, and added a friend to my list of blessings. Between small talk and comfortable silence, we passed the time until Aunt Sis and the others rode up to the truck. Scooter hopped out to open the trailer gate, and Aunt Sis hollered at her dogs. It was another high-pitched squall but without the urgent, driving edge.

"Get in; get in there, Rhett," she said, punctuating the orders with that signature squeal. As they bounded into the trailer, though, she stepped quickly from her horse. "Nash, you see what I saw?"

"Yes'm, looked like an extra dog got in. I thought I seen one working with us out there but couldn't tell for certain in the dark. Say, old Rhett's liable to come unwound."

"He'll not get the chance," Aunt Sis said, snatching the bullwhip off her saddle. "I won't have a stray stirring up trouble and bloodying my dogs."

She darted up into the trailer and her whip cracked like a .22 rifle.

"Ain't made no trouble yet," Nash observed under his breath.

"Get from here, you sorry wretch," she spat, and a dog yelped as the lash connected.

I felt about a moment's worth of pity, and then a speckled blur sailed through the lowered window to land sprawling in my lap. All the air whooshed out of my body and a Breath Saver mint flew across the cab.

"Wh-where did you come from," I wondered shakily.

Just then Aunt Sis snatched the door open and reached for the scruff of his neck. The cab light blinded me, and words wouldn't come. So, I knocked her hand away as gently as possible.

"Watch him, Ches. He may try to bite. I didn't aim to scare you, honey. Never once thought he'd—"

"This poor dog's not gonna bite. You're scaring him to death."

I knew this because of the warm puddle forming in my lap, and soon my aunt noticed it, too.

"Rain-wet, exhausted, and now… I can barely smell roses or honeysuckle anymore, but that wet stuff on your jeans comes through loud and clear."

"He didn't mean to make a puddle, Aunt Sis. Look, I think he likes me."

"Have mercy," she groaned, rubbing her temples. "We can't take in every stray dog that comes along."

"I don't want every stray, just this one. Please?"

Sparking a flame from the little silver saddle, Aunt Sis took in a calming dose of nicotine and studied the trembling animal on my lap.

"Well, he's not bad looking for a half-starved pup. Nash says he might even work a cow. He may belong to somebody, but he ain't seen home in a month of Sundays."

The individual bumps of the dog's vertebrae stood out sharply along his back. An odd mixture of black, brown and gray mottled his coat. I didn't know anything about dogs, but he seemed young and vulnerable. Still, he carried almost as many scars and scratches as Rhett.

"So, can I keep him?"

"We'll take him home and see how he does, but if somebody claims him or he makes trouble, you'll have to give him up."

"He won't cause any problems, Aunt Sis, no he won't," I cooed in the same tone I'd heard her use with Rhett and the others.

Shaking her head, she strode back to thank the deputy for his help. I asked to be dropped off at the house, and while she and Nash tended the horses, I cleaned myself up and went out on the back porch to feed the hungry stray.

"Sorry I kept you out so late," my aunt apologized as she collapsed onto the porch swing.

"It was kind of fun," I admitted.

"Ah, to be young again," she sighed. "You ought to have been with us in the old days. I can remember having a big time on nights like this. Now, I want a hot bath and about a week in bed. I ache in places I'd never even thought about at your age, places it's not very nice to think about."

"I didn't even know I wanted one, but I'm glad we found me a dog."

"For better or worse, honey, I think Puddler found you. Look at him gobble them groceries!"

"Puddler," I protested, "he needs a manly name like Butch or Killer or…"

"Oh, yeah, he's a killer alright. I bet I could make him puddle right here on the porch, but I'm too tired to clean it up."

"Aw, don't scare him, Aunt Sis," I begged before my concern shifted to her. "A week in bed might be a little extreme, but you ought to take better care of yourself."

"Don't lecture me tonight, Ches," she pleaded, exhaling a stream of smoke.

"I'm not even talking about that," I said, indicating the cigarette. "You need more rest, less stress, and some working hours designed for a human being."

She gave me a look full of tenderness and gratitude but laughed off my suggestion with a mock shutter.

"Why, I'm already getting fat and lazy. Just imagine if I let myself sit around all the time." I argued hotly against this self-criticism, but she just hugged me and kissed my cheek.

My aunt's week of rest lasted only a scant few hours. Her morning cough sounded as familiar to me as the electronic click and whir of my wheel chair. It still worried me, but it also signaled my daily chance to pamper her just a little with a hot cup of coffee.

"My dog's still here," I said excitedly, handing her the mug.

"You're spoiling me, Ches. Pretty soon, if you oversleep, I'll just lay here helplessly wishing I could make it to the kitchen." We shared a laugh, and then she acknowledged my news. "So, old Puddler didn't leave us, huh? He'd have to be dumb as a box of rock to wonder off from his new meal ticket."

"He loves me more than leftover meatloaf," I stated definitely.

"Me too," she said with a wink, "me too. If you can make do with yesterday's biscuit and some fig preserves, I'll get up and go help Nash with your mare. After last night's wind and rain a good shampoo and set will do more for me than beauty sleep."

"Golly, Aunt Sis, I forgot about our buggy ride. I hope it's not too hot for Mable."

"If Nash can shoe a horse at seventy-five, old Mable can pull me and you down the road."

"If you say so," I agreed.

A few minutes later, I picked up my biscuit and rolled out onto the front porch behind Aunt Sis. The familiar Stetson covered what she considered messy hair, and she wore a yellow western-style shirt with stiffly starched blue jeans. Impossibly long hours, stress, and loneliness, none of it showed. She looked like the feminine version of a Marlboro advertisement, painting an attractive picture of rugged independence while hiding the costs.

Pausing on the second step, she turned and cleared her throat to speak to me, but her mobile phone rang.

"Sis Durham," she said into the phone.

I waited with idle curiosity for the rest of the conversation. Instead of speaking again, though, she took a couple of quick puffs off her cigarette, reached out to steady herself, and set down hard on the steps.

Chapter Seven

Aunt Sis?"

Concerned, I steered my wheelchair to the edge of the porch and pitched what remained of the biscuit with its sweet, sticky figs into the yard to keep from dripping them onto my lap. I heard only a quiet murmur on the other end of the phone, and my aunt's strange reaction pushed my curiosity to new heights. Not only that, but I felt familiar knots of anxiety forming in my gut.

"Yes sir," she finally said. "Yes sir; I'm on my way."

"On her way where," I wondered silently.

When she snapped the mobile phone shut, it seemed to break some kind of spell. She leaped up off the steps, tossed away her cigarette, and glanced back at me.

"Come on; we'll take your van."

I darted back inside for the keys and then careened down the ramp. Aunt Sis slung dirt and gravel as we left the yard, but I never once feared for our safety. The same quick reflexes that enabled her to handle a whip or ride a bucking horse made her an excellent driver.

"You okay?" I finally asked as we sped along the farm-to-market road toward McKendrick.

"Yes, honey. I'm sorry. That was Uncle Elmer on the telephone. Evidently, Aunt Hattie fell stepping out of the bathtub this morning. She won't let anybody in to help her, but she's asking for me."

"The niece she doesn't even like?" I asked without thinking. "No, wait. I didn't mean that like it sounded. It's not your fault she treats you like dir—"

I went quiet then, and my face flamed red.

"It's okay, Ches. You don't have to be embarrassed. Aunt Hattie and I have our moments, but blood is thicker than water."

"What?" I asked, and then the old saying rang a bell somewhere in the back of my mind. "Yeah, but why call on you after the way…"

"I expect she wants a-another lady to help her. She thinks the world of your mother, but Dallas is a good ways off."

Hattie's house seemed small but neat, covered in light brown vinyl siding, but I didn't look at it long. The sight of Andrew Hollister pacing up and down in the front yard demanded all my attention. Aunt Sis looked from him to me with a what-in-blue-blazes expression but rushed into the house leaving me to figure it out. "Nuts," Andrew muttered as I rolled across the yard toward him. "They're all nuts."

"Who?" I asked politely.

"Oh, Ches, what are you doing here?" Was that—"

"Yep, Aunt Sis," I answered. "The lady who lives here is her mother's sister, my great aunt."

"They're all nuts, and they're all related," he breathed in an undertone. Then to me, "I happened to be walking through the neighborhood this morning, and I heard a woman call for help. I stood under an open window and talked to her. She told me not to kick in the door or call 911 but to go across the street and fetch her brother."

"Uncle Elmer," I supplied.

"Right; he dug a key out of a flower pot and let us inside. That seemed like a step in the right direction, but he stopped around the corner from the bathroom to argue with her."

"Let me guess; she wanted y'all to stay out and wait for Aunt Sis."

"Pretty much, but I assumed they were talking about another sister. Miss Sis Durham never crossed my mind. You never heard such bickering back and forth. 'Elmer Blakely, you stay out of here, and get a hold of Sis.' 'I'm not gonna bother that poor girl. She can't come running into town every time you crook your finger. Are you bleeding?' 'Just a little.' I almost lost it on that one, Ches, but neither one of them wanted an ambulance."

"Well," I answered trying to sound cool and collected like Aunt Sis, "they're used to doing for themselves."

"All my folks were the same way, but I guess I've lived in the city too long."

"Do you think Aunt Hattie will be alright?"

"I'll say this; her constant fussing hasn't slacked off since I got here this morning."

"Probably a good sign," I said with a smile. "Let's go in the house and see what we can find out."

Andrew boosted my chair over the low doorstep and directed me into the hallway just outside the bathroom.

"One, two, three… Upsy-daisy!"

Aunt Sis sounded strained, and Uncle Elmer let out a grunt, but apparently they lifted Aunt Hattie out of the bathtub. I reversed my chair to clear a path, and the two of them supported her, huge flowered housecoat and all, to her recliner. Andrew tried to relieve Uncle Elmer, but the old man waved him away. Though they lowered her as gently as possible, the recliner's springs groaned under her bulk.

"I still say you could have gotten me up by yourself and spared poor Elmer's back."

"Poor Elmer ain't the one fell tryin' to take a bath," he muttered, but Aunt Sis went to her knees beside the chair.

"I'm sorry, Aunt Hattie. Really, I am, but if I'd gotten you part way up and then dropped you… At least we got you all clean and covered up before Uncle Elmer came into the room."

Reaching up tenderly, she brushed a lock of blue-looking hair out of Hattie's eyes and then patted the old lady's hand.

"Mighty small comfort," Aunt Hattie fumed. "I need to take my medicine, but I've yet to have a single bite of breakfast."

"Why don't I throw together a batch of biscuits and scramble some eggs?"

"Pancakes sit better on my stomach, and an egg's not worth eating unless it's fried."

"Yes'm," Aunt Sis said meekly, and I realized my mouth was hanging open.

"I'd fix her a piece of burnt toast and a glass of warm water, darling," Uncle Elmer suggested none too quietly as he trailed after her toward the kitchen.

Aunt Sis gave him a sad little smile and shrugged her shoulders.

"I don't mind," she assured him. "Aunt Hattie's just rattled."

"Just mean," he corrected, "mean as a snake. She's not that-a-way with everybody. Still, it just ain't right."

I tried to follow the others out of the room, but Aunt Hattie waved me back.

"Hi there, Ches," she said sweetly. "I hope my little escapade hasn't messed up your morning. These things happen if you live to get old and feeble."

"Yes ma'am, I understand. I'm glad you didn't break anything."

"I am, too, child. That's a real blessing. Now, tell me, you had enough of Miss high-and-mighty Sis Durham yet?"

Anger surged through my whole being, but I knew Aunt Sis wouldn't want me to be rude. I took a deep breath, trying to imagine what she'd say and how she might say it.

"Excuse me, Aunt Hattie. I'll just go check on your breakfast."

"Like I told Ches," Andrew explained as I rolled into the kitchen, "I was walking through this neighborhood when I heard a call for help."

"Yes," Aunt Sis said, stirring the pancake batter, "but what on earth were you doing in town at this time of the morning?"

"Apparently, Mr. Parmalee owns a lot up here, and he'd like to sell it. I don't have any real use for it, but he's been after me to come up here and take a look. I couldn't sleep so…"

"Giles thinks he's found a live buyer. He'll strip you dryer than a poor man's milk cow if you're not careful."

Andrew threw back his head and laughed. His gray eyes still danced with amusement when they settled back on her face.

"I don't know if anybody ever told you, Miss Durham, but you've surely got a way with words. Strip me dryer than a poor man's milk cow, huh? Well, don't fret yourself. I can look after my own interests."

"Most folks call me Sis, and I don't see anything special in the way I talk."

"Of course not, that's what makes it so enchanting."

"Enchanting? I hope you're not mocking me."

"Hattie's got your dander up, darling," Uncle Elmer diagnosed. "Nobody could blame you for it, either, but cut this fellow a little slack. No telling how long she'd have laid in that tub if he hadn't happened along with a good set of ears. 'Course, it might have helped her attitude."

"You're bad Uncle Elmer," Aunt Sis answered with a broad smile.

"I just tell the truth."

"Might as well stay and eat," she offered. "It's nearly dinnertime. You're welcome, too, Andrew."

"No pancakes for me, darling," Elmer answered. "Watching Hattie peck away at you is hard on my digestion. I'm apt to say something that can't be took back. Good luck to you all," he added and slipped out the kitchen door.

"I believe I will stay if you don't mind feeding me," Andrew said.

"I don't mind the least little bit." Aunt Sis assured him. "How could I after you helped rescue my aunt."

"I didn't do anything."

"That's a matter of opinion, Andrew. I've been meaning to invite you to church."

"I'm on vacation time right now, and that'll end soon. But I plan to spend my weekends up here. I'd love to join you for Sunday services."

Andrew and I tagged after Aunt Sis as she carried a loaded tray into the living room for Hattie: hot coffee, an assortment of pills, pancakes, and eggs fried to order with sausage and bacon.

"Where's Elmer? To think how that brother of mine dotes on you just because you can bang around on the piano… And you won't even feed him?"

"Now, Aunt Hattie, you know how I love Uncle Elmer. He claimed he wasn't hungry."

"You ought to know when he's just acting polite," the old lady said accusingly.

"Try to eat a bite, now, and take your medicine. You still feeling alright?" Aunt Sis asked gently as she sat the tray down.

"Certainly," Aunt Hattie snapped. "I feel fine."

"Well, I don't," Sis finally admitted. "No two ways about it; I've just got to have a cigarette."

"Tell me, Sis," the old lady demanded, "do you ever think of anybody but yourself? These boys don't even have their plates yet."

"Sorry, y'all," she tossed in our direction, already headed for the door. "This won't take long."

"Take as long as you need," Andrew said soothingly. "I'll get Ches a plate and help myself, too."

"Why?" I asked into the silence.

"Sis can't even help it anymore," Aunt Hattie explained matter-of-factly. "She's hooked on those nasty things, well and truly hooked."

Andrew almost choked, holding back his laughter, but my voice vibrated with resentment.

"Not why her," I annunciated clearly, "why you. Does she need to quit smoking, sure, but that's no reason to be so mean to her?"

"Mean," Aunt Hattie repeated in genuine surprise, "is that what you think?"

She rifled through the stacks of books and newspapers on the end table next to her chair.

"I don't think; I know."

Unearthing a Polaroid labeled Easter Sunday, 1975, she thrust it toward me. No bellbottomed jeans or loose sack-type garments for Aunt Sis, not even at sixteen. Her sky-blue dress looked sweet and modest. It fit her figure, though, rather than hanging as if on a rack. The white straw hat, pearls, and gloves highlighted a sort of timeless beauty. Obviously pleased with her place on Daddy's arm, she gazed up at him adoringly, while my grandmother lingered a few steps behind, looking back over her shoulder.

"I snapped that picture without a thought in the world except how pretty Sis looked in that dress," Aunt Hattie admitted, "but the longer I looked at it, the madder I got."

"Wha—"

"Your poor daddy," she explained. "He's eleven years old there, but it was like that his whole life. My sister tried, but even she favored the golden child. As for Chester, the sun rose and set on his darling girl."

Searching the photo for Dad, I finally spotted a blur on the outer edge.

"Oh, but…"

"No buts about it," she said almost gently. "Terry labored under all the expectations a father like Chester Durham has for his only son without any of the extra attention."

"Aunt Sis can't help being the way she is," I protested. "She's a lovely lady with a heart of gold, and people naturally gravitate to her. I'll bet she was sweet to Dad."

"She showed him a good deal of kindness, but let him get out of step with Chester, and she'd turn on him in a heartbeat. I took Terry on as my special project. Little enough I was able to do for him, but I bought his outbound bus ticket when the time came."

"Bashing Aunt Sis doesn't help dad, especially at this late date. She dropped everything to come to your rescue, and now you've got her all upset. Why even send for her today? I mean…"

"Sis and I may have our differences, but I'd call on her in a situation like this even if my own children lived closer. She's levelheaded and fiercely loyal. She doesn't holler nursing home every time you stump your toe, either."

Andrew slipped out at some point during our heated discussion, and when he came back Aunt Hattie smiled at him.

"It's good to hear you say something nice about her," he observed without the least hint of sarcasm.

"Mind your tongue, young man. I owe you my gratitude, but that doesn't mean I'll tolerate snide remarks."

My second breakfast was just about gone by the time Aunt Sis returned, looking almost blissful.

"Anybody want more to eat," she offered immediately.

"I don't know about Ches," Andrew said, "but I'm liable to pop if I take another bite. There's just enough left for you."

"I might fix me a cup of coffee, but I hadn't planned on eating."

"Probably a wise choice, my dear," Aunt Hattie said after a critical inspection of her blue-jean-clad niece.

I longed to throw something and not in just any random direction, either, but Aunt Sis bent down and kissed the old dragon on her forehead.

"I can always count on an honest assessment from you, Aunt Hattie."

Hattie knew her comment was mean-spirited, and she finally looked a little ashamed as she glanced at the wall clock.

"I appreciate all you've done, Sis. I really do. Just leave the dishes and scat on to your beauty appointment."

"For crying out loud, poor Miz Lillian must think I'm dead and buried!"

"Talk like you've got some sense, girl."

"Oh, I moved my shampoo and set up to the morning. I clean forgot about it in all the excitement."

"Lillian won't care. You're her only weekly customer under ninety years old and the apple of her eye. Even I've cut down to once every two or three weeks."

"Get her; get her good," I begged mentally. I could hear several different sugarcoated barbs delivered in my aunt's trademark drawl. Why, bless your heart; I believe I'd go back to a regular weekly appointment, was my favorite.

Of course, Aunt Sis spoke with all her usual sweetness.

"I'm fixing to call over there, ask her forgiveness, and beg for another appointment. Be sure to give Aunt Hattie a hug and kiss before we leave, Ches."

All at once my stomach went sour. Hattie always treated me kindly, and I got along with her, for the most part. Still, I hated the way she hounded and criticized Aunt Sis.

"I'd better get going, too," Andrew said. "Miz Hattie, you be careful now; you here? Miss Sis, always a pleasure to see you. Well, Ches, it's been mighty interesting," and with that he stepped smoothly out the front door.

Evidently Miz Lillian wasn't overrun with business that day because she told Aunt Sis to come on whenever it suited her. She washed the dishes, cleaned the kitchen, and dobbed medicine on Hattie's corns. I wondered for a while there if we'd have to vacuum and mop before making our escape.

"Can I come with you?" I asked as we finally drove away.

"You are with me, silly. Surely you don't think I'd give Hattie the satisfaction of keeping you there."

"No, I mean, can I come to Miz Lillian's?"

"To the beauty shop? I don't know, Ches. Driving Mable and the buggy over there is one thing, but just to ride over in the car… You'd be bored to death. A beauty parlor's hardly a manly environment."

"Well, if you'd rather go by yourself…"

"No, you're welcome to come, but don't say I didn't warn you."

Miz Lillian, an energetic lady with graying hair stepped from her air-conditioned brick house and walked over to join us at the shaded picnic table in front of the tiny frame building that served as her beauty shop.

"Good gravy, it's hot out here!"

"Hello, ma'am, I'm Ches Durham."

"Why, yes, Ches. I've heard so many good things from your aunt."

"You should probably check them with some other people," I advised her, laughingly. "Aunt Sis might be a little partial."

When Aunt Sis casually lit a third cigarette, I shot her a quizzical glance. Miz Lillian caught it and felt the need to explain.

"Several of my ladies used to smoke in the chair, but we finally repainted the inside walls. I feel for you, Sis. Really, I do, but you're the last—"

Despite her reluctance to change, Aunt Sis hated the idea of being the last of anything. She hid her irritation well but spoke quickly to head off that train of thought.

"They're your walls, Miz Lillian. Besides, Bowie like to have worked himself to death on that little honey-do. I wouldn't dream of messing up his paint job. The thing is, I can't smoke in the van or Aunt Hattie's house or…" She trailed off with a sigh.

"We can sit here for as long as you need to, sweet pea. My time is all yours today."

"This one ought to do it." Then smilingly, "No real lady wants to look greedy, Ches, but I'm dangerously close to that line."

"You could never be greedy, Sis," Lillian assured her, "not even if you tried. I don't think it's possible with a heart as big as yours."

I loaded my wheelchair back into the van and grabbed the set of crutches, but I found it easier to navigate the steps on my hands and knees.

"It's alright," Aunt Sis said quickly when Miz Lillian gasped. "Ches gets around like that quite a bit."

"Have a seat right here, Ches," the beauty operator invited, probably glad to have me safely inside her shop. "Forgive me if I show off a little. Working on someone as young and pretty as your aunt makes me look like a real expert."

"Miz Lillian?" Aunt Sis murmured in a far away tone.

"What is it, child?"

"Have your glasses checked next time you're in town." The beautician swatted my aunt on the shoulder like a squirmy little girl. Her swat looked hard enough to sting, but those same fingers moved ever so gently as she began to wash my aunt's hair. "Ouch! Quit whopping on me, and tell me the latest word from Deborah. How's her blood pressure these days?"

"Lordy mercy, whine and moan and gripe. That daughter of mine wouldn't last thirty minutes in your shoes. You wouldn't catch her working her fingers to the bone out there at the horse sale and then running uptown to wash and cook and clean for Hattie."

"It's not that bad," Aunt Sis answered sleepily.

"Oh, yes it is," I asserted, and they both jumped like they'd already forgotten my presence.

"Ches, honey," Aunt Sis tried to explain, "Deborah and I went to school together. She's as sweet a girl as you'll ever find. It's just…"

"Do you know what a hypochondriac is, Ches?" Miz Lillian asked bluntly.

"Yes'm."

"Well, then, you know Deborah. I listen to complaints about her health, her good husband, and their finances. Then she pays big money to have her hair cut up town when I'd do it for free."

"Oh, Miz Lillian, how much can it really cost when she only goes once every five or six months?"

"If you're trying to make me feel better, Sis, you can stop now. If you're handing out smart remarks, though, that was a good one. Neither one," Lillian decided as she examined my aunt's closed eyes and blank expression. "The poor child's just too nearly asleep to filter the truth."

"She needs all the rest she can get."

A little while later, the door opened and a lanky man in overalls stuck his head inside. My aunt's head lolled back over the sink, her mouth gaped open, and her breath made a whistling noise as she slept. I felt suddenly and intensely protective of her privacy, and Miz Lillian must have shared the feeling.

"Get out of here, Bowie Tate. Just because you finally put on a few coats of paint doesn't mean you can come poking your nose in my beauty parlor whenever it suits you."

"Settle down, baby doll," he whispered. "I just wondered if this young man needed rescuing yet."

"Take him or don't take him, but get out."

"It ain't like I never saw any of them asleep in the chair. Tell Sis she ought to slow down on those cigarettes, though. That little rattle don't sound good."

You don't spring from your chair when you've got cerebral palsy and depend on a pair of crutches, but in my mind I did.

"Nice to meet you, sir, I'm Ches Durham. Let's go."

I whispered all that in one breath, and the old man gave me a puzzled look. Even so, he drew his head and shoulders out of the doorway and let me pass through.

"Say what?" he asked as he supported me uncertainly down the steps.

"Thanks for checking on me, Mr. Tate. Did I meet you at church the other day?"

"Glad to, son, but this is the first time I've laid eyes on you. Me and Lillian go to church in the county seat."

Safely on level ground I balanced on one crutch and stuck out my hand to shake.

"I'm not sure how well you know my aunt, but she wouldn't like to be seen looking less than her best."

"Women are a peculiar bunch, and high-toned ladies like your aunt are the strangest of them all. I've known her since she was a little bitty girl tagging after the colonel. Why, I wouldn't think a thing about it if Sis walked in on me kicked back in my recliner, but let the shoe get on the other foot... I'd admire a chance to show you my garden," he ended up with a shrug.

"Sounds good, just let me grab my wheelchair."

"I'll do you one better. Wait right here, and I'll go fetch the golf cart."

His garden was a sight to behold. Vegetables of all kinds sprang in long, straight rows from the rich red earth.

"Wow, you've put in a lot of work here."

"It must be quite a sight for a city boy," he teased. "'Tween that and all this clean country air, you may not ever be the same."

Making a sudden stop, Mr. Tate stepped from the cart into his garden and came back with a couple of tomatoes. He wiped them off on his shirt, grinned at me and produced a salt shaker from one of the golf cart's storage compartments.

"Aunt Sis and I are gonna have a fish fry sometime pretty soon. You and Miz Lillian ought to come," I said as we visited contentedly with tomato juice running down our chins.

"Maybe I'll have some fresh okra by that time. A lot of folks like French fries and hushpuppies, but you can't beat fried okra with fish."

"Really?"

"Uh huh. You see any grass out there?" he asked gesturing toward the garden.

"No sir."

"Well, the colonel always said you couldn't work a garden right without a horse or a mule. Miss Sis still swears to it up, down, and sideways. But I plowed all that yonder with a Farm-All tractor."

I talked just enough to let him know I was interested in what he had to say, and he seemed to enjoy having me as a listener. Eventually, we cleaned ourselves up at a water hose and headed back to the beauty shop.

"Thanks for showing me around, Mr. Tate, but I can manage the steps on my own."

He grinned broadly, catching my real meaning.

"Attaboy, you just keep looking after your Aunt Sis. If anybody deserves it, she does."

Instead of plopping back into the chair I'd left, I walked across the room and glanced fondly down at my sleeping aunt.

"It's time to get her under the dryer, but she looks so peaceful I hate to wake her," Miz Lillian whispered.

"If we're not messing up your day," I said, "just let her sleep."

My voice wasn't any louder than Miz Lillian's, but something about it got through to Aunt Sis. One corner of her mouth twitched upward and her eyelids fluttered.

"She's not in my way a-tall," the old lady said kindly, but Aunt Sis let out a cute little snort and startled herself awake.

"Good morning, sunshine."

Even though my aunt's hairdo probably hadn't changed in years, the weekly shampoo and styling seemed to put a fresh spring in her step.

"I'm as hungry as a bear," she admitted on the drive home. "Surely I deserve a chicken fried steak. These last couple of days have just about knocked me flat."

"Of course you deserve a good meal. There's no reason you should have to cook it, either."

"I don't know… It doesn't make much sense to go right back to town after grocery shopping last night."

"Oh, Aunt Sis," I groaned, seeing a weight-loss shake in her future and a fried bologna sandwich in mine.

"Alright," she answered with a grin. "You talked me into it! Let's run home right quick and check the stock. I'll slip into something presentable, and we'll be on our way."

Puddler's whole body wriggled with delight when he caught sight of me. I played with him a while, fed him, and lost track of my aunt for a few minutes. At the click of her lighter, though, I looked up to see her standing in the doorway.

"Don't you look pretty," I said, taking in her pale pink dress, pearl earrings, and cream-colored heels. "That surely is a fancy outfit."

"This old thing," she joked, spinning around for her own entertainment as much as mine.

Aunt Sis greeted everyone we ran across in the county seat with a lovely smile. Most of them received a handshake or hug, too.

"Somebody's in a good mood this evening," I quipped.

"I guess you're right, honey, but I hope I'm friendly most of the time."

"You always let your little light shine," I assured her, "but I will say the wattage is cranked up tonight."

I watched her enjoy a good-sized chicken fried steak, plus gravy and all the trimmings, without a single worried reference to her figure. Suddenly, I understood. Miss Sis felt pretty, and that made all the difference.

"I love having you here, Ches," she assured me, "but I've been slacking off ever since you came. If I get busy and make some horse trades in the next few days, I think I can fill that order for Mr. Hollister."

"I didn't mean to interfere with your work," I said guiltily.

"Don't worry, honey. It was my own doing. I need to load a couple of good, solid ranch horses in the morning and haul them clear up to Canton. Brother Carlton said he'd come over and go for a buggy ride with you. But if you'd rather burn up the road with me, that's fine, too. Either way, I'll be back by church time."

I still hadn't adjusted to attending every single Wednesday night prayer meeting. A day with the preacher didn't sound too appealing, either, but I thought Aunt Sis might travel faster and accomplish more alone. Preacher or not, Brother Crawford had generously given me his horse. He probably missed old Mable, and a buggy ride seemed the least I could do.

"I'd like a chance to take Mable out if you don't need me on the trip."

Aunt Sis just smiled and nodded as she ate the last few bites of her steak. I thought our heavy meal would make her sleepy again, but even after peach cobbler and ice cream, she remained a bundle of energy.

"Davis Western Wear won't close for nearly an hour," she said with a glance at her watch. "I know a certain young fellow who could use some new duds."

I rolled into my aunt's kitchen the next morning to find Brother Crawford seated alone at the table with a coffee cup and a picnic-style basket in front of him.

"Good morning, Ches."

"Morning, sir. Where's Aunt Sis?"

"Somewhere out of Kilgore on I-20, I expect."

"It's barely even six o'clock," I grumbled.

"Miss Sis seemed antsy, ready to cover some country. She even turned down one of Edna's homemade sweet rolls. I don't know what y'all ate for supper last night, but she muttered something about six months of dieting gone down the drain."

"One good meal won't hurt her."

"I know several young ladies who'd love to be as slender as Miss Sis. She's awfully critical of herself, though, and not just weight-wise. In her book the colonel's daughter should work longer, ride harder, and look prettier...period."

"It's not like she's unhealthy or anything. Well, except for... Do you think it's a sin? Her smoking, I mean."

Brother Crawford blew out a long breath, pushed the basket of cinnamon rolls toward me, and tilted his chair back on its hind legs.

"Well, now, I reckon the Lord's more concerned with spiritual things than physical. I doubt if He favors her cigarettes any more or less than these sweet rolls. Most folks don't eat forty rolls a day, but I can't say I haven't been tempted."

"I see what you mean," I mumbled around a gooey mouthful.

"The Bible does teach that anything we put before God becomes sinful. Only Miss Sis knows the place He occupies in her life, but most of her actions indicate godly priorities."

These words settled a troublesome issue for me. Brother Crawford didn't discount the health concerns attached to my aunt's habit, but he confirmed my own deeply held belief. Aunt Sis was not a bad person.

"She told me we'd shut the horse sale down before she let it keep people out of church, and I'm sure she'd rather quit smoking than throw away everything her daddy built."

Brother Crawford nodded in agreement, and I knew he understood my meaning. He watched me lick the icing from my fingers, clunked his chair back down on the floor, and then introduced a lighter subject.

"I like 'at shirt."

"Thanks; it's brand new. Aunt Sis took me to the western-wear store last night and went a little crazy. I hated to see her spend money on—"

"Miss Sis knows her own mind," he said with a grin. "She loves you an awful lot, and I'd guess it pleasures her no end to buy you presents. Besides, you favor your granddaddy in those clothes. All you lack is the hat."

"Wait just a minute," I said and buzzed out of the room.

I came back with a narrow-brimmed straw hat, not a Stetson but a U-Roll-It, carefully shaped to my aunt's specifications. I grinned at the preacher as I set it carefully on my head, mimicking the angle she'd taught me.

"That does it. If she ever gets you out of your wheelchair and onto a horse, you'll be Chester Durham made over. You happy with your new clothes?" he asked. "The last time I checked young people had notions all their own."

"I'm not exactly your average teenager. Easy to put on and take off, that's my rule. Snap shirts fit the bill, these cast-iron jeans, not so much. I never thought much about a personal style, but if Aunt Sis wants to give me one, I'll take it."

"Good enough," he said, laughing. "Mable's brushed, harnessed, and ready."

"How long you been here?" I asked in surprise.

"Your Aunt Sis didn't want to leave you here alone, and I didn't want to eat all the sweet rolls before you woke up. So, I wandered on down to the barn for a while."

"Sounds about right," I said. "Aunt Sis takes really good care of me. Did you know she tucks me in at night like a baby?"

"You okay with that?"

"It's a little embarrassing to admit. In fact, I'm not sure why I told you, but as long as it's just me and her, I like it fine."

Mable's new shoes rang nicely as she clip clopped along the county road. The early June sky looked robin's egg blue, and a faint morning breeze helped keep down the heat. Brother Crawford told me Miz Edna had gone over to let Miz Lillian fix her hair. He even admitted that he'd begun to worry some about her driving. We talked about their great-grandchildren, the church, and his memories of my dad as a boy.

"Say, you handle the old lady mighty well for a beginner," he finally observed.

"Aunt Sis is a good teacher, but I think most five-year-olds could drive Mable."

"Sis couldn't have been much more than five when she drove that team of wild

Shetlands right through the middle of our big homecoming picnic."

"Do what?" I squawked, eyes rounding.

"You heard right. Chester came up with a pair of beautifully matched black-and-white ponies as wild as the day is long. Nash's nephews nor nobody else could stay on them. So he bought a little cart and some harness. 'Sis'll take the starch out of them.'"

"Did she?" I asked.

"Yeah, but they pretty well scrambled the picnic first. She'd been driving them for a week or so, and Chester called them broke. He wanted to show his fancy little team and their pretty driver off in front of the picnic crowd. I'll say this; some of us got a good, close look."

"What happened?"

"Most folks dressed up in old-fashioned clothes to celebrate the church's 100th anniversary. There we went a-chasing after Miss Sis and her runaway team in our grandparents' Sunday best. Those little horses turned over tables, scattered fried chicken, and came to a stop with both sets of front feet planted in a big vat of lemonade."

"No way; I hope y'all threw out that lemonade!"

Brother Crawford nodded and continued his story with a grin.

"Sis still sat in the buggy, old-timey sunbonnet on her head and driving lines firmly in hand. Most of the folks at that picnic, those of us passed a certain age anyway, grew up with horses and mules, but my Edna is scared to death of anything bigger than a medium-sized dog. You might know she'd be the one serving lemonade. 'I can't go anywhere with their feet in the tub,' little Miss Sis explained patiently. 'Pick them up and move them, please ma'am, one leg at a time.'"

Chapter Eight

I would have paid good money to see Miz Edna's face," I admitted when I finally caught my breath. "What did she do?"

"She froze for a minute there, but Sis sounded so calm and matter-of-fact about it all that Edna finally did what she asked. Those ponies stood there trembling with eyes rolled back in their heads while she fished their feet out of the lemonade. 'Thanks bunches, Miz Edna; I'm sorry about the lemonade. Get up, Jesse. Let's go James. Heavens to Betsy, y'all made a big mess!'"

"What itty-bitty kid says Heavens to Betsy?" I asked, but Brother Crawford just pulled off his glasses and gave me a look. "I know; I know. We're talking about Little Miss Sis."

"She wheeled that team around and came trotting back by me and all the other would-be rescuers as cool as you please. Chester Durham had the steadiest nerves of anybody I ever knew, but he was shaking like a leaf when she passed him. 'Sorry about all this, Daddy. They'll have a different outlook before I let them stop again.' And you know something, they did. Their tongues probably dragged the ground that evening, but I don't think those ponies ever gave another minutes trouble as long as Chester kept them."

When a whitetail deer bounded across the road in front of us, Mable threw up her head and snorted. Potential danger usually catapulted my heart up into my throat. For whatever reason- the preacher's calming presence, my good mood, or Sis Durham's influence on my life- fear never crossed my mind.

"Uh oh, somebody better move the lemonade," I thought, smiling a little as I tightened my hold on the lines. "Here we come."

Fortunately, Mable just looked at the quick-footed critter and kept plodding down the road.

"She's seen deer before," Brother Crawford assured me. "That one startled her is all."

"Startled me, too," I admitted. "What about the picnic, though? Was it a complete bust?"

"Naw, we shared what food didn't get spilled or trampled. Some of us wanted to wring Chester's neck for putting our Miss Sis in danger. Of course, she'd tell you right quick that she was Daddy's Miss Sis most of all. Nash came down there in the next day or two and patched up the picnic tables."

"Nowadays, they'd arrest the colonel for child endangerment or some such."

"A body might still get by with it in McKendrick, but you're right. People today love to meddle in each other's business. Better pull over under this shade tree, Ches, and let Mable breathe a minute."

I didn't really know mom and dad's pastor, and to tell the truth they didn't know him, either. Although their church wasn't quite as big as a stadium, we sat far enough from the front that I had to look up on a screen to see his face.

I spent most of my time trying to avoid the well-meaning youth pastor and his quest for greater participation. So naturally, my easy friendship with Brother Crawford surprised me. I felt totally comfortable with him, even after such a short acquaintance.

"Keep your mouth shut," I told myself, but deep down I knew Aunt Sis was right. My questions needed to be settled. "Brother Crawford, can I ask you something?"

My tone must have sounded serious because the glasses came off again, and he twisted around in the buggy seat to focus his penetrating blue eyes on my face.

"I'm all ears, Ches."

"How do I make sure my salvation is for real? I was six years old when I asked the Lord to save me. That seems like a long time ago now, and I just don't… It worries Aunt Sis. And me, too, to tell you the truth."

"Do you have a clear memory of your prayer?"

"Well, yes and no. I didn't exactly pray out loud."

"No matter about that. The Lord hears what's on our hearts."

"I just remember thinking that I was sorry for my sins and that I didn't want to die and go to Hell. I asked Him please to come into my heart and save me."

"There are no magic words, Ches, but it sounds like you covered all the bases. Now, the question is whether that prayer came from your heart or just your mind. Did you feel differently afterwards?"

"Yes sir," I said as Mable stomped a horsefly off her leg. "It felt kind of like somebody lifted a load off my shoulders. What would I know about that, though? I've never carried anything except maybe something on my lap while I drove the wheelchair."

"Know the feeling or not, you recognized it. Salvation is not based on feelings, but we should certainly feel a difference when the Holy Spirit comes into our lives."

"I felt relieved and happy; I know that."

"What about before? What made you decide to pray?"

"I went to a Bible camp, but I couldn't concentrate on the lessons for thinking about how homesick I was. I just knew if I ever made it home, things would go back to normal."

"But they didn't?"

"No sir. I was glad to be home, but I still couldn't sleep at night, not like I had before. Bits and pieces of those Bible lessons kept floating to the top of my mind. I felt agitated. The butterflies surfaced in my chest instead of my stomach, but come to think of it my stomach didn't feel real good, either."

"We call that being under conviction. Did it go away after you prayed?"

"Yeah, it did until lately. It's not as bad as before but…"

"It's not my place, Ches, or anybody's place to tell you you're saved or lost. I will say the Holy Spirit convicts us for various reasons even after salvation. Do you feel you've made an effort to serve God with your life?"

"No… No, I really don't. Right afterwards… After I prayed, I mean, I wanted to learn all I could about God and tell everybody about what happened to me. Then, I got a little older and realized just how unfair life is. I haven't prayed, not really and truly, for several years, but I prayed for Aunt Sis when she and the others gathered those cattle off the highway Monday night."

"Do you believe God heard and answered that prayer?"

"Well… Yes sir, I do. I don't know why He'd want to answer it after the attitude I've had, but I think… I know He did."

"The only petition God accepts from a lost person is a prayer of repentance. The Lord never promised his children an easy life, Ches, or even a pair of working legs. He did promise to go with us through this life and bring us safely into His presence at its end."

I bit my bottom lip and tried, unsuccessfully, not to cry. Dropping the driving lines, I left them to hang loose over the dashboard and turned my face away from Brother Crawford.

"He g-gives us blessings along the way, too, doesn't He? Friends like you, good parents like mine, and… Aunt Sis," I listed, "but I don't deserve any of it."

"None of us do, Ches, none of us do. As for why God would want to answer your prayer, He's always ready to welcome His children back with open arms. Once you truly accept Him, there's no way to lose your salvation or reverse the process. We may wander away from Him, but He never abandons us."

"No sir," I agreed.

"It's up to you to decide whether you're saved or not, but if you are, the Lord wants you to have confidence in Him. You don't have to wonder about your eternal destiny once He settles it. If you are His child He expects you to serve Him as a vital part of a local, New-Testament church, but salvation is the essential step."

"I took that step a long time ago, Brother Crawford," I said, finally meeting his eyes, "and I didn't even need my crutches."

He reached out solemnly for a handshake and then pulled me into a hug.

"That's good to hear, son, mighty good."

"Want to drive us home," I asked. "I'd like to call Aunt Sis."

"I'd be glad to drive a while, but pick up the lines and hold them while I visit the bushes." I had to think about it for a few seconds but finally snapped to his meaning. "Slide over," he said when he came back. "I don't know why, but the old timers always drove a wagon or buggy from the right-hand side."

"Mable knows a real driver's got hold of her now," I joked as we picked up speed.

"She knows who's got her alright, but that ain't what perked her up. She's headed to the barn. You do what you want, Ches, but I believe I'd call your folks and give Miss Sis the good news face to face."

"You may be right about telling Aunt Sis in person, but I never told Mom and Dad about my doubts. I'll share the whole story sometime, but I don't want to spring it on them today."

Brother Crawford took me to the swimming hole after our buggy ride and even rolled up his pant legs to wade around in the shallow part. We came back to my aunt's house to find Miz Edna in the kitchen.

"Lillian and I got to talking and decided poor, sweet Sis would be worn plumb out from a hard day's work and all that driving time. Bowie sent over a mess of his fresh squash, and I found a bag of potatoes and some canned salmon here. It ain't fancy but... Y'all will have a decent supper before prayer meeting, and she won't have to lift a finger."

Brother Crawford peeled potatoes to cream and I cut up the squash for Miz Edna to fry. He described all our fun without a word about the serious talk. I took this as a signal that the good news was mine to share or keep. The lady's quiet gentleness matched her husband's easy-going way, and I soon decided to tell her. I think a few tears of joy fell into the hot grease, but her reaction was nothing compared to what lay in store.

The two older ladies hit the nail on the head as to my aunt's exhaustion. She swung down to the barn first and finally came dragging in, almost too tired to function. She thanked Brother and Miz Crawford for everything they'd done and insisted they stay for supper. Walking on through the house to the back porch, she plunked herself down in the swing, her usually perfect posture nowhere to be seen.

"It's pitiful to be this tired after nothing more strenuous than driving and talking. I promise you, Ches, that's all I did."

"I don't believe a word of it. You dragged that big trailer, talked long and hard to make your swap, and there's no telling what else."

"Nothing to pulling that trailer," she said, "it follows the pick-up."

"Oh, whatever… I couldn't do it, not on the interstate."

"I rode those two horses of mine long enough to show their good points, but they did all the work. The fellow I dealt with had a pen full of young mules, and we separated the ones I took in trade. Of course he wanted to part with the sorry end of them, and I needed the good ones. We argued back and forth 'Turn that mule out.' 'No, I want her. Bring her back.' That didn't make the sorting any easier, and then we still had to load the wild boogers."

"My point exactly."

"I'm telling you, Ches, there's nothing to all that. It just takes time."

"And energy," I insisted.

"Not much," she huffed. "I can barely hold my head up, and there's no reason for it. On top of everything else, I stopped for a Diet Coke and ended up with a hamburger and fries I didn't need."

I wanted to tell her it was impossible to do the kind of physical work she did without some kind of nourishment to keep her going. I knew she wouldn't hear it, though, to her the fast food represented an inexcusable lack of self control. Instead of arguing with that, I decided to change her mood.

"Remember our little talk about God and my relationship with Him?"

"I sure do."

Her backbone snapped straight like a soldier coming to attention, and she dropped a smoldering cigarette butt into the coffee can. Love and concern filled her eyes as she studied my face.

"Well," I said, quoting one of her beloved old hymns. "I am my Lord's, and He is mine."

Aunt Sis squealed like a little girl at a slumber party.

"Oh, honey," she said wonderingly and popped up from the swing. "Precious honey child... You got saved today?"

"No ma'am, I remembered my salvation today and realized I just need to turn back to my Lord."

"I knew it; I knew it! I knew it," she gushed, squeezing the life out of me in a fiercely tight hug. "I thought you were saved all along, but I couldn't take the chance of giving you a false hope. You're not saved because Aunt Sis thinks you are; you're saved because you placed your heart and soul in the Lord's hands."

All of my aunt's weariness seemed to fall away, and her usual lively interest in life returned. Though back on her diet, she allowed herself reasonable portions of Miz Edna's home cooking and seemed to enjoy it. She washed dishes after supper while I dried.

"Brother and Mrs. Crawford sure are sweet, Aunt Sis. He's the only preacher I ever really got to know."

"Preachers are just people, Ches. They have a special calling from God, and most of them try hard to follow His leading. Still, when it comes down to it, they're just folks like me and you."

"Brother Crawford showed me that today. He even got in the swimming hole."

Aunt Sis cut her eyes at me, and her gentle drawl took on a bit of a stern edge.

"You might as well stop hinting around, Ches. I've got a long way to go before I get back in my bathing suit."

"Who's hinting, but how many eighty-some-year-old men do you see wading around in water up to their knees?"

"He's something else alright," she said as her smile returned. "I'll be running wide open the next few days, halter breaking those mules and trying to buy some more horses before the Friday night sale. Would you like me to ask Brother Crawford to come back and spend some more time with you? As far as that goes, I'm sure you'd be welcome over there anytime."

"Well, if I'm in your way..." I said in an honest effort to be cooperative, not realizing how pitiful it sounded.

My aunt looked like I'd slapped her. She reached instinctively to gather me into a hug but stopped long enough to dry her wet, soapy hands.

"Honey, you can just get that out of your head right now," she said, squeezing for all she was worth. "You're never in my way, never ever."

"I enjoy Brother and Mrs. Crawford, Aunt Sis, and I wouldn't mind visiting them sometime. If it's all the same, though, I'd rather spend my time with you."

"Music to my ears," she admitted, "but you better hang on to your hat."

Joy over my renewed faith and confidence powered her through the remainder of the evening and energized her piano playing during Wednesday night service. She sat on the bench as prim and proper as ever, but the songs seemed to get faster and faster. After an all-out race through "Leaning on the Everlasting Arms," Uncle Elmer glanced over and raised an eyebrow.

"Who's the song leader here, Sis?" was his unspoken question.

They adored and depended on one another. Elmer's eyes twinkled with amusement even as he tried to look stern. Ducking her head meekly, Sis reined in her enthusiasm somewhat, but she put her whole heart into "O Happy Day" while they took up the offering. I recognized a personal message meant especially for me.

> 'Tis done, the great transaction's done.
> I am my Lord's, and He is mine.
> He drew me, and I followed on,
> charmed to confess the voice divine.
> Happy day, happy day, when Jesus washed my sins away.
> He taught me how to watch and pray and live rejoicing every day.
> Happy day, happy day, when Jesus washed my sins away.

I took my aunt's warning about the next couple of days pretty lightly, not really believing she could get any busier. I felt her gentle pat-pats on my back long before daylight Thursday morning and realized I'd miscalculated.

"Good morning, sunshine," she whispered, repeating my own words back to me. "It's awful early but I hated to run off and leave you."

"No," I answered groggily, "I want to go."

"There ought to be a law against these things," she apologized, sliding a microwaveable breakfast sandwich onto my plate, "but I picked up a box the other day while we were in Winn-Dixie. They're better than nothing, I suppose, and we've got to hit the ground running."

The frozen sausage biscuit might be a necessary evil in my case, but Aunt Sis turned her nose up at it in favor of caffeine and nicotine.

"Like you say," I reminded her, "this is better than nothing. Want me to heat one up for you?"

"Honey, if I'm going to take in that many calories, they need to taste better than cardboard."

"You're a mess," I said, laughing as I reached across the table to squeeze her hand.

Nash and a sleepy looking Scooter met us down at the sale barn.

"Miss Volleyball finally got a summer job, but Seth has to pick her up and drop her off. I told him you wouldn't like it none. Anyhow, I made him put me out here first."

"Seth is near-about grown. There's not a whole lot I can say, but I wish he'd let me know."

"I told him that, too, but you can be kinda scary."

"Who, little old me? My bark's worse than my bite, Scooter, and I hope you boys know I'm always here if you need me."

"Right now," he joked, "I need you to step up on your horse and get this show on the road. Nash saddled him while I was ratting out my brother to stay on your good side."

"Why, you little dickens," she said, playfully slapping the Durham-Auction cap off his head. "As soon as I get the least bit soft or mushy, you jab the spurs to me."

Aunt Sis rode into the pen horseback, singled out a particular mule, and caught it with one quick toss of her lariat. Each time she pulled a long-eared head up close to her saddle horn, Nash buckled a halter in place and handed the long lead off to Scooter.

With Miss Sis and her saddle horse to help him, my buddy managed to hold the animals while Nash worked over their manes and tails with a pair of razor-sharp hand shears. No matter how often they repeated the process, it amazed me every time. After the fourth of eight mules, Nash needed a break. Leaning against her saddle horse's shoulder, he asked the boss lady for a cigarette. She handed it to him, and he squinted up at her through the smoke.

"There was a time, Miss Sis, when your daddy and granddaddy made us a good living trading mules, but I just can't see no money in it these days. Ain't hardly no farmers left in this country. What's more, anybody that wants a tractor can get one."

"That's right, but I know a fellow in Tennessee who still loves to fool with a mule. He works his tobacco allotment with them and even raises a little cotton for old time's sake. He also buys and sells Tennessee walking horses."

"We had buyers for them two good cowponies or will have this fall. You've always been quite the little trader but…"

"What's the matter, Nash? You think I'm losing my touch?"

"Now, Miss Sis, I didn't say no such-of-a-thing, and I'm mighty sorry if you took it that way."

"I'm getting old, but not so old my mind's slipping. I happen to have a cash order for some fancy-type walking horses."

"Old," he snorted. "Why, you're still a child, but I don't quite follow your thinking."

"This fellow up at Canton has a-way too many mares and three or four good jacks. He likes to see a pasture full of mule babies every spring. Only trouble is, he's getting mighty feeble. The Tennessee man's just a year or two older than me and in better shape to break young stock."

A wide grin split Nash's face.

"Beggin' your pardon, Miss Sis, I ought to've figured you'd have an angle. After we lost the colonel, I tried to guide you along without poking my nose too far into your business, but you're a-way past that now. Truth be known, you never much needed my help."

"That's not so," she said, returning his smile. "I'll always depend on you."

"No ma'am," he murmured under his breath, "not always."

"Come again?" my aunt inquired, leaning from the saddle in an effort to hear.

"Nothing; we best catch a few more before the heat sets in on us."

Aunt Sis missed her throw occasionally and took some good natured ragging from the other two, but I doubted very seriously if either of them could do half as well. They kept going until the temperature climbed too high for such work.

"Let's you and me put in some windshield time, Ches. Poor Nash can't take this heat like he used to. Besides, I'd hate to kill a mule."

"Of course, you don't feel the heat," I joked, "not Miss Sis Durham."

I learned a lot watching Aunt Sis buy horses. Always a perfect lady, she never compromised her integrity, but nobody ever ran over her, either. She described every horse we looked at in great detail: color, height, weight, conformation, good points and bad.

Because of my lifelong fascination with the animals and the things I'd learned collecting models, most horse terminology made perfect sense to me. Enjoying the musical quality of my aunt's East Texas drawl, I soaked up knowledge almost unconsciously. I certainly didn't realize how intentional it all was on her part, not until a heavy, red-faced man stopped her in midsentence.

"Look here, lady, that's my daughter's barrel horse. He ain't up for sale with the others, so there's no need to talk trash about him."

"I'm sorry, sir. I didn't know you'd come back from the barn. I'm just trying to teach my nephew how to judge horseflesh."

"Well, now, your opinions ain't necessarily the true measure of a horse's quality."

"Maybe not," Aunt Sis said in a dangerously sweet tone, "but those opinions came straight from this boy's granddaddy. What's more, anybody who intends to work for me had better have a good understanding of what I look for in a horse."

The fellow didn't act too enthused, but he got a lot friendlier when Aunt Sis started peeling off hundred-dollar bills. We made several more stops and rolled in home after dark. Aunt Sis unloaded our day's purchase, I fed the dogs, and we ate a bite before staggering off to bed.

"Remember our little talk about motor skills?" I asked before dawn the next morning as my aunt went over the procedures of checking a horse into our auction and issuing a buyer's number. "I can barely write my own name."

"Well, you understand the forms. Show the folks how to fill out their own paperwork. Serena Kate and the other office help should be here about dinnertime. Seth can manage the unloading and penning-off by himself, at least until it gets too hot for me and Nash and Scooter to fool with the mules."

I enjoyed taking an active part in the busy sale-day preparations and most of the customers acted patient and friendly. People I didn't even know called me by name and spoke encouragingly.

"Good job, Ches."

"I'm glad to see you out here."

"Old Colonel Durham would be mighty proud."

Coming up from behind, Aunt Sis dropped a hand onto my shoulder.

"Well, don't you look fresh as a daisy," I observed, gazing up at her.

"I slipped up to the house for a quick bath," she admitted. "They tell me you've done a good job down here."

"I'm trying to follow your instructions and keep things moving."

"You've been a big help, but the café's open now. I'll take over here. You run along and eat with Serena Kate and the girls."

"I had another of those better-than-nothing breakfast sandwiches, remember? I bet you didn't take time for a single bite, not even when you went back to the house."

"I had all the breakfast I needed," she said, pulling out her pack of cigarettes as if to remind me, "but you can bring me another cup of black coffee when you come back."

"Good grief, it's 110 degrees in the shade."

Actually, the June day probably registered a high in the low 90s, but coffee?

"Hot coffee cools a body off better than anything else," Aunt Sis informed me. "Besides, I need something to keep me going."

"You might try food," I thought, but "I'll bring you a cup as quick as I can," is what I said out loud.

Serena Kate moved a chair so I could pull in beside her and advised me to order a hamburger.

"Can't you smell it, Ches," she said in answer to my puzzled look. "They cooked liver and onions for the plate lunch."

"Cooked what?" I asked, swallowing hard.

"Calf liver smothered in onions and brown gravy," she explained, wrinkling her nose, "but the banana pudding is to die for."

Our burgers tasted fine, but we tried not to watch the folks around us as they dug into their portions of liver.

"That stuff gets bigger the longer you chew it," a curly-headed blonde said in disgust.

"Miss Sis made me try some one time," Serena Kate confided. "Hers really wasn't all that bad, but liver is liver."

Thinking about Aunt Sis, I inhaled one bowl of banana pudding, grabbed another with the cup of coffee, and headed back to her.

"Thanks for letting me park by you, Serena Kate, but duty calls. I'll see y'all around."

"Ches, honey," my aunt moaned pitifully when she finished helping a customer and looked up to see the bowl of pudding with its homemade meringue on top. "You know how hard it is for me to resist, but I really don't…"

"What's the problem, Aunt Sis? You asked for a cup of coffee, and this banana pudding is mine."

"Oh," she said, trying not to show her disappointment.

"You can have a bite if you want."

"Well, maybe just a tiny one." I held the bowl while she dipped out a little spoonful. "Heavens to Betsy," she breathed, closing her eyes as the taste hit her.

"Good?"

"Miz Edna made that," she said without the shadow of a doubt.

"You know something else? I ate mine in the café and brought this bowl to you."

"Well, bless your sweet heart," she purred, giving up the struggle as she reached for the bowl.

Aunt Sis retreated into her office with the pudding, so I worked the check-in until Serena Kate and the other girls straggled out of the café. Soon enough, Aunt Sis reappeared and led me off to my next assignment.

"What's all this?" I wondered when she stopped next to a small telephone table.

Tucked back into a corner across the room from the auctioneer's box, it held two rotary-dial phones, a calculator, a couple of ink pens, and- if I'm lying, I'm dying- a Big Chief tablet. Though I'd never seen one, I recognized the red writing pad and the picture of an Indian in full headdress on the front cover immediately.

"Your desk," she answered casually.

"I get a desk?"

"Don't you think the Assistant Manager in charge of Remote Bidding needs one?"

"You just now made that up," I snorted.

"Well, it sounds pretty good."

"It does," I admitted, laughing at her. "I like taking telephone bids, but you know I can't write."

"Can you scribble notes that'll make enough sense to jog your memory?"

"Maybe; my memory's pretty good."

"I'll give you a secretary if you need one, but it'd be a big help if you could manage by yourself."

"I can do it but whether I can keep up with you and Jim Rex…"

"Mmm, good point. You'll have buyer numbers, tag numbers, phone numbers, and prices to keep straight with everything around you happening pretty fast. Of course, once a sale is complete, I'll write it down where it counts."

"My handwriting's not only sloppy, it's slow."

"I've got it," she said, snapping her fingers. "There's an old Underwood typewriter in the colonel's office."

"You mean your office?"

"I just sit behind his desk, honey. I don't claim it. New typewriter ribbon may be as scarce as hens' teeth, but you can hammer out your notes on the thing as long as it'll put legible numbers on the page. I'll make Scooter tote it in here directly."

"Thanks for all this, Aunt Sis," I said taking in my little corner with a gesture. "I'm really excited."

"No, Ches, thank you. This remote bidding business may turn out to be a real shot in the arm for our sale."

"You really think so?"

Lifting her shoulders slightly, Aunt Sis flashed me a we'll-soon-find-out grin.

"I put an ad in the Peddler and on the radio. It lists a partial catalog of horses, gives the phone numbers, and states that you'll be taking bids."

"Wow, I may be busy."

"We probably won't get many calls tonight," she admitted, "but after you build a reputation, you can function sort of like an order buyer. There's no way to assemble a full catalog of horses beforehand. When folks call in, though, you can tell them what we've got that they need. Your bidder from last week left a message for you to call him. He asked for you by name; there's a start on that reputation."

I helped my customer pick several horses and took his bidding instructions. As luck would have it, I bought three of our picks for him but only got two other calls. Both of those, a man and a woman, quit bidding before I ever really got started. My ears perked up as a familiar-looking bay mare entered the sale ring.

"Alright boys and girls give a listen to old Jim Rex, and let me tell you about this good mare. Miss Sis used her two or three times in our friendly little Saturday competitions. If you're huntin' one quick as a cat, here she stands. She ain't no kid horse unless your kid knows how to ride, but when I say Miss Sis Durham rode her, you know she's been rode. Scooter's put some time in on her, too. Who'll give $350 to start?"

I knew the barn, Aunt Sis, had caught the little bay for a $125, but Jim Rex got his $350 and headed for higher ground. After watching her little mare bring $675, Aunt Sis cleared her throat and said something besides "bring one" into the microphone.

"You bought yourself a fine little mare, Randy. If I had the time and energy to ride them all, I'd keep her 'til she died of old age. While I'm talking, though, let me make a little announcement about the Saturday schedule. The sun beats down on that bald arena something fierce this time of year. So, I'm calling off the playdays in favor of early morning trail rides."

"Aw, come on, Miss Sis. Don't spoil the fun for the rest of us just because the little bay rocket sold. You scared of getting beat or something?"

Scooter made his crack from the relative safety of the alley that funneled horses into the sale ring, but his voice drifted out loud and clear.

"That's about enough from the peanut gallery," Aunt Sis snorted, teasing right back even as she laughed. "Don't forget who's running this show. We'll ride out at 7:00 each Saturday morning. Now, after a long sale on Friday night, that'll separate the real cowboys and cowgirls from the ones who learned to ride on a grocery-store quarter horse, but it'll put us back here in time to start loading out at 10:00."

I recognized a challenge in my aunt's words, a challenge to the same high spirits that made folks love the good-natured competition of the playdays. Scooter answered her in no uncertain terms.

"Don't worry about me, Miss Sis. The day I can't go at it, work or play, hard enough and long enough to keep up with your old-lady self is the day I'll hock my saddle."

Instead of handing him a snappy reply, Aunt Sis wilted just the tiniest bit. Nobody in the crowd knew it, but Scooter had pushed things a hair too far with the old-lady business. Suddenly, I felt lonesome and more than a little helpless. I wanted my aunt home in the porch swing where I could comfort and protect her, not on display way up there in the auctioneer's box. Finally, she cleared her throat and spoke once again into the microphone.

"Tomorrow will be the last day of early load out with a playday after dinner. Our Saturday morning trail ride will start next week. Oh," she added, "we'll ride wagon and buggy friendly routes."

A lump rose in my throat as this afterthought told me her real reason for the change. I might never dart around barrels or weave rapidly between poles on an athletic horse, but I could sit in the buggy behind old Mable and enjoy a trail ride as well as anybody.

When pay-out time rolled around on Saturday afternoon, Aunt Sis motioned me over to her desk and slid some bills across it.

"Wait just a cotton pickin' minute," I protested.

"You earned every cent of it, Ches."

"Thumb through that pile of pay slips and read me some of the names."

"Jim Rex, Nash, the McKendrick boys—"

"How much do you pay yourself every Saturday?"

"Well, I don't exactly…"

"I didn't think so. You're the boss here, Aunt Sis, but if all you want is another hired hand, you'd do better with somebody able bodied."

Leaning back in her chair, the colonel's chair, my aunt cracked a tight little smile.

"I never thought I'd say this, but you may be too much like daddy. Not many folks can put me in my place that quick."

As she spoke, Aunt Sis tore my pay slip to bits and dropped them in the waste-paper-basket. I watched as she took up her pen and wrote something with rapid, jerky movements.

"I didn't mean to hurt your feelings," I apologized.

"Hurt my feelings? I'm as proud as an old plow mare with a new baby colt," she said reaching back into the cash box for more money. "Sign this receipt to the barn. If a man's going to trade, he'd better keep some cash on him."

"But Aunt Sis I don't—"

"Back when he cared," she added a little sadly, "Terry lived in fear of folks finding out how much cash I kept. He swore I'd get knocked in the head one of these days, but nobody's tried it yet. Now, go call the rest of them in here."

The five hundred dollars she handed me wasn't exactly a mule-choking roll, but it sure looked like a big wad of cash to me. Even allowing for inflation, I felt sure Colonel Chester Durham had started his trading career with a lot less. The money scared me a little, but my aunt's trust made me square my shoulders, stick out my chest, and ride my wheelchair like it was a prancing stud horse.

I followed Aunt Sis straight through the house and out to our favorite spot on the back porch. She no sooner collapsed onto the swing and lit her cigarette than the telephone rang.

"You look comfortable; I'll get it."

Dad's voice on the other end of the line surprised me, but it sounded mighty good.

"Hey, son," he said cheerfully. "Did you forget how to call home or something?"

"No sir," I answered. "I'm awful sorry, Dad, but we've stayed pretty busy."

"I know exactly what you mean," and his voice lost some of its humor. "Run, run, run; work, work, work from can-see to can't. That's why I knocked the last dust and horse hair out of my clothes a long time ago."

"Oh, but I love it. Aunt Sis is sweet and kind- only not in a mushy, baby-talk kind of a way. She's the coolest aunt any boy ever had, and she's making me a real part of things. I don't know; it's like she… Like she needs me or something."

"She probably does, son, but is Mac Town a good place for you?"

"McKendrick," I substituted automatically, "and, yes sir, I think it is. Brother Crawford helped me figure out for sure that I am a Christian."

"Wha—"

"Yes sir, and I've got a horse and a buggy and a dog here, friends too."

"Slow down, C.J. You've been saved a long time. Where did you get a horse and— Never mind; that's got my sister's fingerprints all over it. If I'd known you were having doubts about your salvation, son…"

"That's okay, Dad."

"No, it's not. A parent ought to pick up on things like that. Looks like Sis figured it out right off the bat."

"I don't know whether she understood the whole problem or not. She knew something was bothering me, though, and I spilled my guts pretty quick when she asked me about it."

"I'm sorry I failed you, but Sis'll come through in a tight, come through every time. I grew up with little Miss Perfect. Now, she's slightly bigger Miss—"

"Watch it," I interrupted.

"Taller, I mean taller Miss Perfect."

"You didn't fail anybody; I worked hard to hide all my doubts."

"She got you up on a horse yet?"

"No sir, we haven't talked much about me riding, but I like driving my buggy. I'm working the sale now, too. Aunt Sis even gave me some trading money."

"Trading money?" he snorted. "I think it's time I had a little talk with that girl."

"She's worn out from a hard day's work." My voice sounded strangely protective, even to me. "Please don't fuss at her."

Chapter Nine

Well, I guess we know who's got you wrapped around her little finger. You better hurry along and light her cigarette. We can't have Mac Town's most precious flower wasting energy."

"Aw, Daddy, don't be that-a-way. She works her fingers to the bone, and you know it. I love you and Mom more than anything in this world, but Aunt Sis is..."

"Don't bother searching for the right glowing terms to describe her. I heard them all from the colonel. Say, though, you haven't said Daddy in a long time."

"That's her coming out, I guess. She always calls you my daddy and sometimes uses Daddy for the colonel."

"I'm hearing a lot more 'yes sir' and 'no sir,' too. I guess my sister's influence ain't all bad."

"I'm learning a lot, Daddy, really I am. Not just horse stuff, either. I'm learning how to live with myself, cerebral palsy included, and stay reasonably happy at the same time."

"That sounds like some pretty important business. I miss you, son, and so does your Papa Joel. We can put up with it a while longer, but I'm not so sure about your mom. You might have to come on home sooner than we planned."

"Oh, no! No, Dad, I can't. Aunt Sis really counts on me."

My aunt's perfume and the clinging odor of tobacco smoke entered the kitchen ahead of her, and soon enough, I felt her presence behind me. She took the phone from my hand, coughed her throat clear, and spoke ever so gently.

"Whatever it is, Ches, I'll take care of it."

I drug a kitchen chair over close to the telephone so she could sit down, squeezed her free hand tightly, and then headed out to play with my dog.

Half an hour passed before Aunt Sis called me back into the house.

"I need another cigarette," she whispered, one hand over the mouthpiece, "and your mama needs to hear your voice. There'll be no more talk of you going home early."

"I don't know how you do it," I said, rolling back out to the porch after a short visit with Mom, "but you can sure put the Miss Sis Durham treatment on them when it suits you."

"Fiddle sticks, if I could really make them toe the line, you'd all be living here." She gave a long sigh, put out her cigarette, and casually changed the subject. "I expect church will be a lot more enjoyable now that you've dealt with your doubts."

"Yes'm," I agreed. "I liked the music right off, but now I'm looking forward to Brother Crawford's sermon. Before, I was caught up in what all God ought to do for me. With that attitude out of the way, maybe I can learn what I'm supposed to do for him. Do you usually enjoy the services, Aunt Sis?"

"Of course, honey. I can't think of any place I'd rather spend my time than in the Lord's house with His people."

"Is it hard to…um… go without…"

I gestured vaguely toward her cigarette and trailed off, more than a little embarrassed by the question. She almost laughed, but her expression turned suddenly serious.

"Ches, honey, you must think I need a constant supply of nicotine. Why, if I couldn't sit through an hour-long church service… Anytime my little habit distracts from the preaching of God's word, it becomes a real problem. I don't think I could ever step out of a service to smoke, no matter how miserable I might feel."

"Not that it's any of my business, but you've got no cause to be ashamed. Concerned about your health, maybe, but never ashamed."

She dismissed the health hazards of smoking, concentrating instead on public opinion.

"Some of the younger folks, people from my age on down, don't act like they want me smoking anywhere around the church house. It breaks my heart that anyone might think I'm setting a poor example. Still, I'm not fixing to up and quit just because society has once again changed its notion of right and wrong."

The next morning Aunt Sis fed what stock wasn't turned out to graze, changed into a pretty Sunday dress, and carried me happily off to church. She seemed confident in her handling of the situation with Mom and Daddy, but the prospect of an early return to Dallas still worried me some.

I loved my parents and thought the world of Papa Joel, but this was my summer with Aunt Sis. I needed every minute of it to learn the lessons only she could teach. With all that on my mind I forgot about my aunt's invitation to Andrew Hollister, but he met her on the church-house steps.

"You're early," I said with a grin before heading on around to the ramp.

"Well, y'all didn't exactly tell me what time it started, but I'm an early riser anyhow. The dogs are set up on automatic feeders. With no saddle stock to see after…"

I heard Aunt Sis apologize for the delay in filling his order, and the conversation continued as they opened the side door for me.

"I ought to have your horses by Tuesday, Andrew, or dinnertime on Wednesday at the latest."

"That's fine, Miss Sis. I can't look at them until Friday evening, and you won't have time to fool with me during the auction. Let's make a date for Saturday."

"Join us on the morning trail ride?"

"Yes ma'am; sounds like a plan."

"You talked me into using your first name, so you might as well call me just plain Sis."

"Your eighty-something uncle calls you Miss Sis," he said with a teasing light in his eyes. "I don't intend to lop off that miss unless you let me slip a ring onto your finger one day."

Blushing, Aunt Sis managed a sweet smile but fell suddenly quiet.

She got the air conditioner going, started a pot of coffee in the kitchen, and ended up gazing perplexedly at her pew. I couldn't possibly serve as a buffer between her and Andrew, not stuck out on the end in my wheelchair. Even if Jim Rex and his kids showed up, it wasn't likely they'd pile onto our bench and rub elbows with the competition.

"I'm going outside, Ches," she said, nervously fingering the clasp on her handbag.

Following her out, I cleared my throat.

"Sometimes I get a little stiff from staying in this chair too long. Can I park it in the isle and sit beside you?"

Instead of answering, Aunt Sis broke the familiar routine of lighting her cigarette long enough to hug me tight.

"Stay out of this heat," she called, spotting Andrew as he strolled our way with two Styrofoam cups. "I'd be inside myself, but air conditioning can't replace a necessary dose of nicotine."

"Well, here's some coffee if you want it. Ches," he questioned, offering the second cup to me.

"No thanks; you go ahead and drink it."

"The building's not all that cool yet," he explained to Aunt Sis. "Anyway, I don't believe you'd stay inside. Cigarette or no cigarette, you're an outdoor person."

"Takes one to know one," she said with a laugh.

"I surely didn't mean to offend you with my little wedding-ring crack."

"They tell me I'm pretty straight-laced by today's standards, Andrew, but I'd be in a mighty sad shape if I couldn't take a harmless little joke."

After that, the tension passed from our little group. Aunt Sis introduced Andrew with her easy, natural grace as other folks arrived for church. Brother Crawford greeted him and then turned to me with an especially warm handshake.

"There's my buggy riding partner."

"Yes sir, I'm ready to go again anytime you are."

My aunt's piano playing was always a treat, but I got an even bigger kick out of watching Andrew watch her. He finally gathered enough presence of mind to start singing along about half way through the second song, and he sang in a fine bass voice. Seth, Scooter, and some more of the horse-sale crowd came in after Sunday school, but I didn't see Jim Rex or Serena Kate.

Brother Crawford preached on how saved folk ought to bear fruit for Christ. Though he used his King James Bible and made no obvious effort to simplify his language, any child old enough to reason could have understood him. I listened, this time, with an open mind. The message pricked my heart without making me feel defensive.

Uncle Elmer's invitation hymn was one I'd never heard before. The old minor-key tune sounded mournful, but I heard a joy there, too.

"I will arise and go to Jesus. He will embrace me in His arms. In the arms of my dear Savior, O there are ten thousand charms."

Aunt Sis and I carried Brother and Mrs. Crawford into the county seat to eat at Golden Corral, and naturally we invited Andrew along.

"If it's all the same to y'all, Brother Carlton, I'd a lot rather sit in the smoking section," she called as the pastor and his wife headed inside to get us a table.

"When have I ever forgotten, Miss Sis," he answered with a fond chuckle.

I stayed with Aunt Sis while she waited for my wheelchair ramp to stow itself.

"People don't feed the preacher as often as they used to, but it's something Mama and the colonel always liked to do. I love spending time with the Crawford's, and you know I'd rather eat than cook so…"

I nodded my understanding and followed her up onto the sidewalk as Andrew swept in to open the door for her. He even pulled out a chair to seat her. My eyebrows went up as Brother Crawford repeated the gesture for Miz Edna. My parents loved each other, but they weren't big on such old-fashioned graces. I'd never seen anything quite like it outside of black-and-white movies.

"I bet the Golden Corral management love to see you coming," Andrew said, teasing my aunt about her bird-like portions. "Now, me, I try to get my money's worth."

Aunt Sis made some kind of light answer, and the two of them ended up talking about his favorite young birddog. I tried to listen, hearing the enthusiasm in their voices, but my thoughts kept drifting back to Andrew's courting manners.

"Ches, say, Ches? I asked you how Mable's doing? I declare, boy, you're mind must be a million miles away."

This came from Brother Crawford, and I looked up with a start.

"Sorry, sir, Mable's just fine. I'm itching for another buggy ride."

"Me too, but that ain't what's on your mind right now."

The old man just let his statement dangle like a big fat worm on a hook. I ignored it as long as I could, checked to make sure Andrew was deeply fascinated by his conversation with my aunt, and bit hard. Clearing my throat, I leaned toward him and spoke in a lowered tone.

"Noticed all the little things Andrew's doing for Aunt Sis? The door and her chair and..."

"As a matter of fact," he admitted, "I have. We don't see near enough gentlemen nowadays."

"Yeah, well, I know one more you're not gonna see. I'll never be able to do those little things for a girl... Um, I mean a lady. It never bothered me before, but Andrew makes it all look so smooth and natural. Of course, my Aunt Sis deserves every bit of it."

Brother Crawford started to pull his glasses off, but reached down for a piece of fried chicken instead. He chewed slowly, thinking over his answer, but Miz Edna beat him to it.

"I wouldn't worry, Ches. For better or worse, most girls your age aren't raised to expect those little courtesies. They'll never know the difference."

"Thanks, Miz Edna, but I'll know. Before coming to stay with Aunt Sis, I never even thought about those things. Now... How will I ever get a girl as strong and loyal and sweet as Miss Sis Durham if I can't treat her the way a lady ought to be treated?"

Aunt Sis glanced around at the sound of her name and favored us with a smile before turning back to Andrew. Taking a long swallow of water, Brother Crawford sat forward a little and tried his luck with me.

"The little gestures of respect are important, but they don't make a gentleman. The lowest varmint ever walked on two legs can tip his hat or fling open a door. I probably wouldn't have seated Edna if Andrew hadn't set a kind of a high mark. She's made it through sixty-two years of marriage and never strained a muscle pulling out her own chair."

"As bad as I hate to admit it," Miz Edna joked, "he's right. Why, Ches, the fact that you want to do those things, even think about them, is enough to make most girls hearts go pitter patter. When that special young lady comes along, just find other ways to show her how much you care. Telling her won't hurt none, either."

Their advice sounded good. My prospects as a date, much less a husband, still looked mighty poor, but I finally pushed the subject to the back of my mind.

Despite a constant quest to regain the flawless figure of her youth, Aunt Sis had all but passed over the salad bar, choosing only some pickled okra and a slice or two of tomato from that section.

"I like all kinds of green vegetables," she explained, "but for pity's sake I want them cooked and seasoned."

"Salad's not bad once you get used to it," Andrew volunteered.

I saw her stiffen a little and read her thoughts.

"Does he think I need salad? I don't look that big, do I?"

Aunt Sis let the moment pass without comment and brightened up considerably when he brought her a desert she'd pretended not to want.

A small war broke out over the ticket. I stepped in and settled things by paying for myself and the Crawfords with some of the traveling money Dad had given me. With that taken care of, Aunt Sis could graciously allow Andrew to buy her meal without feeling that he had to feed everybody she knew. He walked us out to the parking lot, took in the mechanics of a wheelchair ramp, and even closed the driver's door for my aunt.

"I'm no expert," I told Aunt Sis as we pulled away from the restaurant, "but I think you got courted this afternoon."

"You know," she answered, sounding a little surprised, "it's been a long time, but I believe you're right. What do you think of Andrew?"

"He seems like a nice guy. The question is, what do you think about him?"

"I don't know," she finally admitted. "I still get mad as a wet hen every time I think about Uncle Doc's place being sold out from under him, but that's not really Andrew's doing."

"No'm, it's sure not. What was it you said about Mr. Right coming in on a high lope? Don't write Andrew off before the dust settles behind his horse."

"He strikes me as a decent, upright man," she said primly. Then with a long sigh, "and Lord knows he's handsome enough."

"I wouldn't know about that, but you're pretty enough and a whole lot more."

"My best days are long gone, Ches. Anymore, I'm just hanging on as well as I can."

"You're never gonna accept it from me, but maybe you'll believe Andrew when he tells you. He will tell you, too, if you give him half a chance."

We drove along in silence after that, Aunt Sis pondering the possibility of a new romance and me wondering if I'd ever have one at all. As dreamy and relaxed as she already was, my aunt's spirits rose steadily as we left the county seat, passed through McKendrick, and drew closer to the homeplace. This love of the land proved as contagious as any disease. Feelings of peace and wellbeing chased away my gloomy thoughts as we stopped in the front yard.

"Why don't you go call your mother, honey," Aunt Sis suggested as I motored my way into the house.

"But what if she wants me to come home?"

Aunt Sis answered with a wry half chuckle, fishing out a cigarette as she opened the front door.

"Don't worry; I got that little piece of business squared away with your Daddy. Jenna just wants to hear from you more often. So, run along and make that call."

"Yes'm," I answered. "Are you headed out to the back gallery?"

"I'll save your seat," she said with a nod and a smile.

I talked to Mom for a good while but eventually scooted into the swing beside my aunt.

"I don't know how you managed it, but Mom never said a word about me coming home."

"I told you I'd take care of it, honey, and that's what I did."

Aunt Sis cooked a big breakfast the next morning and ate her fair share without a word of regret.

"I've got to clean house and try to catch up on some paperwork. You might call Scooter and see if he wants to take a buggy ride down to the swimming hole."

"Do you have to work all day long? Scooter's alright but I'd rather go with you."

"Aww, Ches, how come you always know the exact words to melt my heart."

"You'll go with us?"

"Melted heart or not, this house is going to wrack and ruin, and my books are far enough behind to make an accountant like your daddy pull his hair out."

Wrack and ruin, to her way of thinking, meant a little dust around the base boards, a few dirty dishes in the sink, and a couple of saddle blankets hung out to dry on the back-porch railing. I couldn't say one way or the other about her book keeping, but when Scooter needed a ride, she took time to drive over and get him.

"What if I ride the buckskin colt down to the swimming hole and back?" he demanded almost as soon as he climbed into the truck. "Will you pay me for the time on him?"

"I'm not paying you to go a-swimming, Scooter McKendrick," my aunt retorted. "I'll give you ten dollars for the ride, but you'll have to slow lope him around the pond for a while to earn it."

"Tightwad," Scooter grumbled, but Aunt Sis had something else on her mind.

"Ches, honey, are you comfortable driving Mable by yourself?"

"I think I'll make it just fine if Scooter'll ride along close by."

That's the way we did it, too. I felt about nine feet tall sitting up in that buggy with just my dog for company, and Puddler looked kind of proud himself. Mable, grand old lady that she was, did everything I asked of her.

"Be sure and wear your lifejacket, Ches," my buddy mimicked in a high, falsetto tone that really sounded nothing like Aunt Sis, "and make sure Scooter earns his ten dollars. I don't want that colt standing around all day."

"Don't make light of her," I chided, holding back laughter myself.

"Oh, if anybody really poked fun at her, I'd break his nose, but it ain't like that with me. We pick at one another, but your aunt has helped me all my life. She's crazy about you, Ches, 'round the bend over the moon crazy. Miss Sis ain't exactly known a lot of happiness these last few years, but since you came…"

"I know, but I don't really understand why. You and your family and even old Nash are more help to her than I could ever be."

"Don't ask me," he said with a shrug. "Maybe it ain't about help. I expect she's glad to have some family around, some of her own blood. Can you swim sure enough? Without the jacket, I mean."

"Yeah," I answered with a shrug of my own.

"Well, get after it, only don't drown. Your aunt would never forgive me. This colt's got him a mighty pretty short lope," he called a few minutes later as I worked the tightness from my leg muscles in the spring-fed coolness of the swimming hole. "Like the trader says, he'll lope in the shade of the same tree all day long."

"What are you talking about?" I hollered back.

"Tight circle," he explained. It'd just about kill Miss Sis if she knew I'd ride him for free."

Scooter rode for a while, staked the buckskin out to graze in the shade, and then cannonballed into the water.

"What do you do once school starts? About working for Aunt Sis, I mean."

"Keep right on," he answered, "as much as I can."

"It must get kind of busy."

"I don't play ball or toot no horn in the band. Sale Barn Science is my only extracurricular activity."

"Aw, foot," I guffawed, splashing him a good one.

"No, really," he said spitting water. "I'll never forget the day Seth asked Pop if he ought to go out for football. The old man kind of grinned at Miss Sis before he answered."

"Yeah, and what did he say?"

"'Play football, huh? How much 'at pay?' Trev stood there and looked at him like a possum caught in the high beams, so Pop told him some facts of life. 'When you work up a sweat, sonny boy, make darn sure somebody's paying you.'"

As if to cap off his daddy's statement, Scooter returned my splash with full force.

"Well," I said, pausing to cough and sputter and wipe my eyes, "that's a pretty sensible way to look at it. There are a few sports that might be possible for me, but I like Sale Barn Science better than anything else I've found." We swam right through dinnertime, but eventually, both of us wore down. "Is that an eagle?" I asked excitedly and then sucked in a sharp breath to keep myself from sinking as I floated on my back.

"Nah," Scooter answered, "just a hawk. "They're cutting hay in the Parmalee bottom. He's circling around to catch the mice and rabbits or whatever tasty bit of dinner the mower might jump from cover. Speaking of dinner, did you say something about leftover sausage and biscuit?"

We sat on the bank, eating, for about half as long as it takes a couple of boys and a wet dog to air dry. To my surprise, we met the boss lady on our way back. Her delicate-looking little form perched comfortably atop a fancy palomino, just like she'd been born there.

"I thought you were cleaning house," I said innocently as she rode up alongside the buggy.

"And I thought I told you to wear that lifejacket," she countered smoothly. "You're still a-drippin, but it's dry as a bone."

With that, she wheeled her mount and put him into a rocking-chair lope that Scooter just had to match. The two horses made a pretty picture as they traveled along side by side in front of old Mable.

The palomino was a rich, golden yellow with a platinum-blonde mane and tail and a white star on his forehead. The buckskin was a more muted, earthy shade of yellow with black mane and tail and black stockings halfway up his front legs. Being older, the palomino held the advantage in muscle and frame, but the colt was no slouch, either.

Aunt Sis soon pulled her horse down to a walk and motioned Scooter to do the same.

"What's the matter," he challenged. "Don't tell me you're too out of shape to hold the pace?"

"There's nothing the matter with me," she replied, her mind on more important things than his smart mouth, "but does he look a little off in the left front to you?"

He studied her horse for a minute as they walked along, and a frown creased his forehead. A few of their terms still escaped me.

"What do you mean off, Aunt Sis?"

"Limping, or at least not traveling right," she explained shortly.

"I can't tell, Miss Sis," Scooter finally admitted. "If he is, it ain't much. I ain't been looking at them forever and a day like you. Let's swap horses, and you can study him for yourself."

The old age crack registered, and Scooter would probably pay for it later. At the moment, though, she took his suggestion.

"He's crippling," she finally decided, "or I'll eat my good hat."

"Straw or felt?" Scooter asked with a grin.

Our little group reached the front of the sale barn to see Nash and his tall, broad-shouldered nephew standing together in relaxed conversation. Aunt Sis dropped lightly to the ground, flipped the colt's reins around a welded pipe hitching rail, and ran a hand up and down the palomino's left foreleg.

"Feel that leg," she snapped, tossing a look at Nash.

"Now, Miss Sis, don't you go hunting every pimple and scratch," Little Herman protested. "That horse is sound, fancy broke, and dog gentle just like you wanted for your—"

I wondered if he might say, "your nephew," but he never got the chance. Nash straightened suddenly, and the easy family feeling between the two men fell away.

"Lie to Miss Sis one more time, and I'll knock your head plumb off. This horse ain't feeling that sore leg, or he wouldn't put it on the ground a-tall. He's had a shot, sure as you're born."

"Just pain killer, I swear," Little Herman said emphatically. "I didn't give him anything to settle his nerves. He don't need it."

"Well, I can see that. He ain't the first doped horse I ever looked at, but he's sure crippled."

"If you know so much, fix him. The right kind of trim and a set of shoes'll do the job."

"Maybe," Aunt Sis bit out, "but I told you I wanted using horses, not trade stock."

"It ain't easy finding a pair of flashy, matched geldings without a real fault between them. You couldn't do it on short notice, or you'd never have called me."

At the words matched geldings, I looked around and spotted another palomino horse tied farther back in the shade of the barn.

"What's wrong with him?" my aunt asked, and her voice sounded like ice as she gestured toward the horse I'd just noticed. "I want it straight this time."

"Well, nothing really, but he's got a little buck to him if you push all the wrong buttons. Surely the colonel's daughter ain't scared."

"It is not in your best interest to talk to me about the colonel right now. I am trying awfully hard to act like my sweet, gentle mother." She annunciated every word with care, obviously holding her temper in check, but her hands shook slightly as she lit a much-needed cigarette. "What if I'd put Che— somebody else on the one with a little buck to him?"

"You asked for one sure-enough gentle riding horse and another to match him. Now, quit preaching, and get to the point."

Taking in as much nicotine as possible, Aunt Sis seemed to weigh her options.

"I'll give you a thousand for the pair," she finally said, "but not a penny more."

"That's the same as stealing 'em," he squalled. "The crippled is registered! They'll bring more in the sale."

"Not when I get through calling the faults on them, they won't. What good is a registered gelding anyway? I'll take a chance on them at a thousand. Otherwise, you can trot your horses and whatever money you've got tied up in them on down the road."

"Hand me the cash, and get 'em out of my sight. The Durham family started cheating me about the time I got big enough to sit a saddle. Why should today be any different?"

My aunt's already stiff backbone suddenly got a little straighter. I don't know what she planned to say because Nash beat her to it.

"If you're gonna talk that-a-way, you just don't have to come around here no more."

The old man took a step forward as he spoke, and the hairs on the back of my neck stood up. I figured Nash somewhere on the downhill side of seventy-five. Aunt Sis, for her part, looked tiny up against Little Herman. He stood something over six feet tall and carried 200 odd pounds of solid muscle. For all that, though, he just stood there looking kind of surprised.

"You'd take her part against your own flesh and blood?"

"Any day of the week and twice on Sunday," Nash answered without the least hesitation, "but since you are my brother's boy, I'll ask you one time to apologize. A good chunk of your living comes from the Durhams and this auction; always has."

"Well, I'll be— This ain't the only horse sale in the country, even if I do have to drive a hundred and fifty miles."

Grabbing a stack of bills from my aunt's outstretched hand, Little Herman flung a set of registration papers to the ground. He spun on his heel, then jingled a set of big-roweled spurs over to his rig, and made the straight pipes roar as he left.

"I'm sorry, Miss Sis. Big Herman never whuped that kid hard enough or long enough, but I sure thought I made up for it."

"Oh, he'll be back, Nash. Don't let it bother you, and don't let it turn into something bigger than it is. I hate to see kinfolks fall out."

"He got lippy with you," the old man answered. "That's plenty big enough for me."

"He's not the first horse trader ever tried a slick deal, and he won't be the last."

"No, but not many of them come back to the folks that raised them and—"

When Nash walked off shaking his head, Aunt Sis stepped into the buggy beside me. She laid a hand gently on my knee.

"I meant these yellow geldings for a little birthday surprise, a gentle gelding for you and a lookalike for me. I'm sorry things turned out kind of uncertain, but that's the horse business. If these two work for us, they're cheap. Even if they don't, they ought to make a little money."

Busy keeping up with Aunt Sis, I'd never once thought about my upcoming fourteenth birthday, and I had to smile at her idea of a little birthday surprise. Suddenly, though, an important question popped into my mind.

"You really think I'll be able to ride?"

"There's not a doubt in my mind, honey, if it's something you want to do. The surprise is shot, now, but if old yeller's leg gets right, he's all yours. I won't give you a crippled, and I'm sure not going to put you on anything that might buck."

"Maybe you ought to go ahead and sell the bucker," I suggested hesitantly. "There's no need for you to take unnecessary chances, either."

"Pshaw, somebody's let him get away with it. A slap or two across the rump with my bridle reins and he'll be a different horse."

"I hate to see you go to all this trouble when we don't even know if I can ride."

"I tell you what," she answered with a sudden grin, "we'll just put an end to your doubts before that perfectly good shot wears off."

Fear grabbed at my insides. But her hand still lay on my knee, and those big brown eyes still held my gaze. If I couldn't trust my Aunt Sis after all she'd done for me, I belonged in Dallas and not in her world.

"Hey, Nash," Scooter hollered, "come back here a minute. Ole Ches is fixing to ride his horse."

"Drive on around to the arena," my aunt instructed. "Scooter, you bring the horse."

In less time than it takes to tell it, we were gathered in a little knot at the center of the big outdoor arena. Scooter held the palomino's head, and we trusted Mable to stand still while Nash and Aunt Sis lifted me from the safety of the buggy seat into the uncertainty of the saddle.

Chapter Ten

My insides quivered as I gave up all control. This was a matter of trust. My personal safety depended completely on one arthritic ex-horsebreaker and my 5'3" aunt who rarely lifted anything heavier than a cigarette. Well, maybe not completely. I did some praying as I hung in the air.

"Dear Lord, please don't let them drop me. Bless them with the strength they need, and give me the courage to make a good ride for Aunt Sis. Oh, and Lord, take away some of this fear so I can enjoy it."

God answered part of my prayer immediately. They didn't drop me or even come close. Stoop-shouldered Nash Holloway had muscles like iron, and my aunt's delicate hands held a surprising strength as well. I felt a little like a sack of potatoes as they swung me into place, but everything worked out fine.

"We gotcha, Ches. Don't you worry none," Nash murmured soothingly.

My gelding wasn't tall, just over 14 hands or maybe 57 inches at the point of his shoulder. When I chanced a look toward the ground, though, it seemed an awful long way down there.

"Aunt Sis, Aunt Sis, I don't know if I can…"

"I'm right here, honey," she almost sang, rubbing a hand up and down the center of my back. "Aunt Sis ain't going nowhere."

Aunt and ain't sounded like the same word from her lips, and that made me smile if only for a moment.

"It's alright, bud," Scooter said, trying to comfort me. "That horse is a real pet."

"How do those stirrups feel, Ches?" Aunt Sis asked.

"I don't know," I sputtered, still a little panicky. "I don't know how they're supposed to feel."

"Try to stand just a little, raise your behind up out of the saddle. Can you get your weight down in the stirrups, or do they need to come up some?"

"Stand up?" I gulped, "out of the saddle?"

"Just rock forward and see if you can put weight on your feet. I won't let you fall. If the stirrups are too long you won't be able to do it, but if they're too short your feet'll go to sleep after a while."

"Like this?" I questioned, pulling myself up by the saddle horn.

"That's it. They look about right to me, but how do they feel."

"Fine, I guess."

"You got a hold of him on your side, Nash?"

"Like a bulldog on a fresh bone," he assured her.

"Alright, Scooter, we didn't put Ches up there to sit like a bump on a log."

Before I could do more than think, "Whoa, wait a minute," my good buddy turned nonchalantly and walked off, leading the horse after him. We eased away from Mable and the buggy, but she didn't seem concerned.

"The saddle maker put that horn there to tie a lariat rope onto," Scooter teased, "not for you to hold in a death grip."

"Hush your mouth, Scooter McKendrick. Why, the first time we slung you up on a horse by yourself, you screamed your fool head off."

"All kids probably do that at some point," he shot back.

"Not all of 'em," Nash grunted almost under his breath.

"Well," Scooter challenged, "go ahead and name one that didn't."

"Miss Sis; she just laughed and smiled and laid over on that pony's neck to hug him. I think faster come somewheres between Dada and Mama. We turned her loose at about three and a half because none of us could run flat out for as long as she wanted to ride."

"But she ain't human. I swear, the colonel raised her on mares' milk."

Their back and forth banter and the smooth motion of the horse beneath me calmed me down some. My first horseback ride, a dream come true, and on such a horse! Aside from the lameness in his front legs, the palomino seemed perfect in every way. He was gentle, friendly, and eager to please with enough flashy looks, athletic ability, and training to suit any rider. I almost snorted out loud as a new thought came to me.

"Yeah, and I'd be a heck of a rider, too, if not for the lameness in my own legs."

Add to that poor balance which made the possibility of falling a fearful reality with every minute I rode. My electric wheelchair seemed incredibly safe by comparison. It would go where I pointed it, but this beautiful golden horse, no matter how docile, was a living breathing creature with a mind of his own.

I felt the muscles in my left leg twitch and convulse, my foot involuntarily patting up and down in the stirrup. It didn't make any sense. I was scared, sure, but not nearly as terrified as I had been a few minutes ago, hanging suspended in the air over the saddle. My stomach soured, and my mouth went dry as cotton. Add shame to fear. Aunt Sis, my brave, unstoppable, almost unbelievable Aunt Sis would see that leg jumping up and down and know me for the coward I was.

"It's alright, Ches," she said, stroking that treacherous leg. "You're fine, your horse is fine, and this is just a nice little stroll around the arena."

"I'm sorry, Aunt Sis," I managed, biting the inside of my lip to control the tears that wanted to fall. "I never meant to disappoint you."

"Disappoint me?" she almost laughed. "Child, how could you ever think you've disappointed me?"

"That leg," I said and cursed it.

"Watch your mouth, Ches Durham," she snapped automatically but couldn't hold back a tender smile. "Don't you think I know you're scared? You'd have to be plumb crazy not to feel a goodly amount of fear right now. A rider is supposed to control the movement of his horse's body, and you have a hard enough time just controlling your own."

When Aunt Sis finally choked up and trailed off, Scooter surprised everybody, himself most of all, by agreeing with her.

"She's right, buddy. I look at you and wish I was that brave. If I couldn't put my legs and hands and tail-end exactly where I need them and keep them there, I wouldn't touch a horse with a ten foot pole. But my friend who can't even walk good, here he is riding and doing a pretty fair job of it."

"We don't mean to say that you can't learn to control your horse," Aunt Sis put in hurriedly, "just that a rider in your condition faces extra challenges. I'm not disappointed because you're scared, honey. I'm proud you're up there making a try, so proud I'm apt to burst a button. I see that look, Scooter McKendrick," she added in a totally different tone as he tossed a grin back over his shoulder, "not one word about biscuits and gravy."

"You said it," he retorted, "not me."

She gave him a queenly glare down her nose and shifted her attention back to me.

"Starting out at fourteen makes things that much harder for you, Ches. I learned to ride before I could walk. Little kids don't know enough to be scared. By the time I got big enough to understand the dangers, tearing across the country on a horse was second nature to me."

"I am scared, Aunt Sis," I admitted, "but I asked the Lord to take away enough fear that I could enjoy my ride. He did; He answered my prayer. I've dreamed about this all my life, and still it's more fun than I ever imagined."

"Aw, honey, this ain't nothing," she quipped and then spoke to Scooter. "Unsnap that lead rope and go tend to old Mable."

This time my doubts found a voice.

"Hold up! I can't—"

"He's all yours, bud."

"Aunt Sis?"

I'm sure the two desperate words squeaked out of me, but nobody mentioned it.

"I'm still here, Ches, and so is Nash. Just settle down and listen. Grab your reins at the middle. Keep them even on both sides. Remember what I told you, now. It's a little bit like the joystick on your wheelchair. Move your hand left to go left; that'll lay the right rein against his neck."

I did as I was told, kind of, and the horse whipped around in a complete circle to the left. Aunt Sis must have let go of me at some point to avoid being stepped on, but her hands were back in place so quickly I never missed them.

"Not all t'once," Nash spat gruffly.

"Easy, Ches," my aunt clarified. "He's got power steering. It don't take much pressure to spin him plumb around."

"I… I'm scared, Aunt Sis."

"I know, honey, but he ain't done nothing wrong. You've just got to learn how to ask for what you want. Try it again, real easy."

I did and managed a smooth quarter turn to the left.

"'At a boy," Nash congratulated. "Now, stop him."

I made a few starts and stops and turns before Aunt Sis changed the game again.

"Rest your legs for a spell, Nash. I'll stay with him."

"Miss Sis, I don't mind—"

"Go rest your legs."

"Yes'm," and just like that it was down to the two of us.

"Look who I found," Scooter called a few minutes later as he and Jim Rex came around the corner.

"One of y'all throw me a saddle on that other yellow gelding."

"Always giving orders," the auctioneer teased.

"Pretty please," Aunt Sis wheedled. "I haven't walked this much since Peanut unseated me way over on the back side of the place."

"Your Welsh pony, Peanut?" he wondered aloud.

"I'm telling you; it's been a long time."

"Sorry, Aunt Sis," I broke in.

"Quit apologizing, Ches. I've waited and prayed for this day. I'd walk to Dallas and back if the colonel could see you up on that horse."

"Not if she could figure out another way to get there, she wouldn't," Jim Rex snorted.

When Scooter brought the other gelding around, he and Jim Rex stood with me on the far side of the arena. Aunt Sis stuck her foot in the stirrup and swung herself into the saddle like she'd never even heard horses could buck.

Sure enough, her palomino walked off like a perfect gentleman, and soon we were riding side by side.

"Go up to the house and find my camera," she told Scooter offhandedly.

"For somebody who thinks exercise is a dirty word, you sure don't mind running the legs off me."

"Do like you're told," she retorted and turned her horse away so he wouldn't see her grin.

Scooter took several snapshots of me and Aunt Sis, and then she sent him to fetch the buckskin colt around.

"What do you want him for?"

I shared my friend's curiosity, wondering apprehensively if she planned to throw open the arena gate and turn me out on the wide world for some kind of group ride.

"You and Nash and Jim Rex are gonna have your pictures made, too."

"That colt's coming along pretty good, but he ain't gonna pack all three of us."

"How come you only pop off like that when I can't reach you?"

"'Cause I ain't as dumb as I look, and you're almighty quick on the swat."

"We've got a gracious plenty of horses, but somebody would have to take the picture anyhow. Y'all might as well use the buckskin. And yes, smarty britches, I mean one at a time."

After the picture taking, Aunt Sis encouraged me to ride a little more.

"I could ride way up into the night without getting tired of it, but I'm sure y'all have other things to do."

"Don't you worry about us, honey," Aunt Sis said reassuringly. "That's a nice horse with a Cadillac handle and a sweet disposition. Enjoy him while you can. Once that shot wears off, it'll take some time to get him straightened out or find something else good enough for you to ride."

"Why don't you trot him a little, bud?" Scooter called later.

I hoped my aunt would shoot the idea down, but the eager light in her eyes told me she was all for it. Reluctantly, I asked the palomino for a little more speed with the same cluck I used on Mable and nudged him as best I could with my slightly stronger left leg. He started off briskly in a straight line. I reined him to follow Scooter, and he ducked around without slackening his pace.

The cerebral palsy affects my balance and not in a good way. I felt myself sliding off the horse's right side and saw the hard-packed arena dirt coming up fast. At the last possible moment somebody grabbed the back of my shirt and snatched me up into the saddle. I knew instinctively that it was Aunt Sis.

Given time, she might have loved me up and told me everything was okay and said what a brave boy I was. Such well-meant mollycoddling could have ended my horseback days right there, but the Good Lord had other plans. My butt landed securely back in the saddle, but the sudden rescue maneuver set her horse off like a firecracker. Bawling his displeasure, he covered a good quarter of the arena in a long, high leap.

"Quit... you infernal... yellow... idiot."

Her angry words came out in short bursts, timed to the rhythm of the horse's bucking. She had saved me from disaster, but I knew I had to ride my own horse while she fought for control of hers.

"That rascal can pitch," Nash observed almost casually, "but he'll never shake Miss Sis."

"I'll… teach you… something… about throwing a fit with me," she gasped as the ground-shaking leaps jarred her tiny body.

The gelding I rode stood like a statue in spite of all the excitement. My heart hammered for Aunt Sis, but I felt no fear at all for myself. Nobody else seemed particularly worried about me, either. Scooter finally eased the buckskin colt up alongside.

"That was a pretty good stunt you pulled," he said teasingly, "but Miss Sis has got to be the center of attention."

"Stunt," I shot back, "I was just trying to follow you."

"Well, you know what they say about bad company."

Aunt Sis finally got her horse's head up and forced him into a flat-out run around the perimeter fence. Wheeling the would-be bronc, she sent him back the other direction.

"I think you might catch him now, Scooter."

"Shoot fire, if she can turn him around like that, she can stop him anytime she gets ready. As much as it may surprise you, Miss blue skies and sunshine is kind of high-strung. Yeller's got her nerves all stirred up, and now, he'll have to run 'til they settle a bit. He went and blew up while she was trying to help her precious nephew; that didn't set too well."

"Y'all seen my cigarettes," Aunt Sis questioned the minute she let her tired mount stop.

"Horse stomped 'em in the ground, Miss Sis," Nash said with a sympathetic shake of his head and extended his own pack for her to take one.

"Remember all the horseback work Daddy did right up until he died?" Aunt Sis asked. "He didn't act half as old then as I feel this evening. Once upon a time, I considered that kind of little fit good entertainment. Now, I'm all wrung out."

"Well'm," Nash began hesitantly, "it ain't quite the same for a lady. The colonel's old bones could still take a pounding from a stiff-legged bucker like that, but your poor insides…"

Aunt Sis blushed slightly at the mention of her insides, so I changed the subject with my own two cents.

"You were wonderful, and besides, yeller looks kind of used up himself."

"I ain't half got his attention yet, but I guess I've gone soft," she said as both of them sucked air in great, wheezing gulps.

"Old, soft, or whatever, you're still Miss Sis Durham. I don't think anybody really doubted you'd stay on top," Jim Rex said seriously, "but Ches nearly hit the ground. I'm not sure he's got enough balance to ride on his own."

"I'll be the judge of that, Jim Rex McKendrick," Aunt Sis snapped. "You can just keep your know-it-all opinions to yourself."

"Aw, Sis, don't get sore. I know I'm supposed to pat you on the head and deny it six ways from Sunday every time you admit to being middle aged and a little out of shape, but don't risk your nephew's safety just because I forgot to sooth your vanity."

"Vanity?" she almost spat. "You've got some nerve."

"Settle down," he drawled. "Remember the leather man and saddle trader from up around Marshall? Had a stroke or something…"

"Yes," she answered, suddenly distracted from her catty mood. "What is his name? They used to host a good many trail rides up that way."

"Still do," he corrected.

"What? Does he ride in a wagon?"

"Horseback like always. He rigged up some kind of special saddle with a chair-back and a safety belt."

"You can just put that out of your mind right now," she said, all of her aggravation returning in a rush. "Ain't nobody strapping my nephew to the saddle, not while I got breath in my body. What if his horse goes down?"

"I can't remember that fellow's name, either, but he ain't no dummy. I'm sure he's figured out some kind of quick release to get himself out of a bind. We ought to wonder up that way and see him one of these days."

"I'd probably lash myself into the saddle and take my chances if it was the only way I could ride," she finally admitted. "But Ches doesn't need any such thing, and he's safer without it. Why, getting hung up and dragged is probably a horseman's biggest danger."

"I know—"

"You know, and you still want to strap this precious child to his saddle? Jim Rex McKendrick, I never heard of anything so foolish in all my life!" You saw for yourself how well the boy rode for his first time."

"Yeah, and I saw him come almighty near a broken arm or leg or neck. Just don't set your mind against safety saddles until you see one, that's all I'm asking."

"Could I trouble you for another cigarette, Nash," Aunt Sis asked sweetly, and that closed the subject.

She probably never planned for me to venture outside the arena on my first ride, but my palomino behaved so well I rode him right up to the gasoline Mule.

"Maybe if I rubbed your back," I offered, hearing my aunt's muffled groan as we pulled into the carport.

"No thank you, honey. A hot bath will do just fine, but first I've got to sit here and gather enough strength to walk into the house."

"No you don't," I said with a smile, my eye falling on the motorized wheelchair sitting where I'd left it. Climbing into it, I patted my lap. "Come on; I'll carry you."

"There was a time… But do you have any idea what I weigh these days, child? If your legs don't operate well, now, they won't work for shucks after this wide load."

"Oh, baloney!" I countered. "Most forty— A whole lot of young ladies would give almost anything to be as slim and trim and youthful-looking as you. Now, hop onto my lap like a good little girl."

The last part tickled her, and she scooted gingerly into place, twisting to a sidesaddle sort of position so I could still see and holding on with an arm around my shoulders.

"This is ridiculous. I'm much too heavy for you, and you're just too sweet to say so. The extra load might do something to the wheelchair. Besides, your Mama would pitch a runnin' fit if she could see us right now."

"You're as light as a feather, Aunt Sis, and Dallas is a long way off. Now, hold on tight."

Once accustomed to the idea of riding in my lap, Aunt Sis started to like it. I even buzzed her around the kitchen while she threw together our simple supper.

"You're awfully sweet to me, Ches. A girl could get used to this kind of treatment pretty quick. It saves a lot of pointless steps and makes me feel pretty special, too."

"You are pretty special, but the question is, are you really and truly comfortable? It almost looks like this might hurt worse than trying to walk on your own."

"Oh, I feel just like a princess, but your poor legs…"

"Hush, now. Let's see… You're too straight-laced to let me, your own flesh-and-blood nephew, rub your sore back, and you've had your claws in Jim Rex this evening. I bet Andrew gives a good massage, though. I can call over there and ask."

"No… D-don't you dare, Ches Durham!" I didn't know my aunt's pretty, pale face could turn so red, but she laughed as soon as she saw my grin. "A hot bath and some liniment will ease the soreness and preserve my sense of decorum."

"Liniment like they use on horses? Be careful you don't take the skin right off your back."

"The colonel swore by it, and I surely need some relief."

Before heading off to soak in the tub and apply horse medicine to her sore back, Aunt Sis put in a call to her farrier and explained the situation with my palomino.

"From what you say, Miss Sis," I heard on the other end of the phone, "I believe we can fix him up, but I'll have to look at him before I can say one way or…"

While they talked, I replayed my first horseback ride in my mind. Only then, looking back on it, did I realize God had removed some of my fear, allowing me to enjoy the experience just like I asked Him. Even as I bowed my head in a silent prayer of thanks, fear and doubt pushed into my thoughts.

"I'll have to stay off my gelding until he heals. What if he turns wild like the other one? What if I'm too chicken to ride again? What if I disappoint Aunt Sis after all?"

"Wednesday morning suits me fine," she told the shoer after clearing her throat. "I've got a load of horses coming in tomorrow."

"You don't like the idea of a safety saddle, do you, Aunt Sis?" I ventured when she got off the phone.

"Safety saddle," she snorted. "I'm not sure if that's the actual term or something Jim Rex came up with, but it don't make much sense. Strapping a body to his saddle is anything but safe. No horseman wants to think about getting hung up and dragged or caught under his horse, but a contraption like that just invites it."

"How many horses have fallen with you over the years?" I asked.

"Plumb down to the ground, you mean?"

"Yes'm."

"Well, none, but—"

"How many horses have you fallen off?"

"Fallen off?" she gasped, and her scandalized tone took me by surprise. "I've been drug off by low-hanging limbs, pitched off, and jumped out from under. I have never just fallen off a horse."

"Okay… Okay," I said hurriedly and rephrased my question with her own words from earlier in the evening. "How many times have you been unseated?"

"Over a lifetime of riding anything that came through the barn… Half a dozen, maybe eight or nine times."

"You're the boss lady, and I trust you absolutely. Still, don't you think Jim Rex might have a valid point?"

"Oh, Ches," she said, reaching up a little dramatically to rub her temples. "Every muscle I own is begging for relief, my head is throbbing, that fool horse pounded half a pack of perfectly good cigarettes into the dirt, and I'm in a mighty poor frame of mind to discuss tying my closest living kin to a horse."

As she talked, my aunt fished a new, or at least un-pounded, pack from her shirt pocket.

"Don't forget Daddy."

"What about him?" she asked with a puzzled frown.

"I'm not exactly your closest living relative."

"Well, you know what I mean," she snapped. "I'm in no mood for word games."

"I'm sorry, Aunt Sis. I didn't mean to—"

"Oh, honey," she cried, voice already full of regret for the sharp tone and reached an uncertain hand toward me before drawing it back to shake out a cigarette. "It's not your fault. A few quick puffs will fix my nerves right up, but it'll take hot water and time to do the rest of me any good."

Scooting to the edge of my wheelchair seat, I leaned forward to place a kiss on her cheek.

"You've taught me a lot in the past few weeks, but I still don't know much about horses or saddles, certainly not these so-called safety saddles. I never meant to argue with you, only to see both sides of the coin."

"Don't ever apologize for arguing with me, so long as you do it respectfully. Nobody else, except maybe Scooter, feels comfortable enough to contradict me.

Ever since the colonel died, it's pretty much been yes'm or nothing."

"I'll bet."

"I'm serious, Ches. It's not good for a person to go unchallenged in all her opinions, decisions, and actions. I didn't just wake up one morning and decide to see how much I could smoke. I'd get so nervous and lonely and… Nobody ever dared say, 'Uh, Miss Sis, you ain't been long put out the last cigarette.'"

"Well, you ain't," I chanced with a grin.

"You're a-way too late for that battle, honey. It takes a certain amount of nicotine to get me through life's little ups and downs. Still, it's good to have somebody around who loves me enough to call my bluff."

"Bluff my foot, I just figure you love me enough not to take my head completely off."

"You needn't ever wonder about my love, Ches."

I drifted sleepily into the kitchen the next morning to start my aunt's coffee but found her there ahead of me.

"Hey, early bird, I thought you might sleep in some after the hammering you took yesterday evening, but I see you're A-okay."

"Oh, honey, my whole body hurts. No time to worry about that today, though. Andrew's walking horses are due in, and we've got to knock a little more edge off those mules before they get here."

After a hurried breakfast of yesterday's leftovers, I drove my aunt down to the home pens. Leaving me on the gasoline Mule, she caught and saddled her palomino. Aunt Sis needed to bring the real, flesh-and-blood mules in from a small trap pasture. More than that, I figured, she wanted to show the horse, and me too, just what she thought of him.

"Please be careful, Aunt Sis. He may blow up again, and you're still sore from the last time."

"Not as sore as he's gonna be if he pulls that stunt on me again."

She swung up lightly but moaned under her breath as she settled into place. Despite her brave words and ready smile, the little groan shoved aside my nervousness and sent a bolt of real fear through me.

I doubted my aunt's poor aching body would afford her the quick reaction time needed to ride out another pitching storm, but the unpredictable gelding rode off as if he'd never had a mean thought in his life. He answered to the lightest touch on a bridle rein as Aunt Sis gathered the little bunch of long-eared equines.

"What are we going to call our palominos?" I hollered across the corral as she closed the gate behind all eight mules without stepping down from the saddle.

"I would say not to name them until we make sure yours will turn out sound in his legs," she answered, riding across the pen in my direction, "but he's already got a registered name, Vernon's Twisted Gold."

"There's a mouthful."

"It ain't all that long compared to some of them. Why not call him Vern?"

"Because he's a golden palomino quarter horse," I objected, "not Uncle Jed Clampett's third cousin twice removed."

"Well, I've probably named a thousand, but if you think you can do better…"

"I knew you weren't totally lacking in creativity," I answered with a sigh of mock relief. "You've just used up all the cool names."

"There's nothing wrong with Vern," she sniffed. "He's your horse, though, or he will be if he straightens up alright."

"Twister," I said suddenly. "I'll call him Twister."

"Say, that's pretty good. Mister Ed… You know, the TV horse, was a palomino. Mister rhymes with Twister."

"No offense, Aunt Sis, but you may have named a couple hundred too many. Call him Trouble, Twister and Trouble."

"He gave me a double handful of trouble yesterday evening," she said, accepting the name with a snort, "but he's meek as Mary's little lamb this morning."

The McKendrick boys pulled up about that time and Aunt Sis set them to haltering and brushing mules. Having gentled down quite a bit from daily handling, the mules didn't put on much of a show, and the work went along smoothly.

My aunt glanced up at the morning sun, checked her watch, and peered out toward the county road. I knew something was troubling her, but I couldn't quite put my finger on it. Seth McKendrick finally cleared up the mystery.

"Where's old Nash?" he asked, looking around suddenly.

"I don't have any idea," Aunt Sis admitted. "We ought to've seen or heard from him by now."

"That's about right," Scooter popped off. "If I laid up in bed, you'd talk about me like a dog. He'd be right in there with you, too, 'That boy, that boy, that boy.' When it's him late for work we get, 'Oh, poor Nash! I'm just so nervous. I just don't know— I think I'll have another smoke.'"

"That's it, Scooter McKendrick," she snapped whirling to face him with fire in her eyes and a braided leather quirt in her hand. "You've let your mouth overload your wagon this time."

"You might've caught me, too," he taunted, hopping up to scramble over the corral fence, "five or six years ago."

"Aunt Sis," I called sharply enough to get her attention and then took on a peacemaker's tone. "Would you like for me to go check on him?"

"I can see him," she explained, half exasperated with my apparent stupidity, "but I want to get my hands on the mouthy rascal."

"No… No'm. Do you want me to go see about Nash?"

"Would you?" she asked, suddenly sounding grateful even as she paused for a desperate-looking drag from her cigarette. "He really should've been here by now."

"I'll be glad to find out what's keeping Nash. Just don't wring Scooter's neck before I get back."

She sighed, coughed, and finally let out a tiny laugh.

"I'd have to saddle a horse and take down my lariat rope to ever catch the little dickens, and that's a-way too much trouble."

"Come on, Puddler," I called to my speckled dog, and he leaped readily to the seat beside me.

"Be careful," Aunt Sis hollered as I cranked the machine, "and come right on back."

Mom and Dad didn't particularly like the idea of me crossing a room unattended, not without my wheelchair.

Now... Me and old Puddler crossed two pastures in the bright summer sunshine, following cow trails through small stands of timber and stopping to open and close each gate. The lessons from my aunt were starting to take hold. I noticed the dust we raised, saw a brown tint creeping over the green meadows, and knew our summer had turned off on the dry side.

Aunt Sis naturally fretted over Nash, a last link with her girlhood, but I felt very little anxiety. The man worked hard for his age, and if he overslept once in a great while, it was easy to understand. Still, my aunt was genuinely concerned, and I liked the feeling of being useful.

I'd yet to master the art of counting cattle, but I looked over several small bunches without finding any obvious problems and checked the water level in two ponds. Puddler rode happily beside me and shadowed my every step as I maneuvered around on my crutches to handle the gates, but he never once opened his mouth to say he could do it faster. Like Aunt Sis, my dog trusted me to get the job done in my own good time.

I pulled up in front of a weathered frame house, mounted the small porch, and balanced on one crutch to wrap at the door.

"Nash?" I called from just outside the door. "Hey, Nash, it's Ches. Can you hear me?"

I yelled for the old man several times, but no answer came. Slowly, hair stood up on the back of my neck, and a jolt of fear ran through me.

How old was Nash anyway? I wondered. He looked younger, but common sense told me he had to be darn near eighty. My stomach balled into knots as I laid a hand on the doorknob, and a big part of me hoped to find it locked tight. Once again, though, common sense got in the way. I knew my Aunt Sis who owned this house, and I knew Nash who lived here. Most likely, neither one could come up with a key if their lives depended on it. The door swung open easily under my hand.

I didn't know how Nash felt about dogs in his house, but suddenly I didn't want to go in there all alone. One low whistle and Puddler stayed right at my heels. I looked around carefully and called out several times as we made painfully slow progress down the narrow hall.

The shotgun style house looked like the bachelor's home it was, not filthy by any means but a long way from spick and span. Dusty, nicotine-stained windows filtered the bright morning sunlight and gave it a strange dappled look on the hardwood floors. Nash might not smoke as much as my aunt, but he didn't clean house quite as often, either.

Nash's front room held a recliner, two rocking chairs, a consol television, saddles, bridles, and other equipment necessary to his line of work. I checked to make sure he wasn't asleep in either of the chairs and then continued reluctantly through the kitchen. Pausing outside what could only be his bedroom door, I snorted and stomped around like a colt at a new gate. A big part of me wanted to beat it back to the Mule as fast as my crutches could take me and run for Aunt Sis. But how could I?

She'd sent me over here to check on a dear friend, trusted me with that responsibility. How could I go speeding back across the pasture and subject her all too delicate nerves to a terrible shock when the old man might be in there napping?

I swallowed hard, said a quick prayer for strength, and stepped into the room. Window shades blocked out most of the light, but I finally spotted Nash Holloway in his bed under a couple of quilts that were probably even older than him. The strength in my leg muscles exhausted, I sank to my knees beside the bed. I hollered his name almost directly into his ear without any response, and my heart sank, too. How would I ever tell Aunt Sis?

A lump rose in my throat as I thought back over the many little favors Nash had done me in my short time on the homeplace. When I finally pulled my eyes away from him, they went to a framed 8"x10" on the bedside table.

This picture, the only one I'd seen displayed anywhere in the house, showed a teenaged Miss Sis sitting her horse between Colonel Durham and Nash himself. All three of them looked happy and satisfied after completing a day's work together. Knowing then that I had to be sure, I swung my gaze back to the old man and reached out a trembling hand to touch him.

Chapter Eleven

I looked at Nash there on the bed and realized I'd never talked to him about his faith. He'd shown me a consistent gentle kindness that I felt sure came from a Christian heart. Now, remembering his devotion to Aunt Sis, I figured he might have treated me kindly even if he were the most hardened sinner who ever lived. My hand shook harder as I wondered where my friend would spend his eternity. Finally, I dug up enough courage to place my unsteady fingers on his shoulder.

The old man's eyes popped open at my touch. I let out a startled yelp, but he never missed a beat.

"What's the matter, boy?" he asked sleepily, looking not at all surprised to find me and my dog in his bedroom. Then, a slow grin spread across his face. "You thought I'd crossed on over, didn't you?"

"Yes sir," I admitted a little awkwardly. "It sure looked that-a-way."

I reflected in passing that I'd never heard Aunt Sis call him, sir, but at the moment surprise, relief, and affection for the old man overshadowed any artificial division between us.

"Sorry I scared you," he apologized. "Woke up with a misery in my back this morning and didn't feel like hobbling into the kitchen to use the telephone, so I just rolled over and went back to sleep."

"They say back pain is some of the worst you can have," I told him sympathetically. "People look at my bent legs, a body that doesn't work like they think it should, and they figure I must hurt something awful. I don't, though, not now anyway. It may come later in life, but I'm hardly ever bothered with any kind of pain."

"Bet you sleep good, too, don't you?"

"It may take me a few minutes to drift off, but once I do I'm usually out for the night."

"Those are blessings of the young."

"I don't know; you're a mighty sound sleeper yourself."

"Every now and then," he admitted with a chuckle.

"You know, Nash," I began and drew in a deep breath for the conversation I thought I'd put off too long, "I'm not sure if you heard, but I finally figured out once and for all that I am saved."

"Heard? Well, I reckon so. Anybody who knows Miss Sis or has even passed within hollering distance of her lately heard that, and it's mighty good news, too."

"Yes sir. Yes sir; it is. Do you… I mean…"

"Hey," he said earnestly, "you really did think I'd kicked the old bucket, didn't you? Well, I know the Lord, Ches. I'm right sorry we never came out and talked about it before, but you can rest easy now."

"I'm glad to hear it."

"I go over yonder to Antioch Baptist Church. We have preaching on the first and forth Lord's day and Sunday school on the others."

"Wow, only twice a month? Back when I was trying to duck and dodge, Antioch would have been my kind of church."

Throwing his head back on the pillow, the old man laughed loud and long.

"I'll say one thing for it; a quarter-time church will make you appreciate the Word. Everybody works up a hunger for good Bible preaching in between times." Suddenly Nash drew in a sharp breath. "What time is it? Poor Miss Sis is the one took the pounding from that yellow bronc yesterday, and I'm the one turns up late for work."

"Poor Miss Sis is worried about you. She'd be over here to check on you herself, but she's in the mule pen with Seth and Scooter."

"I wish she'd take it easy for a day or two, rest, and recoup a little."

"A day or two," I scoffed. "Aunt Sis can't even sit still for five minutes, not without a cigarette."

"Bless her heart; she can never do quite enough. Between keeping the horse sale afloat and living up to her notion of what it means to be Colonel Durham's daughter… She probably ought to cut back on her smoking, but doggoned if I'll be the one to tell her. Like you said, a cigarette is the only thing that'll sooth her nerves."

"I worry about her health," I admitted a little uneasily, "but I love to see her relax if only for a second. Can I do anything for you, Nash?"

"Just knowing you'd like to help means a lot, boy, but there ain't nothing for it. These miseries come on me out of nowhere, and take their sweet time about passing off."

"Well, I'm sure Aunt Sis will want to check on you herself as soon as she gets a minute."

"You tell that sweet child not to fret over me. I'll be back to work in a day or so." I turned to go, but his voice stopped me. "Say, Ches, she sure was proud of you up on that horse."

Retracing my steps into the room, I knelt back down beside the bed.

"I'm not sure what she saw to make her proud. Hopefully I didn't look as scared or clumsy as I felt."

"I reckon you looked alright for somebody who never sat a saddle, but that ain't the important part. You've got a powerful lot of grit. Most folks in your shape would just throw up their hands and quit."

"That's pretty much what I did back home, but it never really seemed like an option down here."

"Not with Miss Sis on the place," he agreed. "There ain't no quit in that child, and she can't accept it in anybody she loves. Now, you'd best get on back to her before she worries herself plumb sick."

Puddler braced with his front legs and leaned back against the seat as we re-crossed the pasture at some speed. My aunt rode out to meet us on a tall, fine-boned black horse.

"Nash is okay," I yelled while she was still a good ways from us, and I heard her happy laughter ring out on the hot morning air.

"Praise the Lord," she said as I stopped the Mule beside her, "and thank you for going to check on him."

"He's my friend, too," I reminded her and received a nod of silent understanding. "That horse you're on must be crippled up worse than my Twister, the way he slings his feet around."

"He ain't crippled, just gaited. A Tennessee walker is supposed to move that-a-way. They're a smooth ride, but don't ever try to catch a cow on one."

"Can't be done, huh?"

"Oh, it can be done, but you talk about a pain in the neck! It's kind of like driving an automobile with a standard transmission. You can whip him over and under with a lariat rope until you give slap out, and he'll still hit every gear he's got before he breaks to run. A good quarter horse can go from a standing stop to a flat-out run in one jump."

"Why would anybody ever try to rope off a gaited horse?" I asked, laughing.

"Sometimes you use whatcha got," she answered lightly.

I accompanied her back to the pens and found a large man in overalls sizing up the mules. Looking around for Scooter and Seth, I quickly guessed they must have ridden off in another direction trying other horses.

"They're good looking mules," the big man twanged in a surprisingly high pitched voice, "but as raw as rough-cut lumber. It'll take a lot of work to break and train them." Then, his gaze swung to me. "Hello, sunny, I take it from the smile on Miss Sis that old Nash ain't left us yet."

"He's fine, just got the misery in his back."

"Good; I brought him a twist of home-grown chew he'd sure hate to miss. I think a lot of that old man."

"We do, too," I answered. "We do, too."

"Ches, honey," Aunt Sis said a little breathlessly as she swapped her saddle to another horse, "this here's Ransom Clark, the Tennessee mule man. Ransom, meet my nephew, Ches Durham."

The huge, friendly bear of a man ran backwards a few stumbling steps in a show of mock fright.

"Uh oh," he yelped, "trading with one Durham at a time is scary enough."

"How are these horses around gunfire?" Aunt Sis asked, swinging gracefully into the saddle.

"The big black gelding was used in birddog field trials. As for the rest of them, a body ought to be able to shoot off of them...at least once."

"It's a good thing you came along when you did, Ches. He'll take advantage of a poor, helpless female. Why, Ransom will have all our sweet-natured mules plowing a garden before I get even one of these fool horses to stand steady for a shotgun blast."

"At least my horses arc broke," he interjected. "These mules ain't never felt harness."

"We could've broken them easy enough," I fired from the hip, "but Aunt Sis told me the Tennessee mule man liked a challenge."

My aunt positively glowed with pride, and even Ransom slipped me a wink.

"Well, Miss Sis," he said an hour later, "I'm gonna haul your rejects on down toward Houston and see if I can't pawn them off on some trail riders. I'll be back Friday evening to see your sale and pick up my mules."

"We won't charge him much to keep the mules 'til he gets back, will we Aunt Sis?"

"Just a small fee," she teased in her most demure and ladylike tone.

My aunt put out some feed for the new walking horses, gave us three boys a .22 rifle, and told us to target practice near their pen while she went to get her hair fixed. Some adults might have considered this a little dangerous, but Seth was nearly grown. We were all old enough to know better, and besides, beauty shop day was beauty shop day.

"Seth," I admitted to the older boy, "I never shot a gun before."

"Miss Sis know that?" he questioned.

"Probably, if she sat and thought about it, but this rifle is as common a tool to my aunt as her lighter or a lariat rope."

"I expect she'd want to teach you herself if she knew this was your first go 'round," Scooter put in, "but there's no reason we can't show you how it's done. Line your front sight up with that Diet Coke can, and put 'em both in the rear-sight notch."

"A little ol' .22 bullet can travel a mile or better," Seth warned me. "They ain't anywhere near accurate at that distance, but they're still deadly. See how we sat the cans just in front of that little rise? Always know where you're shooting, and try to figure where the bullet might go if you miss, 'cause everybody misses sometime."

"Yeah," Scooter agreed, "Miss Sis'd skin us all if any of the livestock came up with a hole where it didn't belong. You might want to close that off-side eye, too, my left handed friend."

"I can't."

"Do what?" he spat in disbelief.

"My eye muscles are nearly as gimpy as my legs," I explained. "I can't even blink one eye without shutting them both."

"Well, durn. How are you s'posed to wink at the girls?"

"I reckon you'll just have to wink for me."

"Don't pay any attention to Scooter. Some of the experts say to shoot with both eyes open. You just figure out what works for you."

"Don't pay any attention to Scooter," the younger brother huffed. "I bettcha I'm a better shot than you these days. I don't waste time hauling my girlfriend clear over to the mall or cookin' hamburgers for her citified friends."

"You don't even have a girlfriend," Seth shot back, "and you won't either as long as you spend all your time following Miss Sis around like a homeless puppy dog."

"What's that supposed to mean?" I questioned sharply.

"Well, we can all see how successful her dating life has been."

Jerking the rifle up to my shoulder, I snapped off a shot in the general direction of our target. Seth jumped backwards and let out a startled yelp.

"Give a fellow some warning, why don't you?"

"You missed the can clean," Scooter said when he finally stopped laughing, "but I'd say that bullet was well spent. Lever another one into the chamber. This time, try aiming at yonder can. Take you in a deep breath, and let it out just before you squeeze the trigger."

"Say, boys," Aunt Sis called a little while later from her back porch, "how about helping me haul these groceries over to Nash?"

All three of us knew her too well to mistake her call for a normal invitation, one that might be accepted or refused. This was a summons from the queen, and target practice ended in a hurry. Sometime after returning from Miz Lillian's, fresh hairdo in place, she'd fixed some potato soup and what she called comfort custard for the sick and shut-in of our immediate vicinity.

"You never fix me anything special when I'm sick," Scooter whined, but nobody paid him any attention, least of all Aunt Sis.

Scooter carried the soup pot down Nash's narrow hallway, Seth packed the custard, and I trailed along behind with a twist of Tennessee chewing tobacco stuck in my pocket.

"Miss Sis, you oughtn't to have gone to all this trouble."

To this day I don't know how the old man knew she was waiting out on the porch, but he hollered so loud that Scooter almost spilled his load.

"No trouble, Nash," came floating back in answer. "You take care of yourself; and get to feeling better. Let me know if you need anything."

"She'll know it by telepathy," Scooter grumbled, still sore over having jumped like a scared rabbit.

Aunt Sis and I carried the McKendrick boys back to Seth's truck, and she paid them for the day's work.

"Y'all take some of this food home," she instructed. "Maybe it'll save Serena Kate a little trouble. Be sure and tell her I said hello, too."

Sitting across from Aunt Sis with our own supper on the table, I looked back on a satisfying day. I'd checked on Nash and found him still alive, made a friend from Tennessee, and felt perfectly safe even when Aunt Sis went off to the beauty shop and unknowingly left me to face a new experience without her reassuring presence.

Miss Sis Durham was nothing if not high strung, yet she'd managed to practically eliminate anxiety from my daily life. I won't say my aunt never worried. She fretted over those she loved and the continued survival of her precious horse sale. Never the less, she placed her health, personal safety, and most other booger bears of life squarely in God's hands.

My aunt made prayerful but confident decisions and seldom ever bothered to look over her shoulder. She might be described as nervous but not in the fearful, self-doubting way I'd known all too well. Lack of physical activity or being forced to wait gave her the jitters. Once free to act, though, she rarely second guessed herself.

Her daily example and a newly secure relationship with my Lord and Savior allowed me to live outside of fear for the first time in years. I still got scared from time to time but no longer dreaded every bend in the road of life.

"Thank you, Aunt Sis," I managed around the lump in my throat.

She looked up, soup spoon halfway to her mouth, and saw tears in my eyes.

"I never saw anybody cry over plain old tater soup," she joked, but her tone was as loving and tender as could be.

"No ma'am. I mean, it's good and all but… Thanks for everything."

"Child, I haven't done anything but put you up on a crippled horse and stir up your hopes, maybe without good reason."

"No, you…"

"I wanted to do so much more. I intended to cook you three good meals everyday just like Mama would have done, and I meant to teach you every little part of our business the way the colonel would if he was here. I wanted to cut way back on my cigarettes, maybe even quit for you, but the summer's sliding on by and—"

"Don't talk like that," I broke in fiercely. "I won't sit by and listen to anybody criticize my Aunt Sis, not even you. Twister might still make me a good horse. If he does or he doesn't, though, you've changed my life for the better."

She sprang from her seat and rounded the table so fast I thought my sharp tone might earn me a slap. Instead, her arms slipped around me and her head rested on my left shoulder.

"Oh, Ches… Oh, honey… Is there anything you'd like to do before our time gets completely away?"

A thought had been nagging at the back of my mind, and somehow, it just came out.

"Well'm… I'd kind of like to study the Bible, I mean, here at home with you." My aunt's tight hug grew even tighter, and her sobs shook both of us. "Did I say something wrong?" I wanted to know.

"N-no," said the muffled, broken voice into my shoulder. "My personal Bible study hasn't been what it ought to be for a long time now, but that's not your fault. With the sale to run and the house to keep, Daddy and Mama gone… Oh, there's no excuse, I just…"

Supper dishes done, my aunt picked up her large leather-bound Bible and motioned me out to the porch swing.

"We're starting tonight?"

"No time like the present, honey. We can match our personal study time to Brother Crawford's Wednesday night lessons in the book of Acts and get kind of a double dose, or you might enjoy the Gospel of John."

"If I have questions about what we go over on Wednesday night, I can always ask you. Let's study something else at home. Seems like we'd cover more ground that way. Why not just start at the front of the book, 'In the beginning God created,' and so forth."

"Well, we can, but John deals with the earthly life and ministry of Jesus in a fairly straight forward manner. I think it would be a good study for you."

I expected to miss the shared laughter over Ben K. Green's sharp country wit. As it turned out, though, I truly enjoyed learning more about my faith. Aunt Sis read the scriptures in her honey-sweet drawl and explained away any little confusion over King James English. We started and ended with prayer, and I felt a whole new world opening up to me.

Aunt Sis cooked our usual early breakfast on Wednesday morning. I trailed after her as best I could while she oversaw the never-ending round of horse feeding and other chores. Then, she settled herself reluctantly behind the colonel's desk. She showed me what she called our books for the first time. I found it interesting, even if the profit looked kind of slim, but her ashtray filled up awfully fast.

"You okay, Aunt Sis?" I asked as she reached for the next cigarette. "You don't have to show me the books, you know."

"It's important for you to see them, honey. I enjoy having you with me, but I do not enjoy paperwork. I'm so far behind on everything. If some salty bronc broke my neck tomorrow, you'd never get this mess straightened out. Just for instance, I can never keep up with the payroll, but I can't just quit paying the boys. So, naturally, it's all in my head until I take a day like today and make myself catch up on the books."

"You look absolutely miserable, and there's enough smoke in the air to fill a Saturday night pool hall."

"Oh, I'm alright. The colonel hated paperwork, too, so I've been doing it most of my life." Suddenly, a worried frown crossed her face. "Is my smoke bothering you, honey? We can open the window."

"What about my daddy? Profit and loss is his thing."

"Terry worked on our books some and seemed to like it," she said, getting up to open the window without any further comment on my part, "but the colonel kept him outside."

"Trying to force him to make a hand?"

"Force is a strong word."

"Colonel Durham was a strong man."

"Terry can handle horses, always could, and that's what makes it so exasperating. He's able but not willing."

"So he can ride, trade horses, and whatever else, but he hates it. Kind of like you and paperwork."

Astonishment, understanding, and sympathy chased one another across my aunt's face. She drew deeply on her cigarette and finally let the smoke out with a sigh.

"Somehow I never thought about it just that way, Ches." The moment passed, and all her agitation returned. She crossed the room, snatched open the office door, and stuck her head out to look both ways. "That cotton pickin' horseshoer said he'd be here early this morning, and here it is almost dinnertime."

I realized suddenly that as soon as the cotton pickin' horseshoer showed up, she'd have an excuse to quit the desk and leave her paperwork behind.

"Why don't you call him?" I suggested hesitantly.

"He doesn't carry a mobile phone, wouldn't have one if you gave it to him. Besides, you can't rush a horseshoer." She started to sit back down in the desk chair but couldn't quite make herself do it. "Go find the McKendrick boys and tell them I want to start catching horses for the shoer."

My wheelchair made its small electronic click as I moved to obey. I met Nash just outside the office, though, and he dropped a hand on my shoulder.

"I'll help Scooter. You let Seth keep riding those colts."

"Nash," my aunt called before I could form an answer, "you oughtn't be working today."

"I don't aim to work. Ain't quite mended enough to charge you for no time, but I've looked at them four walls about as long as I care to look. The day I can't catch a few horses and tie them in the alley, I hope somebody'll knock me in the head."

"They'll have to deal with me first," Aunt Sis said, and all three of us laughed.

Aunt Sis caught Twister herself, and she and Nash stood ready when the farrier arrived. A short, wiry young man, he didn't banter with Aunt Sis like Mr. Ransom Clark of Tennessee or waste many words on me and Nash, either. He did say Twister had good feet and that proper trimming would train their growth to the right angle. In the meantime, special shoes on my horse's front feet raised him up onto his toes and off the tender frog, or flat part, of the hooves.

The limp, barely noticeable with a shot of pain killer, had grown worse almost overnight, but it seemed a little better after the shoeing. Scooter led my horse up and down for our observation.

"How long do we need to rest him?" I finally asked the horseshoer.

"That's up to your aunt. She may want to lay off him for a while and ease the soreness out of those tendons. Was he mine, I'd ride him and see how he does, but I learned a long time ago that Miss Sis Durham's got her own ideas."

"Mostly good ones, too."

Scooter pretended to make the comment under his breath, but we all heard it. Though it looked at first like Aunt Sis might faint dead away from shock, she ended up smiling. Stretching out his back muscles before moving to the next horse, the farrier shot her a question.

"I thought I saw Preacher's old mare turned out in your horse trap that runs down to the county road?"

"Mable belongs to my nephew, now."

"Preacher die or something?"

"Gracious, no. He just decided to part with her."

"'At mare's older 'an water, but she was a good buggy horse in her day. I shoed her a time or two."

"I put a set on her when she first come to us," Nash volunteered, "so it ain't time yet."

"Uh huh," the young man answered, "and here we stand a-scratching our heads and trying to figure out what's wrong with your back."

"Never you mind," Nash said dryly. "We still got a few good miles in us, me and the old mare both. Ain't that right, Miss Sis?"

"Right as rain," she agreed with a big smile.

Nothing could dampen her joy at closing the office door behind her, and the report on Twister was just what she wanted to hear. The unfinished paperwork must have gone unfinished for a while longer. We picked up seven head of consignment horses in Jacksonville on Thursday and bought another off the side of the road on the way back. Friday, with all the fast-paced action of a sale day, provided Aunt Sis plenty of excuses to stay on the move.

I usually sat alone at my little desk or the remote bidding station or whatever a body might choose to call it, but on that particular evening Ransom Clark acquired a folding chair and kicked back beside me. It surprised me to see him bid on one of the mules he'd refused earlier in the week.

"I didn't think you liked that one?" I ventured.

"She's the best mule out of the bunch, but I didn't like where Miss Sis had her priced," he said from the corner of his mouth. "Maybe tonight I can buy her on the open market."

"Aunt Sis will set the price if you buy her."

"And rightly so," he agreed. "It's her mule. Still, I can give more for the animal than most folks around here, and your aunt knows it. I've got access to a stouter market, but there's always a chance some rich old codger will decide she looks just like his granddaddy's mule."

"She does," I joked. "I can see it from here."

"You've got horse trader in the blood, just like Miss Sis," he said with a big grin as Jim Rex hollered sold and called out his number, "but it didn't do either of you any good on that deal."

Andrew came in late, hunted up a folding chair of his own, and flanked me on the other side. I introduced him to Ransom, and they shook hands across me.

"Bidding for people who aren't here seems like a big responsibility for someone who's only been exposed to the horse business a few weeks," Andrew observed after watching me take a call.

"Aunt Sis is teaching me something all the time," I assured him, "and we're not exactly swamped with phone-in business just yet."

"Anybody crazy enough to buy a nag without looking at him, and I've done it, ought not care who does the bidding," Ransom offered, firing a stream of tobacco juice at the nearest spittoon.

"I guess that's true enough," Andrew agreed. "You excited about the trail ride, Ches?"

Without actually admitting any fright, I told him of my first horseback ride and a nagging suspicion that Aunt Sis wanted me to take Twister on the next morning's jaunt.

"He's a great horse, Andrew, and I loved riding him. But as far as the wide open spaces, I just don't know."

"Use a little common sense, Ches. Your aunt's not going to throw you out on a trail ride the second time she ever puts you in the saddle. You know as well as I do she cooked up this whole trail ride business so you'd have more chances to enjoy your buggy."

"Thanks, Andrew, you're right."

"My walking horses here yet?"

"Up at the house," I said and saw Ransom sit up straight.

"Well, I'll be an egg sucking hound! I knew she had 'em sold."

"Did she ever tell you any different?" I asked lightly.

"Not in so many words, but she smiled and batted those eyelashes and refused to comment one way or the other."

"There not exactly sold," I clarified. "No money's changed hands, but we've got Andrew's order."

"Are you the breeder?" Andrew asked, leaning across me excitedly.

"Y'all can talk bloodlines all you want," I said with a sort of half smile. "Just remember, I'm sitting right here. You're not about to cut Aunt Sis out of the deal."

"Now, that wouldn't be much of a way for me to win her heart, would it?" Andrew asked, giving me a wink.

"No, but trying to buy the homeplace and sale barn wasn't much of a way to start, either."

Ransom lost all interest in bloodlines, and slapped Andrew on the back with one of his bear-like paws.

"'At a boy," he bellowed. "Miss Sis will make a heck of a wife if she ever lets herself be caught."

"We'll be in the old folk's home by then. She finally called me by my first name last week."

"You just hang in there. Any horseman knows a high-strung filly's worth all the extra time and effort."

Aunt Sis woke me at daylight the next morning, and nobody could have guessed she was operating on only a couple hours' sleep. She'd sent me home as soon as Jim Rex dropped his hammer on the last horse, so I felt more or less rested. Some of the other trail riders, though, looked like cowboy and cowgirl zombies.

Seth McKendrick's volleyball-playing girlfriend snoozed on the back seat of my buggy, and she hadn't even put in an appearance at the sale. She slept in back because old Puddler commanded the space beside me, nose to the wind and tail wagging. Aunt Sis led the way on her Trouble gelding, and after a few tense moments I decided she pretty well had his number. We circled around behind the swimming hole and took a winding path through a narrow strip of woods.

"This trail's really something," I called up the line to Aunt Sis.

"Glad you like it, honey."

"You better like it, honey," Scooter's voice mocked from somewhere behind me. "Me and Nash spent a half a day hacking it out wide enough for your buggy."

One way or another he managed to ride around some folks and come up next to me.

"Next time do a little better job," I teased. "A few of the little limbs you left are slapping Mable in the face."

"You get any more like your aunt and it's apt to strain our friendship."

With that, he tossed a pinecone at his brother's girlfriend, passed us, and rode up innocently behind Andrew and Aunt Sis. Eventually, we went through a pasture gate onto the county road and circled back to the sale barn. I stayed in the buggy and followed Andrew around while he tried the rest of the walking horses, but Aunt Sis went off to supervise the Saturday checkout.

"So, the black is the only one proven steady around gunfire?" he asked.

"According to Ransom, he's already been used in field trials. We exposed them all to several .22 rounds, and it didn't seem to faze them. You don't actually plan to fire a shotgun from their backs, do you?"

"No, not under normal circumstances, but there'll be shotguns going off in close proximity."

I knew my aunt's asking price on the little bunch of horses and managed to make the trade without giving up a dollar. Since Andrew had his eye on my beautiful, charming, and independent aunt, I'm not sure how much that actually says for my skill as a salesman.

Aunt Sis cleared the barn of livestock and paid her staff before exhaustion finally caught up with her. Skipping our usual visit on the swing, she went straight to bed. I'd never used anything but the microwave in Dallas, but I managed to heat up some leftover biscuits and gravy before waking her. My aunt barely held her eyes open long enough to eat.

"I'm sorry, honey," she said with a yawn. "I bet your Mama and Daddy never nodded off at the supper table."

"We hardly ever sat down to supper, not together like me and you. Besides, they never closed out a horse sale at two o'clock in the morning and got up for a trail ride before daylight. You rest now, and we'll catch up on our Bible study tomorrow."

I said a special prayer for my aunt that night, thanking the Lord for her influence on my life and asking him to restore her strength. Reason told me a night's rest would fix her up, but I felt a lot better after putting it in the Lord's hands. In spite of this peace of mind, I couldn't quite shut down for the night.

I made a round through the kitchen, checked to make sure everything was turned off, and picked up my aunt's well-used Bible as I turned on the porch light and headed out to the swing. It didn't seem quite right to read ahead in the gospel of John without her. Besides, Brother Crawford's lesson from Wednesday night still stewed in the back of my mind. I flipped back and forth through the pages of the old Bible and finally found Acts chapter 8.

Rereading the account of Philip and the Ethiopian eunuch, I easily put myself in the eunuch's place. He went down to Jerusalem without a clue of what he was searching for, knowing only that something was missing in his life. In the same way I'd come to Aunt Sis for no better reason than to get out of my parents' hair. Thanks to my aunt, Brother Crawford, and the people of McKendrick in general, I found much more than a fun place to spend the summer.

The last couple of lines in verse 36 kept catching my eye. "See, here is water; what doth hinder me to be baptized?"

I'd found eternal salvation as a youngster but never bothered to make a public profession of faith. When my eyes finally grew heavy, I realized I couldn't change the past by sitting out here on my aunt's porch in the middle of the night.

Aunt Sis woke bright-eyed and bushy-tailed to feed the livestock. Morning chores taken care of, she made her usual smooth transition from the rawhide-tough stand in for Colonel Durham to the soft-spoken church pianist wearing her mother's pearls. Andrew showed up for church once again, but this time Jim Rex and Serena Kate were there as well.

I wondered how my aunt might handle this delicate situation but didn't have to wonder for long. She moved quietly to another pew, took me with her, and left them all sitting together.

They'd all met at the horse sale, so it wasn't too awkward except for the fact that Jim Rex and Andrew both coveted a spot beside Miss Sis. Enjoying my newfound closeness to the Lord and to the church family at McKendrick, I didn't think much about the two would-be suitors, but Serena Kate caught Aunt Sis in the church yard after services.

"Why didn't you sit with us like always," she questioned, pouting a little, "and why is that Hollister man hanging around you?"

"Andrew's a visitor, sweetheart, and we all need to make him welcome. I'm the only one around here who's had any dealings with him, aside from Giles Parmalee. How would you like to depend on Giles as your main connection to the community?"

"I guess you're right, but I still say you could have sat with us. Oh, I almost forgot. I had that roll of film developed just like you asked me to, Miss Sis. Y'all wait a minute while I get your prints out of the car."

"From the day I rode Twister?" I asked eagerly, and my aunt nodded.

Soon enough, Serena Kate came back and a little group gathered around us.

"Does your mother know about this?" Aunt Hattie asked looking down over my shoulder. "Horses are a mighty good way to get hurt, especially for somebody in your condition."

"Aw, now," Brother Crawford said easily, "he looks natural up there. Puts me in mind of his granddaddy."

I did look natural, too. Not scared to death, not anxious, and not even crippled. The pictures showed a boy on a horse with his pretty aunt and their good friends, nothing more and nothing less.

It didn't take a genius to figure that Aunt Hattie would tell Mom about my horseback ride the very first chance she got. In the past little things like that had preyed on my mind, even keeping me awake nights, but lately, I enjoyed the peaceful slumber of a tired and contented thirteen-year-old boy. On Monday morning, though, I woke to a racket I can only describe as the noise of battle.

Chapter Twelve

Aunt Sis had declared war on dust, the clutter of daily life, and even the faint but persistent odor of cigarette smoke. I'd seen her clean house before, but this... Room spray hung heavy in the air and the electric purifier I'd almost forgotten hummed busily. She didn't even offer to fix my breakfast, and that should've tipped me off right there.

I missed another big sign the next morning when Aunt Sis delayed her first cigarette. Instead of reaching for it the moment her eyes opened, she donned her housecoat and headed for the back gallery.

"You'll want a new pair of jeans and a good shirt today," she volunteered later as we sat together at the breakfast table. "We may have some horse buyers coming."

I looked her up and down taking in the 1950s style, white summer dress dotted with red cherries. A narrow emerald belt at her waist brought out the little green stems on the cherries, and white high heeled sandals afforded a bit of added height.

"They must be important buyers," I said with a grin. "That's a right fancy getup."

"Right fancy," she repeated in her thickest drawl, "if Jenna ever hears you talk that-a-way, she'll skin me alive and sign you up for private grammar lessons."

"Well, I still say the dress looks right fancy, and you do, too."

Our good clothes flew right under my radar like all the other signs. Later, when she suggested a buggy ride, I reminded her about the potential buyers.

"Oh, you know how it is. They may show up, and they may not. I don't intend to fiddle away a perfectly good day just waiting around, not when I can spend it with you."

Mable clip clopped along at a slow jog trot, morning air already warm but not unbearable thanks to a steady breeze. The flowery presence of Miss Sis Durham's perfume alongside me mixed with the smell of fresh-cut coastal and bahia grass in the hayfields we passed. A dry, dusty odor in the air raised the possibility that this second cutting of hay might be the last if we didn't get some rain.

"If you're worried about missing those buyers," I said reluctantly, "we can go back."

"I told you, Ches, I want to spend this time with you. Anybody with earnest intentions of buying a horse will wait around till we get back or take enough initiative to call my mobile phone."

"Thanks, Aunt Sis. Any day spent with you is a great one, and driving a good horse makes it that much better." After a while, though, my stomach began to grumble. "Why didn't we bring along some kind of snack?" I asked and then borrowed a phrase I'd heard from Nash. "My belly's eating my backbone."

"I reckon it is about time we head back," Aunt Sis admitted after a glance at her wristwatch. She spoke up again as we neared the house, taking me completely by surprise. "Push old Mable up to a trot, but hold your lines just a little snug so she'll carry her head right."

"You've told me more than once to hold her to a walk coming in to the barn. Besides, it's really starting to warm up."

"Just this once won't hurt. Now, do like I tell you and stir her up a bit."

Aunt Sis placed one arm casually around my shoulders while the other gloved hand smoothed her dress in a familiar, ladylike gesture. About the time I finally started to get suspicious, I caught sight of our front yard. People, two or three deep, lined both sides of the short driveway.

"Wha—"

"Don't slack her off for the turn," Aunt Sis whispered, voice brimming with enthusiasm. "Wheel us in there like an old time stagecoach driver, and don't forget to smile. Happy birthday, Mister Chester Joel Durham, Aunt Sis loves you."

"I love you, too, but my birthday's not until Friday."

"I happen to know your boss, and- birthday or not- you're working Friday."

Aunt Sis needn't have worried about whether or not I would smile. Her little joke tickled both our funny bones, and we came in laughing. She planted a kiss on my cheek just as I noticed the Happy Birthday, Ches banner hanging over the porch.

Eyes wide, I spotted some beloved faces in the crowd. Daddy, Mom and Papa Joel stood together in a little knot.

"What in the world," I wondered as Daddy stepped up and pulled me into a rough hug.

"Hey, son, you drive this rig pretty good!"

"Pretty well," Mom corrected automatically.

I felt Aunt Sis stiffen beside me and then force herself to relax.

"I'm fixin' to drop some catfish in Lake Crisco, Ches. Reckon your folks'd enjoy a buggy ride?"

Aunt Sis laid it on pretty heavy with the "fixin' to" and "reckon." I knew she'd fired her warning shot.

"Oh, it's too dangerous for him to take off without you or somebody who knows what they're doing."

"Dangerous?" Daddy snorted. "Why, that looks like Brother Crawford's Mable. She must be a hundred and three in people years."

Grabbing Aunt Sis at the waist, he lifted her from the buggy, spun her around, and set her on her feet.

"We may have our differences, Sis, but I knew you'd be just what the doctor ordered for my boy." Then to Papa Joel, "Hop up there next to him. The back seat'll be nice and cozy for me and Jenna."

"Why, Terry Durham, we've got company," Aunt Sis chided with a playful swat. "Straighten up, now, and mind your manners."

Laughing, Papa Joel slid into the seat next to me.

"Where we going, sport?"

"Nowhere until I get my hug," Mom answered for me.

"Love you, Mom," I murmured, almost loosing the lines as she pulled me to her.

"Oh, it's so good to… C.J. Durham, you smell like an ashtray. Serena may claim to love you, but her cigarettes will always come first."

I felt a surge of protective anger. How could anybody question my sweet aunt's love after all she'd done? Papa Joel read my expression and stepped in quickly.

"Miss Serena's smoking has nothing to do with her love for C.J. Now, get in the buggy. You're holding up our ride."

"We can go anywhere y'all want," I said, answering his original question, "but I'd just as soon not stray too far from the house. Mable's already had a good workout, and it wouldn't do to miss my own party."

"You should've sat up there to help him," Mom grumbled as she and Daddy settled into the back seat.

"He'll be fine, Jenna. You probably drive the old mare all over creation by yourself, don't you, son?"

"Well, I've been alone in the buggy, but there's usually a horseback rider or two around. I'm not exactly by myself now, either, not with the whole wagon load of y'all. Aunt Sis wouldn't send me off if she didn't think I could handle it."

Mom let out a little squeak as I turned Mable around in a short circle to head back out on the road. My eye fell on Andrew crossing the yard with fresh flowers and a box of assorted chocolates under his arm. He shot me the thumbs up sign.

"When you promise a fella a fish fry, Ches," he called, "you deliver in a big way."

"Who's the guy with the flowers, and what's he talking about?" Mom asked, over her momentary panic.

"That's Andrew Hollister, late of Georgia," I explained, "and he's been hunting an excuse to come a-calling on Aunt Sis."

"I can't tell you how good it is to see you, and I really hate to nag during your birthday celebration. Still, I wish you would speak English."

"What he said makes good sense to me," Daddy told her, "and it sounds pretty serious. Jim Rex got his dander up yet?"

"What?" Mom asked in genuine confusion.

"He ain't put up much of a fight so far," I said, hoping to answer both questions.

"I knew him for a lazy rascal, but I didn't think he was that lazy."

Mom threw up her hands in despair at our grammar, or lack of it, but a few minutes later she complimented my driving skills.

"Even with all these real horses around," Papa Joel said in a voice meant just for me, "I thought you might be getting a little lonesome for your collection. I brought along three or four of our favorites."

I didn't have the heart to tell him that model horses hadn't crossed my mind for nearly a month.

"Thanks, it'll be good to see them." Then, my excitement turned real as an idea hit me. "Did you happen to bring Blaze?"

"Naturally, she came along to graze the home pastures."

The real Blaze, a sorrel blaze-faced mare, was Colonel Chester Durham's all-time favorite roping horse, and the Blaze in Papa Joel's suitcase was an original model he'd constructed from a photograph.

We rolled back up to the house in time to see Aunt Hattie struggle ponderously out of her Oldsmobile. Mom and Dad helped her to the door while Nash went with me and Papa Joel to tie Mable in the shade.

"Miss Sis is workin' too hard," he grumbled. "She oughtn't to get herself in such a tizzy."

They'd worked livestock together in freezing weather, blowing dust, and stirrup-deep mud. Let her put on that little ruffled apron, start bustling around, and get red in the face from the heat of the kitchen, though, and he'd holler for old Doc Parmalee every time.

"Colonel Durham would be mighty proud of the way you've taken care of her, Nash."

"I sure hope so," he answered, fervently, "but you'll have to take over one of these days."

"Don't you worry," I assured him. "I reckon they'll be a bunch of us standing in line."

"Not that Miss Sis can't take care of herself," he added hastily, glancing at Papa Joel who looked like an outsider to him. "In a lot of ways she's the one who sees after me."

Knowing the level of courtesy Aunt Sis expected for our guests, I got in my wheelchair and worked through the crowd like a man running for dog catcher. Mr. Bowie Tate grabbed my hand and shook it like he was pumping water from a well.

"We fetched along a big mess of okra, just like I told you. Lillian's in the kitchen now, cutting it up to fry."

"Thank you, sir; I'm sure proud y'all come."

"Well, my Lillian thinks the world and all of Miss Sis, and you seem like a mighty fine young man yourself."

His kind words put a lump in my throat, and I paused a minute to look around at all the friendly faces. In a city of over a million people, I'd counted my true pals on one hand. Now, in little-bitty McKendrick, Texas, I had a house and yard full of them.

"You gonna high hat me all afternoon?" a familiar voice called from somewhere over my shoulder.

"That's the plan," I said, whirling the chair around to face Scooter. "A fellow with this many folks at his birthday party don't have to put up with your lip."

"Half these jokers came for the free food. Who'll be here tomorrow and the next day? I'll tell you: Miss butter-won't-melt-in-my-mouth Sis Durham, crazy old Nash, and yours truly. Now, how about taking me to meet your folks?"

I returned his friendly punch to the shoulder, but before we could make our way over to Mom and Daddy, Aunt Sis rang the old dinner bell.

"Get it while it's hot," my aunt called. "Where's the birthday boy?"

"Right here, Aunt Sis," I answered with a wave and started over toward her.

"How about saying the blessing," she asked me quietly.

I'd never prayed in public before, but somehow I felt a peace about it.

"Yes'm."

After my short but sincere prayer of thanks, she bent down for a hug.

"Your plate's a-waiting at the head of the table, honey. There's more fish to fry, but first I've got to sneak out for a cigarette."

"You don't have to sneak or even go outside," I said softly into her ear. "This is your house, remember?" She gave me a conspiratorial grin, but slipped out anyway. "No use waiting on me," I told our guests. "Aunt Sis probably fixed me the biggest helping. I hope y'all aren't too shy to catch up."

I overheard a brief conversation between Mom and Dad as they brought their plates over to sit with me and Papa Joel.

"C.J. shouldn't have to play host here, but we all know what's on Serena's mind."

"Give it a rest, Jenna. Did you hear that prayer or see him laughing and talking in the middle of this crowd? I'm telling you; he's a different boy from the one who left Dallas."

"What's happening in the big city these days," I asked as they sat down.

"Plenty, I'm sure," Papa Joel answered, "but our little corner of it's gotten pretty dull without you."

"Thanks, but it was pretty dull before I left."

"What a thing to say," Mom objected, but Scooter, Seth, and Miss Volleyball walked up just in time.

"Mom's always worried about the lack of close friends my own age. Believe it or not, Scooter, you're the answer to her prayers. Mom, Dad, Papa Joel, meet the McKendrick brothers and…"

I expected some smart response from Scooter, but he reached up and snatched off his cap.

"I'm plumb tickled to meet y'all."

"We are pleased to meet you, too, Scooter," and if his countrified speech annoyed her even a little bit, I couldn't tell it.

"Y'all must be Jim Rex's boy's," Daddy put in happily. "He and I spent many a day together."

"Yes sir," Seth responded. "We've heard some of the stories. This is my girlfriend, Valery."

"Valery the volleyball star," Scooter added with a solemn nod, and it earned him a quick glare from his brother.

Mom spoke to Seth, and then fell happily into conversation with Miss Volleyball while the rest of us turned our attention to the groceries. My aunt's fried fish, okra, and other trimmings tasted as good as anything I'd ever eaten. Dad, Papa Joel, and I stayed pretty quiet for the first few minutes, but we had a lot of catching up to do.

"Well, son, I guess life on the homeplace agrees with you," Daddy finally ventured between bites.

"Yes sir; it's hard to even think of Dallas as home anymore. Don't get me wrong," I qualified quickly. "I miss you three every day, but I'm as happy as I've ever been."

"Mac Town ain't a bad spot to grow up," he admitted. "My mama called it an easy place to live and a hard place to make a living. 'Course, she usually followed that statement with, 'I quit worrying about money the day I married Chester Durham. I've seen him rich one minute and near-broke the next, but me and my babies never wanted for anything.'"

"The colonel must've been some kinda man," I reflected. "He sure won undying loyalty from Aunt Sis."

"Daddy was a pistol, alright. I wish now I'd taken more time to enjoy him instead of trying to live up to him, but you just think about growing up with a father like that and Miss Sis Durham to boot."

"This fish has bones in it," Mom exclaimed when she finally got around to taking a bite.

"Sure, sweetness," Daddy answered. "Sis cut it into steaks for the skillet, but she never filleted a catfish in her life. I'm sure they fried a few whole, crispy tail and all, if that suits your fancy."

"How disgusting," she said with a shutter, and then a fresh horror struck her. "C.J. can't eat anything with bones in it. He'll choke!"

"I don't know if he can eat it or not, ma'am," Scooter drawled, "but he's sure putting it somewhere. By my count he's a-workin' on the fourth piece."

Mom could be overprotective and even a little pushy, but she was also a pretty good candidate for mother of the year. She helped provide for our family, cared for her aging father, and made our house a home, all the while acting as nurse, advocate, and cheerleader for me. Unfortunately, she and my wonderful aunt somehow managed to bring out the worst in each other.

Mom worked as office manager for a well-known dietician. So, naturally, she acted as our nutrition guru. Scooter's unwitting comment on my portion sizes drove the danger of bones right out of her mind.

"Four pieces?" she demanded. "Serena cooks just like her mother. If she can't fry it, she'll pour grease in it. Moderation is always important, but it's absolutely essential at her table."

"Aw, now—" Daddy started to object but never finished his thought.

"It looks like she's finally plumped up some. Of course, I knew it was just a matter of time; cigarettes could only postpone the inevitable for so long."

This little speech earned Mom a wide-eyed stare from the McKendrick boys and a sharp "Jenna!" from Papa Joel.

"Fortunately," she added without missing a beat, "the lifestyle doesn't seem to have caught up with you yet."

Sucking in his breath, Daddy tried again and made it stick.

"Jenna Suzanne! Leave Ches alone; he's a growing boy. Another thing, you can either stop criticizing Miss Sis or sit here while I announce to the table your weight on our wedding day and just what the scale reads now."

Mom suddenly needed several long gulps of her ice water, and the rest of us sat there in awkward silence. Finally, I turned to Papa Joel with a quiet question.

"Would you mind very much if I gave the Blaze model to Aunt Sis? I don't think she's ever seen it, and I know it would mean the world to her."

"This is your party, sport. I doubt Miss Serena is expecting a gift."

"No, but she's done so much for me and—"

"Every model horse I ever built I built for you. They're yours to do with as you please."

Several old friends came around to see Daddy, and Mom slowly got over her embarrassment. Even though his remark toned her down some, I ate my peach cobbler and homemade ice cream out on the front porch. I talked to Mr. Giles Parmalee for a while, and soon, Aunt Sis found me again.

"Come on back inside, Ches. It's time for the birthday presents. Giles, you've always got plenty of hot air; gather everybody in for me."

I parked my wheelchair in the middle of the old parlor. Folks brought in chairs from other rooms to supplement the rocker, settee, loveseat, and piano bench, but Aunt Sis stood beside me with the attentive Andrew not far from her elbow. She cleared her throat, made a little speech to thank the folks for coming, and then turned to speak directly to me.

"Ches, you know the gift I planned to surprise you with and why I can't give it today. I wracked my brain for the right substitute. Anyhow, honey, here's the colonel's good hat, a real John B. Stetson." She started to say something else, choked up, but finally managed a laugh. "You can open the rest of your presents, now, while I go off somewhere and have a good cry."

I looked at the light-colored, narrow-brimmed felt hat and realized how many memories it must hold for her. My throat got tight and my eyes stung at the thought of all she was giving me.

"Wait just a minute, Aunt Sis," I managed. "Let's not cry but once. I don't know any words good enough to tell you how much I appreciate everything you've done for me or how proud I'll be to wear the colonel's hat this fall, but I've got something to give you, too."

My aunt's eyes grew wide, shimmering with unshed tears. She shook her head vigorously as if rejecting the very idea.

"Th-this is y-your birthday party."

Wanting to take her hand, I reached up without thinking and set the hat on my head at just the right angle. She pulled in a ragged breath and began swaying slightly on her high-heeled sandals.

"Andrew," I called sharply.

"I got her, Ches; I got her."

Andrew stepped up quickly to support Aunt Sis, and the gesture must have struck a jealous chord in Jim Rex.

"There ain't nothin' wrong with her," he said gruffly, swinging a straight-backed chair into place for his lady. "Get it together, Sis. Plop your behind down here and dry up the waterworks."

"Thank you," she murmured sweetly, sinking into the chair.

If her mind and heart hadn't turned so fully to bygone days, his tone and very public reference to the back of her front would have earned him an icy stare.

"Aunt Sis? Aunt Sis," I repeated gently, patting her hand.

She straightened in the chair, cleared her throat again, and seemed to gather some strength.

"I'm fine, honey, just fine."

"I know you are, and like I say, I want to give you something."

"You don't have to give—"

"It ain't nothing but a little toy horse," I said casually, slipping Papa Joel's model into her hand, "but she might look familiar."

"Blaze… Oh, Ches, I can see the colonel on her now."

Aunt Sis buried her face in my shoulder so nobody else could see her cry, and I hugged her tightly, hiding tears of my own.

"Well," Scooter announced after a minute or two, "y'all might as well give the rest of this stuff to me. Offerin' regular, run-of-the-mill presents when she's done give him old Colonel Durham's hat is kinda like following a bulldozer with a spoon."

I felt my aunt's body shake with laughter and a smile stole across my own face as I realized Mister Mouth had saved the day for both of us. Stetson still atop my head, I opened a portable CD player with headphones from my folks, a stack of Louis L'Amour audio books from Papa Joel, and a card with the usual ten-dollar bill from Aunt Hattie.

I unwrapped presents from folks I never expected to get me anything in the first place: a big jar of pickled okra from Bowie and Lillian Tate, a white western dress shirt from Uncle Elmer, and another stack of CDs from the Crawfords.

"I talked to your sweet mother on the telephone, Ches," Miz Edna explained, "and she told me about the new gadget. If you get tired of shoot-'em-up westerns, you'll have some gospel music to play."

"The Chuck Wagon Gang is your aunt's all-time favorite group," Brother Carlton volunteered. "We love their sound, too, and thought you might enjoy those tapes."

"Yes sir, thank y'all."

Andrew presented my very own bone-handled Case pocket knife with three sharp blades. The knife cost him considerably more than the bouquet and candy he bought for Aunt Sis, but knowing her, it probably did more good for his courtship, too. My buddy, Scooter, proudly held up a horse-hair halter.

"This is from me and old Nash. He's the one hand braided it, but I thinned the tails on four horses to get all the different colored hair."

"Wow, thanks; it'll look great on Twister."

"May be too big," he worried. "We made it for Mable's big-headed self."

When all the other gifts had come and gone, Dad sprung a little surprise of his own. His mysterious-looking package stumped me right off the bat. Long, narrow, and lightweight, I couldn't even guess at its contents but tore off the plain brown paper to reveal a perfectly-balanced, expensive-looking buggy whip with a black lash and tassel on the end of it.

"Don't you go whuping old Mable just because you can," he cautioned, "but Sis told me your buggy had a whip socket on it. That doodad will look better than an empty bracket and be right handy if you need it."

"It's great, Dad, light and easy-handled."

"I'm sure glad you like the little whip, son. It came out of a fancy tact store that caters to those high-booted English-rider types. The sales clerks probably thought I was crazy, but I laughed the whole time just picturing your Aunt Sis and good old Nash wandering around in there. 'What in blue blazes is that little-bitty, flat piece of leather goods?' 'Heavens to Betsy, Nash, I think maybe it's supposed to be a saddle.'"

He pegged them both to a tee, mocking their voices with the kind of pin-point accuracy that only an aggravating little brother could manage, and a ripple of laughter moved through the room.

"That's about enough of that," Aunt Sis said, but her own giggle drained the usual authority from her bossy tone.

"Hey, y'all, I want to thank everybody for coming and for my gifts. It means a lot to have you here whether you came from just up the road or down from Dallas."

"Your aunt put out the word, Ches. Anybody who didn't come 'round for your birthday needn't bother comin' back no more a'tall," Uncle Elmer answered teasingly.

"Well, sir, I sure wouldn't put it past her."

"Say, Miss Sis," the old man burst out with a sudden thought, "you don't aim to let a gathering of this size get by without a little singing?"

"I suppose that's up to the birthday boy," she answered with a smile.

"What kind of singing?" I wanted to know.

"Gospel singing around the piano," the old man answered, "but I reckon we could work happy birthday in there."

"Gathering around the piano sounds fine if we only knew somebody who could play the thing."

The words took on a teasing tone as I gazed adoringly at my favorite piano player in the whole wide world. Singing those old church songs thrilled my heart, and, though I wondered what my voice might sound like without the effects of cerebral palsy, I chose to enjoy myself in spite of its imperfection.

My aunt took the same worry-free approach. She, the lady who never sang in church but devoted all her attention to the piano and kept a mint in her mouth to quiet her troublesome cough, finally let me hear her deep, rich alto. I'd caught small doses of it around the house and sale barn, but the full effect nearly took my breath away.

Aunt Sis played for us and sang the alto lead on "I'll Meet You in the Morning" with her eyes closed through most of the song. Joy shown from her face as she contemplated, not only a Heavenly reunion with Colonel Chester Durham and other loved ones, but also the first look at her Lord and Savior.

"This is the best birthday ever," I declared when we were all about sung out, "and it ain't over yet. Who all wants a short buggy ride?"

"There's a plenty of food left. Y'all stick around, wait for a turn in the buggy, and eat again before you go," Aunt Sis invited freely, and most folks took her up on it.

"Scooter gave me the halter," I told Nash as we made our way to the barn to unhitch Mable from the buggy. "It's a beautiful piece of work, and I want you to know how much I appreciate it."

"Beautiful don't count for much," he muttered, "but I reckon you'll find it stout enough."

Though most of the locals had drifted on home, I noticed a fire-engine red BMW convertible still parked in the yard next to Mom's Ford Explorer.

"Who's Beemer?"

"Don't you know?" he asked with a grin. "Your Daddy come a-driving that thing in here, but I reckon it belongs to Miss Sis."

An early picture of my aunt, cigarette in hand and the weight of the world planted firmly on her shoulders, floated up from my memory, and I heard the words, "Show him the little car, Jim Rex."

"Where did Aunt Sis ever come up with that thing? Why, she couldn't even fit a saddle in the trunk."

"I don't think she's ever sat in it, Ches. You know, somebody done decided smoke-smell cuts the price of an automobile. Miss Sis'd a lot rather travel everywhere a'horseback than do without her cigarettes."

"Yeah," I agreed, thinking a little guiltily of all the times she'd driven the van just to make things easy on me, "but you ain't told me how she got it."

"Aw, some high roller got to owing the barn a good chunk of money, and Miss Sis ended up with his toy rocket. I never figured we'd have no earthly use for it, except to cash it in, but I reckon Terry had to get home some kinda way after he left your van."

I found the family gathered on the back porch and earned a glare from Mom as I slipped in to the swing beside Aunt Sis.

"You have a beautiful voice. How come I never heard you sing like that before?"

"Did you see my can of Diet Coke?" she questioned. "I do pretty well as long as I've got something to keep my throat clear. That's why there's a coaster on the piano."

"Why not keep a coke handy during church? People wouldn't mind it, especially if they got to hear you sing."

"A can of Diet Coke sitting atop the church piano hardly shows the proper level of respect. They've all heard me sing before, and besides, I wouldn't want to take a coughing fit and mess up the song service. It doesn't matter so much here at home."

"If you'd just quit—" Mom started, but Daddy cut her off with a grin.

"You want to know the real reason she won't take a Diet Coke into the church house, Ches? Mama didn't do it that-a-way."

"Oh, Terry," Aunt Sis breathed, and I saw a mixture of fondness and exasperation in the shake of her head. "I'm trying to set the boy an example of respect for the Lord's house, and here you are making jokes."

"I'm sorry, Sis. Church ain't no place for snack time, but," he added with another grin, "I still say if Mama had played standing on her head, you'd do it or break your neck trying."

"Say," I asked in an effort to change the subject, "how do you like driving your sister's little hotrod?"

Daddy jumped up off the porch steps, tossed me a smile, and snapped his fingers.

"I need to take you out for a spin."

Mom heaved a long sigh and spoke from one of the rocking chairs.

"I guess almost anything's safer than breathing Serena's nasty smoke, but keep a close watch on your Dad. He crawls behind the wheel of that red-hot car and becomes a teenage boy again, darting in and out of traffic, ignoring the speed limits, and…"

"Rest easy, Jenna," Aunt Sis said on an exhale. "Us poor little old country folk seldom make enough traffic for anybody to dodge around."

"I'm awful proud to see you doing so well, son," Daddy said as we zipped over a Farm-to-Market road in the BMW, "but I hope you know the most important things you've learned here can be used in Dallas or anywhere."

"Yes sir. I mean, I guess so."

"Sure they can. I'm not talking about whatever you've picked up on how to run a horse sale or make a trade. It's more the lessons you mentioned on the phone the other night, how to live."

"I reckon some things stay the same no matter where you are."

"That's right. You look a man in the eye when you shake his hand, son. You hold your head up and be proud of who you are. I never found the right words to help you understand such things. I know a man ought to do this-a-way and never that-a-way, but I don't always know why. Sis is probably more demanding in her expectations than I would ever be. Even so, she's a whole lot better at explaining herself."

"Aunt Sis is a humdinger," I agreed, borrowing a word I'd heard her use to describe the colonel, "but don't sell yourself short. You and Mom have always been there for me."

"We've tried, son, and we miss you at home. I'm tickled you got to spend a while down here with Sis, but I think it's time to come on back to the real world and apply the things she's taught you."

Chapter Thirteen

I felt the sudden rush of anger, but my aunt's unfailing example of respect forced itself to the top of my mind.

"What makes her world, this world, any less real than yours?" I asked quietly, and my voice only shook a little. "If she doesn't get up every morning and tend to her business, real, live animals go without feed and water. Those animals are entrusted to her care by real customers."

"Now, son, I never meant—"

"No sick days or vacation time for Aunt Sis," I continued, scarcely pausing for a breath. "She's a nervous, delicate lady, but if she doesn't hustle every week and then get in there on Friday night and make it all come together, there won't be any horse sale. Her living and the colonel's legacy will go straight down the drain. I'd call that pretty real."

Daddy slowed down and glanced over at me. Finally, he grinned.

"Somebody ought to tell Sis about the difference between teaching and brainwashing. I feel like she just got through chewing me out, her or the colonel one."

"Oh, I didn't mean to—"

"She don't either, son, she don't either." He waited for what seemed like several minutes and then spoke again. "You know you'll have to be home sometime in August to start school."

"Yes sir. I figure to cross that bridge when I come to it."

As if in answer, Daddy punched the accelerator, and the car surged forward.

"Boy howdy, but this is a sweet little ride. Look at that RPM gauge, Ches. Why, she's just floating along at ninety. Wait till we hit that straight stretch just this side of Mac Town, and I'll nudge her up past a hundred for you."

I laughed happily, then, but maybe not for the reason he thought.

"You called me Ches. It'd be nice to answer to just the one handle." Suddenly, though, my thoughts turned serious. "Daddy, I really wish you and Aunt Sis could get along. I love her so much it almost hurts."

He slowed the car, matching our speed to his cautious answer.

"I'm glad you and Sis have a strong family feeling. As for me and her, we get along best by staying out of each other's way. I miss my big sister sometimes but don't quite know how to patch things up. Then too, she and your mom are about like oil and water."

"Yeah, I know." We drove along in silence until an idea struck me. "Nash says she's never once sat in this fancy little car of hers. Why don't you take me back home and show her what it'll do?"

"Home?" he asked, and I saw a touch of sadness in his questioning smile.

"Home to the Durham place," I said, nodding just a little.

"Your mom's not going to like that one bit."

"Surely she won't care if you take Aunt Sis for a ride."

"You know that's not what I'm talking about. She's all set for you to start back to Dallas with us this evening. If she heard you call Mac Town and the old Durham place home…"

A thought struck me, and I scrambled for my billfold. Thumbing through it, I pulled out the new, wallet-sized print of me and Aunt Sis together on horseback.

"You've just got to make mom understand," I begged and handed him the picture. "Look at that and then tell me it's time I headed back to Dallas. Aunt Sis bought that horse especially for me, but I've only ridden him once because there's some kind of problem with his front feet."

"How did the ride go?" he asked, smiling in spite of himself.

"Oh, I'll be honest; it was a little scary. My wheelchair will go where I point it every time, but a horse has a mind of his own. You know something else, though? I loved it! I felt free and I don't know…normal."

"That's great, Ches! They have therapeutic riding programs in the Dallas area, you know."

"Oh, yeah, that'll go over real good. I'll just let you look into your sister's eyes, those deep brown ones big enough to hold her whole heart, and tell her you aim to let some city-raised professionals teach me how to ride."

He appeared to give it some serious thought before answering in a gloomy tone of voice.

"I believe I'd rather deal with Jenna."

"That's kind of like the rock and the hard place, but thanks for understanding, Daddy."

We found everybody still on the porch, and Daddy jumped in with both feet.

"Ches ain't— I mean, C.J. isn't coming home this trip."

"What?" Mom and Aunt Sis jumped to their feet in the same motion, speaking almost as one, but my aunt added a postscript.

"...in the Sam Hill are you talking about? Of course he's not leaving yet."

"It makes perfect sense and will save us a long drive back down here," Mom countered. "He's sure to get homesick sooner or later, and school starts in August."

"Now, Jenna, our boy don't act homesick to me, and as for school... Well, it's a while yet 'til August."

Aunt Sis sat back down, hands folded contentedly in her lap, but Mom paced up and down the porch. Finally, she whirled on Daddy.

"I need to speak to you in private, Terry."

She stormed off, and he followed her reluctantly down toward the home pens. Aunt Sis cleared her throat as he passed and joked in a lowered tone.

"There's a quirt hanging just inside the saddle shed door. It's okay to defend yourself, little brother." I pictured the braided leather riding whip and shot my aunt an I-can't-believe-you-just-said-that look. "Sorry, honey," she said with that twinkle still in her eyes, "but he may need all the help he can get."

Papa Joel sat silently through the whole little exchange, and I couldn't help wondering what he thought about it all. I guess my aunt's mind drifted in the same direction because she turned in her seat to face him.

"Mr. Joel, can I get you another glass of tea? How about some more cobbler?"

"No ma'am, but I would take another slice of that good, cold melon if there's any left."

"I'm not sure how cold it is, now, but I'll bring you a piece."

"Still sweet and juicy," Papa Joel observed a minute later as he bit into the watermelon.

"Well, I'm mighty glad you like it," Aunt Sis said in her best southern belle hostess tone and sank down beside me once again. "Ches," she began hesitantly, "if you want to go home with your Mama and Daddy—"

"No ma'am. I wish I could promise to stay forever, but I'll stay here as long as I can. In fact, I want to talk to you about something. The Lord's been working on me. I think it's time I got baptized."

"Now that you're sure of your salvation," she answered slowly, "the next logical step is to join a Bible-believing local church. Even so, I can't help but wonder how your folks would feel about your getting baptized here in McKendrick."

"I think they'll want to be here. Maybe if we set it up for tomorrow night, they'd stay one more day."

"Baptism doesn't save you, Ches, you were as saved on the day you put your faith in the Lord Jesus Christ as you'll ever be. This ain't something you've got to rush."

"I know it, Aunt Sis, but I want to be baptized here at home and become a member of McKendrick Missionary Baptist Church. I may not get to live here forever. We don't even know for sure if I can stay the rest of the summer, but I want my church membership to start here. The way you explained it, I can always move my membership later."

"Sounds like the boy's put some thought into this, Miss Serena," Papa Joel interjected.

"My poor little ol' heart's pounding for joy," she answered with a smile, "so I reckon I'll quit trying to change his mind. We'll check with Brother Crawford first thing in the morning. You'll need to walk the isle and be baptized all in one night. It kind of seems like taking the vote for granted, but I reckon we can get by with it under these special circumstances."

"Well, then," I answered happily, "it's all settled."

"Not quite," Papa Joel reminded me. "Take my advice, sport, and give your mom a chance to cool off before you spring another shock on her."

"Yes sir. I'll sure try, but I've got to say something before they get ready to leave."

My parents came back a few minutes later, walking hand in hand. Mom pointed her index finger at me but smiled a little as she did so.

"You can stay here until the week before school starts, young man, and not a day longer."

"Oh, thank you, Mom. Thank you, thank you."

"It doesn't exactly help my feelings for you to act like I just commuted your prison sentence," Mom pouted, but Daddy changed the subject.

"How about a ride, Sis?"

"Sure thing; I've got lots of horses that need it."

"Not that kind of ride, I'm talking about a cruise in that Beemer you acquired from some misguided wanna-be horseman."

It looked at first like Aunt Sis might laugh the notion off, but she finally tilted her head to one side and studied Daddy for a moment.

"Why not, little brother."

"There's the Sis Durham I know," he said with a grin, "ready for anything."

Mom and I followed as they trooped around to the front yard and piled happily into the tiny convertible, laughing and carrying on the whole time. Daddy fiddled with some buttons, the top slid down, and old-time country music blared out into the air.

"Will she scat?" Aunt Sis asked him with a wink.

"Like a scalded dog," he hollered over the engine noise and radio.

Standing beside me, Mom shook her head.

"Two irresponsible middle-aged kids," she fussed. "I didn't worry half as much about him going off with you, but I can just hear Serena squealing, 'Faster, Terry; punch it."

"I'm glad they're off having a little fun together," I said almost tentatively.

"Probably a good thing," she admitted. "You and I don't have brothers or sisters, but I suppose it's an unbreakable bond. I just hope they don't wrap that little red Christmas ornament around a pine tree."

"Aw, don't fret. Daddy's a pretty good driver no matter what the speed."

"Don't fret?" she mimicked. "I love you, son, but I feel like you've changed a great deal since leaving home."

"Yes'm, and I hope I've changed for the better. I've learned how to think on my feet, on my wheels rather. I can do a little more than just sit around and wait for you and Daddy to come home from work."

"Miss Sis Durham, life coach and general expert on everything," she said, rolling her eyes. "Yet all she does is cling to the past and puff constantly on a cigarette to deal with the stress of feeling it slip slowly from her white-knuckled grasp."

I drew in a long breath and let it out slowly.

"That's the first time I ever heard you call her Miss Sis instead of Serena."

"Well, in case you didn't notice, I'm being a bit sarcastic."

"Aunt Sis has never claimed to be perfect, but she expects me to conduct myself like a Durham. Those expectations have been good for me."

When we made our way back around the house to sit with Papa Joel, I considered inviting Mom to join me in the swing, but somehow I hated to give away my aunt's spot. I parked my wheelchair between the two rockers instead.

"Is it down to just the three of us?" Papa Joel asked.

Mom answered his question with one of her own.

"That's not such a bad thing, is it?"

"No ma'am," I replied automatically.

"The people around here may talk slow and adapt to change even slower," she declared, "but I'll say one thing for your aunt and her neighbors. They believe in manners."

"Aunt Sis sort of demands respect; there's just something about her. I mean, it's not like she goes around quoting Emily Post all the time. I can say yeah or nope to her if we're out working, but if I ever said it with just a hint of the wrong tone, she'd probably slap me cross-eyed. Or she might cry, and that would be at least ten times worse."

"Emily Post," she reflected, "I haven't heard that in years. It's amazing what all you've picked up from Serena in such a short time. Just don't take up smoking or absorb her narrow-minded prejudices."

"What do you mean prejudices?" I demanded. "Plenty of black folks come to the horse sale every week."

"That's business," Mom countered. "Nash is one of the dearest friends she's got left in the world, but did you see him in the house today, mixing freely with her other guests?"

"He was around," I answered defensively, "and I saw her fix him two or three plates full."

"Did she fix anybody else's plate beside yours? No," Mom answered her own question, "and she carried his outside."

"A whole bunch of folks ate outside."

"Uh huh, and every one of them came in to fix his own plate, not Nash."

"That's as much on his part as it is hers. It's the way they were raised, both of them."

"Maybe so, but that doesn't make it right. Anyway, I wasn't necessarily speaking of racial prejudice. You're the one who took the conversation in that direction."

"What other kind of prejudice is there?"

"Your Dad took me to Niagara Falls on our honeymoon," she said, pulling my hand into her lap. "When I try to tell Serena how beautiful it was, she hooked one leg over the front of her saddle, squinted against the smoke of her cigarette, and looked way down her nose at me.

"If she's a'horseback and you're on the ground, down is pretty much the only way to look at you."

"You didn't hear that condescending tone. 'All that cotton pickin' water's too far from home to do us a lick of good. You ought to smell the honeysuckle around here come late spring, or sit your mount on a little rise while Daddy and the boys drive a big bunch of loose horses across the open ground below. No piddling little waterfall could ever hope to compare.' That kind of prejudice has nothing to do with race."

"Maybe it's just how she felt," I insisted stubbornly.

Mom frowned momentarily, and then a light bulb seemed to click on.

"Let's make a deal, C.J. You remember that your aunt might not be absolutely perfect, and I'll try to show my appreciation of everything she's doing for you."

"Fair enough, but you try hard or no deal."

Mom laughed then, and the sight and sound of it did my heart good. When I asked how things were going for her at the office, she launched into stories about two ditzy young receptionists in training. The tales were kind of funny, even if they didn't involve horses or dogs, and Papa Joel chuckled right along with me.

Daddy and Aunt Sis roared back into the yard right around dusk-dark. We heard them come in through the front door and clatter down the length of the dog run. Laughter floated out on to the porch ahead of them and seemed somehow to annoy Mom. Come to think of it, I probably didn't help matters by scooting into the swing and waiting expectantly for Aunt Sis.

"That little car will flat get it," she told Mom, running a hand over the top of my head as she took her usual place. "You ought to go a-riding with Terry. It'll sure get your blood pumping."

"My blood pumps just fine, thank you," Mom sniffed as Daddy dropped into my vacated wheelchair. She paused for a moment, and then pounced like a cat. "Tell us about your new boyfriend, Serena. What does poor, clueless Jim Rex think?"

"I don't know what you're talking about, Jenna, but I won't hear a word against Jim Rex. He's a fine man, a good…um… pretty fair auctioneer, and he makes a nice date, too."

"I want to know about the dark-haired guy with the flowers and candy."

"Who, Andrew Hollister? He's just another money man, wandered off out here in the country to try and buy up the world, but my little piece of it ain't for sale."

"I only talked to the Hollister fellow for a minute, Sis," Daddy objected, "but he's not your enemy. In fact, he looks love-struck to me."

"Pshaw," my aunt spat, attempting to wave away the notion, but I knew part of her hoped it might be true. "He's probably squired around all kinds of sophisticated city girls."

"Maybe so, but I'm fairly certain he never dated anyone like you."

Mom's voice dripped with sarcasm, but Daddy drew a positive meaning from her words and used it to support his point.

"It's a mighty rare privilege to date the Mac Town homecoming queen and valedictorian, class of '76."

"There'll never be another Miss Sis Durham," I said, "and that's for sure."

"Believe it or not, Sis," Daddy continued, "I understand what family land means to you, but it wasn't Andrew who did Uncle Doc dirty. If you've just got to be mad at somebody, blame Giles Parmalee."

"Oh, I do," she answered halfheartedly, "but I've dealt with the old rogue all my life. It's hard to cut him off at this late date."

"He's right about one thing. What good can Uncle Doc get out of his land at this point? It would have been sold off eventually."

"But there's always a chance, isn't there Serena?" Mom's tone took on a cruel, mocking edge. "The old man might have left it all to you."

"Try harder," I hissed at her.

Patience suddenly evaporated, Aunt Sis whirled on Mom like an old-time duelist ready for a sword fight to the death.

"You shut your mouth, and quit sticking your nose into things you don't understand. Whatever happened to that place should have been Uncle Doc's decision. That old man, as you call him, still thinks he's coming home one day soon. He'd be almighty surprised to find some bird-hunting stranger living in his house."

"Now, Jenna, you know there's not a greedy bone in my sister's body," Daddy said quickly. "How about a smoke, Sis?"

Movements still jerky with anger, she snatched a pack from her pocket and extended it to him.

"Here, take 'em. When will you grow up and start buying your own?"

"Sis," he said, speaking in a concerned tone as he tried to pull her back into the present. "I haven't smoked a cigarette in years. I thought you might want something to ease your nerves."

"It's not a bad idea at that," she answered, a half smile playing across her lips as she realized what he meant.

"If Uncle Doc had left his place to you," Daddy ventured, "and I know that's not your main concern, it would've only delayed the outcome. Should anything ever happen to you, Ches has got a whole lot more than he can deal with right here."

A pained expression washed over her face at the mention of my name, and she dropped the pack, contents undisturbed, back into her pocket.

"He's a Durham," she snapped. "He'll manage just fine. You could, too, if you half tried." With that, she dismissed Daddy altogether and turned apologetically to me. "Ches, honey, I had no right to speak to your mother like I did, especially not in front of you. I hope you can forgive me."

"You know what they say," I answered with a grin. "All the best horses are a little high strung. If you're trying to apologize, though, you better point it at her. As far as I can recall, I've never felt the rough side of your tongue."

My aunt's noble little shoulders squared like she was fixing to mount a bad bronc. She heaved a pitiful sigh and turned once again to face Mom.

"I am truly sorry, Jenna. I've begged y'all to come and visit for years, and the first thing I do is jump down your throat…"

"I'm sorry, too, Serena. I'll never understand all that business about blood ties to the land. It sounds like something out of the dark ages to me, but you've dedicated your life to perpetuating the system. Perhaps you're right; I'd do better to stay out of things that don't concern me."

"The system, if that's what you want to call it, does concern you, Jenna. As Terry's wife and Ches's mother you'll never be without a place to call home. At least stay one night, please?"

I reached over and squeezed my aunt's hand. Whatever happened, she wouldn't be left alone to watch the dust settle behind them, not this time. Mom may have noticed my gesture and read something into it because her sudden decision surprised us all.

"We'll stay the night, Serena, and thank you for the invitation."

A few minutes of almost comfortable silence passed before Papa Joel stifled a yawn, and Aunt Sis got to her feet.

"Y'all come on in, and we'll get everybody settled for the night."

Later, when she tried to slip back outside, my aunt caught a lecture on the evils of smoking. Mom just couldn't seem to appreciate the restraint it took for Aunt Sis to step out of her own house every time she wanted a cigarette. When the lecture finally ended, I trailed along after her, told her what a wonderful aunt she was, and reassured her that things would be back to normal by tomorrow night.

As I settled into bed, I expected my aunt to step in as usual, smooth my covers, and say goodnight, but Mom and Daddy beat her to it. They came into my room together, and Mom sat down on the edge of the bed.

"You're not going back on our deal about being nicer to Aunt Sis, are you?" I asked looking up at her.

"N… Why do you ask?"

"When you caught her heading outside… Well, it's okay to scold me or the girls who work in your office, but Aunt Sis is a grown lady. More than that, she pretty well runs things around here to suit herself."

"I didn't mean to be rude, C.J. Serena needs to take better care of herself. Those cigarettes are hurting her more than they help her, but she sucks them down like her life depends on it."

"At least they make her feel better," I defended, but Mom arched an eyebrow at me. "Okay… It's not the healthiest habit, but she's still a wonderful lady. Besides, this is her house."

"I never said she wasn't— I didn't mean to imply that smoking made her a bad person."

I started to respond, but Daddy choked and snorted and made my point for me.

"You beat Sis over the head with her smoking like it was a broom and she was a stray dog. I don't know how Ches ever managed to jump to the wrong conclusion."

"Am I that bad?" she asked with a sigh.

"I know you mean well, Mom. I worry about Aunt Sis, too, but it doesn't help matters to chew her out every chance you get."

"I never thought I'd miss this place, son," Daddy said, changing the subject, "but it's good to be here, especially with you."

"Yes," Mom agreed, "it's good to be anywhere with you, even way out here in the sticks."

"Thanks; I'm awful glad y'all came."

"Goodnight, C.J."

"Hold on, Mom," I said, reaching up to catch hold of her hand. "I need to talk to you and Daddy about something."

"What is it?"

"I want to be baptized."

"Oh," she said a little breathlessly, "I think that's wonderful."

"Here," I added quietly. "I've decided to join McKendrick Missionary Baptist Church."

"Are you sure that's the wisest course?" she asked, straining to keep her voice level.

"I'm at home, Mom. I really think I ought to make my public commitment to the Lord here."

"Are those your thoughts or Aunt Serena's?"

"Try harder," I warned.

"What?" she sputtered. "This has nothing to do with our deal."

"Think for a minute, Mom. Do you really believe Aunt Sis would interfere in something so personal, or are you just badmouthing her because you're not happy with my decision?"

"Well, I'm sorry, but your dad and I would like to remain part of your life."

"Yes ma'am," I said gently. "That's why I want to set it up for tomorrow evening.

Y'all can stay that long, can't you?"

"Sure we can," Daddy answered for both of them, "and we're proud of you."

"Yes, very proud," Mom agreed quietly and smiled down at me.

The next morning I made coffee as usual but didn't bother to look for Aunt Sis in her room. I found her on the porch, smiled good morning, and handed her a steaming cup.

"I want to fix a good, home-cooked breakfast for your folks, Ches, and then y'all can go on over to see Brother Crawford."

"You're not coming?"

"I will if you want me to, honey, but we've still got a business to run. Friday'll be on us before we know it, and besides, me and Jenna could do with a little time apart."

"Yes'm, I understand."

"I mean it, though, Ches. I can go if you want me along."

"I'll always want you along, Aunt Sis, but I don't guess there's any particular need on this trip."

"Always is a long time," she said, pausing to sip at her coffee. "I'll remember that when you're dating some cute little girl, and crazy old Aunt Sis is nothing but an embarrassment."

"You could never embarrass me," I assured her, "and any girl I date will have to meet your approval."

"I love you, Ches, more than you'll ever know."

Aunt Sis outdid herself with breakfast and then took Papa Joel down to the sale barn while Mom, Daddy, and I headed off to visit the Crawfords.

Miz Estelle entertained Mom and Daddy in the house, but I bounced my wheelchair along a rugged path, accompanying Brother Crawford down to his pond.

"Baptism is a church ordinance, Ches," the old man said gravely. "It pictures the death, burial, and resurrection of Jesus Christ. Our Lord wants all His children to follow Him in scriptural baptism and become an active part of one of His local New Testament churches, but I'm sure you know that no amount of water can save a person."

"Yes sir. I'm already saved, and I'd like to become a member of McKendrick Missionary Baptist Church. Sorry to rush things up this way, but my parents want to be here."

"And rightly so. Don't trouble yourself about the rush, but as much as I'd like to be your pastor, I wonder if you wouldn't be better off to wait and find a local church back home."

"McKendrick may not be my permanent residence, but it is my home."

"That's all well and good, Ches, but I'm gonna give you some advice that might sting a little. Just remember, I count you as my friend. Don't join the church at McKendrick because of your family's history there. That's not the right reason."

"I feel at home in the church here, Brother Crawford. I've prayed about it, and I believe I'm following the leading of God's spirit."

"I'm mighty proud to hear you say that, Ches."

"Thanks for everything," I said, giving him a firm hand shake.

"Uhhh," he grunted, favoring his creaky joints as he pushed himself upright. "I ain't done nothing. Thank you for being so good to our Miss Sis."

"Shucks, if it wasn't for her I'd still be that poor boy in the wheelchair." Glancing down at me, Brother Crawford raised his eyebrows. "Yeah, I know. But now I'm Ches Durham, horse trader in training and the apple of my aunt's eye. This chair's just a tool to get me from one place to another, makes a pretty handy seat once I get there, too."

"You sure got a plenty of that old Durham spark in you," the preacher snorted. "Say, would it be any easier for you if we held the baptism at the swimming hole there on your aunt's place."

"It might, but how will the folks know where to come?"

"We'll meet at the church as usual. That-a-way I can explain things and offer an invitation. You come forward and, after they vote you in, we'll all head for the swimming hole."

"Sounds like a plan," I agreed. "It'll be a lot easier than going up and down those baptistery steps."

"You got time to wet a hook with me?"

"Maybe we'd better go fishing another day, Brother Crawford. I feel like I ought to spend time with my folks while they're here."

Returning home we found Aunt Sis in her office at the sale barn. She listened with a distracted smile as I explained the plans for my baptism. Soon, though, she dropped her eyes back to the desk. Daddy crossed the room to gaze over her shoulder for a minute or two, and his facial expressions were priceless.

"Goodnight, Sis, that's got to be the worst set of books I've ever seen!"

"Maybe so," she answered tartly, "but I know where my money's at."

"I'm glad you do," he shot back, gesturing down toward the desktop, "because nobody else could ever decipher that jumbled mess."

"Well, mister smarty britches," she challenged, slapping her pencil down on the open ledger with a thwack, "if you know so much about it, fix 'em to suit yourself."

"You're our daddy made over, Sis. The real records are in your head just like his were, and you know it. I'd love to help out with the books, but you can't just dump them in my lap, swing up on a horse, and ride away."

"You sure know how to take all the fun out of it," she sighed, reaching for a fresh cigarette, "but I would appreciate some help." Then, she swung her attention to me. "Hunt up Nash and get him to hitch Mable, Ches. Your Mama and Mr. Joel might enjoy another little ride."

Mom stayed nervous, still doubting my ability to handle the horse, but we enjoyed our time together considerably more than Aunt Sis enjoyed being cooped up in the office. That night, my aunt apologized several times for our supper of cold fish, but she ate hers standing up and hurried off to bathe and change. She and I took my van to church just like always while the others followed in Mom's Explorer.

"You know how I hate bookkeeping, Ches, but it sure did my heart good to see your daddy take an interest in Durham Auction Company again."

"Please don't get your hopes up," I warned. "Daddy's interested in anybody's accounts. The worse they look, the greater his interest. Don't ask me why, but he enjoys that kind of challenge."

"Still, I really appreciated his help. You should see the difference it made."

I'm pretty sure Aunt Sis visited with every single person as they entered the church, but they acted suitably surprised when Brother Crawford took the pulpit first thing.

"Good evening, folks. Tonight's services are going to be a little different. It happens that someone has a need to bring before the church so we'll start with a song of invitation."

A big smile lit Uncle Elmer's face as he stood, called the page number, and led us in a song. I was about to do a right thing, and everybody in the room loved and supported me. Still, my heart flopped like a catfish in a tow sack. Aunt Sis slipped me her horse trader's wink from the piano bench, though, and that gave me the courage to send my wheelchair up the aisle.

"Coming home, coming home, nevermore to roam. Open wide thine arms of love, Lord I'm coming home."

"Chester Joel Durham has come forward," Brother Crawford said when the music stopped, "professing Christ as his savior and expressing a desire to be scripturally baptized into the membership of this church. You all know Ches. What's the mind of the church in this matter?"

"I move that we accept the young man as a candidate for baptism and after baptism full fellowship with the church."

The welcoming words came from a lean, baldheaded gentleman I'd met in church and seen around the sale barn, but in the excitement of the moment I couldn't recall his name.

"I'll second that motion," Uncle Elmer called hardily from where he stood.

"All in favor let it be known by the usual sign," Brother Crawford said, and church members raised their hands as one. "Opposed, likewise," he invited. My throat tightened as he paused for a moment, and I was glad to hear him finish with, "Of course, there is no opposition. We're mighty glad to have you, Ches."

"I'm glad, too," I managed, clasping his hand.

"Terry and Jenna Durham, Ches's parents, are only with us for a short while, so I took the liberty of making special arrangements for the baptism ahead of time."

"Amen," came from a couple of members as they voiced their approval.

"Because the steps leading down to the baptistery might prove difficult for our brother, we're going to leave here and assemble again in church capacity at the old swimming hole on Miss Sis Durham's place. Most of us have been there at one time or another, so if you're not sure of your directions just tag along with somebody. First, though, I'd ask that you come by and give Ches the right hand of church and Christian fellowship as Brother Elmer leads us in another song."

"Amazing Grace how sweet the sound, that saved a wretch like me. I once was lost, but now am found, was blind but now I see."

The congregation filed passed me in a blur of handshakes, hugs, and happy congratulations, but a few of them stood out sharply. Mr. Bowie Tate spoke into my ear as he pounded me on the back.

"Miss Sis called Lillian this morning, and we wouldn't have missed this for the world."

"Thank you, sir," I managed and squeezed his hand for all I was worth.

Daddy, Mom, Papa Joel, and Aunt Hattie all took their extra few seconds with me. A few more folks filed by before I noticed that Uncle Elmer had stopped singing, leaving the rest of them to carry on without him.

I looked up in time to watch him step down off the platform and over to the piano. Tears ran openly from my aunt's eyes, but she kept playing until he reached down and took her by the hand.

Uncle Elmer lifted his niece off the piano bench and drew her close, almost supporting her as they walked toward me. A lump rose in my throat, and I moved to meet them. Elmer Blakely was a plainspoken man, almost gruff at times, but his tender, caring way with Aunt Sis touched my heart.

If I knew my aunt, she was laser focused on doing her job well.

"You can cry, Sis Durham," she'd tell herself, "but don't miss a note."

Uncle Elmer knew how special this night was for her, and he knew she would regret not making it through the line to hug my neck. So, being a practical, get-things-done type fellow, he just gathered her up and brought her to me.

"Oh, Ches," was all Aunt Sis managed as she hugged my neck, but she proved more talkative on the way out to the swimming hole. "I'm very proud of you, honey, and I'm proud of your parents, too. They may not think too much of me or the way I've spent my life, but Terry and Jenna truly want what's best for you."

The long summer evening afforded us plenty of daylight, and Brother Crawford supported me as we waded out into the swimming hole, both of us fully clothed.

"Oh happy day that fixed my choice on thee, my Savior and my God. Well may this glowing heart rejoice and tell it's raptures all abroad."

I thought the lack of my aunt's fine piano playing would really hurt the singing, but added enthusiasm in the voices made up the difference.

"Once again," Brother Crawford said when they finished, "Ches has come forward professing Christ as his Savior and desiring to become a member of McKendrick Missionary Baptist Church." His words ran together for a moment as my eyes locked on Aunt Sis standing there with Daddy, Mom, and Papa Joel.

"Thank You, Lord," was my grateful prayer. "Oh, thank You!"

"I baptize you my brother," the old preacher continued, "in the name of the Father, the Son, and the Holy Ghost. Buried with Him in the likeness of His death and raised to walk in a newness of life."

"Well, Ches Durham," I thought as water ran off me, "just how do you intend to live this new life?"

Chapter Fourteen

Nobody lives a perfect life. Miss Sis Durham taught me that by example, but she also showed me the way to a better life. Even as Brother Crawford raised me, dripping wet, to the surface, I vowed I'd be a stronger Christian going forward.

"That's a fine thing, honey," Aunt Sis said when I shared my resolution the next day, "but your new life began way back when you placed your faith and trust in Jesus Christ."

"Yes'm, I know. It's just… My spiritual growth kind of stalled out until I found McKendrick and you."

Never comfortable with praise for herself, my aunt brushed off the statement and rode up beside me in the center of the large arena. She stopped her palomino gelding and surveyed mine with an expert eye.

"Twister's traveling pretty well on those new shoes. What say we try him outside?"

My parents and Papa Joel had gone home, leaving us to our normal routine, but there was nothing normal about Aunt Sis riding over to the big gate and reaching casually down to open it.

I felt my stomach muscles tighten and tasted fear at the back of my throat, but good old Nash spoke before I could.

"You mighty sure about that, Miss Sis?" he asked from just outside the arena.

"We won't get out of a walk, and he can hold on to the saddle horn," she answered. "I just thought we'd ease down yonder and look at the cows. Of course, it's entirely up to Ches and what makes him feel the most comfortable."

Swallowing hard, I mustered a grin from somewhere.

"Open the gate, boss lady. I'm right behind you."

Observing the smile that lit my aunt's eyes and softened her features, I felt well rewarded for hiding my uncertainty. We left Nash to finish up some chores around the barn and rode out into the cow pasture. Twister seemed content with our lazy pace, but Trouble danced and pranced as Aunt Sis held him back. I clung to the saddle horn with my right hand, held the reins loose in my left, and slowly started to enjoy our ride.

Aunt Sis pointed out the dry conditions but remarked that her cows had picked up some flesh since we pulled the big calves out of the pasture. The cattle were scattered out grazing or hold up in small bunches in the shade. When my aunt spotted one bunch across a small creek, she turned in the saddle to face me.

"Do you feel like moseying over there, Ches? I'd like to look at those cows, but it's not something we have to do right now."

I surveyed the creek crossing and swallowed hard. The streambed was narrow and almost dry, but the red-clay banks looked plenty steep.

"It's whatever you think, Aunt Sis. I hate to hold you back. Still, this ain't Saturday, and I don't really want a bath."

Aunt Sis rocked back in the saddle and then leaned forward over her horse's neck. I wondered briefly if she might be fighting for breath but soon recognized her laughter.

"That does it, Ches. It's over. Your poor mama's won a lot of battles, but she's lost the war. You're about as country as they come." With that, she relaxed her hold on the bridle reins and allowed Trouble to start down into the creek. "Hold tight to that saddle horn," she called back over her shoulder, "and trust your horse. He'll carry you across in good sh—"

I started obediently after her, but Trouble put a sudden end to the reassuring words. About halfway down, he stuck his head between his knees and let out a blood-curdling bawl. Twister understood the situation better than I did. He wheeled suddenly and plunged back up the near bank.

By the time he stopped, with the creek safely between us and Trouble's rodeo show, I was almost completely out of the saddle. I must have dropped my reins and latched onto the horn with both hands. Only that white-knuckled grip kept me from hitting the ground. Twister stood perfectly still while I clawed my way back up to an upright position and then sat there shaking.

Aunt Sis couldn't pull her horse's head up. It was too far gone, but that didn't keep her from raking the yellow hair from his sides with her spurs. I sat there watching and wondered what in the world I would do if she got hurt. I felt safe enough for the moment but didn't know if I could ride back to the sale barn, even at a slow walk.

I managed to work my left foot back into the stirrup, but the right leg and ankle refused to cooperate. Giving up on that useless task, I gathered my reins from up around Twisters ears and tried to gather my thoughts as well. The tears on my cheeks didn't mean much until I saw somebody bouncing toward me in the gasoline Mule. Then, I wiped hurriedly at them with my sleeve.

"You alright, Ches?" Jim Rex asked as he pulled alongside.

"I reckon so. We started down into the creek, and—"

"I saw most of it. Let me get you down off that horse."

"No sir," I said, surprising myself a little, "not while Aunt Sis is working so hard to stay on. If you'll just slide my foot back into the stirrup, I believe I can ride home with her after the dust settles."

"Hard headed as a rock," he muttered, "just like every Durham I ever knew." Even so, he slid my booted foot firmly into place and gave my britches leg an encouraging little tug as if to say, "I'm right here with you, pard."

"Do you think she can ride him," I asked, hating the doubt in my question even as I spoke.

"I know she can, but whether she ought to or not is a different story."

Trouble finally got enough of Aunt Sis and those spurs. He picked his head up and decided it was easier to play by her rules. She rode him back and forth across the creek about ten times but never did stop to look at that little bunch of cattle.

"Hello, Jim Rex," she said brightly as she finally stopped beside us. "Where did you come from on this fine morning?"

"Fine morning my big toe," he grumbled. "Little Herman sold you a crippled and a fool. With enough special care, the crippled may make a horse for Ches. That one you're on… He might make good soap, but that's all he's fit for. He'll never be dependable, and you know it."

"He's sure got a loose wire somewhere," she admitted, "but he's a dead ringer for Ches's horse. I can handle him."

"Well, you've never had any sense where your own safety was concerned, so I don't expect any different now. This boy, though… That's twice you've nearly let him fall off." Aunt Sis stiffened, and her easy smile died. She took the words fall off as an insult to our family name, but Jim Rex didn't give her a chance to tear into him. "You were a little busy at the time, Sis, but I had a real good view of Ches hanging from the side of his horse."

"He's in fine shape now," she countered, "sitting right square in the middle."

"Yeah, and if that gelding of his didn't have such good sense, he could have ended up right square under your horse's feet."

Aunt Sis sucked in a sharp breath and looked to me for confirmation. I nodded regretfully, and she glanced away, reaching for a cigarette.

"Don't feel bad, Aunt Sis," I said quickly. "It's not your fault. I don't have much balance or leg strength."

Seeing her weaken, Jim Rex pressed his advantage.

"Why not at least check into safety saddles, Sis? It's about time I went steppin' out with a pretty lady anyhow. You bring Ches, I'll bring my kids, and we'll make a date of it Monday. We can see that guy at Marshall who built himself a safety rig and then go eat or take in a movie or some such thing."

Aunt Sis tried to speak casually as if she were more interested in her cigarette than any possible plans for Monday, but I could tell it hurt her to admit she might have misjudged my ability to ride a regular saddle.

"That fellow used to be a fairly good customer at the barn. I reckon it wouldn't hurt to pay a call on him. If he wants to show us one of those contraptions you keep talking about… Well, it wouldn't be polite not to look."
"Translation," the auctioneer quipped, shooting me a wink. "You're right, Jim Rex. I'm sorry I've been so dead-set against your very reasonable suggestion."

"Come along, Ches, we can't sit around all day and listen to the wind blow."

"Yes ma'am," I answered stoutly and clucked Twister into motion.

Given her druthers, Aunt Sis would have galloped off, leaving Jim Rex to sputter in our dust. I couldn't manage anything much faster than a walk, so we rode away with heads held high and dignity intact. She did, anyway. I looked back with a grin and a shrug. Anyhow, we didn't get very far before he overtook us in the Mule.

"Wait up a minute, Sis. I came out here hunting you for a reason."

"I know," she sniffed, stopping her horse, "to clown around and make your little jokes at my expense."

"No, no, there was something besides that. Oh, yeah," he said with a snap of his fingers. "I need you to come up to the bank and co-sign on Serena Kate's car note."

"That girl needs a brand-new car like I need the horse market to bottom out."

"She really wanted that little hotrod you put Terry in, but I wouldn't even let her ask you to price it. I figured you'd try to let us have it way too cheap. A new Cavalier makes more sense for her first car, and this deal will be fair to everybody."

"Especially fair to the Chevrolet house," Aunt Sis commented. "Why can't you sign for her? I remember a time when the McKendrick name and a handshake were good enough to get you a blank draw note."

"Ex-wives are hard on the credit, and Amos Earl says these newfangled bank examiners don't put much stock in a handshake. You know I'm good for it, Sis, but if you don't want to sign, I'll see about a loan from the car dealer."

"We'll meet you up there directly," she answered with a sigh. "I need to put Ches on my bank account incase... When the colonel... Well, you know, they froze his accounts. I'd have likely starved out and the horse sale along with me if we hadn't had a plenty of cash on hand."

"Don't talk that-a-way, Sis. You're good for fifty or sixty more years."

"Just so I live long enough to see this car note paid off; that'll suit you and Serena Kate."

A gentle, teasing tone took the sting out of her words. Still, the sudden talk of putting her affairs in order made me uncomfortable and seemed to bother Jim Rex, too.

The Friday night horse sale wasn't anything special. Aunt Sis said the summer heat was hard on our business. Sunday, though, I experienced my first service as a member of McKendrick Missionary Baptist Church. People who hadn't made it out for my baptism welcomed me to the church family, and I felt more at home than ever.

Without putting her wishes into words, Aunt Sis made it clear that she'd rather sit beside me than favor one interested gentleman over the other. Andrew found a seat with some folks he'd met at the horse sale, but Jim Rex and family crowded onto our bench.

Andrew finally managed to catch a word with her out at the van.

"I hate to talk business at church, Miss Sis, but do you have anybody who could ride my horses and keep them legged up for me while I'm working?"

"What about the man you hired to see after the dogs?"

"News travels fast. He's good with the dogs and handy around the place, but riding is above his pay grade."

"Scooter can do it," she said with a smile. "He's a pretty good little hand, especially if you're gone clear down to Houston and don't have to listen to his motor mouth."

The tall, dark-haired bird hunter grinned in response to her little joke.

"I'll pay whatever you think is fair to compensate the boy for his work and you for the loss of his time."

"You needn't worry about compensating me. Five dollars an hour will take care of Scooter, and I'll see that he earns it. If you'd like, I'll even take a look at your dogs every now and then."

"Thank you, ma'am, I'll rest easier knowing you've got your eye on the place while I'm gone."

"That's what neighbors are for," she said lightly, "and we can be good neighbors as long as you've put aside the notion of scarfing up my land."

She turned away then, but he stopped her with a hand on the elbow.

"I'd like to be more than good neighbors, Miss Sis. Won't you let me take you out sometime? With your permission, Ches," he added with a quick smile. "If she's interested in going, I mean."

"She's interested," I assured him, making my aunt blush prettily.

"That's good news," he said. "Still, with our conflicting work schedules…"

"I'll be available next Saturday afternoon," Aunt Sis put in, "but I may not be very good company the day after a horse sale."

"You're always good company, Miss Sis, as far as I'm concerned."

"Two dates in one week," I said, teasing my aunt as she drove us home.

"Do you think it's disloyal?" she asked worriedly. "To Jim Rex, I mean."

"Disloyal to the fellow who married three other women while you stood patiently by, loving his children and supplying him with a steady job? Not hardly! I'm a little put out, though, because I finally get to spend some time with you and the doggone wedding bells start clanging."

"They'll both break and run before it comes to that," she quipped. "You've seen how Jim Rex and I can get under one another's skin. And poor Andrew… Well, it won't take him long to get tired of a chronically nervous, hopelessly old-fashioned, hard-headed country girl."

"You're always listing your so-called bad points, and I'm about tired of it. My Aunt Sis is quite the catch: independent businesswoman, fearless cowgirl, and the truest definition of a lady I've ever known."

"You better quit, Ches," she sniffled. "You'll fool around and make me cry."

When the phone rang early Monday morning, I buzzed into the kitchen to answer it.

"Durham residents, this is Ches."

"Hey—"

"Hi there, Serena Kate, hold on a minute. I'll get Aunt Sis."

"In case you haven't noticed, Ches, your aunt is one of those strange people who take pride in getting up before the rooster. I don't want to hear, 'Good morning, sweetheart! Ain't it a beautiful day?' while it's still dark outside."

"Turn off the lights," I suggested, "and then look out a window. It's not as dark as you think."

"Whatever; I'm up way too early and thinking about our little trip this afternoon."

"We're going to Marshall to look at a saddle, right?"

"Yes, but I want it to be more than that. Pop and Miss Sis have danced around each other for most of my life. He's kinda in awe of her, thinking he ain't good enough. Miss Sis likes him fine, but she's too much of a lady to do the asking herself."

"Yeah," I said slowly into the silence. "but where do we come in?"

"We can all squeeze into your van, see a man about a saddle, and let it turn out like most of their so-called dates, or we can make it something special for them."

"Special sounds good to me, but I would like to look at the saddle."

"No wonder you and Miss Sis get along so well. You've got her one track mind. We'll look at the stinkin' saddle."

"Okay… What's the rest of the plan?"

"Seth can drive your van: me and him, you and Scooter. We'll put the love birds in my new car. The saddle man's name is Darrel Lancer. I just about turned the office upside down, but I found an old auction ticket with his address and phone number on it. Mrs. Lancer said they'd be looking for us sometime this afternoon."

"Thanks for setting things up, Serena Kate."

"Somebody had to do it. Your aunt doesn't think much of this safety saddle business, and Pop's nearly helpless without her to nudge him along in the right direction. Their first real date was at a bowling alley, and we're going bowling after you see the saddle."

"It sounds like a good plan, but what can I do?"

"No plan sounds good to Miss Sis unless it's hers. I need you to bring her around to the idea of taking two cars. Tell her you want to spend a little time with the younger set, or think of something better."

"Well, it wouldn't take much to do better than that."

"I guess not. Anyway, she and Pop won't know about the bowling alley. They'll just follow us on into Marshall and right down memory lane."

We talked on for a minute, and then I hung the receiver back in its cradle with a smile. Despite her super-cool teenage attitude, Serena Kate adored my aunt and wanted her for a real stepmother.

"Who was on the phone?" Aunt Sis inquired as she bustled in from feeding the dogs.

"Serena Kate," I answered, and my aunt glanced wryly at the wall clock.

"Is she awake early, or up late?" Then, a frown creased her forehead. "They all okay over there?"

"Yes'm, everybody's fine as far as I know. Are we sure enough going with them to look at the saddle? We don't have to if you're uncomfortable with the whole idea of safety saddles."

"Uncomfortable don't half get it, Ches, but I'll do things for you that nobody else could ever talk me into. Besides, I already told Jim Rex we'd go."

"Well, Serena Kate thinks she and I and her brothers should take the van over there while Jim Rex drives you in the new Cavalier."

"If we're not all gonna ride together, I'd as soon take the colonel's old pickup and smoke whenever I feel like it."

"I don't know… She's got this plan."

Surprisingly, my aunt gave in with a smile.

"My signature's on the note," she quipped. "I might as well ride."

Mr. Lancer, a big man with a head full of salt-and-pepper hair, drug his left foot badly when he walked. Talking gave him fits, too. But his bright-eyed wife seemed willing and able to get his point across. She told us how they missed making their rounds to the various horse sales, and he reminded her that Durham Auction Company was the only one of their old haunts still putting on regularly scheduled sales. He stepped up and hugged Aunt Sis, though I gathered they'd never been particularly close.

"Darrel says he's mighty proud of you, Miss Sis," his wife explained, "and your daddy would be, too."

"Thank you, sir," Aunt Sis answered, speaking directly to him. "I thank you, too, Mrs. Lancer, for having us here."

"Y'all have already made our day," the lady assured her. "We don't get much company around here, or many customers, either, in the hot summertime. If you could see your way clear to buy something and pay just a little too much, it would keep Darrel happy for a month."

"I'll say one thing, Darrel," Jim Rex guffawed. "If you can get the best of Miss Sis Durham, you've done something. She'll squeeze a nickel 'til the Indian rides the buffalo."

A broad grin spread across Mr. Lancer's face, and it finally spilled over into a loud laugh that we all understood. He and his wife showed us an old but well-made western saddle with what looked like a receiver hitch sticking up behind the cantle. The back from an office chair, with its own hitch attached, slid into place and bolted there.

"A flank strap is generally attached to the riggin' on a rodeo bronc," Mrs. Lancer explained. "It makes the horse buck harder. They put quick-release latches on 'em so as to snatch 'em off in a hurry. This here flank strap is anchored to the chair back and makes a seatbelt for the rider."

My aunt's face showed a genuine fondness for these folks, but right alongside it I detected a polite, determined rejection of the whole business. Mr. Lancer picked up on it, too. Pointing and gesturing, he showed me how to pull the quick release and get myself out of a bind. I glanced toward Aunt Sis and, for the first time, saw a flicker of doubt. Normally, Jim Rex would have pounced on her weakening resolve, but I was the one who finally spoke.

"The design looks workable to me."

"Do you really think it's something you want to try, Ches?" Aunt Sis finally asked. "Things can happen awfully fast. Why, you could be mashed under your horse before your hand ever finds that cord."

"I'll never have your quick reaction time, Aunt Sis," I reminded her gently. "I'm liable to get hung up, even in a regular saddle. If I'm going to ride we'll just have to take all the precautions we can and leave the rest in the Lord's hands."

"Darrel says that's the only way to look at it," Mrs. Lancer put in as her husband nodded his head to back me up.

"A good, gentle horse is one precaution," Jim Rex added, "and it looks to me like this safety saddle is another. Maybe if the boy's not so worried about staying on top, he can actually learn something about how to handle a horse."

"Well," Aunt Sis said with a sigh, "I can't fight all of you. Mr. Lancer, would you mind if we brought my nephew's horse over here sometime and let him try your saddle?"

Either Mr. Lancer didn't like that idea or he had a better one. We waited uncertainly for his wife to bridge the communication gap.

"I ordered Darrel a handmade tree for his birthday last year, and he built himself a new saddle from scratch."

"Handmade tree?" I questioned.

"The tree is the skeleton or frame of a saddle," Aunt Sis explained. "They're made of wood or some other material and covered over with the leatherwork."

"Darrel wants Ches to take this old modified rig home and try it there. Then, if you're interested in buying it, he'll take six-hundred."

"Six-hundred dollars?" Aunt Sis shied away from the saddle like a colt from a new gate.

Mr. Lancer laughed until he almost cried, even going so far as to point at her.

"He says you're just as tight-fisted as your daddy was," Mrs. Lancer admitted, sounding more than a little embarrassed.

Aunt Sis seemed to brighten up under this odd, left-handed complement. Before we left she handed Mr. Lancer six crisp one-hundred-dollar bills.

"If the rig don't work out for Ches, I'll re-sell it." Mr. Lancer's eyebrows shot up in an exaggerated questioning look. "I'll make money on it, too, or my name's not Sis Durham."

Tears showed in the big man's eyes, and Aunt Sis reached out uncertainly to lay a hand on his arm.

"Darrel wants to thank you. Nobody else will joke and carry on with him like they did in the old days. Old friends look at his condition and feel sorry…"

"Sorry," Aunt Sis snorted, "anybody who's still got enough nerve to ask six-hundred dollars for a wore-out stock saddle with the back off a busted chair bolted onto it don't need my sympathy."

"You'll do, Miss Sis."

These four words came out slurred and uncertain, but Darrel Lancer got them said without help from his wife or anybody else. Seth toted the saddle, and Aunt Sis hung close beside my wheelchair as we drifted back toward the cars in a bunch.

"Are you glad we came, Ches?"

"Yes'm," I answered whole heartedly.

"Then I'm glad, too," she said, resting one hand lightly on my shoulder. "That old saddle may or may not be the answer, but we'll sure find out. I promise you this: As long as you've got the want-to, I'll keep you a'horseback one way or the other."

"So where do we go from here?"

Jim Rex directed the question to my aunt, but Serena Kate answered in a teasing tone.

"That's not for you and Miss Sis to worry about. Just climb into the car and follow us."

"Kinda bossy today, ain't she?" Jim Rex asked, looking around at the rest of the group.

"I don't much care where we go," Aunt Sis admitted, "but I'm smoking before I get back in that car."

The hour-long drive followed by another hour of visiting meant nothing to me except a new saddle, time spent with good friends, and the anticipation of Serena Kate's surprise. Now, for the first time, I considered the discomfort my aunt had endured without so much as a single complaint.

Though she obviously enjoyed smoking, it also caused her a great deal of misery. Of course, to her way of thinking, it was doing without her cigarettes that made things hard. Everybody in our little group loved her, but the others made jokes and tried to rush her while I worried over her distress. Aunt Sis bore their teasing good-naturedly and, instead of worrying, took a direct approach to fixing the problem. She smoked two cigarettes in rapid succession, and we went on our way.

When we pulled up and parked in front of the bowling alley, Serena Kate could barely contain her excitement.

"This'll be great; they're going to love it!"

The girl usually moved a bit slower than average, showing the same languid grace as her father. Now, she bounded out of the van and over to the passenger door of her little sports car.

"You gonna let Sis get out, or not," Jim Rex asked quizzically as the rest of us came up to them.

"Not until you come over here and open her door."

"Oh, right."

Slapping his cowboy hat into place, he hurried around the car and snatched the door open. Aunt Sis extended a hand to him and rose from her seat like they did it every day.

"I declare," she drawled, "these children do listen when we get to reliving the good old days."

"Every now and then," Scooter qualified, "but I still don't believe you walked two miles to school, uphill both ways."

"I never told you that," she said, wrinkling her pretty nose at the distasteful thought. "I would have loved to ride my horse to school, but I never did that, either."

"Sorry, guess I got you mixed up with some other old lady."

"It won't be so funny, Scooter McKendrick, when I snatch you up by the ear. You can holler, 'She's not my mama,' all you want to. Nobody's gonna help you."

"Well, that's what the teachers at school told us to do if somebody grabbed us. I still say it would've worked if I'd tried it somewhere besides the sale barn. That bunch of crotchety old horse traders just enjoyed the show. Instead of coming to help a poor kid out, they hollered things like, 'hit him a lick for me, Miss Sis.'"

Even as I laughed with them, I realized that the McKendrick kids enjoyed memories of my aunt that I could never share. I felt a pang of jealousy but pushed it aside. The years I'd missed with Aunt Sis were gone, and I could never get them back. What I could do was cherish our time together in the here and now.

"You did too ride a horse to school one time," Jim Rex said as we all trooped inside. "In fact, you rode him through the school."

"Well," she answered demurely, "you held the doors open."

"One of them, anyway," he admitted.

"That's right," she remembered, pausing significantly as she turned to face him.

"And now I've said too much," the auctioneer intoned regretfully.

"My real good friend was supposed to run around and let me out the other end, but you turned yellow. There I was, straight-A student and everybody's favorite, bottled up in that hallway on a wild-eyed appaloosa pony. Mr. Stephens would have caught me, too. Only, I squalled like I was callin' the dogs, and Terry heard me. He came hotfooting it over from the junior high and let me out just in the nick of time."

I got to keep my boots because they would stay safely on my wheelchair's footrest and off the bowling lanes, but the rest of the bunch had to rent shoes.

"We need a picture of all them cowboy boots lined up on that shelf," I joked.

"Would you believe I left my camera at home," Serena Kate asked, slapping her forehead dramatically.

"I bowl better with my spurs on, Ches," Jim Rex told me.

"He's only half kidding," my aunt said. "Jim Rex took me to a bowling alley on our first real date, and we went a'horseback."

We all got something to eat, chose our bowling balls, and divided into two teams. Finally, Jim Rex picked up the story again.

"We slipped off from a playday at the riding club and rode on into town. Not McKendrick, I'm talkin' about big town. It was darker than the inside of a cow, and here we go clippity-clop down the side of the highway. Kids can be awfully thickheaded when it comes to danger, and our heads were two of the thickest."

"I wouldn't have gone a-tall," Aunt Sis protested, "but you'd come up with an empty loop in the ribbon roping, again. I felt so bad for you, and those pitiful puppy dog eyes got to me."

"Go on now, you know it was my cowboy charm."

"Well, it sure wasn't your ropin' skills that impressed me."

"Hey," he joked, the pain of boyhood failures softened by the years, "I never caught my horse's front feet but once."

"That, sir, is quite an accomplishment. No wonder I lost my heart."

"Did you really, Sis? I never lost mine; it's been safe and sound in your pocket all along."

I missed hearing whether Aunt Sis returned his tender words in kind or said something like, "What about these young'nes and the three women you married?" because Serena Kate rolled the prettiest gutter ball you'd ever want to see and hurried back to whisper in my ear.

"This is good stuff, Ches. What did I tell you?"

I couldn't quite share Serena Kate's eager optimism, but things rocked along nicely until Aunt Sis rolled a strike.

"Yes siree, Bob! Don't never bet against Miss Sis Durham," Scooter yelled at the top of his voice. "I'll take a spot on her team any old day."

Aunt Sis laughed, hugged him, and gave me a squeeze for good measure.

"On that triumphant note," she said, "I believe I'll go have a cigarette."
I waited for Jim Rex to say he'd go along and keep her company, but the offer never came. Even if I couldn't always open up doors or pull out chairs, I knew better than to let a lady stand outside a public place in the cold or hot or whatever all by herself.

"Mind if I come," I asked.

"Why, no," Aunt Sis assured me, but Jim Rex had to put his two cents in.

"Taking up smoking, Ches?"

"Not tonight," I answered dryly.

None of us had paid much attention to the big celebration taking place a couple of lanes over, but an elderly lady with balloons tied to her walker blocked our path to the exit.

"Happy birthday, ma'am," Aunt Sis said sweetly and tried to slip around her.
"Thank you, young lady," the birthday girl replied, whipping that walker around like a cutting horse locked onto a cow. "Did I hear one of those little boys say your name was Durham?"

"Yes ma'am," Aunt Sis said, working hard to ignore her pressing need for a cigarette. "I'm Sis Durham of Durham Auction Company in McKendrick, Texas. This is my nephew, Ches Durham, and we run a weekly horse sale."

"I can't feature anybody buying a horse in this day and time," the old lady observed, but she moved on quickly. "Ches? You say this boy's name is Ches?"

"Yes ma'am," I interjected.

"I knew it was worth a try!"

"What's that?" Aunt Sis asked politely.

"Cornering you this way," our new acquaintance answered. "It was a long shot but… My name is Gladys Coleman, and many years ago, I met a handsome young cowboy named Chester Durham."

Aunt Sis forgot the cigarette, she forgot Jim Rex, and I think for a second there she might have even forgotten me.

"There never was but one," she said in a husky voice, reaching across the walker to clasp the old woman's hand. "You met my daddy, and I'd like very much to hear about it."

"Well, it's my birthday party, but I don't think the grandkids and great-grandkids will even know I'm gone. What about you two? Y'all looked to be on a mission."

"I was just stepping out to smoke, but that can wait."

"Don't wait, child." Gladys advised bluntly. "You'll feel worse, not better, for the delay."

"I expect you're right."

"You know I am. Now, lead the way."

"You don't need to tell me twice, Mrs. Coleman," my aunt quipped and sailed on toward the exit.

"Mrs. Coleman was my mother-in-law, and not a particularly loving one," she quavered as Aunt Sis settled her gently onto a convenient bench. "Call me Gladys."

"The colonel raised me to give respect where it's due," Aunt Sis explained, finally lighting herself a cigarette, "and I've expected no less from his grandson. We'll do our best to remember, Gladys, but you'll have to pardon any little slips."

"The kids all think I've quit," Gladys said, watching my aunt with obvious envy. "They're the ones who've quit, quit buying me any. Picking them up from the store, I should say. It's my money."

Aunt Sis made a sympathetic noise in the back of her throat and quickly extended her pack to Gladys.

"I suppose they think they're helping you but…"

My aunt trailed off with a little shudder that made Gladys chuckle flatly.

"If I hadn't let Chester Durham get away, I might've ended up with a daughter like you, one who would understand. You say he made a colonel? I never figured him for an army career, too independent."

"Not a military colonel, Daddy spent his working life as an auctioneer. By saying you met him, do you mean y'all exchanged pleasantries on the sidewalk?"

"It wasn't much more than that. I was young and impressionable, and he was… Well, you knew him longer than I did."

"Yes'm, but this business of letting him get away sounds pretty serious."

"Foolishness really, I married well and spent fifty-two years with the love of my life. Still, when a young girl gives a piece of her heart… Let's just say your daddy captured my imagination."

"I wish I'd been around to study his method," I announced, and both ladies laughed.

"We met back in the late '30s. My Papa ran the railroad depot here in town. On this particular day, Mama sent me down there with his lunch. This was cotton-raising country then, and the railroad wasn't particularly accommodating to livestock people."

"Before stock trailers and paved highways, railroads were the only game in town, so to speak," Aunt Sis put in for my benefit. "They weren't real strong on customer service, and they didn't have to be."

"That's right," Gladys agreed. "Papa followed the unofficial policy of the T&P. Company men up here in the farm country considered it a favor to even haul live freight. Nowadays, people will go to a lot of trouble for the privilege of living on a little piece of land. Back then, and I'm ashamed to admit it, some of us here in town thought we were just a little bit better than the rural folks."

"Funny thing," Aunt Sis said a little icily, "every businessman in this town depended on the rural trade for his living. Farm folks probably ate better than ninety percent of the townspeople, too."

"Right or wrong, that attitude didn't make things any easier for Chester. Like I said, this was farm country, but anybody who kept more than a milk cow or two eventually wound up with some cattle they couldn't pin. Chester made a swing up through the country and bought a bunch of these half-wild animals. He brought a friend with him, a boy called Harman Lee, and traded with the understanding they would catch the animals themselves."

"Parmalee, Miss Sis corrected. Uncle Doc was a pretty good cowboy, too, in his day."

"They'd gathered their cattle, brought them through town to the rickety little set of pens at the depot, and ordered a stockcar. When the car finally came, they loaded their cattle, only to have them sidelined to make way for a shipment of perishable goods."

"Daddy took that?"

"Chester wasn't your daddy yet, child. He was a raw country kid, maybe nineteen or twenty, and my Papa held all the advantage."

"I see," my aunt said, but her voice still held some doubt.

"Chester didn't like the situation, but like you he'd been raised to respect his elders."

"I never knew the colonel," I admitted when the old lady fell silent. "I know his daughter, though. Manners and respect mean a lot, but if they're all one-sided it's, 'Pass me that quirt; he'll sing a different tune when I get through.'"

"Now, Ches," my aunt chided gently, but Gladys threw back her head and laughed.

"When I swished my new pink skirt through the door, Chester quit wrangling with Papa. Like I said, he was fresh from the country, but he stepped right up and spoke to me."

"Daddy was nothing if not direct."

"In Fort Worth or somewhere further west, I suppose he might've looked like a farm boy with his narrow-brimmed southern hat and low-topped boots, but here in Marshall he looked like a real cavalier of the range. He pulled off that little Stetson and held it over his heart when he spoke to me. If memory serves, he even made the tiniest of bows in my direction. 'How do, missy? I'm Chester Durham from over around McKendrick, and I'd be mighty pleased to make your acquaintance.'"

Gladys smiled at the memory and then gazed down regretfully at what little remained of her cigarette. Noticing, Aunt Sis reached quickly for the pack, but the older lady seemed to hesitate.

"Please help yourself. After an hour I've got an impossible case of the jitters. Two hours will bring on a sick headache and a mighty short fuse. I don't even want to contemplate a situation like yours."

"Thank you, child, your daddy was thoughtful and so are you."

"Trust you and Miss Sis to find the only senior citizen around," Scooter whispered in my ear, and I jumped. Louder, he said, "We gave up on bowling when y'all didn't come right back. The rest of them wondered into the arcade to part with their quarters and put their eyes out on them little bitty screens."

"This boy talks sense," Gladys decided. "Is he some kin?"

"He might as well be," Aunt Sis sighed, and made the introductions. "Gladys met the colonel when he was a young man, and she's telling us about it."

"He had a blue roan cowpony with him that day," the old lady continued. "I wouldn't know the difference between a bay and a dun if they trotted up here, but

I'll recognize a blue roan every time. Chester told me what color his horse was, and I've never forgotten it. Before the afternoon ended, I saw him throw his handkerchief down in the street, gallop back by, and pick it up without stopping."

"Daddy always had a good handle on his horses. Did he show you the pony's quick stop and spin him around for you?"

"How did you know?"

"He taught me to ride, and that's what I'd do if I wanted to impress somebody with my horse. I've watched him show more horses than I could count, but he'd aged passed the handkerchief trick before I came along."

"Later," Gladys told us, "he lifted me up onto his horse and jogged us down to the drugstore for an ice-cream soda. Now, that was one hot date in 1938 or '39. We'd have gone to the picture show, too, but Papa finally found a place for the Durham stockcar."

"He probably wanted to get that wild cowboy away from his pretty daughter," Aunt Sis guessed with a bright-eyed smile.

"I don't know what all your uncle told him while we were gone, but Papa got them hooked up and hauled out. I almost invited Chester to call on me again. When I thought about the fifty or so miles between us, though, it seemed like a lot to ask. I regretted my shyness for a long time."

"Well, I can't say Mama had an easy life," Aunt Sis ventured, "but she had love and protection. Nobody messed with the colonel's lady."

"Or his little girl, either," Gladys surmised. "The Lord gave me a fine family, and after meeting you all, I'm convinced Chester's life was every bit as full."

"I'll say this for him," Scooter remarked, "the man cast a mighty long shadow."

"He sure enough did," I agreed.

Neither of us had known my grandfather, and yet the colonel was almost a tangible presence in our lives. Before Gladys or Aunt Sis could respond, the bowling alley door banged outward.

"Miss Sis," Serena Kate ordered through angry tears, "get yourself in here this minute."

Scooter shrank back, not so much from Serena Kate as from the wrath he figured her tone would draw from Aunt Sis. As it turned out, though, my aunt's first reaction was one of concern.

"What's the matter, sweetheart? Is something wrong with Seth or Jim Rex?"

"Seth's alright, but Pop… You've done it to him again."

Chapter Fifteen

Done it to— Settle down, Serena Kate, and tell me what's wrong."

"You sat around with your hands folded sweetly in your lap and let Pop fall for the wrong kind of woman three times. All you ever had to do was crook your finger at him, but no, it was the colonel this and the horse sale that. Now, you're out here smoking your precious cigarettes and gabbing while he stumbles into the same trap again."

I expected some major fireworks, but Aunt Sis turned calmly back to Gladys.

"Please excuse this young lady. She was raised better. I've truly enjoyed visiting with you, but it seems I'm needed inside. Keep the pack," she added as an afterthought. "They won't let me smoke in the car anyway."

"Poor child, that's how it starts. Not in the car, not in the house, and then they cut you off altogether." My aunt paid little attention to this warning, but Gladys's next words stopped her with one hand on the door. "Sis Durham, whoever he is, if you can't leave him alone for thirty minutes…"

"Yes'm," Aunt Sis replied, glancing sadly over her shoulder, "I know."

Scooter's face showed a deeper concern than I had ever seen there before. He and I started after the boss lady, but Gladys called me back.

"Wait a minute, Ches. I'd like to stay in touch with you and your aunt."

I fumbled around trying to swap contact information until Scooter whipped out one of my aunt's business cards.

"Sorry to run off, ma'am, but we got trouble. Get a move on, Ches."

Jim Rex's white, button-down shirt stood out in the dimly lit arcade room. He had turned in the bowling shoes by then. I noticed because he seemed to be giving his boots a lot of attention. Seth drifted over to stand solemnly with me and his little brother.

"Looks as guilty as an egg suckin' dog, don't he?"

Scooter didn't try to answer, and I sure couldn't come up with the right words. Seth's analogy pretty well summed up the scene. Old Jim Rex stood there with his head hung down mumbling some kind of response to Aunt Sis. Behind him, time ran out on his chance to snag a small stuffed animal with an automated claw. The machine squealed and flashed, wanting more quarters.

My aunt's voice hardly rose above a whisper, but her back and shoulders looked like they were set in concrete. Maybe, if Miss Sis had stuck her finger in Jim Rex McKendrick's face, stomped up and down and pitched a general hissy fit, the well-built young blond would've unpeeled herself from his side. As it was, she just hung there, trying to turn his attention back to the claw machine and her prize.

Suddenly, I found myself shaking with anger and wishing I was physically able to thrash Jim Rex within an inch of his life. The colonel wasn't here and never would be again. Somehow, I felt responsible. Jim Rex had been good to me, and Scooter was my best friend, but all that mattered was my Aunt Sis and the scattered pieces of her tender heart.

I considered all kinds of ways to make Jim Rex pay, but none of them would have done Aunt Sis a bit of good. All she wanted was to get out of there with as little public fuss as possible. She swept out of the arcade, and we three boys followed along in her wake. Serena Kate tried to stay with her daddy, but I caught his parting words.

"Go along with Miss Sis, sugar bear. She may need you. Now, don't cry; I'll see you sometime tomorrow."

"I'll drive," Aunt Sis insisted when Seth started to climb behind the wheel of my van.

Those two words were all she said between there and home. The country oldies station played an awful lot of Hank Williams, Sr. while the McKendrick boys and I talked in respectful whispers like we might have used at somebody's funeral. Serena Kate wept noisily, but Aunt Sis never made a sound. Occasionally, though, the glow of a streetlight showed her tear-wet cheeks.

"Home again," I said softly as old Puddler ran from under the house to meet the van.

"Yes, we're home," my aunt echoed in a surprisingly strong voice. "Y'all might as well spend the night," she told the McKendricks. "No use going back to that big, empty house."

The word empty came on a sob, but this small sign of weakness passed quickly.

"Pop might come—" Serena Kate started doubtfully, but Scooter cut her off.

"I'm stayin' here."

"We got nobody waiting up town," Seth observed, laying a gentle hand on his sister's shoulder. "Pop'll be back when he's good and ready, but I think we're better off here for the time being."

Because Aunt Sis never locked her door, Serena Kate was able to run inside and give it a good slam while the rest of us watched from the yard. A few minutes later, though, she took my place in the swing. Clinging close to Aunt Sis, she never even fussed about the smoke.

I can't say who slept and who didn't, but we passed the night. Seth and Scooter made quick work of morning chores, taking me with them to supervise from the Mule. The previous evening's ordeal didn't damage their appetites much. They ate everything Aunt Sis put in front of them.

My aunt looked exhausted, and the cigarette between her fingers seemed almost permanent. When she spoke to us, though, the words came out in a cheerful tone like nothing had ever happened.

"As soon as you boys can get up from the table," she said in a friendly jive at the overstuffed McKendrick brothers, "go catch Ches's horse and get that saddle from the back of the van. Be sure to put a good, thick saddle blanket on him. Those bolts that hold the receiver hitch stick out some on the underside."

"Aunt Sis," I protested weakly, "nobody wants to mess with that this morning."

"I do, and the last time I checked I was still calling the shots around here."

This could have sounded like a reprimand, but she laughed when she said it, running a hand lightly through my hair as she passed behind me to gather the dirty dishes. As it turned out, everybody seemed to enjoy helping me ride. It took our minds off other things.

"That-a-way, Ches," Seth called encouragingly. "Spin him around. Those feet ain't hurting him no more, and he knows how to do it."

Even Serena Kate got in on the fun, snapping more pictures with my aunt's camera. It didn't take Aunt Sis long to come around to the safety saddle once she saw me ride with it.

"I declare, honey, if I'd known that rig would make things so much easier, I'd have gotten you one to start with."

"Well'm," I tried to explain, "in a way it's like driving the buggy. I can concentrate on handling my horse without holding on for dear life."

"Are you comfortable enough to ride outside?" she asked.

"If I'm not ready now, I doubt I ever will be."

"Y'all heard the man; everybody catch a horse. You, too, Nash."

"I haven't been on a horse in six months," Serena Kate moaned, "and I sure can't ride like this," she added indicating the sundress she'd put back on after yesterdays outing.

A frown puckered my aunt's forehead, but Nash offered a solution.

"I'll take her in the buggy, Miss Sis. That'll be easier on these old bones anyhow."

"The day you get too old to ride, Nash Holloway, I'll quit the horse business altogether."

"Not likely," he muttered, smiling as he moved off to catch and harness Mable.

Riding stirrup to stirrup with my aunt, I enjoyed a newfound confidence, and Twister's gentle willingness only added to the feeling. He moved across the pasture without any sign of pain, and did everything I asked of him.

"Little Herman may have tried to cheat me," she said as we rode, "but he did us a favor after all. Horses like Twister don't come along very often. He'll always be a little bit gimpy, but that's because he's had a job and been used hard. On the other side of the coin, he's a good one because he's had a job. We'll keep him shoed right and mix a little bute in his feed when he needs it. You'll never ride him hard enough to know he's crippled."

"Bute?" I questioned.

"It's good for pain and swelling in a horse. You can give it several different ways. I imagine Little Herman mainlined him, put a shot of the stuff right into his jugular, but it's simpler to mix it in the feed."

Everybody bragged on the safety saddle and how well I rode in it, but none of us were foolish enough to credit Jim Rex for his determined promotion of the idea. Aunt Sis and I spent the whole day with the man's kids, and his name never came up once. Sometime after supper, they climbed in Seth's pickup and headed back into McKendrick.

"We alright, Scooter?" I asked quietly just before he shut the passenger door.

"You know it, bud," he said with that easy grin, and they left in a cloud of dust.

The boys showed up for work, regular as ever, all week long. We bought horses, compiled a partial catalog, and answered the inevitable phone calls from people who wanted to know what time the sale would start.

"We've only been doing this on the same day, at the same time, in the same place for nearly fifty years," Aunt Sis told me wearily, but a smile played across her lips as she said it.

I happened to be near my aunt when Serena Kate blew in on Friday afternoon.

"Did you fire Pop? Because if you think I'll just keep on running the office—"

"I didn't fire him, sweetheart. If Jim Rex isn't coming it's because he doesn't want to be here."

The girl's shoulders slumped and all the starch went out of her.

"I was afraid of that. You mean he didn't even let you know he wouldn't be here?" Aunt Sis shook her head slowly in answer. "C-can you still use me in the office? I wouldn't blame you a bit if you ran me off and the boys, too."

"Oh, sweetheart." my aunt said brokenly, and Serena Kate fell into her arms. When the moment passed, I reluctantly raised a question.

"What'll we do without…"

"Just keep the Diet Coke coming," she said with a whimsical little grin. "I'll call the bids myself."

"And keep the books, too?" I wondered.

"He's right, Serena Kate. I can't use you in the office tonight. You know the other girls better than I do; pick somebody reliable to leave in charge. I need you up there beside me."

"Yes'm," the girl answered with a radiant smile.

Aunt Sis cleared her throat a lot and coughed some, but she was an excellent auctioneer. The sale went faster than I had ever seen it, and overall, the horses seemed to bring a shade more. I grinned and chuckled to myself until Andrew Hollister poked me in the ribs.

"Say, what's got into you?"

"Nothing," I answered. "We should've run Jim Rex off a long time ago."

"Run… Where's he at tonight?"

"Don't know and don't care," I answered shortly. "Just look at her sell them horses, Andrew."

"Come on, Ches, what's happened around here?"

"That's for Aunt Sis to tell you, if she will. I wouldn't push it."

Before bed that night, Aunt Sis insisted she'd take me out horseback for the next morning's trail ride, but I said I'd go in the buggy so she could stay home and rest up for her date with Andrew.

"If I'm not as vivacious as I might be," she said trying and failing to hide another yawn, "the gentleman will just have to forgive me. I'm not about to pass up a chance to ride beside you and show everybody what a hand my nephew's making."

"You've been through a lot this week," I said in the sternest tone I dared use with her, "and there'll be other times for us to ride together. I like Andrew. You do, too. He deserves a fair chance, but he won't get one with you dropping off to sleep every couple of minutes."

This was the first, and maybe the last, out and out argument with her I ever won. Of course, we hardly ever disagreed in the first place.

"We all drag our tails over here for a trail ride, and she lays up in bed," Scooter teased mercilessly the next morning.

Serena Kate, generally a late sleeper herself, seemed to be sticking close to her brothers for mutual support during the latest family crisis. Spearing Scooter with a glare, she hoisted herself onto the buggy seat beside me.

"Just shut up."

It put Puddler's nose out of joint, but he clambered into the backseat. Seth led the way, and we all did our best to pretend everything was normal. Andrew matched his walking horse's gait to the speed of the buggy and spoke to me without raising his voice any more than necessary.

"I hope Miss Sis isn't under the weather this morning or, worse, avoiding me."

"Just the opposite," I said reassuringly, "she's resting up so as to be bright-eyed and bushy-tailed for you this afternoon. What have you got planned?"

"Well, Ches, I've wracked my brain. I considered taking her as far as Tyler to one of the fancier restaurants, but she wouldn't like leaving you for so long."

"I'm not completely helpless, you know."

"Talk to your aunt, not me," he said with a shrug.

"What did you finally come up with?"

"This may seem a little unconventional, but I planned a short hike and a picnic lunch for us."

"Hike?" I asked in disbelief.

"Sure, we've cleared some nice trails on my place and rehabilitated Dr. Parmalee's prize rose bushes. We can cut through the woods from her place and end up in the rose garden for our picnic."

"Aunt Sis can't walk all the way over... Oh, she might do it, but she'd end up exhausted and thoroughly unimpressed."

"So, you think it's a bad idea?"

"A shady spot in Uncle Doc's rose garden should be right up her alley. Miss Sis loves the beauty of nature, and she'll be able to smoke without feeling self-conscious. You just need some way to get her there with a whole lot less sweating."

"I could always come around by the road and pick her up in my car, but I wanted her to see some of what we've done with the place."

"If you can't think of anything else, I'll loan you Mable and the buggy, but that's kind of like taking a girl out in her own ride."

"It does seem that way," he admitted. "I know your aunt gave you the rig, but she bought and paid for it. Besides, it'll be awfully warm by this afternoon."

"Too warm for old Mable," I teased, "but not too warm to drag your lady out across the pasture on foot. You've got a lot to learn about Miss Sis Durham."

"Alright," he grumbled, "you've made your point. I'll think of something."

Serena Kate kept quiet through the whole exchange, but as he rode on ahead she gave me a supportive pat on the back.

Aunt Sis changed her outfit three times and fussed endlessly over her hair and makeup. She finally settled on the pale pink dress with white ruffled collar that she'd worn the night we visited the western-wear store.

"Oh, Ches, I probably stink like cigarette smoke, but my nerves..." She paused just long enough to light up again and then continued on a slightly different line. "I don't know what's wrong with me. I haven't acted like this since high school."

"Well, I'm no expert, but you wouldn't feel this way if you didn't think a lot of him and want things to turn out well."

"I suppose you're right," she agreed. "Pray for me, honey."

"Yes'm," I answered, squeezing her hand.

I started praying right then and prayed even harder when Andrew pulled up out front in what looked like a monster truck with an open platform where the cab should have been. Only old Rhett stood bold and true, advancing halfway across the yard to meet the threat with hackles raised. The rest of the dogs scurried under the front porch.

"What kind of monstrosity," Aunt Sis muttered but her next words told me the strange ride wouldn't be a deal breaker. "Oh, honey, I sat a bottle of perfume down somewhere and walked off from it. Quick, help me look."

"Here it is. Got your mints?"

She nodded and gave me a quick squeeze before floating across the room to answer Andrews knock on the door. I followed her out, and Puddler gathered enough courage to climb the porch steps and press himself against my legs, letting out a warning growl.

"Good afternoon, fair lady. Your chariot awaits."

"I'm glad to see you Andrew," she managed with a smile, "but that chariot looks like it could tear up an awful lot of ground."

"Not if I'm careful," he answered, dropping the act. "This is what they call a swamp buggy, and it's set up for bird hunting. I wanted you to be able to look over the country, especially the improvements we've made on your Uncle Doc's old place."

"I can see all of the country the Good Lord intended me to see from the back of a tall horse," she sniffed.

"It doesn't really matter," he said with a shrug. "There's nothing out there to look at that's half as pretty as you are."

Roses bloomed in my Aunts cheeks as the heartfelt praise melted her.

"Do you think we can get Ches up there? I planned to drop him off to stay with Giles."

"Mr. Parmalee?" I demanded. "I don't want to stay with that old goat. Why can't I just stay here or over at Nash's house?"

"Nash is gone to the river," she explained, "and you'd be the only one on the place. I don't want you thinking too hard of old Giles just because you saw us butt heads. He's been a neighbor, customer, and off-and-on friend all my life. It'll ease my mind to know he's looking after you."

"Come on, Ches," Andrew coaxed. "At least you'll enjoy the ride over there."

I rubbed Puddler on the head and talked to him before Andrew carried me up to the open platform and went back down the ladder to help Aunt Sis. She let out a little squeal as we rumbled from the yard, but I think my aunt enjoyed the bird's-eye view as much as I did.

Junk tractors, pieces of hay baling equipment, and rusted-out vehicles surrounded Giles Parmalee's brick home. The old giant met us on the front porch.

"Hey there, Sis. You didn't tell me you was coming on that thunder wagon."

"I've never laid eyes on this thing before today," she answered, "but it's quite a machine."

"You might as well go find a preacher," he called wryly to Andrew. "You've won her heart sure as the world if she won't say what she really thinks about that loud, rut-making bucket of bolts. If Sis had her way, we'd all be stuck in the horse and buggy age."

My aunt's face turned fire-engine red, but Andrew just threw me over his shoulder and started down the ladder.

"We'll be back before dark, Ches," he said, plopping me onto a wrought-iron bench and handing me my crutches.

"Don't worry," Giles responded. "I'll take good care of the light, hope, and future of the Durham family."

"You better," Aunt Sis called down with steel in her eyes, "or I'll nail your hide to the barn door."

Giles watched in silence until they rumbled out of sight and then he turned to me.

"Sis is a good gal, but she takes things altogether too serious. She'll fret herself into an early grave if them cigarettes don't get her first." As he spoke, the old man settled a fresh wad of chewing tobacco in his cheek. He contemplated for a while before spitting into the yard. "Cat got your tongue?"

"It's not my choice to be here," I told him, "but I am here. This is your home, so I reckon you can say whatever you like."

"Well, now, I don't believe you had that much vinegar in you when you first come here. Miss Sis has done growed you a backbone, or rather she give you room to grow one for yourself. Me and Sis ain't enemies; I love that gal."

"You've got a funny way of showing it."

"I'd do most anything for her, but I just can't see the world the way she does."

"How do you mean?"

"I live here because I was born here. It costs money to pick up and move. I fool with horses because I know something about them. If a feller's dumb enough to let me cheat him, I'll wring him out like a wet rag. My folks, and yours too, was the rich people around here, but they all stayed broker than the Ten Commandments. I don't know nothing about no proud family heritage. Miss Sis, though, she eats, sleeps, and breathes it."

"What do you think about Andrew?"

"He's got money sense. I tried every way in the world, but I never took a nickel off him that he didn't get something of fair and equal value. Them fancy manners ought to please Sis," he added. "Anybody'd be better than Jim Rex. She'd just as well drag around a dead mule as tie herself to that hapless idiot."

"You don't hold back much, do you?"

"That's one of the few privileges of old age. Let's get inside where it's cool."

The house was built with a sunken den, and we both negotiated the step-down carefully. Stacks of photo albums covered the coffee table. Some of them even spilled over onto the couch.

"Going through your pictures?" I asked.

"My late wife was kind of a shutterbug. I drug these out thinking you might like to look at them. There's pictures of your people scattered all through there and plenty of horses, too."

"I'd like that very much," I said, surprised he'd given any thought to my entertainment.

"How about a sodee-water?"

As the afternoon dragged on, I learned what I should have known already. Giles Parmalee was a human being, flawed and imperfect, but not near as much of a hard case as he wanted folks to believe. My thoughts kept returning to Aunt Sis. I prayed for her and Andrew, even while I listened to Mr. Parmalee narrate the story found in his wife's pictures.

After that picnic in the rose garden, Aunt Sis did away with the trail rides altogether. Too hot, she claimed. In truth, though, she needed her beauty rest. Saturday afternoons became her regular time with Andrew. She usually left me with Nash or even Scooter, but somehow I didn't mind ending up back at Mr. Parmalee's now and then.

Aunt Sis replaced the trail rides, at least as far as I was concerned, by taking me with her whenever she went out on horseback. With the weather hot and dry, she kept stock work to a minimum, but when she did ride out in the early morning to gather a few horses for the sale or do something with her own cattle, I was right there at her side.

"I wish you'd run Trouble through the sale Friday night," I said after one of his frequent stunts. "He scares me."

"That's why you ain't riding him," Aunt Sis pointed out dryly.

"No, I mean it scares me for you to ride him."

"That's awfully sweet, honey, but him and Twister look so good together. I'll make him do to suit me until a better one comes along."

If a given situation required some real help, Nash and the McKendrick boys rode with us. Other times, when Aunt Sis could have easily done the job by herself, she depended on me.

We tried several auctioneers but none worked out as a regular replacement for Jim Rex. Aunt Sis gradually fell into the pattern of calling her own sales. The kids stayed around all the time, but we never saw hide nor hair of him. Finally, sometime in July, the dry spell broke and it rained for a solid week.

"Craziest darn weather I ever did see," Mr. Parmalee grumbled one Saturday evening when Aunt Sis stopped by to pick me up, "floodin' right here in the middle of the summer."

"Mmm, but it sure is nice," Aunt Sis countered. "Ought to keep the grass from withering away."

"Any other time I'd be tickled to death, but the old Dolly mare ain't come up. She's due to foal any day. The bottomland's done turned to soup and I can't get down there to check on her."

"Dolly must be twenty-years-old."

"Eighteen," he admitted. "Late breeding back, too, or the baby wouldn't be coming this time of year. This'll probably be her last, and I don't want to lose it."

"Ches is about due for a little ride anyhow. We'll ease down there after church tomorrow and take us a look-see."

The McKendrick siblings gave each other uncomfortable looks when Andrew finally claimed a spot on our pew, but they stayed close by. Jim Rex didn't come to church at all.

"I wish I could go along," Scooter blurted when Aunt Sis mentioned our plan to ride the Parmalee bottom that afternoon, "but Pop's taking us to meet— Well, anyway, he told us to come straight home."

Andrew couldn't go, either. He told us to have a good time and squeezed my aunt's hand warmly before heading back to Houston to prepare for an early morning conference call.

"Looks like it's just me and you," I said with a smile.

I thought we might ride out from home, but Aunt Sis jumped our saddled horses into the stock trailer and drove over to Mr. Parmalee's house.

"Them clouds is working up to another gully washer," the old man said without preamble. "Y'all are liable to wind up soaked to the bone."

"Giles is right," Aunt Sis said after a quick glance upward. "Maybe you ought to stay here with him."

"I won't melt. Besides, I counted on getting to ride."

"Tell you what," my aunt compromised, "if Giles feels like staying down here to watch, you can ride your horse in the pen. I'll make a swing through the bottom and see about Dolly. If it blows up a storm, you can just ride into the barn."

"I'd rather go with you, Aunt Sis, but you're the boss."

"Aw, come on, Ches," Mr. Parmalee said, lending his support to her plan. "Stay here and show me what that yellow nag of yours can do."

"Nag?" I shot back. "It's that horse of Aunt Sis's that ain't fit for making soap. My Twister is a sure-enough Cadillac."

"Cadillac's only as good as its driver," he challenged.

Though hindered by age and arthritis, Giles still seemed as strong as a bull. He and Aunt Sis set me in the saddle and shut me safely into a pen before she swung up on her horse.

"Come on, Rhett," she called, following it with a long whistle. "Hunt her up."

"Don't you let that cur dog jump on my baby colt," Mr. Parmalee cautioned.

Aunt Sis just shook her head at him and rode away.

A lot of horses will pitch a fit when somebody takes their buddy off, but Twister never once acted like he cared if Trouble came or went. My speckled pup ran along with Rhett for a short ways but soon stopped to look back over his shoulder.

"Up here, Puddler," I called, and he boogied on back.

"Nothing like a good dog," Mr. Parmalee said with a chuckle. "Old Rhett will likely be the one to find the mare and baby if they're found. He ain't fixing to jump on that colt, but I've got to jab at Sis about something."

The rain held off, and I enjoyed my ride in the small pen. I rode figure eights, circles, and a sort of zig-zag pattern, weaving through poles that weren't there. Mr. Parmalee hollered out advice and encouragement from his lawn chair.

"Told you he was a Jim-dandy," I bragged.

"Two cripples, but from the looks of things I'd say the pair of you could get a lot done."

Instead of striking me as an insult his words sounded like the biggest complement anybody could ever give me and my horse. We might not be the quickest or the stoutest, but in spite of our problems, we could make things happen.

Time passed quickly. Before we knew it, I'd been riding an hour and a half.

"Reckon the storm blew around us?" I asked, pausing beside the fence.

Mr. Parmalee studied the sky for a minute and then placed a stream of tobacco juice between Twister's front feet.

"I expect so. Hope that mare and baby ain't in trouble," he added with a glance at his wristwatch. "Sis ought to be getting back in here."

The old anxiety reared its head, and my throat got a little tight.

"I didn't much like Aunt Sis riding off by herself."

"Aw, Sis likes to put on that helpless lady act when it suits her, but she's tough as nails. Besides, you get her and old Rhett stirred up, they're meaner than anything in that bottom."

"You're probably right," I admitted and managed a smile.

"See 'at billy goat?" he questioned, pointing it out as it nosed around the outside of the barn for loose feed. "There ain't a pen on the place that'll hold him, but I'm fixing to toss him in there with you. Let's see how long you and that yellow pony can keep him out in the middle. Ever let him get to a fence, and he'll slip right through."

"I hope Aunt Sis comes back before your goat dies of old age 'cause he ain't fixing to get by me and Twister."

Sneaking up on the goat, Mr. Parmalee grabbed him by one horn and the loose hide on his back. He hoisted the animal up and literally tossed it over the fence. The goat landed on his feet, and I rode to him.

Twister caught on right away, and we hazed Billy out toward the middle of the pen. We held him out there for a good little while before he darted around us. He beat us to the fence and looked like a gone goose, but Puddler nipped him on the nose and turned him back.

"Hey," Mr. Parmalee guffawed, "that's cheating."

"No sir," I called back over my shoulder as Twister pinned his ears and went for the goat. "Why do you think I keep a dog?"

When the goat finally got by me again, Puddler wasn't there to stop him. My pup had jogged out to meet Rhett as the dingy red dog came up from the pasture. I stopped Twister, gave him time to breathe, and waited expectantly for Aunt Sis.

"Rhett's showing his age," Mr. Parmalee observed with a regretful sigh. "He must've tired out and come on in ahead of her."

The old dog hung back, not coming all the way up to the pens, and when Puddler tried to play, Rhett bit the fire out of him. My dog yelped in pain and slunk back with his tail between his legs.

"He wouldn't come in without Aunt Sis if he had any choice about it," I said with sudden certainty. "And the way he chomped down on Puddler just now, he'll nip at him but…"

Mr. Parmalee spat out what remained of his chaw and raked dirt over it with the toe of his boot.

"Well, he ain't Lassie, nor Rin Tin Tin, neither. He's just a rough old cur dog."

My aunt's description of Rhett came back to me. "He's loyal to his last drop of blood. That's what Aunt Sis says, and I think she's in trouble."

"Alright," he said slowly, "I'll drive up to the house and call Nash. He can saddle a horse and lope off down there if it'll ease your mind."

"Hurry," I urged. "Rhett'll head back in a minute whether anybody goes with him or not."

"Don't get your drawers in a wad. I'm a-going."

I didn't bow my head or close my eyes because I wanted to keep a watch on the old red dog, but I prayed right there in the saddle.

"Dear Heavenly Father, you made my Aunt Sis tough and quick and smart, but she'd be the first to admit that she needs You. I don't trust that horse of hers, Lord, and I'm scared. Please keep Your hand on her and show me what to do."

When Mr. Parmalee came back, I heard concern in his voice for the first time.

"That blasted phone line," he explained, "water gets in it and then… If you're alright here, I'll drive over to y'all's place and start Nash on his way."

I had remembered something, and a cold knot of dread formed in my stomach.

"He's still at church."

"That's right," Mr. Parmalee said, slamming a huge hand against the dash of his pickup. "This is big meetin' day at Antioch. I'll have to fetch one of them McKendrick boys."

"They're gone, too," I said, feeling sick.

"Hollister then."

"On his way back to Houston," I answered shortly. "We've got to go, now."

"Even if I had a horse ready to hand," he admitted in disgust, "I couldn't lift my foot high enough to put it in the stirrup. We'd stick this old truck within three hundred yards."

Forcing myself to think calmly, I considered our limited options. The decision came slowly. I didn't know if I was up to the task, but I figured Aunt Sis needed me.

"Open the gate."

Chapter Sixteen

Boy, you've never even ridden that bottom," Mr. Parmalee protested, his mouth falling open.

"Rhett knows where he left Aunt Sis."

"What could you do to help her if you found her? You can't even get off your horse unless you pull that rip cord and just let yourself fall."

"Hunt up some help, or figure out a way to get to us. If Aunt Sis is okay, I'll ride back and let you know. If she's in some kind of trouble, at least I'll be in it with her."

When Mr. Parmalee made no move to open the gate, I sidled Twister up to it and leaned from the saddle like I'd seen Aunt Sis do.

"Ches! Come back here, boy."

"I'm gone," I called, trying to take charge of the situation as my aunt would have done, "and sombody'd better be coming on behind me." I managed another gate going out into the pasture and spoke encouragingly to Rhett. "Alright, old fella, go to her. Where's Miss Sis?"

I put Twister in a long lope, trying to keep up, but quickly slowed his pace. I'd never ridden anything faster than a walk, not out in the open. Puddler stayed right with my horse, and Rhett doubled back every few minutes. Suddenly, it dawned on me what I was doing. I was riding off alone into a pasture I'd never seen before, following a dog for my direction and hoping to help an aunt who was tougher and more capable than I would ever be.

Rubbing Twister's neck, I prayed he'd stay steady. He hadn't made a false move yet, but I knew if he turned silly now, I'd be in a real bind. I rode for what seemed like hours before I heard Rhett's excited yelp up ahead and caught sight of my aunt's palomino gelding.

Trouble stood there with his bridle reins dragging the ground. The saddle, pulled oddly to one side, looked somehow darker than I remembered. Riding closer, I realized the leather was thoroughly wetted. I turned my gaze from the horse and looked for Rhett, figuring he would be as close to his lady as possible.

Seconds later, I found him nuzzling her face. Aunt Sis lay on her back in a nearby creek. The stream wasn't deep or swift-moving but it held enough water to soak her clean through. She seemed unconscious at first, but the old dog's attentions brought her around. He growled warningly at Puddler. Not sure what had hurt his lady, he guarded her against anything and everything.

"Hey, old fella," she groaned. Where you been? Oh, Rhett, it hurts. It hurts something awful."

"Aunt Sis," I called, knowing she couldn't see me from where she lay. "I'm here, Aunt Sis. What do you want me to do?"

"Ches, honey, how did you get here?"

"Rhett came after help, and I'm all the help he found," I answered apologetically.

"I'd rather have you and Rhett than a whole rescue squad," she gritted through obvious pain. "We're not likely to get any rescue squad, either. I must've landed right smack on my mobile phone. Ride up beside me, and let me catch hold of your stirrup."

I obeyed quickly. Aunt Sis pulled on the bottom of the stirrup and then on my ankle. Finally, she clawed her way up the stirrup leather to a standing position. Her face went white as a bed sheet, and she sucked in a ragged breath. Unable to bare any weight on her right leg, she clung to my saddle horn to stay upright.

"Are you okay, Aunt Sis?" I asked stupidly, but she didn't seem to mind the question.

"Something's busted; I'm not sure what. I've got us into a fine mess, honey. If I pass out you'll just have to use your own judgment because I don't know…"

Her voice held regret along with the pain. Aunt Sis felt like she'd let me down because she didn't have a set of marching orders ready and waiting. The thought twisted my heart strings, and I stroked her white-knuckled hand as it gripped the saddle horn.

"Mr. Parmalee's bringing more help, but I think we need to get you out of this water. Can you walk out on the bank?"

"If I can't," she said grimly, "drag me."

Swallowing hard, I spoke to Twister.

"Step up, easy. Nice and slow."

"Aim for that white oak. Maybe I can…"

Aunt Sis trailed off, biting her lips to hold back sobs of pain, but I got enough of the message. When we finally reached our goal, she turned loose of my saddle and leaned against the large tree trunk. Nothing but pure grit and determination kept her on her feet.

"You go ahead and cry, Aunt Sis. I know it hurts."

"Not too bad," she lied. "It's a long way from my heart. Now, go catch that yellow crow bait. He's fixing to pack me out of here, and I don't much care if he likes it or not."

"No ma'am, you can't—"

"Just catch him," she wheezed, the pain making her breath come short, and I knew better than to argue anymore.

Riding over to the aptly named Trouble, I leaned down and fished for a bridle rein. I talked to him in the soothing tone I'd learned from Aunt Sis, but the words themselves were anything but complimentary.

Aunt Sis took the reins from me and wrapped them around her wrist.

"I don't think I can pull the saddle over. You straighten it up, Ches, and I'll try to tighten the girth." That done, she passed the reins back to me. "Now, you hold him while I get on."

"Please don't do this, Aunt Sis. Mr. Parmalee's coming as fast as he can."

"I found his mare and a pretty little stud colt. As soon as I get myself a'horseback, we'll drive them out to meet him."

"You're in no condition to fool with…"

I gave up, watching with helpless tears in my eyes as she made her try. The shock of standing on her right leg, even for a second, nearly sent her to her knees. Still, she managed to hang her left foot in the stirrup and start up into the saddle. Swinging that injured leg across the horses back proved too much for her. She gave one sharp cry and crumpled into a heap.

Rhett never made a sound or gave any warning. Almost before his lady hit the ground, though, he latched onto the yellow horse savagely. Trouble squealed in pain and kicked out, but the old red dog refused to turn loose. Seeing my aunt's foot fall free of the stirrup, I let the horse go, thankful Rhett hadn't lit into Twister or clamped down on my leg in his blind rage.

This time it was Puddler who nuzzled Aunt Sis awake, whimpering as he applied a slobbery tongue to her face.

"What happened, Ches?" she asked pushing the pup back to look up at me.

"You didn't quite get on."

"Well, I gathered that. Did he jump out from under me or…"

"No'm, you blacked out. Trouble left right after that with Rhett hanging from his hock."

"Why, that old fool," she murmured with a faint smile, "I hope he don't get himself kicked."

She lay there in silence until I decided maybe I could take her mind off the pain.

"What started all this?"

"Rhett found the mare and colt, and we headed them home. What with the weather blowing through, Trouble acted a regular fool. I handled him alright, though, until we started across the creek. He threw himself over backwards. It's a dirty trick, but I should've been able to step out of the saddle."

"There's no way you could have known what he was about to do."

"He caught me, Ches, and that's all there is to it. I'm getting old and slow."

"Yes, and fat too, I've heard it all before. Now, you be quiet and listen to me. You are the bravest, strongest, kindest, and most elegant lady I ever hope to know. Like you said earlier, we're in a mess here, but I want you to remember two things. None of it is your fault, and there's nobody I'd rather be in a mess alongside."

My words opened the floodgates, releasing tears no amount of pain could make her shed. I wanted to go to her worse than I'd ever wanted anything in my life, but I knew I'd never get back into the saddle. Rhett came out of nowhere, knocked Puddler rolling, and licked the tears away almost as fast as they fell.

Suddenly, my ears caught the welcome sound of a big engine.

"Hey," Giles Parmalee hollered from atop Andrew's swamp buggy, "y'all need a ride?"

Moving almost like a young man, he came down the ladder, gathered Aunt Sis into his arms, and carried her up again.

"We need to get a hold of Aunt Hattie," I told him. "She'll call Daddy and whoever else—"

"Ches?" Miss Sis called weakly from the platform.

"Yes'm, I hear you."

"You bring in the mare and colt. Pick up that yellow nag, too, if you can. I'll want my saddle."

"Thank You, Lord," I thought. "She's still giving orders."

Joy and relief washed over me, as I rode away smiling, but they proved premature. Mr. Parmalee told me later that, 'I'll want my saddle,' was the last intelligible phrase she spoke between there and the emergency room.

Rhett started off after the swamp buggy, and it took my best imitation of Aunt Sis's trademark squall to fetch him back. Eventually, we found old Dolly drifting slowly toward the Parmalee headquarters with her baby.

The pair made painfully slow progress, but I backed the dogs off and gave them plenty of time. When we finally reached the pens, a badly shaken palomino gelding stood by the trailer, waiting to go home like he'd been an innocent victim of the whole unpleasant affair. I turned Dolly and her colt into a pen and stuck Trouble in another one to avoid any chance of losing my aunt's saddle.

Opening what looked like the feed room door, I hoisted a half-empty sack and managed to balance it in front of me. I poured some groceries into a trough for the hungry-looking old mare, put the rest of the feed back where I'd found it, and began to wonder what to do next. I needed to go to Aunt Sis, but how?

Unless I wanted to risk a bad fall, I was pretty well stuck in the saddle until somebody came along to help me down. I rode Twister over to stand under a shade tree, laid the reins down on his neck, and talked to my Lord.

Despite the seriousness of the situation, I laughed out loud when I caught myself praying for patience one minute and begging God to send somebody quick in the next. I was still chuckling a little when my minivan bounced down the driveway. I heard Scooter hollering before the mud-spattered van even stopped.

"There's Ches; I see him! Just look at him a-sittin' up there like the picture of a cowboy and them dogs laid out on either side of his horse."

To my surprise, Jim Rex McKendrick stepped from behind the wheel. All three of his kids piled out talking at once, but my gaze locked on the auctioneer.

"I'll swan, Ches. I'm sorry. I never figured anything like this…"

"Don't tell it to me. I'd like to spit in your eye, but I need you to get me off this horse and take me to the boss lady."

"You can spit in his eye if you want to," Scooter assured me. "Me and Seth will still get you down."

"I'll haul the horses and dogs home in Miss Sis's trailer," Seth offered. "The rest of you go on to the hospital with Ches."

Aunt Hattie, Uncle Elmer, and the Crawford's sat huddled together in the waiting room, but Mr. Parmalee levered himself up on a heavy wooden walking cane and limped across the space to meet me.

"Sis wasn't making too much sense, Ches, but I know she wanted them to wait until you got here."

"What do you mean wait?"

"To do the surgery," he explained. "See, the orthopedic surgeon's fixing to leave on vacation. He's aiming to replace her hip right away. I caught Hollister about halfway to Houston, and he's headed back now."

"Good, did Aunt Hattie call my folks?"

A touch of humor crept into his worried face.

"She got them and then called anybody else who ever even heard of Miss Sis Durham. You better check in with your Mama, though. Hattie told her I left you out in the wild to fend for yourself."

"Do you think they'll let me see Aunt Sis?"

"If they don't, they'd better figure on dealing with me." His voice dropped to a whisper then and lost its grumbling tone. "I can't hardly stand to look at her a-laying there in that hospital bed, Ches. Mrs. Crawford will go with you."

We found my aunt sleeping peacefully under the anesthetic, ready to be taken to the operating room. Maneuvering my wheelchair as close as possible to the bed, I reached out and took one of her hands.

"I brought in the mare and colt, Aunt Sis. Got your saddle back, too."

"She can't hear you," the anesthesiologist informed me.

His tone was more matter-of-fact than unkind, but Mrs. Crawford placed an arm around my shoulders.

"You talk to her anyway, Ches. Just the sound of your voice might be a comfort."

"Well," I continued shakily, "you've nearly filled up the waiting room, and some more of our bunch is on the way. I'm here, Aunt Sis. I'm here, and I love you. Miz Edna's here with me, and everybody's praying for you."

An electric wheelchair can be a wonderful thing. I never let go of my aunt's hand until they wheeled her through the operating room door. I called Mom, but she and Dad were there with us by the time a surgeon came out to give his dubious report.

"The hip looks great," he started in a hopeful tone. "Ms. Durham is younger and stronger than ninety percent of my patients. She shouldn't have any trouble regaining full mobility. However, at the moment, she is running a high fever and her lungs are awfully congested."

"Serena's been a fairly heavy smoker for as long as I've known her," Mom volunteered.

"She also spent an hour or better on her back in the creek, part of it with a horse on top of her," I defended hotly.

"There's springs all up and down that little creek," Mr. Parmalee added. "That water stays cold year round."

"With the exposure and her history as a smoker," the doctor said, "pneumonia is a big concern. I'll start her on an IV antibiotic. She should be coming out from under the anesthetic anytime now."

"Can we see her?" I asked eagerly.

The doctor sized me up uncertainly and then frowned.

"One or two adults can visit her, but I don't think it would be a good idea for you to—"

Mr. Parmalee nearly swallowed his chaw, but he turned the situation over to a steadier head.

"Preacher, if you don't talk to this upstart right quick, I will, and he won't like it none."

"The boy's been staying with his aunt this summer," Brother Crawford explained patiently, "and they're mighty close." He paused briefly to look around the little group of family and friends. "Not a one of us would want to go in Ches's place."

Aunt Sis always did have a mind of her own, and her body simply refused to wake up. My original five-minute visit turned into hours and then days of terrible uncertainty.

Once they moved us into a room, I stayed by her side, praying, whenever I wasn't trying to run the horse sale.

Without Aunt Sis as the driving force behind the operation, our sale didn't amount to much, but we kept the gates open. I didn't turn away a single horse, or one buyer, either. Dad called it pointless and a little crazy, but he pitched right in and kept the books. Jim Rex even convinced me to let him auctioneer for us again.

"I hurt Sis mighty bad," he told me on that first night, "but I've never yet left her in a jam. If the old Durham horse sale's got any kind of chance, we're all gonna need each other."

I never even tried to answer, but I sat beside him that night and did my best to read the market for him as Aunt Sis had done. Meanwhile, the boss lady seemed to grow weaker by the day. She lost weight rapidly, and the sight of her hooked to all those tubes and wires nearly turned me inside out. Not knowing what else to do for her, I called Miz Lillian.

"Of course, Ches," the old lady responded to my hesitant question. "That's a fine idea. You and I both know she'd want us to keep her hair fixed."

"You need some rest," Mom suggested gently after the beauty operator had come and gone. "Why don't you come back to Dallas for two or three days."

She did a fair share of nursing herself, wiping my aunt's face with a damp cloth and swabbing out her mouth to keep it clear of phlegm. She and Daddy stayed on hand as much as they could, and Andrew did the same. They drove back and forth to their jobs when necessity demanded it.

"No ma'am, I'll rest just as soon as Aunt Sis gets back to herself."

The boss lady stirred and moaned every once in a while but never opened her eyes. She'd squeeze my hand, and one time her lips formed the words, "I love you," but that was as much response as anybody got out of her.

Nash avoided the hospital as long as he could but finally decided he had to see her. His reaction summed up my own feelings. He stood looking down at her from the foot of the bed, and his powerful shoulders shook as he sobbed.

"Sweet Lord Jesus," he finally moaned, "what are we gonna do now?"

I'm not sure he even knew I was in the room, but I took it upon myself to answer his question.

"We'll have a horse sale Friday night and another one the Friday night after that. She's gonna get up out of this bed one day, Nash. I sure don't want to be the one to look into those eyes and tell her we just shut it down."

A day or two later, I looked up to see a tall, broad-shouldered figure standing in the doorway. Little Herman Holloway stood there crushing the brim of his carefully shaped straw hat as he searched for the right words.

"Ches, I never meant… I've known your aunt all my life. I never thought she could walk on water the way Uncle Nash seemed to figure but… I guess you know he's looking for me 'cause I'm the one sold her that horse."

"Well, lay low," I advised. "Aunt Sis wouldn't want to cause any trouble in your family."

"Sis was always decent to me. I never went to hurt her. Guess I figured she could ride anything with hair on it, but time gets by. She's puttin' on some years now."

"She's not old," I answered hotly, "and she can still outride you."

His even white teeth gleamed in a grin, and soon I found myself laughing with him. The indirect role he played in my aunt's accident was just part of the horse business, but the little crack about her age roused my temper.

On Monday of the second week, Jim Rex stopped by to find me and Andrew sitting with Aunt Sis.

"I'll come back when the weekend farmer clears out," he said nastily.

Andrew didn't rise to the bait. Instead, he came out with a sudden inspiration.

"Sell a horse," he said excitedly to the auctioneer.

"What horse?"

"The old grey mare that ain't what she used to be," Andrew retorted. "Any horse, just make like you're fumbling around trying to start one."

Jim Rex shot me a questioning look, but I'd caught Andrew's fever of hope by then.

"Do it," I ordered. "Do it now."

"Here goes," he answered with a shrug. "Well, alright now boys, whatcha gonna give for the good grey mare?"

"Louder," I hissed.

"Turn her around there Nash, and let the folks have a look at her. Who'll give me a price to start her? How much for her?"

He rolled into an auctioneer's chant that included no real numbers, just rattling like he was hammering around for a bid. Watching Aunt Sis intently, I saw her hand tap against the bed rail.

"A hundred and a half," she tried to say.

The words came out as a croak but sounded no less decisive for it. Repeating the opening bid to Jim Rex, I motioned frantically for him to roll on up.

"It's working! Keep a-rattling."

I was leaning over Aunt Sis when her eyes drifted open. She smiled at the sight of me, but it turned into a puzzled frown as she took in her surroundings.

"Where am I," she mumbled around the tube in her throat, "and what's that fool trying to sell?"

"Nothing," I admitted, kissing her forehead as my tears came. "He's trying to wake you up, sleeping beauty."

Things happened fast after that. When the tubes came out, Aunt Sis started taking a little nourishment. Clear liquids at first, but she soon graduated to peach ice cream. One bite slid down a little too fast as panic gripped her.

"Heavens to Betsy, what about the sale? How long have I been laid up?"

"Ches kept the horse sale running," Andrew said reassuringly, "and he even got a lady in here to fix your hair."

Her deep brown eyes filled with tears as they fastened on me.

"Thanks, honey. You sure came through in a tight and handled yourself like a Durham."

"I didn't do anything much," I told her shakily. "But I begged the Lord to bring you through, and he did it."

"I'm grateful He saw fit to let me stay around a little longer. You know Aunt Sis loves you."

"Yes'm," I answered, swallowing hard, "and I love you."

Tuesday evening as she picked nervously at the bed sheet, the inevitable question finally came.

"Ches, honey, how long has it been since I had a cigarette?"

"You don't even want to know," I said gently. "Just try not to think about it."

When she dropped the subject, I figured she hated to ask me for something I couldn't give. The young doctor on duty the next morning received no such consideration.

"Send a wheelchair in here," she said in her Colonel Durham's daughter tone of voice, "or tell that therapist I'm ready for a longer walk."

"The therapist will determine an appropriate amount of activity. Do you want to go anywhere in particular, ma'am?"

"I need to get out of this hospital, feel the sunshine warming my bones and… You may not like to hear it, but I need to smoke."

"Your respiratory system is significantly compromised, Ms. Durham. Why do you think a scant hour of summertime exposure resulted in pneumonia? Our tests indicate some early-stage emphysema."

Aunt Sis blinked, swallowed, and gave him a long-suffering look.

"If you're trying to scare me, it's working," she stated flatly. "Now, I really need a cigarette."

"You've already gone a week without nicotine," he said on his way out the door. "Look at it as an opportunity to quit."

"I want my cigarettes, Ches, and the use of your wheelchair." Her voice spurred me to obedience, but she raised an uncertain hand. Wait, honey... I'll see Uncle Doc first."

Giles Parmalee arrived shortly after my phone call, pushing his uncle in a wheelchair. The old man had a head full of white hair, alert blue eyes, and hands that trembled from Parkinson's disease.

"I heard what happened, Sis, and I'm sorry."

"Not half as sorry as I am," Giles rumbled from behind him. "It was my mare and colt she rode out after."

Aunt Sis smiled briefly, shaking her head to dismiss any blame, but came right to the point.

"Uncle Doc, they're trying to scare me into giving up my cigarettes. I want you to look at the x-rays and see if they're really as bad as all that."

"I don't need to look at the tests, sugar. These boys don't have any reason to lie to you." He indicated the hospital's medical staff with a general wave of his hand. "They may put a little scare-talk into it, but what they say is based on the facts."

"That's not exactly what I wanted to hear."

"'Course, they don't know you like I do. You're all Durham, hardheaded and strong. Lord willing, you'll live to see this boys children whether you put the cigarettes down or not."

"Say, Uncle Doc," she interrupted when he flicked a glance at me. "Ches has grown some since you saw him last."

"Yes'm, but there's still the matter of his children. They could very well remember you rooted to a rocking chair with your cigarettes, lighter, and ashtray in easy reach. On the other hand, they might grin at one another and say things like, 'Plumb crazy, ain't she?' while they try to keep up with you a-riding through the brush."

When the old man fell silent, I rolled up to the other side of her bed.

"Nobody but the colonel ever had any luck telling you what to do. I knew you'd have to make up your own mind, so I brought these."

As I spoke, I laid her saddle-shaped lighter and a fresh pack of cigarettes on the bedside table. Her wonderful smile brightened the whole room, but for the first time ever, I wasn't glad to see it.

"Why, bless your sweet heart," she said gratefully.

Tapping the pack firmly against her palm, she removed the cellophane, took out a cigarette and placed it between her lips. She flicked the lighter experimentally, checking to see if it had dried out from soaking in the creek, and raised it toward her cigarette.

"You know they're gonna have a fit if you light that in here."

I guess my voice carried a note of disappointment or maybe defeat because she let the lighter go out and looked up suddenly.

"Ches, honey," she asked reluctantly, "do you want me to quit?"

My answer should have been immediate, but doubts crowded my mind. Can she quit? Will she think I look down on her for smoking? Do I really want to give up all those special times together, her little breaks? Finally, I swallowed hard and nodded.

"Yes'm."

"Oh, Ches…"

Taking the cigarette from her lips, she held it under her nose for a good whiff and then gazed longingly at it. Unbeknownst to any of us, Daddy stood at the door watching. He chose that moment to play the caring, protective brother.

"Now you've done it, Ches," he said in a severe tone. "Aren't you ashamed of yourself? Your Aunt Sis has been awfully good to you, but to go and ask for the impossible... She'd like nothing better than to give you whatever you want, but she's too weak and pitiful to even think about doing without her cigarettes."

"You leave that sweet boy alone, Terry Durham," Aunt Sis ordered curtly, but Daddy spoke to her in a gentle, understanding tone.

"Go right ahead and smoke, Sis. I expected more of Ches, but he's just another ungrateful young upstart."

I was starting to catch onto Daddy's game, but his words stung just the same. Some of the pain probably showed in my face because Aunt Sis looked like she was fixing to come up out of that hospital bed.

"Weak and pitiful, huh?"

Hands trembling with anger, she stabbed the cigarette back into its pack, dropped the pack into a pink plastic bedpan, and hurled the bedpan across the room with one quick motion of her wrist.

"You missed," Daddy taunted from the relative safety of the hallway.

"Go back to Dallas," she called, "and take those dratted things with you. If Ches wants me to quit, that's just what I'll do."

"You know he tricked you," I guessed after a while.

"I figured it out as soon as I settled down, but I'll not go back on my word. I've still got two and a half cartons in the cabinet over the sink; give them to Nash."

"What about your cigarette lighter?"

"The colonel gave me that on my twentieth birthday. I don't want to part with it, but I'd rather not look at it for a while, either. Why don't you keep it?"

Quitting proved an uphill battle, but I never once heard my aunt complain. Andrew spent a good deal of time with her, and she may have told him how miserable she felt under the strain of near-constant cravings. All I ever got was, "I'm fine, honey, just fine. But, Heaven help, I'm eating like a horse."

"Look, Sis," Jim Rex started when he finally came to see her at the house, "I'm sorry for all—"

"Ches says you rattled me awake?"

"Yeah, but it was Hollister's idea. He seems to know you pretty well, no longer than he's been around."

"Oh, Jim Rex… I think Andrew and I have found something special, but whether we have or not, my heart won't stand anymore of waiting around for you to grow up. I hope we'll always be friends."

"You can count on it, Sis. No cigarette?" he asked raising an eyebrow.

A hand lifted automatically to the pocket of her blouse, but she drew it back with a wistful little smile.

"They're gone; I lost 'em in the Parmalee bottom."

"Well, something good came out of that mess." Then hesitantly, "Can I still rattle for you?"

"As long as there's a Durham Auction Company," she assured him wholeheartedly.

The extra weight that had melted off Aunt Sis in the hospital found its way back, and a few more pounds followed. She fretted and fumed until Andrew sat her down for a talk.

"You are a beautiful lady, Sis Durham, and as far as I'm concerned, you get more beautiful with each passing day. I'd a lot rather see you go up a dress size than worry and agonize over that all-important next cigarette."

"A girl can't fight everything at once," she finally admitted with a sigh.

Physical therapy looked suspiciously like exercise, and my aunt hated it with a passion. Even so, the goal of getting back in the saddle afforded powerful motivation. Seth McKendrick worked Trouble almost every day, but Aunt Sis swore she'd ride the horse at least once more.

Her big day came a week or so before I was to go back to Dallas and my old routine. A proud and strangely quiet Scooter accompanied her on the ride while Andrew and I waited to greet her like a returning hero. After three hours in the saddle she could barely stand up, much less walk. Even so, she turned back to stroke the gelding's sweat-stained neck.

"Might as well pat on a rattlesnake," I grumbled.

"I'll get as rough as need be, Ches, but I won't hold a grudge against a horse. Anybody who don't love and admire these beautiful animals had just as well stay away from them."

"Yes'm," I answered meekly, realizing she was right as usual.

As Scooter led the horses away, she collapsed against Andrew for support.

"Miss Sis," he said, looking down into her face, "you hard headed, independent, exasperating beauty, I've got a question for you."

"Mmm?" she inquired, still breathless from the effort of a hard ride.

"Will you marry me?"

Her eyes widened as she gazed up at him, but none of the surprise found its way into her voice.

"Oh," she drawled almost lazily, "I expect so."

"Great day in the morning, Ches," he shouted. "I think that was a yes."

"I expect so," I mimicked with a smile.

"I'll be opening the new Dallas office," Andrew told his fiancé, "and that'll put me close to Ches when he goes back to his parents."

"I always swore I'd never do it, but I guess there's no way around it. I'll have one more big sale and then close the barn. Nash can look after the place for as long as…"

"Why, my precious silly darling," Andrew said, laughing at her with his eyes. "How will Ches ever know whether or not he wants to take over the horse sale one day if you throw in the towel now?"

"Please don't tease me, Andrew. A wife's place is with her husband, and your work will be in Dallas."

All trace of humor left his face.

"Oh, no. No, baby doll. I'd never ask you to… You're my little wild rose. If I cut off the roots and carried the bloom away to Dallas, you'd dry up and crumple to nothing. "

"But how…"

"I'll keep an apartment in Dallas just like the one I've got in Houston and drive home to you every weekend. That'll save Ches catching the bus with a saddle over his shoulder."

"You put in for a job transfer just so you could bring my nephew home to me every weekend? Oh, Andrew, I love you so!"

"Our nephew," he corrected. "We'll roll in here every Friday evening in time for the sale, won't we, Ches?"

My heart filled up as I looked at the two of them standing there together, and I don't think they ever doubted my answer.

"Well, Aunt Sis, I reckon we've finally crossed our bridge."

Acknowledgments

The Lord has truly blessed me beyond measure. My parents, Kenneth and Rhonda Keeling taught me about God's saving grace early in life and have supported me in every endeavor I ever undertook. They also raised me to live beyond any preconceived limits associated with my handicap. To extended family, friends, neighbors, and a handful of excellent educators I am just Jake, a person, not a disability. The members of Friendship Missionary Baptist Church in the Jumbo Community also deserve special thanks for their continual prayers and support. I am grateful to John Cunyus at Searchlight Press of Henderson, Texas for his partnership in this project. Lastly, I want to express my gratitude to each and every reader for inviting my characters into your life. I hope you enjoyed making their acquaintance.

Author's Note: This novel is intended as a tribute to the people and culture of rural East Texas. However, it is a work of fiction. Any resemblance to actual persons or events is purely coincidental. My aunts (Donna Howeth, Linda Sledge, and Lorene Pless) read the manuscript and offered valuable suggestions as did my mother, Kevin Plaster, and Nell McCarson-Langford at the Mount Enterprise branch of the Rusk County Library, but all errors are my own.

About the Author

Despite physical challenges and limited mobility, Jake Keeling is actively engaged in his family's ranching operation. He pursued an education, earning a Master of Arts in history. While recognizing the importance of hard work, he credits any and all success in life to the support of his family and a personal relationship with the Lord Jesus Christ.

Searchlight Press
Who are you looking for?
Publishers of thoughtful Christian books since 1994.
PO Box 554
Henderson, TX 75652-0554
214.662.5494
www.Searchlight-Press.com
www.JohnCunyus.com

CPSIA information can be obtained
at www.ICGtesting.com
Printed in the USA
FFHW02n1054131018
48762890-52893FF